After a career as a beauty therapist and aromatherapist, Carole Matthews is now a bestselling novelist. She lives happily in Milton Keynes with her scuba-diving instructor, who is living proof that romantic men do exist, and a cat, whom she's allergic to. She describes herself as a typical Gemini – daydreamer and realist – whose passions include cooking (more domestic disaster than goddess), T'ai chi, dancing, rollerblading, cars (anything fast, sporty and totally impractical), cycling, gardening and travel (particularly involving the words 'basic', 'adventure' and 'wilderness'). She is an evening-class-aholic; goes to the cinema at least once a week; and follows Feng Shui and horoscopes when all else fails. In between all this, she finds the time to write hugely entertaining novels and scripts for television and film. Not surprisingly, she is a stranger to housework.

A Whiff of Scandal
and
Let's Meet on Platform 8

Carole Matthews

First published in this omnibus edition in 2001
by Headline Book Publishing
for WHSmith plc

10 9 8 7 6 5 4 3 2 1

HEADLINE BOOK PUBLISHING
A division of Hodder Headline
338 Euston Road
LONDON NW1 3BH

www.headline.co.uk
www.hodderheadline.com

WHSmith plc
Greenbridge Road
Swindon
SN3 3LD

www.whsmith.co.uk

ISBN 0 7553 0076 9

Printed and bound in Great Britain by
Clays Ltd, St Ives plc

A Whiff of Scandal

Carole Matthews

To

Annie Murray and Linda Taylor for much needed support and humour. Vivien Garner for friendship and more plots than I could ever feasibly use in one lifetime. Darley for helping to keep my sensible head on in times of crisis.

Sheila and Pauline for broad shoulders, words of wisdom which I constantly ignore to my cost, an unending supply of Kleenex and for helping me maintain some semblance of sanity in what has been a truly *annus horribilis*.

Chapter One

ANISE

A pale yellow oil with a sweet spicy fragrance reminiscent of liquorice. In large doses it has a narcotic effect. It should be used with extreme caution and in moderation only. Anise is good for aches and pains, particularly in the neck.

from: *The Complete Encyclopaedia of Aromatherapy Oils*
by Jessamine Lovage

'She's had men popping in and out of there *all* day,' Anise said over her shoulder. 'They're more regular than our cuckoo clock.'

There was a sharp edge to the winter morning, complementing perfectly the tone in Anise's voice. Outside, cobwebs, rigid with frost, hung along the hedge like starched doilies bereft of fairy cakes, flung there with careless abandon after some wild tea party. The chill sun bounced off the ice crystals and glinted in her face, making it difficult to see. In her sitting room, Anise squinted and lifted the binoculars up to her eyes, her reading glasses clinking as they knocked against them. The binoculars were heavy and her arms were aching already.

She watched the postman puffing up the hill, his breath making more steam than Thomas the Tank Engine. Shifting her position, she took her weight on her good leg

1

and pointed the binoculars at the house across the road, whizzing them fuzzily across the barrier of leylandii and the spindly skeletal trees before focusing on the front door of number five Lavender Hill.

'Nine fifteen.' She glared at her younger sister who was reclining in an armchair, apparently staring into space. 'Write it down!'

Angelica sighed and picked up her notepad.

'First one of the day. Tall. Caucasian. Male,' Anise barked.

Angelica paused with her pencil. She looked up at her sister. 'What does Caucasian mean?'

Anise turned and glared at her. 'White, Angelica. *White*. Tall, white male. Don't you ever watch *NYPD* or *Hill Street Blues*?'

'No.' Angelica shrugged and her face took on a ponderous look. 'I've seen *The Bill* and the repeats of *Heartbeat* and I don't remember them saying it on either of those.' She put the pencil back to her notebook. 'How do you spell Caucasian?'

'Just put white,' Anise snapped, returning to her binoculars. 'Just put white.'

'I've never seen a black man in Great Brayford. Do you think you need to specify white?'

'The world is changing, Angelica,' her sister replied crisply. 'We could soon be overrun by foreigners. Vietnamese boat people or a tribe of South American Indians with wooden plates in their lips. There are thirty-five thousand Hong Kong Chinese moving into Milton Keynes. I read it in *Buckinghamshire on Sunday*. A few of them are bound to find their way to Great Brayford. She balanced the binoculars on her hip and wished fervently that the pins and needles would go out of her hands. It would hardly be on to rub them in front of Angelica and lose face. 'And what about Mr Patel at the post office?'

'He's not black. He's Asian. I don't think that counts. But I suppose it just depends what the Cauc bit means really.' She put her pencil in her mouth and chewed the end of it thoughtfully. 'And he doesn't have a wooden plate anywhere about his person, as far as I can tell.'

Her sister glared at her again. 'Are you deliberately being obtuse, Angelica?'

'I just think you're being rude about Mr Patel. He's a very nice man. You should get to know him better. He always helps to tear the page out of my pension book. They don't make perforations like they used to.'

Anise tutted. 'Let's get on with it, shall we? I only have so long left to live.' She raised the binoculars again. 'Tall, *white* male. Light-grey pinstripe suit. White shirt. Not tailored. Loud, flashy tie. Too vulgar by half.'

'Is it absolutely necessary to write down what he's wearing?'

Anise turned to glare at her sister for a third time. 'How will we know if he comes out wearing the same clothes?'

Angelica sat back in the armchair and languorously crossed her legs. 'How will we know if he comes out at all unless you're planning to keep watch all day?'

'I thought I'd draw up a rota.'

'Oh no, Anise.' Angelica waved her hand emphatically. 'You can count me out of that one. If you want to do this, you can do it by yourself. I don't mind taking a few notes but you're not getting me up there doing your dirty work. You know I don't like heights.'

'It's four steps, Angelica. Four steps. I'm not asking you to scale the Eiffel Tower without a safety harness.' She craned forward with her binoculars. 'He looks suspiciously like Melvyn Bragg.' She turned and snapped at her sister's inertia. 'Quick, quick – write it down. Write it down!'

'Does he look like Melvyn Bragg now or before he grew his hair too long?'

'What does that matter, for heaven's sake?'

'I would have thought it was quite important.' Angelica brushed her hair from her forehead with a languid movement. She had seen the young Grace Kelly do it years ago in *Dial M For Murder* and it was an affectation she had practised ever since. She had it down to a fine art after all these years. Not that anyone ever appreciated it. It drove Anise insane. Partly because it drew attention to the fact that her hair was still generously flecked with soft honey tones rather than the harsh ice-grey that Anise's had gone just after she turned sixty. She had looked remarkably like Catherine Deneuve until then – everyone used to say so. Fifteen years later, Anise's skin was also grey but she hid it skilfully with a liberal application of Max Factor, but people no longer made the Deneuve comparison. Her seventies had turned Anise old, cold and as hard as a boiled sweet.

'If we're noting down everything including the colour of his socks, the length of his hair seems quite pertinent. You could be a bit more specific, Anise. You haven't said how old he is either.'

'It's hard to tell. He's looking shifty, moving his head from side to side. Bugger. This hedge is in the way, we'll have to get Basil to top the leylandii again.'

'I think he's getting too old for it.' A look of concern crossed Angelica's face. 'Perhaps we need to get someone else in.'

'*We're* getting too old for it, that's why we pay the lazy blighter to do it for us. Although the only thing I ever see him doing is leaning on his blasted spade watching the grass grow.'

'Every time I see that *Yellow Pages* advertisement on television where they're looking for a replacement lawn-mower for their doddery old gardener, I think of Basil. I know he's not been with us for very long, but I'd hate to see him move on.'

'I'd love to see him move, full stop! I've seen garden gnomes that are more animated than Basil.'

'Why don't you speak to him then?'

'You know what he's like, Angelica. He can be so difficult.'

'I would have thought you'd have a lot in common,' Angelica said pleasantly.

Anise eyed her sister, checking for any hint of sarcasm. Angelica stared innocently at her notebook, pencil still poised.

'I must say though, I thought it was a tad out of order that he took a double-barrelled shotgun to the squirrel. After all, we put the nuts out specially for him. I miss his fluffy little tail.'

'So do I, but unfortunately Basil didn't.' Angelica felt moved to find her lace handkerchief, but dared not leave her notebook unmanned while Anise was still looking at her.

'I know, but what can we do? We need help and help is very hard to find. Good help is a myth perpetuated by the romanticism of *Upstairs, Downstairs*. It simply doesn't exist. The BBC have a lot to answer for.' She adjusted the binoculars. 'Anyway, never mind Basil or the Beeb, that woman at number five has opened the door at last. She probably just fell out of bed. It looks like it.'

'Do you want me to write down what *she's* wearing or should I just stick to Melvyn Bragg?'

'She's got that same skimpy little white thing on again.' Anise curled her lip in distaste. 'I don't know when it sees the washing machine. It seems to be permanently welded to her back.'

'She could have more than one,' Angelica pointed out helpfully.

'Spendthrift!'

'Anyway, it's not skimpy. It looks like a uniform. All the hygienists at the dentist's wear them. I think it's quite smart.'

'How can she be in uniform with hair that untidy? If she was a professional she'd have it tied back in a neat ponytail.'

'That's the fashion these days, Anise. The tousled look. It's only the men that wear neat little ponytails. If you went to a hairdresser that had trained after the Great War, then you would know these things.'

Anise resented Angelica's snubbing the delights of Suzette's Tuesday Pensioners' Special, a five pound fright of rollered curls, barely combed out to a Mrs Mertonesque bouffant and lacquered rigidly into place so that it would last a week. 'All I know is that I don't want a haircut that means I have to re-mortgage the house,' she retorted.

To be fair, Anise came off quite well, Angelica thought. Suzette swept her hair into a sort of side chignon which, although it looked harsh, didn't look stupid. For herself, she much preferred to go to one of those trendy salons in Milton Keynes where she was more likely to come out looking like Anthea Turner – despite the fact that the music was too loud and all the stylists wore black clothes and make-up like Morticia Addams.

'And when did you last see a professional showing her knees?' Anise went on. 'That skirt barely covers her bottom.' She put the binoculars down. 'Damn! I've missed it! They've gone in now. I don't know whether she kissed him or not.' She pointed at Angelica's notepad. 'Just put, erotic contact unknown.'

'You said she normally kisses them on the way out.'

'She does. But she makes it look all innocent. Nothing more than a chaste peck. I'd like to know what she does to them while they're in there.'

'Mr Patel said she's an aromatherapist.'

'Mr Patel talks out of his jolly bottom.'

Angelica found it hard to imagine Mr Patel's bottom as jolly. 'Why don't we simply ask her what she does?'

'Do you think she'd come clean? And, besides, if you were running a . . . a . . . *bordello*, would you want the world to know?'

'I think it would be useful for attracting business.'

'Attracting business!' Anise made a humphing noise. 'She's the sort of woman that advertises in phone boxes.'

'You seem to know an awful lot about running a bordello, Anise.' Angelica closed her notepad and pushed the pencil through the spiral binding at the top. 'I thought you'd led such a sheltered life.'

'I know something suspicious when I see it,' she said, wagging a malevolent finger. 'And I will get to the bottom of this, Angelica, with or without your help!' She snapped the binoculars closed decisively.

'Would you like a hand getting down?' Angelica offered. 'That stepladder's awfully high.'

'Yes, dear.' Anise had already held out her hand before she saw the smile that twitched her sister's lips.

Chapter Two

ROSE

A pale oil with a rich, sweet, floral and slightly spicy aroma. Rose is well-known for its healing properties and as the symbol of Venus – the goddess of love and beauty – often inducing feelings of wellbeing and tolerance in its user. Emotionally, it will bring out your deepest feelings and gladden an aching heart. Physically, it is good for cooling inflammations and swellings.

from: *The Complete Encyclopaedia of Aromatherapy Oils*
by Jessamine Lovage

Unlike Sinead O'Connor, it had been considerably more than seven hours and fifteen days since he had taken his love away. It was actually getting on for three months now. But at least Sinead was right in one respect. *Nothing Compares 2 U*. Or 2 Hugh, in this case. Rose wondered if Sinead had shaved her head as an act of retribution. If so, it seemed a much stronger statement than simply moving out of London into a pleasant little village just south of Milton Keynes. Perhaps she should shave her head too. Hugh would have hated that. But that might just serve to make the locals even more suspicious of her than they seemed to be already. Goodness knows why. They were hardly all straw-chewers. There were only a couple of born and bred Great Brayforders left. In fact, most of the residents seemed to have been 'Lunnuners' themselves before they forsook their roots and became pseudo-country folk. So they really had no right to treat her like a two-headed intruder.

Head-shaving did seem a bit drastic though. Besides, her mother had told her she had a head full of tiny bald spots where, as a child, chickenpox scabs had pulled her hair out and it had never regrown. Whenever her mother saw her, which was mercifully little these days, she examined her head for evidence and the doleful tutting told Rose that she was never disappointed.

Rose had never managed to find one herself. She had persuaded various hairdressers to look for these corn circles in her hair but no trace had ever been found. In fact, they had gone as far as to tell her that she had nice hair. Hair to be envied. It was blonde and was best left to do its own thing rather than have fruitless hours spent on it trying to tame it. Generally, all things considered, it was quite reasonably behaved.

Perhaps Sinead should have waited a bit longer before taking the BIC razor to her bonce. The pain of longing certainly did get less. Out of nowhere tiny gaps would appear in the seemingly endless queue of pain, allowing healing to squeeze in almost unnoticed until suddenly one day you realised that you had gone for a few hours without feeling hollow and sick. Rose could now go for days – well, one day – without her stomach lurching every time the phone rang. Or wishing that he was here with her rather than who knows where. But these things hadn't just happened since Hugh left. They had happened all the time he was supposed to be with her as well. And to be fair, he hadn't exactly jumped out of their relationship, he had been given an almighty shove over the edge. She knew full well that it was impossible to expect everything in life to be as reliable as a Volkswagen but Hugh took the biscuit. In fact, he took the whole packet. There were limits even to the bounds of unreliability. Surely.

Okay, so he was devastatingly handsome, intelligent, charming, witty, the life and soul of the party. He was successful, rich, powerful and even influential. And, of course, he was great in bed. He had to be, didn't he? When have you ever met a man who scores so highly in every other area and then is lousy between the sheets? It goes with the turf. But was he reliable? No. It was not a quality that you could attribute to Hugh. He was about as reliable as a British Rail timetable.

Rose moved a row of small brown bottles to one end of her shelf. The smear of oil was thick and sticky and would need large amounts of Jif and elbow grease to shift it. She should have mopped it up as soon as it was spilt. A whoosh of surgical spirit and that would have been it. But, no, she had been too busy; it had congealed and now she would pay the price of coaxing it away, hoping that it hadn't left a telltale yellow ring on the white Formica shelf. Still, she shouldn't complain about being busy. She had thought that business might tail off when she moved from London, but she had been lucky enough to have a steady stream of clients virtually from day one, mainly thanks to her established clients recommending her services to outlying friends and relatives.

The doorbell rang and she put down her J-cloth, frowning at the clock as she did so. No one was due yet according to her diary; she had a gap of about an hour after Mr Sommerfield – who she always thought looked suspiciously like Melvyn Bragg – unless she'd made a cock-up with her appointments. She took her apron off and smoothed her white cotton uniform over her hips as she headed for the door.

There was a man – well, more of a guy – standing there, leaning on her doorframe, smiling at her. Lopsidedly. 'I've come to look at your fireplace,' he said, smile widening. 'I understand you want it opening up.'

It was certainly an original chat-up line. Her eyebrows headed for the bridge of her nose in an involuntary frown. 'I'm sorry. I don't think I know who you are.'

He cocked his head in the general direction of up-the-hill. 'Dan Spikenard. Number fifteen. Builder's Bottom.'

'Oh! You're the builder?'

'Got it in one.'

She looked at him critically. He didn't look much like a builder. If he did, he was the Hollywood version. Crisp, clean, checked shirt, possibly Gap – definitely not Mister Byrite. His jeans had just the right amount of stone-washed fade and no rips in the knees. His hair had just the right amount of golden flecks that caught the light as he moved, his eyes the right amount of mischievous twinkle. The designer stubble had grown to perfection. And if there had been a camera present, it would have been catching his best side. He wasn't like other builders she had met, who all had bald pates – not à la Sinead – one eye, two earrings, four fading tattoos and a beer belly that had been expensive to acquire. There was also a distinct lack of greasy donkey jacket and mud-caked Dr Marten boots.

'Have we met before?' Rose asked politely. She would have definitely remembered if she had met him.

'No. But if you're wondering why I know all about your fireplace, you haven't lived in the village long enough.' He pushed himself away from the doorframe. He was tall, too. Very. 'Did you mention it to anyone?'

A puzzled look crossed her face. 'Only in passing, at the post office.'

'Ah, Mr Patel.' The smile widened. 'Our village tele-graph. Well, let's see. He probably told Mrs Devises, who probably told Mrs Took, who probably told Cassia Wales, who probably told the Lavender Hill mob, who probably told Gardenia – who definitely told me.'

Rose returned his smile. 'Who on earth are the Lavender Hill mob?'

'The snoop sisters.' He gesticulated backwards with his head. 'Anise and Angelica. They live just across the lane. You must have met them.'

She nodded. 'We're on nodding terms.'

'They're Great Brayford's answer to Hinge and Brackett. They don't miss a trick. MI5 have a lot to learn from those two. It's fair to say that they've been a bit slow with you. You're still known in the village as that nice young lady at number five.'

'I am a name, not a number!' She wished he would stop smiling like that, it was stopping her brain from functioning properly.

'Unless you do something scandalous to outrage the residents, like paint your front door a different colour, you'll remain the nice young lady at number five for ever.'

'I think I might resent that!'

'I wouldn't if I were you.' He shrugged and she noticed how wide his shoulders were under his pristine checked shirt. 'Don't take it personally. It just takes a long time to be accepted into village life. Look at Mr Patel. They treat him as if he's just come over on a banana boat from Bombay, despite the fact that he's had the post office for over five years, is one of the nicest blokes round here and, by all accounts, is third generation Slough.'

Rose laughed. It sounded strange. How long had it been since she had spontaneously burst into giggles? It was probably easier to remember when she had last spontaneously burst into flames. It certainly wasn't in the last three months. And before that there was the bit where it was all going horribly wrong and there hadn't been many laughs then either.

'Anyway, back to your fireplace,' he continued. 'Do you want it opening up or not? Sometimes the messages passed along are a bit like Chinese whispers – you know, bring three and fourpence we're going to a dance.'

'What?'

'Bring reinforcements we're going to advance.' He grinned. 'Something usually gets lost in translation.'

She laughed again. This was ridiculous. She was starting to sound like a hyena on laughing gas. It was probably because she had been using her namesake Rose oil this morning, which always made her feel slightly euphoric. Thankfully, given the price of it, it hadn't been the one she'd spilt. She tried to calm herself down. 'Well, they were right this time. I do want my fireplace looked at.'

'Good to see that the jungle drums aren't failing.'

'Come on in.' She held the door open for him and he suddenly made the hall seem very small. 'Through here.'

'Phew,' he said, following her into the room. 'It smells like a tart's handbag in here.'

'I'll take that as a compliment, shall I?'

He picked up one of the small brown bottles and examined it carefully. She took it from him, fearing that in those large hands it would soon be heading towards the floor with an unhealthy crash. 'What do you do?' he asked.

'I'm an aromatherapist.'

He raised an eyebrow. 'Ah, one of these new-fangled, New Agers.'

'Something like that.'

'We go for that sort of thing round here. This isn't your typical farming community – we like to play at it, green wellies and Barbours, preferably without the farmyard smells and mud.'

'I've noticed.' She laughed again. Why couldn't she think of something intelligent and witty to say?

'Will you have enough business to keep you going here?'

'I hope so. I've had some good contacts from the clients I left behind in London and I've started to advertise in the local paper.'

His face darkened momentarily. 'You want to be careful. This might not be the big city smoke, but there are still plenty of cranks about. You're here on your own – you ought to think twice about having strangers trekking through your house.'

'You sound like my mother.'

'Sensible woman, is she?'

Rose groaned.

'Seriously,' he continued. 'Gone are the days when you could leave your back door open all night.'

Rose gave an involuntary shiver. 'I know, but there *are* pluses to being out in the sticks.' She walked to the window and looked out. 'The garden's wonderful. I lived in a poky flat in London.' Executive apartment complex with roof terrace and underground parking. And Hugh. 'I've got birds, foxes, badgers and deer. And the view across the vale is stunning.'

'These are the things that remind us we live in the country.'

She turned back to him. 'I must admit it's not quite as rural as I had expected.'

'Not so much milking maids and cow pats as advertising executives and bullshit.'

'Well, yes.' She felt a bubble of laughter again. 'There certainly seems to be a larger percentage of Mercs than moo-cows. And everyone looks like they've just walked off the set of *Dynasty*. Apart from Melissa, the girl that cleans for the vicar. You can tell she's a country lass through and through. She's still got that fresh-faced, tumble-in-the-hay sort of look.'

'Mel's probably one of the few true villagers left. Certainly the youngest. If you cut her in half she'd probably have, "Welcome to Great Brayford" stamped right through her middle.'

'We've had coffee together a couple of times. She's been very friendly,' Rose said.

'Oh, and the sisters grim,' Dan continued. 'They were born and bred just down the road in the manor – the one that's the golf course clubhouse now. Their father was a big landowner round here. Owned half the vale, and had his eye on the rest of it.'

'So there are a few country folk still left.'

'A few.' He shook his head sadly. 'Not many though.' He hooked his fingers through the belt loops of his jeans and his smile broadened again. 'Well, I'm sorry we don't live up to your expectations. Would you be happier if I went to get some straw to chew?'

'No, but I'd be happy if you looked at my fireplace.' She smiled sweetly.

He nodded solemnly. 'I'm a builder, that's my job.'

She walked over to the fireplace. 'I'm afraid the Philistine who lived here last obviously got some cowboy firm in to brick it up.'

'Sure did, ma'am.' He twirled imaginary guns from his imaginary holster. 'A and D Spikenard. A is my brother Alan.'

'Oh, I'm sorry!' A flush spread over her cheeks and Rose put her face in her hands. 'That was *so* thoughtless!'

He winked at her. 'Well, as long as the Philistines pay the bills, I do what's required.' He crouched down and nodded at the offending fireplace. 'This won't take long. Can I come back at the weekend and do it for you?'

'Well, yes. That'll be fine. What sort of price are we talking about? I'm a bit strapped for cash after the move and everything.'

He pushed up again. 'Well, just to be neighbourly and prove that we're not a cowboy outfit, you can have it on me.'

'Oh, I couldn't possibly do that!'

'Well, I can't bake apple pies or make jam with bits in but I can knock a hole in your wall to say welcome.'

'That would be very nice of you.'

'I'm a nice sort of guy.' He winked at her again. 'But don't tell everyone. They'll all want holes knocked in things.' He headed for the door. 'I'd better be going. I'll see you Saturday. Early. Early-ish.'

She followed him. 'Thanks. I really appreciate it.'

He turned at the door and leaned on the doorframe again. 'By the way, are you going to tell me your name or do you want me to call you that nice young lady at number five like the rest of them?'

'I'm sorry. I didn't introduce myself, did I?' She held out her hand. 'I'm Rose. Rose Stevens.'

He took her hand. Was it her imagination or did he hold it longer than was absolutely respectable for a first meeting?

'Dan,' he said again. He pushed back the stetson that he wasn't wearing with the butt of the six-shooter he didn't have either. 'Me and my horse Trigger will see you on Saturday.'

Chapter Three

SPIKENARD

An amber-coloured oil with a distinctly animal attractive odour. Spikenard is an excellent antidote for insomnia, nervous indigestion, headaches, stress and tension. It is useful in fighting withdrawal from addictive substances, helping to alleviate symptoms such as palpitations, breathing difficulties, distorted vision, confusion and panic attacks. Emotionally, it can soothe aggression and anger, speed the healing process and induce a positive state of mind.

from: *The Complete Encyclopaedia of Aromatherapy Oils*
by Jessamine Lovage

Once she had completed her index fingernail with the requisite three strokes, Gardenia looked up from painting her nails. 'What are you smirking at?'

Dan walked past her to the kettle and filled it with water. 'I'm not smirking.'

Gardenia's eyes narrowed. 'Yes, you are. You're making the Cheshire Cat look like Victor Meldrew.'

'The Cheshire Cat grinned, he didn't smirk. And I'm doing neither.'

'You're remarkably sunny for some reason,' she said sullenly.

'I'm delirious because it's Monday and in a moment, when I have drunk this delicious cup of coffee I am so skilfully making, I'm going to go and play bricks with the big boys.' He poured water into the cup.

'Why aren't you at work already? And where have you been for the last half hour?'

'And why am I smiling?' Dan saluted and did a dubious impersonation of an army officer's voice. 'I'm British. I will only give you my name, rank and serial number. Nothing you can do will make me talk, you fiendish swine.'

'Grow up.' Gardenia went back to her nails.

He brought the cup of coffee and sat next to her at the table.

'Have you taken your shoes off?' she said without looking at him.

'No, I haven't taken my shoes off. I am wearing them in deliberate defiance of house rules.'

She glared at him over her polish bottle.

'And, anyway, they weren't muddy,' he said quickly.

She smiled coldly at him. 'You might be smiling, but you're still an awkward sod at heart, aren't you?'

'If I wanted a fight – another fight – I might say it takes one to know one.'

She ignored that. 'So. Where *have* you been?'

The ends of Gardenia's fingers were developing into hideous chocolate-coloured blobs. It was probably the latest fashion. These things mattered to Gardenia. She took a painstaking amount of care over painting them so that it all stayed on the nails – mainly – and she didn't get bits round her fingers that she had to pick off later. It looked absolutely frightful, but it would take a braver man than he was to tell her so. He took a sip of his coffee and shuddered, not entirely sure whether it was because of the nails or the taste of the coffee. It was some awful decaffeinated stuff, because real coffee, real *tasty* coffee, clogged your arteries or took ten years off your life or gave you wrinkles. Something like that. And these things mattered to Gardenia.

'I have been spending a congenial half hour with our new neighbour further down Lavender Hill.' He took another sip of the coffee and decided that it definitely was the culprit.

Gardenia looked up and blobbed her nail. She didn't notice and he wasn't going to point it out. 'That woman at number five?'

'The prefixes nice and young are usually used, but yes, that woman at number five.' He pushed his coffee away from him. 'She's called Rose.'

She wrinkled her nose. 'What sort of a name is that?'

He shrugged. 'An English country one, I suppose. And you're hardly in a position to cast the first stone with a name like Gardenia.'

'I was named after my great-aunt.'

'What was she called?'

'Gard—' She looked at him with disdain. 'Arsehole.'

'Perhaps Rose was named after someone who was a complete prick.'

She smiled through narrowed eyes and narrowed lips. It was Gardenia's 'look'. 'Then she'd be called Dan, wouldn't she?'

He stood up. 'Well, I can't sit here all day exchanging social pleasantries when there are bricks to be laid.'

'What did you go to see her for?' She affected a sickly smile. '*Rose.*'

'I'm going to knock her fireplace out for her at the weekend.'

'Is that some sort of crude joke?'

'No.' He tried to look suitably offended. 'You were the one that told me she wanted it doing.' He headed towards the door. Fresh air. A blessed relief from cloying perfume competing with acetone. 'I bricked it in a couple of years ago for the Palmers. It'll only take five minutes to knock it out again for her.'

'Up to your usual standard of workmanship then?'

21

He acknowledged the jibe with a rueful smile. 'I said I'd do it for nothing.'

'You always were a charmer.'

Dan sighed. 'She's nice, Gardi. You'd like her.' Though what she'd make of you is a different matter, he added to himself silently. 'You ought to pop along there and welcome her. She's an aromatherapist. You like that sort of thing.'

The nailpolish brush was still suspended over the blobbed nail. 'Anise thinks she's running a brothel.'

Dan threw his head back and laughed. 'In Great Brayford? Do me a favour!'

Gardenia's face darkened. 'Apparently she's got men popping in and out of there all day.'

'They're clients! Hasn't that woman got anything better to do with her day than snoop on her neighbours?'

'Anise said you can't help but notice. She's got some very strange types going in there. And they come out looking all flushed and pleased with themselves.'

'Gardenia, she's a very good and well-respected therapist, from a huge, swanky practice in London. She's had all sorts of celebrity clients.'

'Really?' Gardenia was grudgingly impressed. 'Like who?'

'Like . . . like, er,' he scratched his stubble distractedly. 'I think she mentioned Cliff Richard.'

'Cliff Richard?'

'You know how young he looks.' He glanced at his watch. 'I'd better be going. I'm late. Alan will wonder where I've got too.'

'Why's she moved out here then?'

'I don't know. I didn't ask.'

Gardenia looked back at her nails. 'Oh shit! You've made me blob!'

'I've got to dash. 'Bye, Gardi.' He slammed the door behind him and breathed a sigh of relief.

The sound of 'And don't call me Gardi!' came drifting after him on the air. Fresh country air. Chill and crisp. It was depressing when the inside of your house was more polluted than the outside. He jumped into the Land Rover Discovery he had recently bought, enjoying the smell of new leather. What a discovery it had been too. He hadn't had so much vehicular fun since he grew too big for Tonka toys. He put it into gear and swung out of the drive. They had been building a new Tesco in Milton Keynes and the job was coming to a close. Pretty soon, he thought, there would be a line of Tescos stretching as far as the eye could see from Land's End to John O'Groats. Not that it worried him. People had to eat. The next job he did would be smaller, but even more contentious. And, unfortunately, closer to home.

He pushed in the cassette that jutted precariously from the tape player. 'Good loving gone bad,' screeched Bad Company at full volume. Yeah, yeah, yeah. Gardenia hated this song. That was probably why it had been ejected with such violent force. It was indicative of their relationship. No, it was less subtle than that; she just hated his taste in music. End of story. She also hated his taste in clothes, his friends, his job and most of his family. Except for his younger brother Alan who flirted with her and told her she was young and gorgeous – which she was. It was just that Gardenia liked to hear it a lot. An awful lot. And Alan was a tireless splashing fountain of compliments. Unfortunately, his own fount had dried up years ago. Dan wondered for the millionth time how it was all going to end. When it was all going to end. And why hadn't it all ended already? How long was it till you knew it was the end of the road? Very philosophical for a Monday morning.

His thoughts strayed back to Rose. She had been the guilty party who had put a smile on his face on an otherwise bleak and cheerless day. He must have looked particularly chirpy for Gardenia to notice. Normally things that happened on the periphery of her personal stratosphere simply failed to register. It wasn't even that Rose was particularly attractive – well, she was, but in an ordinary sort of way, not a Gardenia sort of way.

Gardenia was perfection personified. If you took Helena Christensen, Claudia Schiffer, Elle Macpherson and Kate Moss, rolled them all together, pushed them through a person-shaped extruder like Play-Doh, what would pop out would be Gardenia. That good. But a bit older. A bit more brittle. She always looked as if she had spent three hours in the bathroom before venturing a foot out of the house. The trouble was he knew that she *had* spent at least three hours in the bathroom, which sort of took the edge off it. He'd had to build a second bathroom at Builder's Bottom just to make sure he got to work in the morning.

Rose was different. She was fresh-faced. Her make-up didn't look as if she had spread it on with a trowel. She had pale blue eyes that weren't surrounded by neon stripes of colour or thick clumps of black gungy mascara clogging her eyelashes. Her lips were more or less their natural colour rather than cerise or burgundy or scarlet. Her hair was pretty too; it looked as if it was a virtual stranger to hair gel. She was bright and bubbly and would have been a wonderful person to present the National Lottery show. Such as it was.

Amazingly, she had laughed at his jokes. Really laughed. He was so used to Gardenia sneering at him, he had forgotten what it was like to get a laugh. She would have been a useless straight man. And he had lied blatantly for her when normally he was quite an honest man. He didn't know if she was a well-respected aromatherapist. She could have trained two weeks ago, for all he knew. Or she could have been one of those bogus practitioners that the *Daily Mail* was always going on about. And he had absolutely no idea whether she had ever clapped eyes on Cliff Richard in the flesh, let alone laid hands on his body. What on earth had possessed him to say that? You only had to mention minor celebrity and Gardenia was like a dog with two tails. She had a friend whom she had coffee with religiously every fortnight because she was second cousin once removed to Bryan Adams. She couldn't stand the woman! But she had to keep in touch with her just in case Bryan ever happened to be passing and decided to drop in. That still didn't explain why he was so anxious for Gardenia to be impressed by Rose, did it?

And why had he felt so light and funny and interesting when he was talking to her? Why had his stomach churned as if he hadn't had any breakfast when, in fact, he'd eaten three Shredded Wheat? Yes, he was a man who could eat three without batting an eyelid – even four at a push. And why, when it was only Monday and he had the joy of building a new Tesco's, was he looking forward so damn much to knocking a few bricks out of a fireplace on Saturday?

Chapter Four

MELISSA

A pale yellow oil with the light fresh fragrance of lemons, which helps to induce a sense of calm and sensitivity. Care must be taken when purchasing Melissa, as this is one of the most frequently adulterated oils, usually with the addition of lemon, lemongrass or citronella. It is difficult to find true, pure Melissa.

from: *The Complete Encyclopaedia of Aromatherapy Oils*
by Jessamine Lovage

'You're getting through gallons of this stuff, Mel. You're supposed to rub it on, not drink it.' The tip of Rose's tongue licked her upper lip while she concentrated on pouring almond oil from a five-litre plastic container through an unhelpful funnel into the much smaller glass bottle on the shelf. 'Your Frank must be the luckiest man alive. Well, certainly the most massaged.'

'He does like a good rub-down,' Melissa giggled.

'Show me a man who doesn't,' Rose replied sagely. 'What do you want me to put in this one?' she asked, looking over her shoulder.

Melissa was perched on the edge of the treatment couch swinging her legs while she leafed aimlessly through *The Complete Encyclopaedia of Aromatherapy Oils* by

Jessamine Lovage. She reminded Rose of a schoolgirl. A naughty one.

'You know I like the saucy stuff.' She giggled again. 'Something to get them ... him, going. Those dizzy things.'

'Aphrodisiacs.'

'That's the ones!'

Rose smiled. 'I'll use some rose oil, it's one of my favourites.'

Melissa looked up. 'So it should be!'

'And ylang-ylang – that's really exotic. You like jasmine too, don't you?'

Melissa's nose twitched the air like a cat testing the scent. 'I love it. It reminds me of my Mr Sheen.'

'I don't think that's really the desired effect.' Rose measured the drops carefully into the waiting bottle of almond oil. 'But whatever turns you on, I guess.'

'My Frank loves it too,' she said, abandoning Jessamine Lovage.

'Mr Sheen?'

'Silly!' Melissa jumped down from the couch and walked to the window. Spreading her hands on the sill, she looked out of the window. 'Jasmine oil. Well, he likes all the aromatherapy oils I've tried so far. He says they make him feel sexy.'

'I didn't know Frank was such a goer,' Rose teased.

Melissa turned and looked at her, perching her bottom on the windowsill, and Rose noticed there was a slightly wistful look in her eye. 'He's not really.' She shook her head. 'I think he just says it to make me feel better.'

'Well, there's a lot to be said for having a rock steady eddy rather than an unreliable raver.' Didn't she know! Rose thought for a minute, her pen poised over the specially printed gold label that stated 'Rose Stevens – Hand-Blended Quality Aromatherapy Oils.' She decided on 'Secret Passions' and her mouth turned up at the corners as she wrote it with indelible ink in the appropriate space.

It really was quite difficult to imagine Frank and Melissa together. They were a fairly unlikely couple. Frank was so steady you probably could have built a house on him. He was tall, stocky and had dark hair flecked with grey, cropped short to suit the dictates of his job. Frank was the local policeman. Not a race round in a squad car and kick down doors type of policeman, but a serious, nineteen-sixties-style one. He rarely smiled with his mouth, but did so constantly with his clear, kind eyes. He had been a confirmed bachelor until Mel bowled him over and whisked him down the aisle before he had a chance to say no.

Melissa was fun, frothy, flirty, feisty and any other frivolous words you could think of beginning with f. She had long fair hair trailing almost to her waist in lazy, natural curls and she had the kind of naive chicness that people in soap operas spend three hours in make-up trying to achieve. Ignoring the vagaries of fashion, her eyebrows remained steadfastly unplucked rather like Brooke Shields'. Her figure was round in a childish, puppy-fat way, not plump, but probably in a few more years she would be heading that way.

Melissa shrugged. 'I think sometimes the age difference bothers Frank and he pretends to like things that he can't really be bothered with for my sake.'

'Come on, there's not that much between you.'

'Fifteen years.' Melissa said it with a kind of hushed reverence.

'That's nothing these days.'

'He'll be forty soon,' Melissa protested.

'That hardly makes him the old man of the sea.' Having dripper-plugged and capped the bottle of 'Secret Passions', Rose started on the next blend.

'Sometimes Frank treats me like I still wear knee-length

white socks and a school uniform.'

'It could just be one of his fetishes.' She gave Melissa a 'you-know-what-I-mean' look.

'You know a lot about men, don't you?'

'You're making me feel very old, Mel.' Rose sighed. 'I've had one or two in my time. Although, I have to say that I've had considerably more hot dinners.'

'I wish I knew a bit more about life, like you.' Melissa twisted the wispy ends of her hair between her fingers, plaiting them and unplaiting them with a dexterity that made the habit look as if it was a longstanding one. 'I've only had one serious relationship and that's with Frank. We hardly knew each other when we got married. People say I rushed him into it – I know they do. Before that it had just been a few furtive fumbles with some spotty local lads who weren't ever sure whether they'd rather be shoving a hand down your blouse or shoving a frog in your face that they'd caught in the village pond. I bet you've known some really sophisticated men.'

'Sophisticated?' Rose gave a wry smile. 'That's one word for it. Cads, scoundrels, bastards and complete gits are others.'

'I sometimes think that Frank was the original model for Mr Plod.'

'Well, you can give me reliability over sophistication any day of the week.' She abandoned the unwieldy plastic container of oil, which was glugging far too enthusiastically for her liking and looked set to glug on to the work surface if she didn't give it her full attention. Instead, she joined Melissa on the windowsill.

'Don't you miss the glamour of London, Rose?' Melissa's lower lip was starting to pout.

'There isn't any glamour in London. It's dirty, busy, expensive and you spend most of the time on the Tube getting your bottom fondled by perverts in pinstripe suits. Where's the glamour in that?'

She turned and looked out of the window at the garden. There was possibly more moss than lawn and some of the well-established shrubs looked as if they hadn't been threatened with a pair of secateurs in years, but it was all hers. In London the flat had the grand embellishment of a roof terrace but once you had installed four Homebase wrought-iron chairs, a wobbly table and half a dozen tubs of struggling nicotiana, there was barely room to stretch your legs. Besides, there had usually been a gale force wind up there and, when there wasn't, the pollution that drifted up from the congested road below hung heavy in a pall of smog and nearly choked you to death. That was not gardening as God had intended.

'I mean, look at this, Mel. Wide open spaces, fresh air in your lungs, little furry animals rustling about in your borders. A view to die for. What more do you want?' Melissa looked unimpressed, which was a bit disheartening. Perhaps she would have to get some help with the garden if she was going to illustrate her point.

'The little furry animals usually wreck your plants and having lived with that view for the last twenty-five years, it does lose some of its appeal.' Melissa looked at Rose with doe eyes. 'Eventually,' she said, trying to be kind.

'Don't join the "grass is greener" school of philosophy, Mel. You'll always be disappointed in the end. The other side of the fence may look a deeper, richer shade but it usually isn't once you've taken the leap.'

'So is that what made you want to move out of London? The urge to plant pansies in the morning and watch the squirrels eat them for their tea?'

Rose looked at her sideways. Quite often it seemed that Melissa knew more than she was letting on. Rose hesitated before replying. This was getting on to sticky ground. She had moved out of London purely and simply to get away from Hugh. The fact she had ended up in this green and pleasant farmland had been a secondary consideration. The thing was, did she really want to tell Melissa that? She was trying to bury her past, sever all connections, kick over the ashes and make bonfires out of all her bridges. You couldn't get much more emphatic than that. The best thing would be to keep her mouth shut, claim brainwashing by the covers of *Country Life* and let the locals be none the wiser. But there was this persistent, nagging, itching, needling urge to talk about Hugh that squirmed through her. Both her mother and her sister were unaware of the tangled life she had been living in London, so there was no chance for any filial confidences and ensuing comfort there. However, there would be endless recriminations and lots of 'I told you sos' if they ever did find out. She had bored most of her friends to death with the ins/outs, the will he/won't he, the could I/would I and all the other dichotomies that had been part and parcel of life with Hugh. And that had been part of the deal too. No more contact with friends. Particularly mutual ones. Consequently, since arriving here she had mentioned him to no one. His name had not passed her lips. It had circumnavigated her brain several thousand times but not once had she ever let it out. The ivory tower that she had built for herself didn't include a connection to the Hugh helpline – an 0898 number for sad and lonely addicts, pathetic people who weren't strong enough to give up Hughs on their own. Did she really want to tell Melissa all this? Yes, she did.

She tossed her head back and looked at the tidy stipple of Artex on the ceiling. 'I left London because I was too cowardly to shave my head.'

'What?'

'Sorry.' She turned back to Mel. 'I'm being flippant.' Rose leaned towards her new confidante. 'Promise that you won't breathe a word of this to anyone.'

'Cross my heart and hope to die.' Melissa's heart took some crossing, covered as it was by an ample supply of bosoms. She performed some ancient pagan ritual in front of her which was probably supposed to replicate the sign of the cross. It was clear that Melissa hadn't been in a church for some time.

'I've come here to get away from a relationship.' Her voice sounded hoarse, as though she was unused to talking, rather than just unused to uttering the H-word.

Melissa was rapt. 'With a man?' she said breathlessly.

'Yes,' said Rose, suppressing a smile.

'Was he *sophisticated*?'

Rose laughed. 'Oh, yes. The word sophistication was invented for Hugh.' Why was her voice cracking now that his name had passed the hallowed ground of her lips once more. Bloody traitor!

'*Wowwwww!*' Melissa whispered.

'He was sophisticated. Devastatingly handsome. Intelligent, charming, witty. He was successful, rich, powerful, great in bed.' She paused for breath. 'Shall I go on?'

'And you left him to come *here*?'

'Well . . .' She might be spilling the beans, but it was worth leaving a few lurking in the bottom of the can. 'That's the crux of it. Really.'

'Wowwww!' Melissa's eyes were shining with awe. 'Get them keen, treat them mean!'

'It wasn't really like that.' Rose's voice wobbled as much as the wrought-iron patio furniture on their roof terrace had.

Melissa flung her arms wide. 'This is *so* romantic!'

'Romantic?' Her eyes widened in disbelief. 'It wasn't romantic at all.' She shook her head, shuddering as the last few days she had spent with Hugh shot past her eyes like the frames of a video on fast forward. 'It was horrible. Painful. Stomach-churning.'

'Oh, but it is! It's so desperate!' Melissa jumped down from the windowsill. 'I can't wait to tell Frank.'

'Melissa! It's supposed to be a secret – i.e. just between

us. Don't you remember? You crossed your heart.'

'There's no need to worry, Frank won't tell anyone. He's a policeman.'

'I know he's a policeman. And I'm not doubting his integrity. It's just that it's private. I wanted it kept strictly between you and me.'

'Oh.' Melissa looked crestfallen.

'I needed to get away from Hugh. He has no idea where I am. It has to be kept that way. I don't want to be a source of gossip in the village.'

Melissa made an unhappy, huffing sound.

Rose could understand perfectly why Frank envisaged her in white knee-length socks and a school uniform. It wasn't a perversion, he probably couldn't help it. 'Is that too much to ask?'

Melissa tutted. 'No,' she said reluctantly. 'But it's the most sensational piece of gossip I've heard for ages. Nothing ever happens here. It seems such a waste to keep it to ourselves,' she pleaded.

'I really would prefer it like that.' Rose could do a fair amount of pleading herself when push came to shove.

'Okay.' Melissa was suddenly sunny again. 'What time is it?'

Rose felt slightly perplexed as if she'd pushed an on/off switch which she couldn't see. 'Just after two.'

'Oh hell! I need to go. I'm due at the vicarage. I'm doing an extra day for Dave.'

'The Reverend Allbright?'

'Mm,' she nodded. 'I have to go in the afternoon today because there's a bible study in the mornings and they can't hear themselves think when I've got the radio on loud. And I can't hear the radio over the Hoover unless it's on loud. Dave didn't think that Job and Jon Bon Jovi went together that well.' Melissa pulled a roll of notes out of her pocket. 'Personally, I thought it livened the whole thing up a bit. But there's no accounting for taste. What do I owe you for my oils?' She waved the roll in front of Rose.

'Heavens above, Melissa! You couldn't walk around London with a wodge like that, you'd be mugged within five minutes.'

Melissa flushed. 'It's the money I get from Dave.'

'You must do a darn sight more for him than rub round with a bit of Flash to warrant that lot.' Rose winked knowingly.

Melissa's skin surged from radish red to beetroot. She straightened her sweatshirt over her leggings. 'I'd best be off then.'

'Aren't you going to wait till I've blended your other oils? It won't take a minute.'

'No. I best not. I'll take the one you've done and leave this on account.' She thrust fifty pounds into Rose's hand. 'I'll pop back for the others in a few days, if that's all right. We can have a cup of tea.'

Rose looked in astonishment at the crumpled notes. 'Fine,' she said hesitantly. 'Fine.'

Melissa headed for the door. 'Oh, and Rose?'

'Yes?'

'I promise I'll keep your secret, if you'll keep mine.' She swallowed deeply. 'Don't tell Frank that I spend so much money on oils, will you?'

Rose's forehead creased into a puzzled frown. 'Of course not. Client confidentiality and all that.'

Melissa crinkled her eyes. 'You're a pal!'

'Here.' She handed her the small bottle of oil. 'Don't forget this.'

Melissa looked at the label. ' "Secret Passions"?' She gave a wry smile. 'Thanks. I'd better be off. Catch up with you later.'

Rose closed the door behind her and slumped on to the nearest stair. Melissa certainly had a strange view of life. Rose wondered if there was a certain amount of unavoidable inbreeding in country folk, a bit like royalty but without the Germans. Perhaps she had been wrong to confide in her. Perhaps it was like Dan said and you couldn't sneeze without the whole village coming to offer you a tissue. Only time would tell. She hoped someone else would do something scandalous to whet Melissa's suppressed appetite for adventure and let her off the hook. Still, at least she hadn't told her everything. She probably would never have believed it anyway. There was a certain childlike innocence about Melissa and it was so rare these days – a bit like naturally blonde hair. It seemed churlish to spoil it.

How many people would view the tortuous end of an affair as romantic? It was beyond belief. It was only on the big screen that pain and suffering in the cause of love could be deemed enjoyable. Who was it that said love is ten per cent joy but ninety per cent suffering? Too damn true. There were a lot of adjectives that could have described the end of her affair, but romantic was definitely not one of them. The truth had been pain, suffering, blood-letting and begging.

And doubt? Perhaps out of all the hideous little emotions that could sneak up on you when you weren't looking, doubt was the worst. Nearly the worst. Had she done the right thing? Would Hugh eventually have been able to deliver all the promises he had so glibly and so frequently made? Now she would never know. Ever. She was an ex-lover, ex-city girl and contemplating ex-directory. Even if he wanted to find her he couldn't. Her eyes welled up with tears – which seemed so harsh because she hadn't cried for days now. Well, not really cried. A few measly, easily sniffed-away tears didn't count.

The problem with devastatingly handsome, intelligent, charming, witty, successful, rich, powerful, influential men who are good in bed was that they were usually bastards. And Hugh was no exception.

Chapter Five

BASIL (EXOTIC)

Exotic basil is a yellow or pale green oil with a coarse herbaceous odour with a tinge of camphor. It is moderately toxic and irritating to the skin. No therapeutic benefits have yet been found. True basil has far more value.

from: *The Complete Encyclopaedia of Aromatherapy Oils*
by Jessamine Lovage

Reg, the landlord of the Black Horse, considered himself on good form. He'd won a few bob on the horses yesterday, the beer was flowing through the pipes with relative ease, and business was booming due to the influx of yuppies bored with the soulless watering holes of Milton Keynes.

There was only one immediate and unavoidable blot on the landscape and it had just walked through the door. Reg could tell by the smell before he turned round. It wasn't entirely unpleasant, just the faint whiff of someone having left the lid off a jar of Vicks Vapour Rub.

'Good morning, Basil!' Reg said gamely.

'Is it?' Basil snapped. 'What's so flaming good about it?'

Reg was just about to tell him, but thought better of it. 'Usual?' he asked, reaching for a half-pint jug.

'Does it taste any better than usual?'

'Not really.'

'Then half a pint of your finest cleaning fluid it is, landlord.'

Reg pulled the pint and passed it to Basil who looked at it suspiciously through his monocle. The monocle was a relatively new addition to Basil's inexhaustible list of peculiarities and it suited him down to the ground. It went well with the horse's head cane that he liked to brandish on his walks round the village. Obviously satisfied that his beer wasn't about to kill him, Basil raised it to his lips. 'Up yours, landlord!'

'Up yours too, Basil,' Reg said laconically and continued where he had left off – attempting to arrange the pork scratchings artistically on their cardboard display in order to persuade his customers to buy them before they reached their sell-by date.

It was a time-honoured English tradition that all villages should have an idiot, and Great Brayford had honoured the tradition for some considerable time in the shape of Basil. Village idiots no longer had to be possessed of matted hair, Igoresque features and a hump that would do Quasimodo proud. Nineties style village idiots could just as easily come in the form of a retired civil servant, wear a monocle (definite advantage), a rather threadbare tweed suit and Nike Air Pump trainers – although that wasn't the only mode of dress considered suitable. Equally disturbing to the equilibrium was Basil's alternative of a lilac shell suit and brown leather brogues. In these politically correct times, however, village idiots were more likely to be called eccentrics.

Eccentricity had always been something that the English excelled at. You could admire the French for their sense of dress, the Italians for their food, but where were they when it came to extravagantly weird behaviour? Nonstarters. In fact, the English could probably be classed as world leaders at it. It was the kind of eccentricity that surpassed all intelligence. And Basil possessed it in huge quantities.

Great Brayford was a pretty village. Not extremely so. And certainly no more so than several other villages in the surrounding area. The village green was no more than a rough triangle of scruffy grass that the council ran its mower over periodically. There was a pond which once may have been sparkling and pure but was now dank and choked with duck weed. This made it slightly smelly. There was an unattractive concrete bench where the village youths hung out at night, but as there were only two youths it didn't create much of a problem for the residents. They were more into chewing gum than crack cocaine, and even they went home to watch television at nine o'clock, thinking that something more exciting might happen on the BBC after the watershed.

The green was bordered on one side by the post office and general store – nothing less than the prime site for Mr Patel. On the other side was the Black Horse. Reg was an equal opportunities publican and was just as happy serving a pint of mild as he was a Pimms and lemonade. If your kind of fun was having cucumber floating in your drink, he was not about to argue the toss. The menu board catered for similarly eclectic tastes. There was the traditional Ploughman's Lunch – sweating cheddar cheese, lettuce that was predominantly green and sensible, a large brown pickled onion and, the only attempt at exotica, French bread. The other extreme was the Advertising Executive's Platter – smoked salmon, Parma ham and prawns, an abundance of florid Lollo Rosso adorned with more frills than Mrs Reg possessed on her Ann Summers negligée, all served on ciabatta bread with soured cream dressing. (It would have been focaccia but Mrs Reg felt it sounded too much like an Italian swear word.) Still, it was very popular with the estate agents, oil men and lawyers who had started to frequent the pub since the arrival in Buckinghamshire of two major oil companies. It was equally popular with Reg who couldn't believe how much people were prepared to pay for what was essentially red lettuce. If only he could convince them that pork scratchings were *de rigueur* he could go out and happily roll in the clover. For a man whose taste in carpet ran to brown with red and orange flowers, Reg was surprisingly astute.

On the last side of the isosceles was the church. St Botolph's of the Annunciation. Attractive, mellow stone, old, possibly mediaeval. Next to it was the churchyard. Rows of tombstones tilted like crooked teeth that hadn't had the attention of a good orthodontist, weeds stretched up, tangling round the remnants of decaying bunches of daffodils – an early indicator of spring in Tesco's – that had been left in the few plots that had been inhabited, if that was the right term, this century.

Next to that, in an equally shabby state, was the church hall. It was as unattractive as the church was attractive. The mellow stone that it was once built of had been repaired by a mixture of what appeared to be wooden railway sleepers, asbestos panels, breeze blocks and corrugated tin in a violent shade of British racing green. It was in constant use: Cubs, Scouts, Brownies, Guides – trainee youths to replace the two rapidly growing ones; Toddlers' Group, Women's Institute, Flower Arranging Club, Line Dancing, and Tums, Bums and Thighs. This was all the more surprising because of the dilapidated state of the building. The gingham curtains at the rotted wood windows flapped in the breeze, even with the windows closed. Illumination was supplied by one naked lightbulb hanging from each of the rickety beams. It was not entirely clear whether the beams were supporting the walls or the walls were supporting the beams, or what exactly was holding the roof up. If anything. The lavatory was outside – pre-war plumbing with a high cistern that objected to being flushed and a smooth wooden seat polished by years of warm bottoms. Creature comforts it had not, but there was usually an assorted assembly of creatures inside it. The sort that David Bellamy would be most interested in. It was just as well that there wasn't a light in there either, though it would have come in useful the time that Mrs Took went in to relieve herself and sat on the lap of a passing tramp who had popped in to make use of the convenience as his bed for the night.

Apart from the odd passing tramp, there were very few tourists to Great Brayford. Most of them stopped at Stoke Hammond where there were three congested locks on the Grand Union Canal and you could watch the long-boats struggle through the murky water at a pace that was only suited to the terminally dedicated. There was also a pleasant pub and, usually, an ice-cream van whose trade roared like a lion. Studies had shown that the time it took for one boat to pass through one lock was equivalent to the time it took for the entire length of a White Chocolate Magnum to pass from one wooden stick to one person's stomach. Very few who had enjoyed such rural delights found anything of interest in Great Brayford. Mr Patel stayed resolutely shut on a Sunday morning in reverence to the church opposite, so there was no ice cream. Plus it was the one day of the week when he took his charming wife and his immaculately-behaved children out for a drive in his P-reg Mercedes.

Those strangers who unwittingly did venture into Great Brayford were usually targeted by Basil for a spot of 'village idiot' treatment. Unfortunately this robbed Reg of some weekend income from the halves of shandy and the packets of plain crisps that the tourists might other-wise have consumed in his establishment, having found that the village shop was shut. But he wasn't a man to bear a grudge.

Reg could no longer feign distraction by the pork scratchings to avoid doing the job that landlords hated to do most of all – talking to the customers, particularly when the only customer within arm's reach was Basil. By way of solace he poured himself a large double whisky. 'So, old chap, what's new?' he asked genially.

'They've given that bloody McCartney chap a knighthood. What do you think of that?' Basil nodded aggressively.

Heaven help us all, it was definitely one of those days. Reg took a swig of his whisky. 'Paul McCartney?'

'Sir Paul to you!'

'Basil.' Reg leaned on the bar and exuded as much patience as it was possible to muster for a weary landlord. 'That hardly counts as new. It was the 1997 New Year's Honours List. You're not still brooding over that, surely.'

'What's he ever done for Britain? Tell me that!' Basil prodded the air violently. 'I spent years pushing paper in the name of Queen and country and what did I get for it?'

A big, fat, index-linked pension, Reg felt moved to say, and a boss that clearly didn't care that you were completely off your bonce. 'It wasn't just for what he's done for Britain, Basil. It was for the world. He's one of the most popular entertainers of our time. His songs have made a lot of people very happy. Babies have been conceived to the sound of Lennon and McCartney. He's sold over a hundred million singles. "Yesterday" is one of the most recorded songs ever.'

'Bloody layabout!'

Reg closed his eyes briefly. 'He's amassed a personal fortune of four hundred million pounds, Basil.' Nearly as much as your Civil Service pension, you awkward old bugger.

Basil looked unconvinced. 'It's about time he got a proper job.'

'He does endless work for charity.'

Basil's eyes widened maniacally. 'He's not as good as Perry Como.'

Reg realised that this was a battle that was lost before it was started. Best to give in graciously and wave the white flag in the form of an alcoholic sop. 'Another half pint of cleaning fluid for you, Basil?'

'Is it your round, landlord?'

'Yes,' Reg sighed. He pulled another half and handed the glass to Basil who nodded in thanks. Well, at least that was what he assumed it was; it could have been just a nervous tic.

'What do you think of the nice young lady at number five, Basil? Have you met her yet?'

Basil shook his head and showered froth over the top of the bar, which Mrs Reg hadn't long polished. 'Anise tells me she's a lady of the night but I've heard she's one of these New Agers. Massage or some sort of funny thing.' He grimaced. 'All we needed in my day was a bit of winter green on the offending spot and you were as right as rain. She's probably friends with that Swampy fellow. Next thing you know we'll have a ruddy tunnel running right under us.' He took another swig of his beer. 'She'll lower the tone of the village.'

'She seems very nice.' Reg mopped up the froth with a beer towel.

'So do they all. At first.' Basil nodded sagely. 'Wait till she's sporting dreadlocks and growing cannabis in her herbaceous borders. See if you think she's so nice then.'

'Mrs Reg went to see her about her feet and it stopped, just like that.' Reg clicked his fingers.

'What did?'

'I don't know,' Reg admitted. 'But if Mrs Reg said it stopped, then you can be sure it stopped.'

Basil snorted.

'The only thing Mrs Reg thought was that she was a bit too young and lively to be living in a place like this.

43

Mrs Reg thought she'd get bored. I think it's nice to have some young blood in the village, don't you, Basil?' Otherwise, they'd all be crusty old buggers like you, Reg thought.

Basil looked down his nose. 'Say that again when we've raves going on all night and hip-hop music frightening the sheep.'

It was a pointless conversation. As most were with Basil. Reg decided to try another tack. 'I understand you've been doing some work for the Weston sisters. Gardening or some such, I heard.'

'You heard correctly, mine host.' Basil wiped a soupçon of froth from the ragged ends of his moustache with the sleeve of his tweed jacket.

'I wouldn't have thought that was your cup of tea.'

'Ulterior motive, landlord. Ulterior motive.' Basil winked alarmingly. 'Fine filly, that one!' He winked again. Perhaps it *was* a nervous tic.

'Angelica?' Reg was stunned. 'You've got your eye on the lovely Angelica?'

'Tish, tosh!' Basil spluttered into his beer.

'Let me get this straight then.' Perhaps he should lay off the Teacher's so early in the day. 'If it's not Angelica, that must mean that you fancy Anise?'

'Ooerooraw.' Basil made several Les Dawson-type noises that seemed to signify general approval.

'You? Fancy Anise?' Reg repeated it just to make sure his incredulity wasn't misplaced.

Basil narrowed his eyes and leered lasciviously. It was a terrifying sight. 'She's the Queen Boadicea of Great Brayford!'

'We are talking about the same Anise here, aren't we?' It always paid to be absolutely sure with Basil.

'I should say so!' More Les-type noises accompanied the statement. 'She's like one of the Spice Girls!'

'I don't think there is an Old Stroppy Spice,' Reg said

with conviction. 'They have to be young and stroppy. That's the point.'

Basil looked perplexed.

'Anise is a cantankerous old bat! I wouldn't have thought she was your type at all.' Then again . . .

'I resent you calling the woman I love a cantankerous old bat! She's a valiant, headstrong, sex-goddess old bat!' Basil downed his half and slammed the empty glass on the bar. This time he didn't wipe the froth from his moustache with his sleeve, or with anything else. Or from his beard. 'In future I shall be taking my business to another, more congenial establishment.' He stood up and headed for the door.

Reg straightened himself up and with a great surge of effort put the glass in the dishwasher. 'You won't get free beer anywhere else, Basil.'

'In that case, landlord, I shall see you at the same time tomorrow.'

'See you tomorrow, Basil.'

Reg turned to tidy the beer towel on the bar and the door banged on its hinges, startling the estate agents at the corner table tucking into their Lollo Rosso. Perhaps he should just have another small whisky. This sort of news couldn't be absorbed when one was entirely sober. Reg knocked the whisky back in a gulp. Tears sprang to his eyes that were incidental to the swift consumption of Scottish water. Basil and Anise! Wait till he told Mrs Reg. He shook his head. If Basil could be that far off beam in his tweed and Nikes, he really should be grateful that it wasn't a lilac shell suit day.

Chapter Six

'Why do you call your house Builder's Bottom?' Rose was perched on the edge of the dust sheet which covered her treatment couch, watching as Dan knocked the reluctant bricks out of the fireplace with a hammer and chisel.

'To annoy the neighbours.' He paused and brushed his arm across his face, smearing it with dust. There was a sheen of sweat on his skin which was glowing slightly pink beneath his tan. He looked a bit like a Chippendale, but without the fake tan. Dan's smooth brown skin was rugged and realistic, acquired from hours sweating outdoors. When he wasn't smiling, tiny white lines showed at the corners of his eyes where the sun had failed to shine. It proved that he normally smiled a lot. 'I have a childish, rebellious streak. They think I'm lowering the tone of the area.'

'And are you?'

He gave her a knowing look. 'I would normally have said no but it's a bit of a contentious point at the moment.'

'Really?'

'I'm looking to knock the church hall down and build a block of flats.'

Rose twisted her mouth in sympathy. 'I can see how that would make you popular. I have to say though that it doesn't sound like a very nice option. The church hall is such a busy little place, there's always something going on. And flats in Great Brayford? Heaven forbid!'

He sat back on his heels, resting the hammer on his knees. 'It's not as bad as it sounds. The block of flats isn't exactly going to be a skyscraper; there's only eight flats planned. Retirement flats. Very exclusive. And I'd rebuild the village hall. It might well be a busy little place, but it's also a complete dump. If we get any high winds during the winter, it'll probably be a goner anyway. Believe it or not, I'm trying to be community-minded.'

'You're concerned about the state of the bottoms and thighs of the village ladies, are you?'

A smile spread across Dan's face, making the white spidery lines disappear. 'I like to think it's for slightly more altruistic reasons than that.'

'Is it likely to go ahead?'

'Yes. But the negotiations are at a bit of a stalemate at the moment and there's some rising local opposition. Fortunately, they only managed to mobilise themselves after the planning permission came through so it shouldn't present too much of a problem.'

'It's causing bad feeling though.'

He shrugged. 'People don't like change. Whether it's good or bad, the general consensus is that change is best avoided.'

She picked aimlessly at some hard skin on her finger and stared out of the window. 'I can empathise with that.'

'Finding it difficult to settle in?'

'No . . . well . . . Yes. I suppose so.'

'Have you always been this decisive?'

She laughed. 'I love it here really. I think. It's just that it's not as friendly as I thought it would be. I thought London was a pretty cold and impersonal place, but this is just as bad somehow. I hadn't really expected that.' She pulled her foot up to her knee and absently examined the yellow stitching round the hem of her jeans. 'I feel people are holding me at arm's length and I don't know why.'

'Give them time. We're not used to strangers round these parts.'

'You should be though. You said yourself that nearly everyone is an immigrant.' Rose scanned the room trying to find something to anchor on to. She still felt so adrift here. Was it the people or was it within her? Her eyes rested on a pretty poster depicting reflexology points that had been hastily put up in a plastic clip frame. It showed the bottom of two dainty feet adorned with flitting butterflies and delicate line drawings of herbs and flowers. The reflex points were marked with pale pastel blobs indicating the general location of vague points of interest such as the gall bladder, the solar plexus and the elusive ileocaecal valve. The feet were marked 'left foot' and 'right foot' in fancy italic writing, just in case you were in any doubt. The poster was a soft and gentle interpretation of something that was, essentially, quite clinical and gave no indication that if you worked some of the reflex points, it would hurt like hell. Like life really.

There was no need for her to feel so restless here. It was a wonderful house. A wonderful garden. And this was a perfect room to do her treatments in, especially once the fireplace was open again. It was decorated all in stark white at the moment, which was clean and fresh, but a bit harsh. She would soften it down eventually, perhaps to lavender or peach to match her towels. She wanted her clients to feel warm, safe, cosseted, loved. And, heaven knows perhaps this was the crux of the problem – she wanted that for herself too.

Dan put his tools down and sat on the hearth, stretching his long legs out in front of him. 'Well ... do you mind if I'm honest with you?'

'No,' Rose said tentatively.

'I think it may have something to do with what you do.'

'What I do?'

'Don't quote me on this. Promise?' She nodded

reluctantly. Dan cleared his throat and Rose suspected that it had nothing to do with the fine layer of dust that was settling comfortably over everything. 'I think they suspect you get up to all manner of salacious things in here.'

'Salacious!' Rose's eyes widened in disbelief. 'I can't even spell salacious!'

'I think they worry about the number of male visitors you get.' Dan raised an eyebrow.

'No!' She clapped her hands to her mouth.

'Well, you know what they're like. Everyone's heard of aromatherapy, but do people really know what it involves? Particularly round here. Perhaps you should have an open evening to tell them about the tricks of your trade and then they wouldn't be so suspicious.'

Rose jumped down from the couch and took to pacing the floor. She flicked her thumb towards the general direction of Lavender Hill. 'I take it that it's mainly those two old biddies over the road that have got me marked down as Cynthia Payne's sister?'

'Mainly,' he agreed. 'Although it's probably Anise more than Angelica. She's the harridan – poor Angelica is just dragged along in her wake.'

Rose flopped on to the stool waiting expectantly at the end of her couch. 'This is pathetic!' She buried her face in her hands. 'As if I haven't got enough to worry about.' There was a catch in her voice that she didn't like the sound of.

'Look . . .' Dan pushed his hammer away from him. 'These bricks won't mind waiting a bit longer. Let me just have a quick wash and I'll make us a nice cup of tea.'

She smiled at him through watery eyes. 'You go and wash, I'll make the tea. If it takes you as long to brew up as it does to knock a few bricks out, we could both die of thirst!'

* * *

She put the teapot on the table in the kitchen as he came through the door. 'Sugar?' she asked brightly, to show that she was perfectly happy and in control again.

He shook his head and sank into the chair opposite her. She'd had to buy all new furniture since she'd been here. If you could call the ancient, scratched chairs with rickety legs that they sat on new. New to her. Hugh's generosity hadn't run to Conran or even John Lewis furniture. It had been MFI or junk shops. The junk shops had won. She had grand plans for those long lonely winter evenings. There was great fun to be had with nothing more than a sponge and emulsion paint these days. So she'd heard.

Dan picked up the spoon from the sugar bowl, shook the few clinging crystals from it and used it, pointlessly, to stir his tea. 'I didn't mean to upset you,' he said, not looking up. 'I just thought you should know what they're saying. I was trying to help.'

'I know.' She nursed her cup of tea to her. The warmth in her hands was soothing. 'I just overreacted a bit. I should be used to derogatory comments about my chosen profession by now. You get the nudge-nudge, wink-wink merchants in every walk of life. They have one thing in common though, they're usually pig ignorant and haven't even tried aromatherapy.'

'I think that's maligning pigs.'

'It upsets me when I work so hard at it.' Her eyes filled with tears again and she brushed them away. 'I'm sorry, I'm being a complete wimp. I haven't slept too well these last few nights, which doesn't help.' She looked up at him. 'I've had a couple of crank calls in the early hours. It's since the ad went in the local paper.' Rose smiled ruefully.

Dan looked worried. 'What sort of calls where they? You should tell Frank.'

Rose waved a hand dismissively. 'Oh, they were nothing

really. It's just me being stupid. Whoever it was didn't say anything when I picked up the phone, there was no "What colour knickers are you wearing?" or anything like that. They were just there. Listening. They didn't even bother to heavy breathe,' she said with a lightness she didn't feel. 'I'll have a word with Frank if it carries on, or I'll try to remember to switch the answerphone on at night. Listening to my message droning on should put anyone off ringing. Even clients.'

Dan continued to look concerned.

'I'm not used to this country lark yet,' she said reassuringly. 'I've come from a busy, noisy block of flats on the corner of a main road to a lone, creaking house down a tiny lane. It's going to take a bit of getting used to.'

'It's really none of my business,' Dan said, looking at his tea as if there was something about to surface in it, 'but what brought you out here? Great Brayford isn't exactly the centre of the universe. This is not a happening place to be for a bright young thing like you.'

She looked up at him sharply, but his face was intent on peering into his mug and all she got was the top of his head – which was now well and truly dirty blond. Brick dust blond.

He continued, unaware of her scrutiny, 'Even the raves we have round here finish at eleven o'clock.'

'Would it surprise you to know that I'm not into raves?'

He looked up then, a slow, easy smile on his lips, and for the first time she noticed his eyes. They were like clear reflective pools. As green and pure as the rolling fields that spread out beyond the boundaries of her garden. Hugh's eyes were deep, shrouded, enigmatic, and showed you your soul – the dark side.

'It's better if you're not into night life at all,' he said. 'Unless you call a quick pint with Reg before last orders night life. There are some clubs in Milton

Keynes, but it helps if you're under fourteen.'

She smiled. 'I've done all that – hitting the heights. I want a quiet life.'

'At your tender years?' He looked unconvinced. 'There are graveyards that are rowdier than this place. And why give up a thriving practice in London to set up out here? It's not exactly a brilliant catchment area for you.' The clear, green eyes fixed her again. 'About the only thing this place is good for is running away from everything.'

'One hit, one nail, one head,' she said emphatically. It was no use denying it. It must shine out from her like a lighthouse beacon – RUNNING AWAY!

'Bad relationship?' Dan ventured.

'The worst.'

'Husband?'

'Yes.' She managed a wry smile. 'Someone else's.'

'Ah.'

She cupped her chin with her hand. 'Do you make it your business to be right about everything?'

'Why do you think I wear this continual smug smile?' The smile disappeared. 'I didn't mean to pry.'

'Yes you did. And in some ways I'm glad. I haven't really got anyone to talk to. I tried explaining to Melissa, but she thinks I'm some sort of Scarlett O'Hara. It's only true love if it's painful and all that crap.'

'And is it?'

'What? True love or crap?'

'I was thinking of the former.'

'True love?' She shook her head. 'It was. Now I don't know.' She shrugged. It was amazing what liars her shoulders were, saying 'Ho-ho, we don't care!' when she did care – desperately. 'Melissa was right about one thing though. I may not be Scarlett O'Hara, but Hugh did a pretty favourable impersonation of Rhett Butler.'

'Hugh?'

She nodded. 'Arrogant, charming, reckless, devil-may-care. Git.'

'You sound like you've been bottling this up.'

'I try sometimes to talk to my clients, but they're not really interested.' Hell, why was this so hard to admit. 'They're paying me to listen to their troubles not the other way round. I know all about their cute cats, ailing dogs, terrible children, errant husbands, difficult relatives, impossible jobs, faulty cars. Most of the time they can't even remember my name.' She stood up and took her cup to the sink. 'Anyway, now I'm being maudlin. You'll get your violin out in a minute and sing "Poor Old You". And that would depress me even more.'

'It would if you heard me sing,' he quipped.

She smiled thankfully, then turned back to Dan. 'What made *you* run away to Great Brayford?'

'My dad.' He picked up his cup and joined her at the sink. 'We moved out here to Bucks twenty-odd years ago to catch the building boom that Milton Keynes promised. My dad wanted to leave us a good inheritance and, for the most part, it worked. I moved into the village about ten years ago, when I bought Builder's Bottom.'

'How long have you been with Gardenia?' It had cost her ten first-class stamps to get the information about Dan's other half out of Mr Patel at the post office. The fount of all gossip. The juiciness of the tit-bit seemed to rise proportionately with the amount of groceries stacked in the tatty wire baskets. She had a lot to learn about village life.

'Gardi? For ever, I think,' he said flippantly. 'We've had what you might call an on-off relationship since we were teenagers. She moved in with me when I bought the house. Occasionally, she makes a great show about leaving. A week later, I'll walk in and she'll be cooking my dinner and life goes on as normal.'

'Oh please, not another "My wife doesn't understand me" scenario!'

'Well, for one, she's not my wife. And for another, she understands me perfectly. That's why she doesn't like me.' They smiled at each other. Rose rinsed the cups under the tap. Dan picked up the tea towel and wiped them languorously. 'We want different things in life. I don't really know why we're still together. I think it's just that we always have been. It's getting to the point where things will have to change though.' He sniffed self-consciously. 'I want kids and she doesn't. Neither of us is getting any younger. I want someone to leave the business to. I know it sounds stupid, but when you've worked this hard, you just don't want to sell out to someone that won't care.'

'What about your brother, Alan? Doesn't he run it with you?'

'Sort of. I supply the brains – and most of the brawn, come to think of it. Alan just likes driving dumper trucks, he's not committed to it like me.'

'Supposing you could persuade Gardi to have a baby, what if it was a girl?'

'I wouldn't be a sexist father. I don't care, boy, girl, as long as it's healthy. If it was a girl she'd just not have to mind breaking her fingernails on bricks.' His smile faded. 'Anyway, Gardi's adamant. She's too bothered about losing her figure. She says she doesn't want breasts like spaniel's ears and a stomach with tramlines. I don't know why she's so worried, we live next door to a flaming plastic surgeon.'

'This sounds like the start of a row you've had more than once.'

He stared into the garden, still rubbing at the cup with the tea towel although it had been dry for the last five minutes. 'We don't row about it any more, we both just ignore it and hope it will go away.' He looked back at her.

'Listen to me! I don't know why I'm talking to you like this – you're an aromatherapist, not a psychiatrist.'

'With some of the things people tell me, I often wonder if there's a difference. Except psychiatrists get paid more.' Rose took the cup from him before he rubbed the pattern off it. 'It's been nice talking to you,' she said. 'I'm glad we've had the chance. I feel a lot better now. Thanks.'

There was a momentary pause. One of those pauses that goes on just that bit too long and starts to border on the uncomfortable.

Without warning he put his hands on her hips and turned her to him. His fingers nearly spanned her entire width and they were so hot! Even through her jeans and her sensible knickers underneath them, she could feel heat emanating from them. Unable to meet his eyes, she looked at his neck. A pulse beat erratically in his throat. A similar one in hers decided to join in, making swallowing, and breathing in general, quite difficult.

'I want you to call me if ever you have a problem.' His voice was earnest and it rooted her to the spot. 'Don't be alone here, Rose. You know where I am. Night or day. Just come and knock.'

'At Builder's Bottom?' she said breathlessly.

'At Builder's Bottom.' His eyes searched hers. 'Promise?'

'Promise,' she whispered. 'Won't Gardenia mind?'

'Probably.' He let go of her as suddenly as he had first touched her. The break in contact was so abrupt that she thought she might pass out. Her skin still burned. She was sure that when she took off her jeans there would be two bright red hand prints seared into her skin, which would last for days. She would have to slap some chamomile and lavender on it.

Dan looked at his watch. His face was flushed and he was breathing more heavily than he did when he was knocking out the bricks. 'I'll have to get on with your fireplace. Gardenia wants to go shopping in Milton Keynes. I said I'd try to finish quickly so that I could take her.' He smiled thinly. 'It's my penance for being happy in a former life. If I'm late she gets very unpleasant. She goes green and her head spins round like that charming little child in *The Exorcist*.'

'I don't mind if you go.' At least her voice still worked. 'You can come back another day.'

'What time is it?'

Rose checked the clock. 'Eleven thirty.'

'I'm late,' he said with a grimace. 'She'll be long gone by now.'

'I'm sorry. I don't want to get you into trouble.'

'It's okay. It's not your fault, I'm always in trouble with Gardenia.' He looked at the fireplace. 'It won't take me long.' He started to peel off his sweatshirt and Rose's heart stopped momentarily. 'I've got to take this off,' he explained as he was pulling it over his head, 'before I blow a gasket. It's absolutely boiling in here.'

Underneath, she was relieved to see, he was wearing a white T-shirt. A tight, white T-shirt. A very tight, white T-shirt. A bit like Patrick Swayze's T-shirt in *Dirty Dancing*. All rippling biceps, bulging muscles and a six-pack for a stomach. Was that the only reason why he was flushed and panting heavily, the fact that it was as hot as a greenhouse in here? Perhaps she had been misreading the signs? Come to think of it, what was she doing even getting close enough to read signs? Hugh's side of the bed was barely cold, metaphorically speaking, and here she was getting hot under the collar about another man. Another attached man. Okay, so they weren't married, but was it really any different at the end of the day? Wasn't one bitter and painful lesson more than enough? How could she even think about going through that again?

She watched Dan from the doorway as he chipped away patiently at the bricks, his face set in concentration, trying to make the least possible amount of mess. Although he had stripped down to his T-shirt, beads of perspiration were covering his brow. The reason that it was always so hot in the house was that the minute her clients came in they were required to take off their clothes and lie on her couch covered only by a towel while she massaged them with warm oil. Now try saying there was nothing salacious in that! She wondered what Anise and Angelica would make of it. Or even Dan. Suddenly she was feeling very hot and sweaty herself. The promises she had made to herself seemed to be ringing as hollowly as Hugh's. Despite her stern warnings to the contrary, her internal thermostat had deliberately disobeyed her and gone into massive overdrive.

Chapter Seven

GARDENIA
A dark oil with a rich, sweet, floral undertone and jasmine-like scent. Almost all gardenia oil is synthetically produced. It is employed only in high-quality oriental fragrances. Therapeutically, gardenia has no obvious benefits.

from: *The Complete Encyclopaedia of Aromatherapy Oils*
by Jessamine Lovage

Gardenia was pissed off and didn't mind who knew about it. Fortunately, Cassia was pissed off too, so they sat and talked at each other, neither entirely listening to the other's sorry tale nor pausing for breath more often than was strictly necessary. Reluctantly, they were in the Black Horse, but were pleased with themselves for having purloined the table nearest the fire. This hadn't been particularly hard; being Saturday there was a sad lack of estate agents, oil men and lawyers, and it was left to the locals to swell Reg's coffers. The trouble with Milton Keynes was that, as far as Gardenia and Cassia were concerned, there was nowhere to be seen. It was all brash, modern junk-food chains that tried to make up for a lack of character and atmosphere by neon paint, loud Tamla Motown music and waitresses who wore men's clothes. There were no bijou little haunts favoured by

Buckinghamshire's answer to the glitterati, no discreet little cafés, no tasteful little wine bars. Well, there was Nicholl's in Woburn but that didn't really count. The food was sublime, but it wasn't so much frequented by anybody who was anyone as by people who thought they were someone. There was a distinct difference. Life in Bucks was proving a constant disappointment to Gardenia. Let's face it, there's only so much posing you can do in a backwater country pub.

Milton Keynes Development Corporation might have devoted millions of pounds and countless man-hours to developing a city where every road was a straight line and there were no traffic jams. It was all very commendable. But where was the heart? Having attracted all these top-ranking businesses to the place, where exactly were all the seriously affluent supposed to go? Back into London, where they'd just been lured out of? Where was the cultural centre? The art gallery, the theatre – the places where you went for tiresome small talk, tinkling laughter and tippling champagne? Entertainment seemed to re-volve around The Point, a neon pyramid crammed with slot machines and video games devoted to bringing sensory relief to spotty thirteen-year-olds in scruffy leather jackets, before they went to watch something equally mindless on one of its ten cinema screens. That was it. The sum and total. The problem with Milton Keynes was that there was nowhere to show off. What was the point of wearing Nicole Farhi to sit in the dark and munch popcorn?

'I'm pissed off, Cassia,' Gardenia said tightly.

Cassia shook her head. 'I know, darling. You said.'

'No, I mean really pissed off this time.'

'I know, darling.' Cassia creased her eyes sympath-etically and raised her white wine to her pouted lips.

'I mean it's Saturday – Saturday, for pity's sake – and what are we doing? Sitting in some down-at-heel pub, drinking Reg's cheap plonk. I mean, it's just not enough, is it?'

'I know, darling.' Cassia picked at the smoked salmon on her Advertising Executive's Platter. 'But at least these days Reg is producing food that doesn't contract your arteries by just looking at it.'

Gardenia, with a pained expression, nodded in agreement and pushed her Lollo Rosso round her plate. She sighed theatrically. 'When I signed up for life this wasn't what I expected at all.'

'I know, darling.' Cassia dabbed the corners of her mouth with her serviette. 'You need a little excitement.'

'Where from? Where exactly do you go round here for excitement?'

'Search me, sweetie.' Cassia shrugged and slurped her wine. 'Greg is in the Bahamas for another bloody world conference on plastic surgery. Why, I ask you, do you have to go to the Bahamas to learn how to cut even more bits off ugly people? Why? And why, if he had to go, couldn't he take me?'

'I know, darling. I know,' Gardenia said sympathetically. 'But at least you have reflected kudos. At least when Greg goes to the Bahamas you can tell people. It sounds very impressive. I mean a plastic surgeon, it's so fashionable. Where does Dan ever go? I can't really tell people that he spends his life in Milton Keynes laying bricks. Where's the envy factor in that?'

'I know, darling.'

They both sipped their wine and gazed longingly into the flames that licked the sooty sides of the fireplace.

'He's round with that woman at number five.' Gardenia tossed her long dark hair in the general direction of Rose's house. 'He was supposed to come shopping in MK with me, but he had a prior engagement to knock bricks out of her fireplace. He said it wouldn't take him long.' She raised her eyebrows and stared pointedly at her Cartier watch.

Cassia looked around her, checking that no one was eavesdropping. 'She's supposed to be a . . . a . . .' she dropped her voice to a hushed tone, '. . . a woman of the night. Anise told me she has a constant stream of dishevelled men coming out of there. Lucky bitch!'

'It's much more boring than that, Cassia.' Gardenia sighed wearily. 'I hate to disappoint you but she's only an aromatherapist.'

'Oh.' Cassia tutted miserably. They both took another swig of wine and stared at the fireplace. 'Still,' she brightened, 'it'll be nice to have some alternative therapies on our very own doorstep. Who knows, we might drag Great Brayford screaming into the nineties yet.'

'I take it you mean the nineteen nineties.' They both laughed brightly. Once the hilarity had died down, Gardenia continued, 'Apparently, she's done Cliff Richard.'

'No!' Cassia was wide-eyed with astonishment.

Gardenia nodded knowingly. 'And Mick Hucknall from Simply Red.'

'Well,' Cassia was astounded. 'I'm simply green. Perhaps she'll be worth a visit.'

'There must be something about her,' Gardenia said tartly. 'She's the only thing that's put a smile on Dan's face in the last few months.'

'Really?'

'He came home smirking and drooling like a teenage boy last week after he'd been to see her.'

'You let him go to her for a massage?' Cassia asked incredulously.

'No. He's not into that sort of thing. I told you, he's opening up her fireplace.' Gardenia stabbed at her smoked salmon. 'He couldn't wait to get round there this morning.'

'So Dan's got a case of the wandering eyes?' Cassia sat back and crossed her legs.

'If only!' Gardenia sneered. 'You know what he's like. She's just another one of his hard-luck stories. Another damsel in distress who needs rescuing by the mighty bricklaying knight in a Land Rover Discovery. He's not happy unless he's doing a good deed for someone. It turns him into a simpering simpleton.'

'She's very pretty, you know,' Cassia conceded. 'In a natural sort of way.' She narrowed her eyes to slits. 'I wouldn't let Greg anywhere near her.'

'Yes, but Greg isn't Dan. Dan hasn't got a deceitful bone in his body.'

Cassia snorted. 'Don't be fooled, Gardenia. They're all the same. Strip away the layers and they're all bastards underneath.' She pushed the plate of food away from her. The Lollo Rosso had gone limp. 'You don't think I'm under any delusions about what Greg gets up to at these so-called conferences. Swaying palms, all those innocuous-looking multi-coloured drinks with flowers in that can have you flat on your back in half an hour, all those dusky-skinned maidens. I'm no fool, Gardenia. I can tell exactly how much he's been misbehaving by the size of the bottle of duty-free perfume he brings me home.'

'Dan would never dream of leaving me. He wouldn't dare.'

Cassia flared her nostrils. 'I wouldn't waste a fiver on it at William Hill's.'

'You don't know him like I do.'

'Why are you defending him now? Only a moment ago you were complaining about him fiddling with someone else's fireplace.'

'It's just that I wanted him to come shopping with me but he wouldn't cancel. He said he'd promised her.' Gardenia huffed. 'Anyway, I've made other arrangements now.' She looked sideways at Cassia.

'You've haven't!'

Gardenia smiled smugly. 'While the cat is knocking bricks out of a fireplace, the mouse must make her own entertainment.'

'Come on then, spit it out – you know you can't keep a secret.'

Gardenia looked coy. 'I don't know if I should tell you.'

'Of course you should, darling!'

'Well . . .' Gardenia moved her Advertising Executive's Platter to one side and leaned forward conspiratorially. 'Ouch!'

'Dan!' Cassia said sweetly. 'How nice to see you.'

Gardenia rubbed her ankle where Cassia had kicked her under the table. Her brow furrowed. Dan was ducking under the low beam that guarded the entrance to the snug by the fire. It was a well-known hazard for the locals but still had a good go at decapitating anyone over five foot two who wasn't paying attention to it. For a moment Gardenia thought Dan looked taken aback. She studied him closely. He was definitely looking a bit sheepish. Perhaps he was feeling guilty for not taking her shopping after all. He looked over his shoulder shiftily and Gardenia followed his eyes. Rose stood behind him, still in the doorway, unwinding a chenille scarf from round her neck and struggling valiantly out of her coat. Dan took it from her and she smiled. He hung it carefully on the coat rack by the door. Gardenia's frown deepened. It had been a very intimate smile. She glanced at her watch. And look at the time. Just how many bricks did one flaming fireplace have?

'Hi, you two,' Dan said, striding over to join them. 'I didn't expect to see you here. I thought you'd be putting your plastic through its paces by now.' He kissed Gardenia fleetingly on the forehead. She'd never noticed before how fleeting his kisses were. When had their mouths stopped lingering together? When had their lips gone from moist to dry? When had they moved on to cheek pecking? And now foreheads? 'Fireplace finished?' she asked tartly.

Dan flushed. 'Not quite.'

Gardenia smiled sardonically. Hesitantly, Rose joined them.

'Gardenia, can I introduce you to Rose?'

Do I have a choice? Gardenia asked herself. 'Hello,' she said to Rose.

'Hello.' Rose pulled up a chair and joined them at their cramped table overflowing with half-eaten platters and lipstick-smeared wine glasses.

'Hello, darling.' Cassia extended her hand. Her voice was gruff and sultry like Mariella Frostrup's – who always sounded to Rose as if she smoked upwards of forty Benson and Hedges a day. 'Cassia Wales. No relation,' she tittered.

'To who?' Rose looked perplexed.

'Charles, Prince of,' Cassia explained patiently.

'Oh,' Rose said pleasantly. 'I thought you meant Killer.'

'I'm sorry?'

'Killer whales,' Rose explained. 'It's a joke.'

'Oh.' Cassia laughed lightly, but it sounded as if she wasn't sure why. She tried another tack. 'My husband's a plastic surgeon. He's at a conference in the Bahamas at the moment.'

'That's nice,' Rose replied, unsure as to whether Cassia was expecting commiserations or congratulations.

When there wasn't anything more effusive forthcoming, Cassia continued, 'I've been hearing so much about you.'

'All good, I hope,' Rose said self-consciously. Neither of them replied.

Dan stepped into the breech. 'What would you like to drink, Rose?'

'Mineral water, please. Sparkling.'

Gardenia narrowed her eyes. There was that smile again. 'It's a good job you moved here after the oil companies did. Before that, Reg had no idea that Perrier was a town in France, let alone that they bottled water,' she said with a forced laugh.

'Perrier *isn't* a town in France,' Dan said. 'It's just a trade name.'

Gardenia flushed furiously. 'I know that!'

'Would either of you like another drink?' he asked, judiciously changing the subject.

Was she getting paranoid or was Dan looking pointedly at the glasses on the table. She stood up quickly. Too quickly. 'I was just going.'

Cassia looked surprised. 'Were you?'

'Are you still going into Milton Keynes?' Dan asked. 'If you wait till I've eaten, I'll come with you.'

'I've made other arrangements,' Gardenia snapped. She was far too overdressed for Milton Keynes and wondered if Dan had noticed.

'Cassia?' Dan moved his hand to signal drink.

'No, no. I'll just finish this.' She downed the rest of her wine in one gulp. 'Sorry to dash,' she said to Rose. 'I must come to see you. I absolutely adore aromatherapy!' She stood up to leave and patted Rose's arm. 'Do give my regards to Cliff.'

Rose looked at her blankly.

'I've always been a great fan myself.'

'Cassia,' Gardenia fumed. 'Are you coming?'

'Yes, darling.' She winked at Rose.

Dan returned with the drinks and sat down next to Rose. Reg followed him with a hangdog expression and a damp cloth and slowly cleared the table. 'I'll see you later then,' Dan said brightly.

'I could be back late,' Gardenia said.

'The shops shut at six o'clock,' Dan pointed out.

Gardenia hussled Cassia out of the door and into the street. The cold air hit her like a slap after the warmth of the pub and she wished she had worn something more sensible than the short-skirted suit she had on. But sensible wasn't what she was planning to be.

'Are you going to tell me now?' Cassia hissed.

'What?' Gardenia was distracted. They had looked so comfortable together, like two old armchairs next to the fire. She peered in through the window; they were chatting animatedly over their drinks.

'Don't be difficult. You know!'

Gardenia glanced at her watch. 'I can't, I'll be late.' It was a lie, but suddenly she'd had enough of everyone. Even Cassia. Like Greta Garbo, she very much wanted to be alone. Well, perhaps not entirely alone. 'Tums, Bums and Thighs on Monday?'

'I can't wait till then,' Cassia tutted. 'Phone me. As soon as you can. I want to know everything. And I mean *everything*!'

'Okay. I'd better go.' They kissed the crisp air at the side of each other's faces. Gardenia watched as her friend clicked back up Lavender Hill towards her house. If she was going to be unsensible in or out of her unsensible suit, the last person in the world that she should ever dream of telling was Cassia Wales unless she wanted the whole village to know by tea-time. She was in no doubt really about the fair-weather allegiance of her friend. One sniff of Cliff Richard and she'd be scrambling over the battlements into the enemy camp quicker than Cliff could sing 'Living Doll'.

Chapter Eight

Gardenia had taken Rose quite by surprise. It wasn't just that she was sitting as large as life in the pub when Dan had quite clearly expected that she would be long gone to Milton Keynes, it was the way she looked. It wasn't what she had expected at all. Dan was so natural, so easy, so unaffected. Whereas Gardenia was totally artificial, and utterly stunning. Everyone – well, mainly Mr Patel – had said she was beautiful. They just hadn't managed to convey quite how beautiful. She was tall and slim – no, not slim. Thin. Very thin. Thinner than Jodie Kidd, if that was humanly possible. But it suited her. She had an oriental, exotic look, delicate like an orchid. Her hair was long and dark, almost black, and shiny like the coat of a well-groomed cat. Her eyes were slightly slanted, adding to the overall feline impression, and they were piercing china-blue.

No wonder she didn't want kids. She had the kind of figure that wouldn't take kindly to being ruined. If there had been supermodels in Great Brayford, she could quite easily have been one. Except that now she was the wrong side of thirty and, consequently, about fifteen years too late. Also her mouth was too bitter. If it had been softer, she would have been irresistible. But it wasn't and it made Rose feel pathetically relieved.

Dan was stretched out, eschewing the contour of his chair, feet dangerously close to the hearth. He nursed his pint to his chest and was looking decidedly thoughtful. The flickering light from the fire caught the few amber tints in his hair that hadn't been entirely caked in brick dust and still had some sort of reflective index left. Rose broke the silence. 'I didn't expect to see Gardenia here.'

Dan looked at her over the top of his beer. 'Me neither.'

'She didn't seem too cross,' Rose said hopefully. 'At least her head didn't spin round.'

'It will,' he assured her. 'She's just saving it for later.'

'I'm sorry if I made you late.'

'It's not your fault. She knew where I was.' He looked at her and his eyes were soft and soporific in the fireside glow. 'Gardenia doesn't have enough to occupy her mind – she let's little things worry her.'

Rose picked up her Perrier. The glass was freezing. What on earth was she doing drinking cold water on a day like this? It was a day for frothy hot chocolate with whipped cream or for boiling up snow and ice and drinking beefy Bovril. She put the glass down again. 'What does she do?'

'Do?' Dan pursed his lips in thought. 'I'm not sure that *doing* is a concept Gardenia understands. She just *is*. She does that very well. If that counts.'

'Doesn't she work?'

Dan shook his head. 'No.'

'But she looks after the house?'

Dan shook his head again. 'No. We have a cleaner.' He took a drink of his beer, smacking his lips as he drew the glass back to his chest. 'She cooks occasionally. When we've had a row. So she's cooking more often these days.'

That woman shouldn't be called Gardenia, Rose thought enviously, she should be called Riley – she certainly had his life. 'What does she do all day?'

'You don't look that beautiful by accident. It takes a lot of time and effort. And money,' he said as an afterthought.

Rose flushed. So they might row and fight and have

different views about what they wanted from life but he still finds her beautiful. 'It must make conversation difficult,' she remarked tartly, regretting it as soon as she'd said it.

'Not for Gardenia. She can talk endlessly about *Neighbours, Home and Away, Emmerdale, Brookside, Coronation Street* – you name it, Gardenia knows about it. For someone who has so many aspirations socially, she's amazingly content with observing the rigours of fictitious people's tangled lives. It's just a shame that I don't watch any of the soaps.' His face hardened momentarily. 'I'm too busy working.'

Rose felt abashed. 'Now I'm the one that's prying.'

'This is the most taxing conversation I've had for a long time.'

'I'm sorry.'

A smile appeared on his lips, a slow, serious smile. 'It wasn't a complaint.'

'I take it Cassia doesn't work either.' It was better to get this back on more neutral ground. Cassia was a different kettle of fish to Gardenia. Trout rather than the finest caviare. Old trout. Not that much older, well into her forties probably but dressed considerably younger. You could tell that her husband had practised his trade on her. Several times. She, too, was beautiful, but somehow you could tell that she'd picked it all out of a catalogue. Her features were perfect on an individual basis, but they didn't quite hang together properly. A bit like Michael Jackson's nose which stuck out like a sore thumb – if that wasn't mixing her metaphors too thoroughly. In Cassia's case, too, the whole was certainly less than the sum of the parts.

'Ah, well, you'd be wrong.' His face held a supercilious look. 'She's a minor celebrity round these parts. Well, Cassia would like to think so. She presents a show on local radio – Bucks County FM or something.'

'What's the show about?'

Dan shrugged his shoulders. 'I have absolutely no idea. I've never had the good fortune to listen to it. Probably gossip – it seems to be Cassia's forte. It's on in the mid-afternoon, I think, when all good builders are hard at their graft.'

'Well, you do surprise me.' Rose gave an approving look. 'Hidden talents.'

'I wouldn't get too carried away. I'd hardly call it a serious job. It only takes her about three hours a week. That's hardly likely to keep her in the style she's become accustomed to.'

'It's a start, though.' A puzzled look crossed Rose's face. 'It doesn't explain why she's had her face all cut up like a jigsaw, if she's only on the radio.'

'I think Cassia's ambition is like her credit card, it knows no bounds. She's ever hopeful of a phone call from the producers of *Richard and Judy* to say that Judy's been given the chop and could she hot foot it instantly to London to sidle up next to Richard "the boy wonder" Madley on the sofa.' Dan drained his glass and put it on the table. He stretched his arms above his head and cracked his knuckles. Rose shuddered. She would have to tell him about the joys of Benzoin oil one day, the Castrol GTX of the aroma-therapy world, before his fingers locked into a mass of gnarled arthritic joints. 'Besides, if you had a husband in the trade it must be tempting to get him to do a few little jobs on the side. Though I'm not sure if I'd be too keen to let my other half loose on me with a sharp scalpel.'

'It would probably be better than a blunt one,' Rose said philosophically.

Dan laughed and stood up. It was obviously time for him to be going, which was a shame. She'd been enjoying his company, but it wouldn't do to forget that he was someone else's. Someone whom she couldn't even begin to compete with.

'I don't know about you but I'm starving. Do you want something to eat?'

Rose contemplated the remains of the blackboard, ridiculously glad of the chance of a reprieve. 'I'll have ham, egg and chips,' she said. 'And beans.'

'Which stable did you get your appetite from?' Dan quipped.

Rose feigned hurt. 'I'm a growing girl.'

'It's nice to see someone with a healthy attitude towards food. Although I'm not sure that even I would class Reg's angina special as healthy.' He picked up her half-empty glass of Perrier. 'Do you want something stronger than this to wash it down with?'

'I'll have a double brandy and Diet Coke, please.'

'*Diet Coke?*'

She clasped her hands over her knees and looked at him through her eyelashes. 'I don't want to grow *too* much.'

'Perish the thought.' He smiled and headed towards the bar, ducking the low beam with practised non-chalance.

When Reg brought their meals they ate in comfortable silence. Dan had shown good sense, and a similar blatant disregard for his cholesterol levels, and had joined her in the angina special. Both shunned the finer points of good breeding and ate with a heads down, elbows out relish. When they had finished, Reg cleared the table with surprising alacrity and piled the fire high with more logs. They hissed and spat in protest and pushed plumes of heady wood-scented smoke past the shining horse brasses that adorned the fireplace and into the snug.

Rose's jeans were bursting at the seams – just punishment for squeezing that final chip in. She relaxed back in her chair and closed her eyes, feeling the warm glow from the fire massage her cheeks. A low, contented groan escaped from her lips. 'I could just do with going to bed for an hour now.'

'Mmm, me too.'

She opened one eye sharply to check for signs of a lecherous gaze, but Dan had his eyes closed too and looked, as far as she could tell, the picture of innocence. 'Or a walk,' she said quickly.

'Well, we could probably do the latter without causing too much of a scandal in the village.' He opened one of his eyes and it met her one open eye squarely. Rose flushed an even deeper shade of red. So he had been thinking along the same lines. Flirt. The butter-wouldn't-melt-in-my-mouth look was just a facade. 'Have you been up to Woburn Woods yet?'

'No,' she said guardedly.

'Do you fancy it?' He clasped his hands behind his head, looking as if he had no intention of going anywhere in a hurry. 'You'll have to get some boots, it might be a bit muddy under the trees.'

'I don't know . . .' Why was she being such a wimp? Was it because there was nothing more in the world she'd like to do right now than go tramping through some muddy woods with Dan? Did the thought of wanting to be with him frighten her so much? Yes, it did. She never wanted to need anyone again. She wanted to be hard, independent, strong-willed, aloof, untouchable, unhurtable. An island.

'Well,' he said lazily, 'do we stay here and become pub potatoes or do we go and be recklessly energetic? The choice, as they say on *Blind Date*, is yours.'

There was another choice. One that Dan had failed to mention. She could say no to both of the appealing options and go back to her own quiet little world and do something safe and solitary, like washing her hair or cleaning the oven or finding some socks to darn.

'Don't you have anything you should be doing?' Her

voice sounded pathetic and feeble. If she was going to make excuses, at least she should make her own and not rely on him to bail her out.

'Probably,' Dan answered. 'But nothing that would threaten the very fabric of Great Brayford if it didn't get done.' He turned to look at her. 'Do you have to get back?'

Think of those holey socks, she told herself, and the grease in the oven – and the grease in your hair. Say yes – now! 'No,' she said, giving a light-hearted shrug of her shoulders to show her conscience that she had completely and utterly defied it.

'Well, that's settled then. Momentous decision made.'

She knew he was joking, but that's what it felt like to her. In her heart, she knew it was a mistake. It was wrong to get to know him, to get to like him, to get close to him. She might want to be an island, but there was no doubt she'd just put her foot on the ferry back to the mainland. Why had she given him the 'poor little me' routine earlier today? Wasn't that the start of her carefully constructed barrier coming down?

'We'd better get going before we lose the light,' Dan said, uncoiling himself reluctantly from the chair and stretching.

'You don't look very keen.'

'It'll be great once we get out there.' He helped her on with her coat and she felt all hot and bothered even though they had moved away from the immediate heat of the fire.

The air outside was strikingly cold against her burning skin, but it felt refreshing, clearing her head instantly. 'Wow, this'll certainly blow the cobwebs away.'

They walked up Lavender Hill until they reached the end of her lane. 'I'll go and get the Discovery while you get your boots. I'll only be a couple of minutes. Do you mind if I bring Fluffy?'

'Fluffy?'

'The hound from hell.'

Rose laughed. 'No. I'll wait for you at the end of the lane, so that GCHQ don't see us going out together.' She nodded towards Anise and Angelica's house.

'We're not doing anything wrong. Gardenia won't mind and you've got no one to answer to.' He was right, after years of bowing to Hugh's sensitivities she was her own person again. She wasn't so sure that Gardenia would be pink and tickled, though.

'Yes, but when did anyone in this village put two and two together and get anything less than five?'

'This is different. This is one and one.'

'Yes,' Rose nodded sagely. 'And just think what they could make out of that.'

Chapter Nine

ELECAMPANE

A dark brownish oil with a woody odour and honey overtones. It is difficult to blend with other oils. Elecampane is widely regarded as a severe irritant. It should never be used on naked skin. Valued as a vermifuge – i.e., for use in expelling intestinal worms.

from: *The Complete Encyclopaedia of Aromatherapy Oils*
by Jessamine Lovage

Coughing briefly to clear his throat, Detective Constable Bob Elecampane pressed the bell. Forcefully. Its ring echoed emptily through the hall of the neat little terraced house. There was a stained-glass plaque stuck to the window in the front door with a clear plastic sucker. It said 'Home Is Where The Heart Is' and this redoubtable statement was reinforced by a big, red heart underneath it. The door was painted red too and next to it was a bare trellis entwined with the equally bare twigs of some sort of climber that waited for the warmth of spring to bring it back to life. A cracked terracotta pot stood next to that. The winter pansies that someone had so lovingly planted in it had collapsed into a sad, green mess under the pressure of several days of hard frost. Their pretty smiling faces were scrunched up and soggy, flopping listlessly over the side of the pot.

He looked down the road while he waited. A Land Rover Discovery drove past, containing a large, woolly dog. It eyed him inquisitively through the rear window. The driver was paying more attention to his pretty passenger than the road. There were five identical houses in the row, each one with a variety of lovingly planted dead things in pots outside. He wasn't much of a gardener. Actually, he wasn't a gardener at all. There wasn't much call to be a gardener when you lived in a bachelor flat in the conurbation of Conniburrow. But he did know a pansy when he saw one. He peered through the frosted glass of the window and wondered if she had been the one to plant them.

The neck of his denim shirt felt too tight, even though his top button was open, and it was chafing him where he had shaved. He had tried to get it as smooth as a baby's bum. Unfortunately, he'd succeeded in not only removing all of his bristles but half of his skin as well. Still, it had stopped bleeding long enough for him to take the bits of toilet roll off. If the glass hadn't been frosted he could have had a quick look to see that it was okay. But, as it was, he'd have to do – she could take him or leave him. He leaned against the wall feeling like something out of *The Professionals*.

Eventually, there was the tap of high heels on parquet floor – he knew she would be no respecter of floor coverings. Her type never were. She opened the door and stood there chewing. He flicked open his warrant card. 'CID,' he said brusquely. He glanced down the village lane to see that no one was watching. Behind him he thought he saw a net curtain flicker. 'Is PC Cox at home?' he asked. 'Frank Cox?'

'No. You know he's not.' She glanced at her watch. 'He'll have just started his shift.'

He swallowed and hoped that she didn't notice his Adam's apple bobbing up and down. She obviously wasn't going to make this easy for him.

'Perhaps it's just as well, Mrs Cox. I'd like a few minutes of your time, if that's possible.'

'There's no need for this, you know. I was expecting you.' She opened the door and let him pass. The hall smelled of Mr Sheen furniture polish, potpourri blended with cheap perfume, and Johnson's baby oil.

He followed her into the lounge. It was neat and tidy, if a bit girly. Everything was covered in flowery patterns and frills – curtains, suite, cushions. There were ornaments on every conceivable surface – china trinket bowls, little glass vases, cute animals made out of what looked like papier-mâché. And squeezed among them, photographs of her and Frank, everywhere. It was all very homely, if a bit fussy for his taste. What had he expected? Red velvet and black satin? Probably. But it wasn't like that these days.

They stood there facing each other and, suddenly, despite going over it in his mind ten thousand times this morning, he didn't know what to say. That would have surprised some of his colleagues back at the station, particularly those who had recommended he visit Mrs Frank Cox. DC Bob Elecampane, lost for words.

She was wearing a short Lycra skirt – very short – black. And high-heeled shiny black shoes. But no tights. Her top was tight and low-cut and red. He hadn't been too far off on the colour scheme then. Quite a bit of her thingys were showing and they were pale and plump and sort of perched on the edge of her T-shirt and looked as if they could pop out at any minute given the slightest encouragement. It did cross his mind that it was a bit of a funny way to dress for this time of year, although it was warm in here. Very warm. He cleared his throat again. 'As I said, Mrs Cox,' his voice sounded high and unnatural, more like a cartoon detective than the real-life rough, tough law enforcement officer that he was, 'I'd like a few minutes of your—'

'You've got an hour,' she said. 'That's what we said on the phone. And you can call me Melissa.'

'Thank you.' He cleared his throat again and hoped that he wasn't sickening for something. There were a lot of nasty bugs about. 'Certain irregularities have been brought to our attention at the local constabulary, er, Melissa.'

She glanced down at the bulge in the front of his faded jeans. 'The last time I saw anything brought so much to attention, it had a flag flying at the top of it.'

'Er, quite,' he said.

'Now then, Detective Constable Elecampane – Bob. I suggest we get down to business. You've only got an hour. We're wasting valuable time chatting like this, pleasant though it is,' she added kindly.

'Er, quite,' he said again. His brain seemed to have jammed on one phrase.

'I think you'll find what you really came for is upstairs.' Melissa looked at him in what he supposed was a seductive fashion. She had smoke-grey eyes. Not cheap smoke. Not Woodbine or Embassy Number One smoke. Something more exotic. Smoke from those expensive black cocktail cigarettes that women don't smoke any more. 'Come on then,' she said. 'Follow me.'

Er, quite, popped unhelpfully to the front of his brain, so instead he said nothing and followed her obediently up the narrow staircase. The bedroom had been decorated by the same hand as the lounge. There were swathes of pink flower-sprigged frilled curtains, which matched the wallpaper, which matched the duvet cover, which matched the cushions, which matched the lampshades on the tables at either side of the bed. It looked as if she had copied it lock, stock and barrel from between the pages of *Bella* or *Woman's Own*. She smiled with pride as she showed him shyly into the room and for a moment he wanted to turn and run down the narrow stairs, out of 'The Home Is Where The Heart Is' front door and out past the frost-bitten pansies. 'It's very nice,' he said.

'Gratton's catalogue,' Melissa informed him. 'Garden of Romance. Appropriate, don't you think?'

'Er, quite.'

She walked to the window and pulled the curtains. 'Nosy neighbours,' she said by way of explanation.

The furniture was stripped pine. The bed had an ornately carved headboard. It reminded him of a *gasthof* in Austria he had once stayed in on a police skiing holiday. Except at the guest house in Austria there hadn't been two sets of standard issue handcuffs threaded neatly through the bedposts.

'Seeing as this is your first time, I'd better explain how I work.' Melissa held up three fingers. 'I do three specials. Wanky Panky – I don't think that needs any further explanation,' she said coyly. 'Hanky Panky, which is full you-know-what with the added benefits of massage with sensual aromatherapy oils. And Spanky Panky, or pervert's playtime, where I beat you with a selection of household objects of your choice.'

Bob flushed. She sounded as if she was selling him double glazing. It was obviously a routine she had been through more than once before.

'Very popular with the uniforms, that is,' Melissa continued. 'You know what you boys in blue are like, always keen to see a bit of law and order. And not just on the streets of Milton Keynes.' She wagged a finger at him playfully. 'Although I'm not very keen on it myself. I have a tendency to break fingernails if I'm not careful.'

She took his hand and pulled him towards the bed. She lay back on the Garden of Romance duvet, sweeping her long hair across the pillows. Her breasts mounted an escape campaign. He stood over her not knowing quite what to do next. How could he tell her that all he wanted was a cuddle, to be held in someone's arms for one blissful afternoon? How could he tell her that? He had his reputation to keep up. Something else was having no trouble keeping up.

When he made no move towards her, Melissa very slowly parted her thighs. Beads of perspiration broke out on Bob's brow. It was obvious that Mrs Melissa Cox, wife of Frank Cox of the Milton Keynes Constabulary, was wearing no knickers. Not like the Sharon Stone film where she does a quick flash and you can't really be sure that you saw anything untoward without replaying the video time after time after time. And you knew that everyone else had done the same thing because every copy in the video hire shop went all grainy and funny at the same place. No, this wasn't a mere flash, it was a good, long, serious look. Either Melissa was wearing no knickers or she was harbouring a small friendly hedgehog between her Lycra-clad thighs. 'Don't you want to arrest me, Detective Elecampane?'

He scratched his head. 'What, like "Anything you say will be taken down and used in evidence against you"?'

Melissa pushed herself up on her elbow. 'Trousers.'

'What?'

'Trousers. You said they'd be taken down and used in evidence. So go on then.'

With a smile, she took out her chewing gum and stuck it on top of the stripped pine bedpost. She reached towards him and he held his breath. With long, unbroken fingernails she snaked into his pocket and pulled out his personal police radio from its previously unplumbed depths. Opening the bedroom drawer, she tossed it carelessly inside. 'Now, Detective Constable, you've been a naughty boy. I think you need my full correction treatment. What do you say to that?'

'Er, quite.' There was really nothing else he could say.

* * *

She straddled him, naked, her hair flowing loose over her full, round breasts and down on to him, tickling his stomach as she wriggled above him. Oh, how lovely she was, fresh and clean, sexy and dirty, sinner and saint, all at the same time. His toes curled and his eyes rolled as she ministered to his every need – and to some needs he didn't even know he had. The handcuffs chafed against his wrists and somewhere in his mind self-pity chafed against his pleasure. Why couldn't he find a beautiful girl like this? Why did no one ever seem to like him? Why had his previous unpaid encounters with women ended in impotent disaster? What was it about the mere sight of a nubile naked female before him that sent him limping home desolate with humiliation? Yet with Melissa, paid for by the hour, he could be a man.

She smiled down at him, her face pink from exertion. 'Is that nice?'

'Yeth,' he groaned, his voice muffled by the bra that protruded from the corners of his mouth and was tied in a neat bow behind his head. Her waist was so tiny that he thought his hands would have spanned it easily. Dear heaven, if only he could have the chance! It curved out to full and voluptuous hips and a bottom as pink and as rounded as any of Reuben's cherubs. Her skin wobbled deliciously as she moved against him. The pain and the ecstasy were unbearable. If only she would let him free to touch her.

'You'd better hurry up.' She gyrated faster, her eyes on the clock on the bedside table. 'I've got to go and do the vicar soon.'

'The vithar?' He shuddered to an alarming orgasm.

Melissa took the bra out of his mouth. 'The vicar?' he repeated incredulously and a good deal more clearly. 'A man of the cloth? I'd never have thought—'

'No, silly! Not this.' She rolled off him and sat on the edge of the bed, struggling to herd her breasts back into their Playtex pen. 'I *do* for him. *Clean.*'

He lay there exhausted, staring at the ceiling. Melissa slipped on a baggy T-shirt and some leggings and pulled her hair back into a ponytail in one of those scrunchy things that kids use. Tugging a tissue from the box of Kleenex by the bed, she wiped the red smear of lipstick from her mouth. It took years off her. The sexy, the dirty, the sinner vanished at once. She looked as fresh and as innocent as the day she was born. Bob Elecampane gazed at her. Mesmerised. To him she had never looked more lovely.

He watched, enraptured, as she put the fly swatter, the slotted serving spoon and the steak tenderiser back in the bottom drawer of the cupboard. She looked round, suddenly aware that he was watching her. 'I'd better get you undone. Your arms can go dead after a while if you're not used to it.'

All of him felt dead, suddenly bereft, now that their bodies were no longer joined in union. His soul ached for her. Other parts also ached, but that was purely physical and would go after a few days and perhaps a spot of embrocation. He rubbed his wrists, trying to encourage some feeling back into them. 'What now, Melissa?' he said throatily. He tried to look earnestly at her, but she was busy throwing the red top and the scrap of black Lycra into the wicker washing basket next to the wardrobe and wasn't giving him her full attention. 'What happens now?'

She turned and produced a machine from under the bed. 'I take all major credit cards – Amex, Visa. Or a cheque with banker's card. I don't mind either way.'

He fumbled in the pocket of his jeans for his wallet. 'RSPCA Mastercard?'

'That'll do nicely,' she said. He passed the card to her. She examined it closely. 'Oh, that's sweet. It's got cute little kittens and puppies on it.'

'And for every pound spent they make a donation to the RSPCA.'

She looked at him, head cocked to one side. 'That's very thoughtful.'

'It's not everyone I let see my softer side.' His voice sounded gruff with emotion.

'That'll be £69.99 please,' she said as she whizzed his card through the machine.

It was money well spent, but how he wished he hadn't had to spend it. How he wished it could have been spent instead on wining and dining her in some secluded candlelit restaurant, before making love to her in a four-poster bed – without being tied to it. Melissa's voice broke into his thoughts and he realised to his embarrassment that he was drooling.

'Sign there, please, where it says signature.'

Obediently he signed the slip of paper with the pen she handed to him. He folded the receipt she gave him and tucked it deep into his wallet – a reminder of their first time together. He had kept cherished souvenirs of his other women – well, all two of them. Now he had a Mastercard receipt to add to his collection. Which didn't add up to much, really. Two times a lover, two times a loser. With a little twinge of excitement that crept up from his toes, Bob realised that this could well be third time lucky. Who knows?

He slipped on his shirt and reluctantly did up the buttons. Why couldn't he prolong this moment for ever? He watched Melissa as she tidied her bedroom, shaking out the Garden of Romance duvet so that it was no longer crumpled by their love – unlike his shirt which was severely crumpled. She took the handcuffs from the bedposts and tossed them into the drawer that contained the culinary sex aids. Soon there would be no trace of their encounter. Gone would be the harlot's boudoir, transformed before his very eyes to *The Little House on the*

Prairie. He pulled on his jeans. This was terrible. If he wasn't very careful, he was going to get seriously maudlin. He would have to find a few unfortunate criminals to give a good kicking to on the way home just to raise his spirits.

'How soon can I come again?' he asked, trying not to sound as desperate as he felt.

Melissa's eyes widened in surprise. 'My, you're not easily satisfied, are you?'

He looked up from tying his shoelaces. 'No, no. I mean, when can I come to *see* you again.'

'I'll have to get my diary.' She pulled it from the bedside drawer. 'I don't do this every day. This isn't my proper job.' There was a certain defensive note in her voice. She flicked through the pages. 'What about next Friday afternoon?'

'The same time?'

Melissa nodded and scribbled a note in her diary.

'Doesn't Frank ever look at that?' he asked, wishing that he didn't need to.

Her face darkened slightly. 'No, he does not. And if he did all he'd see was ironing.' She pointed to the page. 'Friday, two o'clock, the ironing. That's what you are. The ironing.'

The ironing. Bob followed her silently down the stairs. She handed him his police radio, which he had completely forgotten about. Melissa stood on her tiptoes and gave him a kiss on his cheek. 'I'll see you next week, Bob.' She ushered him out of the door and closed it behind him.

The ironing. Everybody knew that was the most hated domestic chore. It was right there alongside cleaning the loo and scrubbing between the mouldy tiles behind the shower with a toothbrush. His heart sank back to his size tens. Why was he always branded as the man to be disliked? At work he was used to it, but even Melissa had jumped on the bandwagon now. Why couldn't he be the man that people wanted to spend jocular tea breaks with, rather than them all moving shiftily away when he came into the staff room? Why didn't they all stand round and slap him on the back and tell him rude jokes and laugh at his stories like they did with Frank Cox? Why couldn't he have been 'putting the kettle on' or 'baking a cake' or any sundry domestic duty that people generally didn't object to? Why did he have to be the bloody ironing? Endless, monotonous, achingly unpopular ironing. Bob Elecampane looked at the wilted pansies on Melissa's doorstep and he knew exactly how they felt. What was it that Frank Cox had that he didn't? Apart from a very beautiful and enterprising young wife, that is.

Chapter Ten

Rose was pleased that she had gone home for her boots, even the car park at Woburn Woods was thick with black, glutinous mud. She had been less pleased to have the suspicious stare of Anise Weston follow her up the lane and into the house and out again. Rose had tried to smile at her, but she had ducked back inside her head scarf and had continued to attack the leylandii hedge with what appeared to be a pair of pinking shears. Rose had, however, felt her beady eyes follow her back along the lane as she strode very self-consciously and very obviously into Dan's waiting Land Rover Discovery.

Fluffy was a cross between something shaggy and a golden retriever. He was the size of a small, but scalable, mountain and only his hindquarters and low hanging tummy were fluffy. They were also, after not quite five minutes in the car park, extremely muddy.

'Come on, Fluff,' Dan shouted and they headed up the steady incline from the car park into the edges of the pine forest.

The ground was soft and dark under a carpet of golden-brown pine needles. The day was turning damp and grey and if Rose's mind had been turning to thoughts of romance, this couldn't be classed as the most idyllic location. Half a dozen teenagers on mountain bikes whooped and hollered their way through the towering pines. A pony-trekking school cantered by, churning the track to mud where the horses' hooves bit hard into the ground, shouting belated 'thank yous' behind them after they had forced all the aimless Saturday walkers to dive into the nearest trees or be trampled underfoot.

The rutted track was narrow, strewn with fallen pine cones, sodden and curled tightly shut, steadfastly refusing to predict anything good about the weather. The ground beneath the trees was thick with golden furled bracken, a stark contrast to the dark green needles of the towering Scotch pines.

There were a couple of families strolling ahead of them – mother, father and two point two children, an ideal representation of traditional family values. Okay, so it was probably mother and her new boyfriend. Or father and his much younger woman, given custody for the weekend and desperately trying to think what to do next with two bored, resentful, disenfranchised kids who would rather be out with their friends or at home playing computer games. Rose studied them closely. You could tell from a mile off that the dark-haired couple with the two fair-haired kids weren't married. For one thing, he was walking along with his arm slung protectively round her shoulders and kept lifting up bits of her hair and trailing it through his fingers as he talked to her. For another, it didn't irritate her when he did it. And for yet another, she was fondling his bottom through his smart Timberland anorak. Show me a married couple that did that sort of thing, in the daytime, in public, Rose thought, and I'll show you a pair who haven't been married long enough to have two kids that age. The woman stopped and bent to the ground, picking up a big gnarled stick. She smacked her 'husband' playfully on the bottom with it and he kissed her on the cheek. Rose fought to tear her eyes away from them. Didn't they know that half the population of Buckinghamshire was watching them? And, if they did, why didn't they care?

And the children might look happy now, but what would they be like in years to come? They'd probably become maladjusted burglars or serial killers, blaming everything on the fact they came from a broken home. Or if they were lucky enough to be sufficiently unscathed to take up a sensible profession, they'd spend the rest of their lives paying for expensive therapy to sort out why they were emotional cripples who couldn't make love to their wives.

Mind you, she was not the best defender of the family unit, having carried out a torrid love affair with a married man for the better part of two years. She was hardly a champion for the impenetrability of the marriage bed. That could just as easily have been her, trailing through damp, soggy woods on a Saturday afternoon after someone else's kids. Hugh's, in her particular case. Except that when push came very much to shove, Hugh hadn't had the slightest inclination to leave his family for her.

At the top of the incline the path opened out to a clearing where a great swath of pines had been razed to the ground. She was puffing enthusiastically and vowed that she would join the Tums, Bums and Thighs class at the village hall, although the thought of exposing her bum to the ridicule of Gardenia and Cassia – they were bound to go – with the mere protection of a Lycra leotard was not a humiliation she was keen to embrace.

'Shall we sit down for a minute?' Dan said. He pointed to a monstrous tree trunk that had been felled and left skewed on its side at the edge of the track.

'Yes.' She had been lost in her thoughts and for a brief moment – a very brief moment – had forgotten he was there. She sat down next to him. A chill gust of wind tucked itself inside her coat and she shivered, huddling into herself.

'Are you okay?' Dan asked. He felt huge and safe next

to her. His face was wrinkled with concern and the greyness of the day made the greenness of his eyes more vibrant.

'I'm fine.' She shivered again. 'I'm just a bit cold.'

'Didn't you put any gloves on?'

She looked at her bare, blue hands. 'No,' she said.

'Have these.' He peeled off big, thick, sheepskin-lined things with fingers the length of bananas and passed them to her.

'Really, I'll be fine,' she protested.

'Take them. I'll put my hands in my pockets.' And to demonstrate his sincerity he did just that.

She slipped her hands into his gloves, wonderfully grateful for the comforting soft warmth. It was possible that she could have put both hands in one glove they were so oversized.

'You seem quiet,' Dan observed.

'I was just thinking.' There should have been some noise to break the silence. The call of a plaintive bird. The call of a plaintive child. Anything. She looked to Fluffy for help, but he was too busy cocking his leg on various tree stumps and failing singularly to produce anything to water them with.

'About Hugh?'

She smiled at him. 'How long have you been a mind reader?'

'When women go quiet it's usually a man's fault.' Dan dragged a stick along the ground and made a letter D in the dirt. 'Or hormones.'

'Well, I think it's safe to say that my hormones are pretty much in control at the moment.' She gave him a wry glance. 'Most of them.'

'So it must be Hugh.'

She stared down the track they had just walked, eyes glassy, fixed on the family that now struggled up in their wake. The father reached forward and tousled the head of his son and they both laughed. 'It must be Hugh,' she agreed sourly.

'Were you together long?'

'Too long.' She sighed heavily. 'Two years.'

'And all the time he was married?'

She, too, picked up a stick and inspected it closely to avoid looking at Dan. 'He was married. He is married. He will always be married.' She pushed the point of her stick in the soft earth for emphasis.

'But you knew that when it started.'

'No,' she said truthfully. 'No. I didn't.' She wriggled her fingers in the huge expanse of glove. 'It was easy to believe that he was single. He's an American. He works over here regularly. And, I have to say, there was a distinct lack of idle chatter about the folks back home.' Her voice sounded hurt even to her accustomed ears.

'How did you meet?' He underlined the DAN he had completed in the dirt.

'One of my aromatherapy clients was a colleague of his and he recommended that Hugh come to see me to help him get over his jet lag. We progressed from treatment couch to cosy restaurants in three short appointments and pretty soon I was a cheaper option for him than the Holiday Inn.'

'Don't be so hard on yourself.' Dan reached out unexpectedly and took hold of her gloved hand. He didn't look at her. He just kept staring straight ahead, his eyes following Fluffy as he padded relentlessly through the bracken, panting with the effort. Rose's mouth was suddenly dry and she could feel her heart beat in her ears – which she was sure were glowing red because of the cold. She could feel nothing but the firm pressure squeezing the acreage of glove against her small hand and she wished that she hadn't been a wimp and wasn't now paying the price of having her hand inside what was, in effect, a dead sheep.

'It's not a matter of being hard on myself,' she said flatly, amazed that her voice had managed to maintain a level pitch. 'I'm just not deluding myself.'

'So what was the attraction?'

'The attraction?' Rose gave a cynical little half snort. 'He wasn't ugly. He wasn't poor. He had a car. And his own teeth and hair. These things get harder to find in a man as you get older.' She poked at the ground with her stick again. 'Hugh is the only man who can wear a hundred per cent linen suit and never ever look creased.'

Dan was impressed. 'I'm impressed,' he said.

'I knew you would be.'

'That's quite an achievement.'

'Now you're taking the piss.'

Dan squeezed her hand, not a hearty, jocular squeeze, a small, tight, uncertain, apologetic movement. 'What does he do?' he continued in a suitably serious tone.

'He's an architect. Very important firm in Charlotte. North Carolina.' She hadn't known where it was until she looked it up on a map to see where Hugh's wife lived. Hugh's wife Ruth. And their children. Abbey and Jordan. She stared sightlessly at the trees. 'His working life is all straight lines, plans and boundaries. Neat. Tidy. Ordered. Yet personally he's a mass of squiggles, doodles and unintelligible scribble.'

'Did you move out here to forget about him?'

'Who?' she said.

Dan twisted his mouth in admonishment.

'Sorry, bad joke,' she admitted with a tired laugh. 'I came here to start a new life, as they say. I'd tried to end the relationship several times, but it was impossible. Hugh can be very persuasive.'

'I bet,' Dan said darkly.

She ignored the remark. 'So I've made a clean break. He doesn't know where I am and he never will.'

'Brave lady.' Dan sounded impressed again.

'Or a ruddy great fool,' she answered. 'I'm not sure which yet.'

'Any regrets?'

'Hundreds,' she said lightly. A sadness descended on her and she suddenly felt as if she'd jogged up the track with a one-hundred-pound pack on her back. She shivered again, in spite of herself.

'Come on.' Dan tugged at her hand. Their eyes locked and they both became aware that he was still holding her hand. Self-consciously, he let it drop. 'It's getting cold,' he said. 'Let's go back.'

They stood up slowly, Rose stretching her back after sitting so long in the chill air. Dan whistled for Fluffy and he followed them as they cut back along the dirt road that bordered Woburn Golf Club.

A grey dampness hung in the air as the light started to fade. The sort of dampness that meant she would have frizzy hair by the time she got home. They wound their way back along the edge of the forest, the spindly twigs of silver birch providing a fussy edge to the taller more robust trees, until they reached the car park.

The dark-haired couple with the fair-haired children emerged from another track, still wound round each other like sex-starved sixteen-year-olds. They converged on the Mercedes parked next to Dan and Rose. 'Mummy, Daddy,' the children cried. 'Look at that lovely dog!'

Fluffy glowed with pride, parading his mud-caked fur in all its glory. The parents, smiling and benevolent, nodded to her and Dan and ushered their children into the gleaming car, curiously unscathed by the sea of mud. Mummy kissed each of them on the head for good measure. So they weren't a single parent family, with delinquent children and a wicked stepmother. They were actually happily married with two perfectly well-adjusted and polite children. Rose's heart sank. When had Hugh turned her into such a cynic?

* * *

They drove back to the village in silence, Fluffy unceremoniously ensconced in the boot. Dan crossed the busy dual carriageway of the A5 then wound through the tight single-track lanes, the edges of the road indistinct, clogged with slippery leaf mulch. The trees entwined their branches overhead, nature's naked trellis waiting patiently for the decorative beauty that spring would soon bring.

Dan swung the car into Lavender Hill and stopped outside Builder's Bottom. Rose slipped off his warm, comforting gloves and laid them on the dashboard. The sky was darkening to evening, turning from a washed-out wintery blue-grey to a rich, deep indigo. It was cut with bold splashes in improbable shades of vibrant pink and flaming orange. The thin sliver of the moon hung expectantly over the golden glow of the sinking sun. The trees stretched delicate tendrils heavenwards, edging the sky with an exotic border of filigree black lace. If an artist had captured it accurately, you would have sworn he'd been taking drugs.

Rose sighed contentedly. It was spectacular.

'It's spectacular isn't it?' Dan said, a hint of awe in his voice.

'Yes,' she breathed. This was the perfect end to a perfect day.

He turned to her and his arm rested casually across the back of her seat. 'It's been a lovely day, hasn't it?'

Rose smiled at him. 'A day that starts with knocking out a fireplace can only get better.'

He laughed. 'No, I mean it. It's been great.' His voice took on a serious note. 'Maybe we should do it again sometime.'

Rose could feel her cheeks turning the same colour as the vibrant pink in the sky. It probably looked more flattering on a landscape. She felt as if she had known Dan for years. They fitted together so well. He was a soul mate – their bodies buzzed with the same vibration, their minds were tuned to the same station. Usually she was on Jazz FM, while everyone else was on some bizarre long-range programme that whistled and faded in and out, so that you never quite caught its full meaning. This was different. They were so easy in each other's company. There was none of the edginess she felt with Hugh, the constant wondering whether everything was all right for him, whether she was inadvertently going to offend him in any way.

'It's made me realise something.' Dan's voice sounded gruff. His eyes were black and inscrutable in the half-light.

The car was getting hot and stuffy. She could feel cold trickles of perspiration under her arms. Why did she always seem to fall for men who were attached? Why wasn't there some uncomplicated single man who made her body sing? This couldn't go any further. She knew how she felt and she knew Dan was feeling the same. This had to stop; the last thing she wanted was to replace one tangled web with another. 'Dan, I . . .' her voice faltered.

'I've realised,' he said clearing his throat, 'that the situation with Gardenia and me can't continue like it is.' His voice was thick with emotion.

'I don't think this is—'

'I'm not being fair to her.' He gripped the steering wheel and stared ahead, not seeing the view any more.

'You've got to be sensible about this.' There was an edge of panic creeping into Rose's voice. 'You mustn't think that you have to—'

'Spending the day with you,' Dan continued, 'relaxing, chatting, enjoying each other's company, has really opened my eyes.'

'Well, it's good that we can be friends.' This was like a fast-moving river, the current white-frothed and surging out of control.

'You're right,' he said with determination.

'I am?'

'So right. It was what you said about conversation being difficult that made me start to think. How can Gardi and I ever begin to talk about things when we never spend any time with each other? We need to get out more. Do things together.'

'You do?'

'I can't blame Gardi for the problems in our relationship when I don't put any commitment in myself. Can I?'

'No.' Her voice had risen to a squeak.

'You've really helped me to see that today.' He smiled at her and his teeth were Colgate white. It was such an innocent smile that it squeezed her heart.

'What I really need to do is make an effort with Gardenia. This isn't all her fault. I can see that now.' He reached over and pecked her on the cheek. 'Thanks, Rose. You've been a real pal.'

She turned and tried to smile at him, but for some reason her jaw muscles had gone into temporary paralysis. Why was it that when she had just heard exactly what she wanted to hear, she didn't feel a surge of immense relief coursing through her? Why had the hollow, empty, desolate feeling that had swamped her when Hugh had left suddenly enveloped her again?

'Come in for a drink,' Dan suggested. 'I bet you could do with a nice cup of coffee to take the chill from your bones.'

It was going to take considerably more than anything Maxwell House could offer to take away this aching chill.

Rose shook her head. 'Thanks, but I'd better be off.' She put her hand on the car door. 'Besides, you'll have all Gardenia's shopping to admire. I wouldn't want to intrude.'

He stared at her with a wounded look. The sort of look that a dog gives you when you won't play with its favourite ball. 'Have I upset you?'

'No,' Rose said, struggling to sound up-beat. 'As you said, it's been a lovely day.'

'I'll pop by and finish off the fireplace next week.'

She was tempted to say don't bother, but she wanted him to bother very much. 'Whenever,' she said airily.

'Rose.' She was halfway out of the car door and had to turn back to face him. 'Could I just ask you one thing?' He took her silence as acquiescence. 'Didn't you ever feel guilty?' He fidgeted in his seat. 'About Hugh's wife?'

'As guilty as hell,' she said glibly.

His eyes held hers. 'But not guilty enough to end it?'

A lump came to her throat. Guilty enough to feel sick every time Hugh had phoned home from the flat. Guilty enough to feel a debilitating twist of pain in her stomach if Ruth ever rang when they were making love, leaving her soft, drawling voice echoing from the answerphone. Guilty enough to lie awake at night wondering what Ruth was like. Was she better than her? Was she brighter, thinner, prettier? Guilty enough to worry what the children would think of their father if they ever found out. What harm it was doing them. Guilty? 'No,' she said crisply. 'Not guilty enough to end it. Why do you ask?'

He sighed and looked away from her. 'I just can't picture you as the other woman, somehow.'

'I bet there are a lot of things you couldn't picture me as, Dan, but I've probably been all of them in my time.' She swung her legs out of the car, dropped to the ground and slammed the door with a hefty thunk.

The electric window slid down. 'Don't go like this, Rose. I didn't mean to offend you. It's none of my business.'

'You're right. It isn't.' Rose turned on her heel. 'Thanks for a great day, Dan,' she called over her shoulder. Striding off along Lavender Hill, her eyes were blurred and stinging and she hoped to God that Anise had finished mutilating her hedge and she could get into the house before she started to cry. She fumbled with her key in the lock, her hands cold and bare without Dan's spade-sized gloves to protect them. Inside the house, she leaned against the closed door and let the tears pour down her face unhindered.

Chapter Eleven

Gardenia was late. A prickle of irritation ran round Dan's collar as he frowned at the clock again. She could have bought up Milton Keynes by now. And brought it home, tried it on, decided she didn't like it and taken it back for a refund. Gardenia was trying to turn 'unshopping' into an art form.

He stirred the bolognese sauce which was now gelatinous and brown and was starting to stick nicely to the bottom of the pan. Spaghetti bolognese à la peace offering. It was becoming a familiar dish on the menu.

Dan sipped the sauce from the end of the wooden spoon and winced as he burnt his tongue. It tasted exactly the same as when he had tasted it five minutes ago. Where was she? The shops had shut hours ago. He wiped his hands on his PVC apron. It had an unrealistic impression of a bosomy woman in stockings and suspenders on the front, which made it look as if he was wearing stocking and suspenders. The apron had been a birthday present from the lads at the site. That and a bright red, three-legged barbecue. Gardenia hated both of them. She said the apron made him look like a prat. Eating burnt sausages and incinerated steak in the unprotected atmosphere of the fresh air, especially when cooked by a prat in a pinny, was not Gardenia's type of entertainment. At all.

It was difficult to know in a situation like this if Gardenia was just being awkward and making him pay in some obtuse way for not going shopping with her or whether she was upside down in a hedge somewhere, the tangled wreckage of an old but faithful Mercedes with over one hundred thousand miles on the clock strewn around her. He stirred the sauce with growing unease. Spaghetti à la peace offering was a dish, unlike revenge, that was best eaten hot.

When the Merc, untangled, swung into the drive twenty minutes later, a mixture of anger and relief flooded through him. By the time Gardenia burst into the kitchen loaded down with bags from John Lewis and House of Fraser, the anger had won. 'Where have you been?' he asked belligerently.

'What's it to you?' Gardenia answered in the same tone, dropping her packages carelessly on the York stone floor that had taken him weeks to lay.

The spaghetti à la peace offering was going to have to work wonders. 'The shops have been closed for hours.'

'I ran into someone I knew.'

'Who?'

Gardenia flushed. An unstoppable thought tiptoed into Dan's brain. Gardenia never flushed. She had skin like porcelain that defied the best attempts of sun, sherry and full-bodied red wine to turn it even faintly pink. It was hard to tell when she was ill, because she was always that pale.

'Someone you don't know,' she said evasively.

'Who?' Dan persisted.

Gardenia frowned and flopped into a chair. 'What's the point of telling you if you don't know them?'

'I might do,' he said petulantly.

'It was Beverly Langford.' She smiled tightly at him. 'You're no wiser, are you?'

'Bonnie's sister,' he tried.

'Get a life, Dan.' Gardenia flung back her head, letting her silky skein of hair drape over the chair.

'I was just about to dish up.'

Gardenia eased herself upright again and prodded the candles on the table. 'What are these for?'

Dan hadn't been able to find the candlesticks. The cupboards in this house were a mystery to him. There were Dennis Potter plays that were easier to fathom. He'd found the candles all right. Pink. Pastel. Matching the dining room. And any person in their right mind would have put the candlesticks jolly near to them, wouldn't they? No. Not Gardenia. Goodness only knew how her logic worked. Her eclectic sorting system wasn't confined to the cupboards either. The address book was no better. The doctor was under H, for Dr Henderson. The milkman was under R, for Ron Miller. The accountant was under T, for Tax. And the vet was under D, for Dog, of course.

This was why the two fine, tapering, pastel-pink candles were now stuck to brightly-coloured saucers with Blue Tac.

'Has there been a power cut?' she asked.

It wasn't an unreasonable question. Great Brayford did seem to have more than its fair share of enforced candlelit dinners. It was surprising that the population wasn't bigger. 'I was trying to be romantic,' Dan said. 'You know, soft lights, soft music, soft-in-the-head?'

'Why?' Gardenia sounded suspicious.

Dan blew out heavily through his mouth. 'It's the sort of thing couples do.'

'We don't.'

'That's my point,' he explained patiently. 'I thought it was time that we did.'

'Why?' Gardenia sounded even more suspicious.

He spread his hands expansively and shrugged. 'Why not?'

She narrowed her eyes. 'What have you been up to?'

'Up to?' he said innocently. 'Nothing.'

Her eyes disappeared totally behind a veil of mascaraed eyelashes. 'What did you do this afternoon?'

It was Dan's turn to flush. He turned back to the cooker. 'This dinner's going to be cold.' More accurately, it was going to be burned.

'What did you do?' Gardenia could be like a terrier with a trouser leg when she wanted to be.

'I went for a walk in Woburn Woods.' He was appalled that he sounded cagey. It was a perfectly innocent and pleasant walk with a friend. A female friend, his conscience prodded him. A female friend he was starting to like a lot, his conscience got out a pickaxe and hacked away.

'Who with?' Gardenia raised one eyebrow. It was a terrifying gesture that meant she knew she was on to something. He couldn't do it himself, despite practising for hours in front of the mirror. Even if he held one eyebrow down for ages, as soon as he let go, it shot up into his hairline, rendering his facial expression merely pleasantly surprised rather than highly intimidating. There were skills that only women had – 'the look' and the ability to be acerbic using only the eyebrows were just the start.

'I took Fluff,' he said brightly. It was pointless trying to deny Rose had been with them, though the thought had crossed his mind; Anise Weston had seen them brazenly get in a car together and drive off towards the woods. He could hear her recounting it in scandalised tones. It would be the main topic of conversation in the post office on Monday morning. 'And Rose,' he added as quickly as possible.

'Another bit of fluff,' Gardenia remarked caustically.

'She's good company.' His girlfriend's lips set in a tight line. And that was another thing. What exactly was Gardenia to him? He didn't really think she'd been his girlfriend since they'd passed the tender age of sixteen. Having a 'girlfriend' when you were thirty-six just didn't sound right. It was like calling your mum, Mummy. Over a certain age and it just sounded stupid. So what was she? Partner? It sounded far too businesslike. If there was one thing Gardenia wasn't, it was businesslike. Lover? Not very often these days. If you were lovers then there ought to be a certain amount of . . . well . . . making love. So she wasn't his girlfriend, she wasn't his partner, she wasn't his lover and she certainly wasn't his housekeeper. And even his mum had given up on her ever becoming his wife. So, he asked himself the question again, what was she? And why had she been it for so long? He turned his mind back to the spaghetti à la peace offering and its original purpose. Wasn't he supposed to be making an effort to jump start the dead battery of their relationship? If so, why was he defending another woman? He tried another tack. 'She likes you.'

'It's a shame the feeling isn't mutual.'

Dan sighed inwardly. There was no point pursuing it further. Gardenia rarely had a reason for harbouring deep and abiding hatred. It was just something she excelled at. 'I thought it would be nice if you and I could do it together.'

'What?'

'Walk in the woods.'

'Why?'

'Why not?'

'It's muddy.'

'It isn't *always* muddy,' Dan insisted. 'We could get you some wellies.'

'Wellies,' Gardenia sneered. 'Do I look like a wellies sort of person?'

'We could get you green ones.' Dan tried to sound enthusiastic, even though he couldn't actually picture Gardenia in wellies, green or otherwise. 'And we could get you a Barbour. You'd like that, wouldn't you?'

The sneer relaxed slightly and there was a flicker of

light behind her uninterested eyes, though Dan was sure it had more to do with the mention of shopping rather than the freedom to tramp about woods warm and unsullied.

'But you always take Fluffy out on your own.'

'I know.' Dan came and sat down next to her. He was tempted to take her hand, but it reminded him that he had done the same thing with Rose in the woods and he thought better of it. 'Wouldn't it be nicer if we did it together?'

Gardenia looked decidedly unconvinced. 'For who?'

'For both of us.' He raked his hands through his hair. This was like drawing teeth – without the benefit of anaesthetic. 'It's just that I really enjoyed myself this afternoon . . .' He could feel Gardenia stiffen beside him and he continued hurriedly, 'And I thought how much nicer it would have been if it had been you who was with me.'

That was a lie. He hadn't realised how much of a lie it was until it sprang forth from his lips. In a blinding flash, he knew it was Rose who had made the afternoon so relaxing, so enjoyable. If Gardenia had been with him, she would have whined and moaned and they would have raced round at breakneck speed so that she could get back indoors before she turned into a block of ice or the lack of centrally-heated air made her giddy. Perhaps what he really wanted Gardenia to say was that she wasn't the slightest bit interested in getting caked up to the eyeballs in mud but that she had no problem if he wanted to go walking every Saturday – and possibly Sunday afternoons – with Rose. Some hope! Gardenia wasn't noted for her humanitarian standpoint. Giving him permission to spend harmless recreational time with another woman would require something in the form of a brain transplant.

'I don't want to go walking in the woods,' Gardenia said childishly. 'Not with you or anyone else.'

Dan's heart soared. The phrase 'you don't mind if I do?' thought briefly about vocalising itself and then changed its mind. 'The point of this is to get us to do more things together as a couple,' he explained with patience that was thinning considerably quicker than his hair. 'What would you like us to do together?'

Gardenia thought for a moment. 'We could go shopping.'

Dan exhaled heavily. 'That's hardly a life-enhancing experience.'

Gardenia pouted. 'It is for me.'

'I want us to be closer,' he said as earnestly as he could manage.

'You haven't been discussing our relationship problems with Rose, have you?' Her voice held an unspoken threat.

He was tempted to say that it would have been a short discussion. 'No,' he said simply. He pushed himself up from his chair. 'I'll dish up. The spaghetti's been in the oven for hours. It's probably like rubber. You light the candles – if you want to.'

'I've eaten,' Gardenia said.

'What?'

At least she had the good grace to look embarrassed, Dan thought bitterly. 'I went for something to eat,' she explained. 'In Milton Keynes.'

'With Bonnie Langford?'

'Beverly.'

'Well, it looks like it's your lucky night, Fluff,' he addressed the dog, waking him from his catnap as close to the warmth of the oven as lax hygiene standards would allow. 'Chum or spag bol? The choice is yours.'

Fluffy barked and wagged his tail.

'I think that was a definite spag bol,' Dan said to Gardenia. 'At least someone appreciates my cooking.'

'I do appreciate it. I'm just not hungry.'

Dan sighed. 'I'm trying to make an effort here,

Gardenia. Would it do you any harm to meet me halfway?'

For once, she looked slightly ashamed and came and wound her arms round his waist. It was a highly unusual gesture that took Dan completely by surprise. 'There is something we *could* do together,' she said seductively. 'We could have sex.'

The words didn't somehow match the tone of voice. Whatever happened to making love or even the old-fashioned tumbling in the hay? Having sex. It ranked up there alongside having double glazing fitted or having a new patio laid. 'We could,' Dan said doubtfully.

'I'll wait in the bedroom.' Gardenia gave him a squeeze. 'Don't be long.'

He wasn't normally so reluctant, but having waited so long to eat the spaghetti à la peace offering, he was going to damn well enjoy every morsel of it. When he eventually joined Gardenia in bed, he felt like an over-stuffed turkey and had about as much energy. A strange feeling of relief washed over him when she appeared to be asleep, but she opened her eyes and turned to him, giving one of her rare cat-like smiles. He didn't actually like cats very much; he was more of a dog man.

Gardenia was usually the reluctant one. Normally she just lay there and looked beautiful. And she did look beautiful, there was no doubt about that. Most men would give their right arm just to look at her naked and probably their left one to be able to do varied and intimate things with her. Tonight, she was more animated than he had ever known her. Well, perhaps animated was overstating the case, but she actually moved. And wriggled. And squirmed. And made little squeaking noises and said 'oh, yes' a couple of times, although the words seemed vaguely detached and didn't necessarily coincide with what he was doing at the time, which was a bit disconcerting. It made him realise, you were the one who made love to

Gardenia and, if you were lucky, she had sex back with you.

Dan wondered what Rose would be like in bed. She was more rounded. Her skin would feel soft and supple and it was unlikely that her hips would stick out sharply like the ends of metal coat hangers. She smelt wonderful with her clothes on, teasing wafts of the exotic essential oils that she worked with clinging to her body. Naked, her scent would be erotic and unbearably heady, like an explosion on a perfume counter. He could imagine her being free and unfettered, sensuous and giving. Unfortunately, he could imagine it too well. Unaware of her sense of timing, Gardenia oh, yessed once more. And then, thankfully, he oh, yessed himself.

Dan lay back on the bed, one arm above his head, cold sweat drying uncomfortably on his chest. Gardenia curled into a ball with her back to him. He had upset Rose this afternoon, when he hadn't meant to at all. It was true, he couldn't imagine her as the other woman but he realised, with a slightly sickening sensation in the pit of his stomach, that the woman he wanted curled up beside him was Rose.

It would mean that Gardenia would have to go. That sounded cruel, but that basically was the crux of it. How could he do it to her? She was totally dependent on him, just as Fluff was. She'd never done a day's work in her life, although she was perfectly capable of doing something. There must be jobs where you could just stand and look totally gorgeous all day. Even for the over-thirties. Would he ever summon up the necessary courage to ask her to leave? And what then? Rose still seemed to have an unhealthy attachment to this slimy bastard Hugh. Would she be interested in him even if he was free?

He could feel himself balanced uncertainly on the hypotenuse of an eternal triangle and it was an awful sensation. His eyes dropped to Gardenia's back, the delicate curve of her backbone under its utterly inadequate covering of skin. When she wasn't being a complete cow, she could be so child-like, so naive. It would kill him to hurt her.

As he watched her sleep, Dan couldn't help feeling that the limitless possibilities for strengthening their relationship hadn't exactly been fully explored. But he had tried. Hadn't he? His paltry attempt had simply made him realise what a truly hopeless case their relationship was. It was clearly dead and, at least, should be buried with some dignity. Waves of shame, guilt and torment washed over him. It was the first time he had made love to Gardenia with thoughts of another woman invading his mind. Mind you, it was the first time he had made love to Gardenia and hadn't thought of football.

Chapter Twelve

ANGELICA

A colourless oil which turns brown with age. Physically, it is used for fatigue, migraine, nervous tension and stress-related disorders. Emotionally, Angelica is useful for balancing erratic mood swings and helping to create a calm, peaceful environment.

from: *The Complete Encyclopaedia of Aromatherapy Oils*
by Jessamine Lovage

'Thank you, dear.' Angelica took the cup of chamomile tea from Rose with a hand that had a barely perceptible tremor. 'It's so nice that you were able to see me. We haven't had a chance for a proper chat yet. You're always so busy.'

You'd be the ones to know, Rose thought as she sat down in the armchair by the fireplace. Not the fireplace that she was still waiting for Dan to come and finish, a different one – the one in the front room, the lounge, the parlour – whatever you wanted to call it – which was kept tidy for unexpected visitors and long winter nights alone watching inane comedy programmes on television in the vain hope of making herself laugh. She glanced at the clock. 'I've got an hour before my next appointment.'

'Oh good,' Angelica said. She stirred her tea absently,

then fished out the chamomile tea bag and put it on the side of her saucer. Tentatively, she put the cup to her lips and took a cautious sip.

'Do you like it?' Rose asked.

Angelica nodded enthusiastically. 'It tastes lovely, dear.' She put the cup back on the saucer and ran her tongue over her lips. 'It's just a shame it looks like urine.'

Rose laughed. 'I'm afraid none of them are particularly appealing to look at.' She peered into her own cup. 'The peppermint tea I'm drinking looks a bit like stagnant pond water. Not so much an acquired taste as an acquired sight.'

Angelica smiled politely and put her cup on the small table next to her. She crossed one delicate leg over the other and leaned forward conspiratorially. 'Actually, dear, I've come to ask you some professional advice.'

'On aromatherapy?'

Angelica nodded. 'I'd be grateful if you didn't tell Anise. She'd go mad if she knew I was here.'

'Doesn't she know much about alternative therapies?'

'Oh my goodness, she knows all about alternative therapies.' She waved her hand. 'Anise says they've been the downfall of the monarchy. I think it's the adultery myself, but Anise won't have it. She says that they wouldn't have been interested in adultery if they hadn't spent so much time having their bodies smeared with oil and their colons irrigated.'

'She could have a point,' Rose agreed good-naturedly.

'Anise thinks its unnatural to have rubber tubing inserted into any bodily orifice. She has a devil of a time when she goes to the dentist.' Angelica risked another sip of chamomile tea before she continued, 'She knows all about chakras and karmas. And Tantric sex. She watched a documentary about Sting on the *South Bank Show* – he talked all about it. Anise was fascinated. I must say it sounded very boring to me. All that heavy breathing.

When I had my day I liked a quick one up against the church wall.'

'There's a lot to be said for it,' Rose said wide-eyed. How on earth did she come to be having a conversation about colonic irrigation and Tantric sex with this very genteel-looking woman who was possibly old enough to be her grandmother?

'Anise says the body is a temple.' Angelica wrinkled her nose. 'Unfortunately, mine's more like the church vestibule – dusty, draped with cobwebs and doesn't get too many people going through it these days.' She rearranged one of the sunray pleats on her skirt. 'More's the pity.'

'What can I do to help?' Rose inquired, trying to get a grip on this tottering conversation and bring it on to a more professional – and steady – footing.

'There's not much anyone can do,' Angelica said sadly. 'I think this poor old dog has had her day.'

'I was talking about the aromatherapy,' Rose said kindly.

'Oh, that! The aromatherapy – oh yes.'

'So, was it a particular problem that you wanted to talk to me about?'

Angelica moistened her lips. 'I'm afraid it is.' She fiddled with the single string of pearls at her neck. 'I'm having a little trouble with my nerves.' She whispered the last word breathily. 'I think the main problem is that Anise is getting on them.'

'Have you been to see your doctor?'

'Yes. He's a lovely man, but all he wants to do is give me dreadful pills to dope me up.' She swept her hair from her forehead with her hand. 'Essentially, it's Anise that needs doping, not me. I just need a little something to help me cope with her more offensive excesses.'

'Have you tried talking to her?'

'I think King Canute had more success with the waves

than one would trying to communicate to Anise that she's a complete pain in the posterior. Anise is not someone that you talk to.'

'How long have things been difficult?'

'Anise has always been difficult, dear. She was a horrendous child. The older she gets, the worse she is. I was always more malleable. I think the word now is "easy".'

'And what sort of symptoms are you getting?' Rose realised she should be writing this down, but she didn't want to interrupt Angelica now. She was talking quite openly, but Rose could sense that it had taken some effort for her to get to this point.

'Nothing very much, dear. Hardly anything, really.' She took another sip of her tea. 'When she starts to go on – and she can go on so – my poor stomach starts to churn and I feel all fluttery.'

'Pretty standard symptoms for anxiety,' Rose reassured her.

'And then I see a red rage in front of my eyes and I want to do awful things to her, like garrotting her with the green plastic-coated wire from the potting shed, or pushing her in the oven and baking her like the witch in the gingerbread house, or I wish we had a coal cellar and I could push her down the stairs and lock her in there for ever. That sort of thing.'

Rose tried to keep the alarm out of her voice. 'How long have you felt like this?'

'Oh, since I was about four.' Angelica smiled sweetly. 'Don't worry, dear, I've never had the courage to do anything about it. Besides, she's my sister. I love her dearly – really. I just enjoy fantasising.'

Rose grinned in response. 'I don't know if there are any essential oils that will help murderous tendencies.'

'I did take a herbal remedy once. It was very good. It was supposed to keep you calm and centred and help to improve your memory.' She plucked at her pearls. 'Now what was it? I can't remember, for the life of me.'

'I think the best thing would be for you to come and have some aromatherapy massages with me. It's a lovely way to relax. I'm sure you'd enjoy it.'

'I'm sure I would, my dear. But Anise would be very resentful if she knew what I was up to. The problem is getting out of the house without her knowing, you see.' Angelica tossed her fringe back. 'I don't suppose you realise, but she has a pair of binoculars permanently trained on your front door.'

Rose raised her eyebrows in acknowledgement. 'It doesn't come as a complete surprise,' she said tactfully.

'This is one of her worst characteristics. She has to know everyone else's business.' Angelica shook her head. 'You must forgive her. It stems from having a sad and lonely life. She hardly ever goes out these days and therefore, takes whatever pleasure she can from things on her own doorstep.' Her lips twisted into a smile. 'I must say, the constant stream of men that tread your path keep her amused.'

'So I've heard,' Rose answered wryly.

'I'm afraid she thinks you get up to all manner of naughty things in here,' Angelica admitted reluctantly.

'I'm sorry to disappoint her. I only wish I did. I could charge extra, which would certainly help to pay the bills.' There were days when people casting aspersions on her highly professional trade and ethics made her laugh out loud. Fortunately for Angelica, this was one of them. Rose hoped she wasn't in as good a mood when she eventually confronted Anise Weston about the rumours she was spreading.

'I think she's peeved that she hasn't seen Cliff yet,' Angelica giggled. 'Or Mick or Sasha.'

Cliff who? Rose thought. Hadn't Cassia Wales mentioned him too? And Mick and Sasha who? She had definitely lost the slender grip she may have once had on this conversation. Rather than pursue it, she changed the subject. 'Haven't you ever thought of living separately? Being together under one roof every minute of the day can't be easy. Perhaps you'd benefit if you only saw each other in small doses.'

'Anise is so poisonous, even minute doses can be potentially fatal. Besides, I don't think we could ever live apart. Anise couldn't cope without me, no matter what she says. She can't boil an egg, poor woman. We had a very pampered background – nannies, butlers, cooks. It was very nice at the time, but it doesn't make you into terribly self-sufficient human beings. We were expected to be married into good families, so the need to learn basic domestic skills never really arose.'

Rose looked at the woman seated in front of her. She was poised, elegant and, for her age, quite glamorous. When she was younger, she would have been a stunner. She must have had her pick of men. 'But neither of you did marry?'

'Unfortunately not.' She sagged a little. A small, barely discernible movement, but a definite deflating of spirits. 'There wasn't exactly a horde of suitors beating their way to our door. Great Brayford wasn't renowned for its eligible young men.' Angelica looked pointedly at Rose. 'It still isn't.'

'So, there was never anyone . . . special?'

'Oh yes. There was someone special all right.' Angelica tapped the side of her nose secretively. 'I had my *grande passion.*'

'But you didn't marry him?'

Angelica sighed heavily. 'He was already married, my dear.' She folded her hands in her lap and twiddled self-consciously with the ruby dress ring on her engagement finger. 'It caused a terrible scandal. Daddy was outraged. He had his first heart attack very shortly afterwards. I blamed myself.' Her clear grey-green eyes had filled with tears. 'I'd always been his favourite.'

'Did he leave his wife?'

'No,' Angelica stated flatly. 'The scandal ruined him. We're talking fifty years ago. Things were very much different then.'

'Perhaps not as much as you think,' Rose said quietly. 'Do you still see him?'

'No.' The answer was harsh and bare again. It was a few minutes before she continued and when she did, her voice held a slight waver. 'I'm afraid he couldn't live with the shame. Or without me, he said. He took his own life.'

Rose felt a lump rise to her throat. 'That's tragic.'

'Yes, it was a terrible waste.' Angelica twisted the ring on her finger. 'It's awfully bad luck to give someone rubies. They represent blood and suffering. Did you know that?'

'No,' Rose said quietly.

'Neither did I at the time.' Angelica swallowed loudly. 'Anyway, as I said, it was a long time ago.' She took another drink of her tea and as she replaced her cup it rattled in the saucer. 'You know, a pretty young thing like you shouldn't be locked away in a place like this,' Angelica said too brightly. 'You should be out having fun. How will Mr Right find you tucked away down here?'

'I've come here to avoid Mr Right,' she answered honestly. It wouldn't be long before they all knew anyway. Mel might be a caring, sharing human being, but it was probably her secret that she would be sharing with the rest of the village.

'Your *grande passion*?'

Rose nodded. 'Something like that.'

'And is he married?'

'Very,' she said miserably.

'Then you mustn't be like me. It's wrong to put everyone else's feelings and happiness before your own. And above all, you shouldn't feel guilty. It's a pointless and totally destructive emotion. Don't ruin your life by running away from this. If you think he's worth it, fight for him! Your own peace of mind and your future is all that matters.' Angelica reached forward and clutched Rose's hand. Her skin was dry and papery, fragile. Brown age spots marred the cream-white delicate flesh. Her fingernails were white and thickened under the immaculate pale pink, pearlised polish. It was a shock after the clear, smoothness of her face. Her hands were telling a story that her face was still refusing to acknowledge. '*Carpe diem*, Rose. Seize the day!' she whispered urgently, grasping at her fingers tightly. 'Don't grow old and lonely like me, riddled with regrets, with nothing but memories for company.' She patted Rose's knee and sat back in her chair. 'Here I am,' her eyes swept over the room, 'looking for solace in a bottle of essential oils.' She smiled sardonically. 'Better than a bottle of gin, I suppose.'

The room had grown cold and dark, even though it was only mid-afternoon. It was time she thought about lighting the fire in here, Rose mused. The shortest day was long past, but it was still some time until the light, bright summer evenings came to cheer the house. The wallpaper was chintzy, covered in pink floribunda roses and green twisting ivy. Normally, the roses looked too fussy and effusive but in this light they looked flat and unwelcoming. It would have to go. She'd been studying paint techniques – only out of a book, nothing too elaborate – principally with the idea of renovating the kitchen chairs. Now that she'd learned about sponging off, ragging off, bagging off and distressing – all terms which she thought sounded like ways of scrounging from the DHSS – no surface in the house was safe.

'I can at least blend some oils to help. Perhaps some clary sage, geranium and ylang-ylang. They're all wonderfully relaxing. Ylang-ylang helps to dispel anger borne of frustration – so my textbooks say.'

'Yes,' Angelica nodded. 'I could definitely do with a bit of that, dear.'

'You can use them at home in your bath – I take it you can get away from Anise then?'

Angelica's lips twitched in a half-smile. 'Armitage Shanks is my only refuge.'

'If you can escape, it would be a good idea to have some massage. The therapeutic benefits are wonderful.'

'It sounds bliss,' Angelica agreed. She stood up, smoothing the perfect pleats until they fell into obedient folds over her knees. 'I must go. Your next gentleman will be here soon.' She winked theatrically and took Rose's hand. 'Thank you for your help, dear.'

'I haven't done anything yet,' Rose protested.

'We've had a nice chat and that's helped me to get a lot off my chest.' She squeezed Rose's fingers with her thin, parchment hand. She surveyed the lounge again. 'This really is a very lovely drawing room, dear. It's so relaxing and soothing. It has much the same feel as a confessional.'

Rose wasn't sure if that was supposed to be a compliment. 'I've had the house Feng Shui-ed,' she said by way of explanation.

'Bless you, dear,' Angelica said. 'Have you got a cold? You should use some of those nice aromatherapy oils yourself.'

'No,' Rose said. 'Feng Shui.'

'I never catch anything. I take vitamin C religiously. Every Sunday without fail.'

'It's the ancient Chinese art of placement. It's a way of designing your home to bring you luck in money, health and relationships. You arrange your furniture to best harness the powers of Chi energy to keep you in harmony with nature and at one with the universe.'

'Very nice, dear.'

Rose decided to escort Angelica to the door. The subtle

mysteries of the Far East were obviously even less interesting than Tantric sex.

'Well, goodbye, dear. Thank you, again.' She turned and looked at Rose earnestly. 'If there's anything I can ever do for you, do please let me know.'

'Actually,' Rose said, 'there might be one thing.' Angelica had already admitted that she and her sister were domestically challenged. It seemed reasonable to assume that they weren't involved too heavily in horticultural battles either. 'I'm having terrible trouble managing such a large garden. I have so much to do in the house, I can't seem to find the time to get outside often enough.' She put aside the thought of last Saturday pleasantly wasted in the pub and strolling round Woburn Woods with Dan when she could have been weeding and digging and whatever else a garden of such enormous proportions required. 'You don't happen to know a good gardener, do you?'

'Well, I know a gardener. Though I'd hate to be responsible for professing that he's a good gardener.' Angelica looked thoughtful. 'We have Basil. You know, Basil Fitzroy-Smith.'

Rose shook her head. It wasn't a name she had come across yet.

'He's not so much a gardener as a garden ornament. I think he only comes to us because he has his eye on Anise. He hides behind the bushes and looks at her with a strange twinkle in his eye and a line of spittle drooling from his mouth. It's quite frightening.' Her eyes took on a mischievous glint. 'I think he has a crush on her – if people over fifteen are allowed to have crushes. Anise is mortified. She was terrible as a youngster; unless they had a lord somewhere in the family she wouldn't even entertain them to tea. Heaven only knows what it would have taken for them to get a hand up her skirt. That's why she's still a spinster of the parish.' Angelica inclined her head knowingly. 'I can ask him for you – if you don't mind taking a risk.'

'I suppose he'd be better than nothing,' Rose said hopefully.

'Marginally,' Angelica agreed. 'He might be tempted to do more work if he doesn't develop a fixation for you. I'll ask him to come over in the next couple of days.' She patted Rose's arm. 'A word of warning. Don't be alarmed at his clothing. He's not known locally for his sartorial elegance. I think he favours the Wurzel Gummidge school of *haute couture*.'

'I'll bear that in mind,' Rose assured her. 'And I'll have your oils ready tomorrow, if you want to pop over again.'

'That would be very nice, dear. I'll bring a spot of Earl Grey, just in case you're kind enough to ask me to stay for tea. If you don't mind me saying, one urine sample a week is more than enough.'

Rose closed the door behind Angelica and rested on the frame. Her client would be here in a minute, it hardly seemed worthwhile walking back into the lounge. Would it be so bad to grow old alone like Angelica? On the whole, she seemed pretty content and well-balanced – if you ignored the psychopathic tendencies towards her sister. Which were understandable, after all. Anise was starting to bring out psychopathic tendencies in herself and she hardly knew the woman. Angelica was smart and self-contained. Wasn't it easier to live like that rather than be dependent on unreliable men? And there didn't seem to be any reliable men around any more. Was Hugh Mr Right? Was he her *grande passion*? She had thought so. God only knows, she had thought so. Why, when she tried to think of him now, couldn't she remember exactly how his face looked? Why did she have to keep staring at pictures of them together to remind her of the way he had been. The easy smile, the hair that flopped endearingly, the bedroom eyes. Why, when she lay in bed alone at night, was it Dan's face that seemed to feature more prominently in her erotic meanderings? Had Hugh expressed any suicidal thoughts just because she had ended their affair? No, quite frankly, he hadn't. The only thoughts he'd had were to watch his own back. Perhaps Angelica was right; fifty years down the line in the 1990s, things were different. Very different.

Chapter Thirteen

'Are we all here?' Anise asked, tapping her notebook with her pencil. She perched her glasses on the end of her nose, thinking that it made her look intelligent and in control. A force to be reckoned with. In truth, it simply made her look old and bossy. She cast her eyes round the spartan little group, incensed that so few people had answered her call to arms. 'Where's the vicar?'

'Dave said he'll be along as soon as he can,' Melissa replied.

'The Reverend Allbright,' Anise said haughtily, 'should be more interested in this than any of us. It is, after all, his church hall that is in danger of being razed to the ground.'

'He'll be along as soon as he can,' Melissa repeated more forcefully. 'He's gone to see Mrs Garner and her funny veins.'

'Varicose,' Anise informed her. '*Varicose.*'

'Very close,' Melissa said. 'Just round the corner.'

'Stupid girl,' Anise hissed under her breath. Melissa winked at Angelica who tried very hard not to laugh.

'Hasn't anyone invited that nice young woman from number five?' Angelica piped up. 'I would have thought she'd be interested. The flats will be right at the end of our lane. The people on the top floor will be able to see straight into her rear garden.'

'It's not what goes on in her garden that people need to worry about, Angelica,' Anise spoke tightly, 'it's what goes on in her house that concerns me. That's what I'd like to know about.'

Angelica tutted lightly. 'It doesn't concern you, Anise. I've told you before, she's an aromatherapist. Nothing more sinister than that.'

'And I suppose you know all about aromatherapy?' her sister asked tartly.

'No, not all about it. But I do know that it involves massage with essential oils which come from herbs and flowers.'

'Massage!' Anise wrinkled her nose in distaste.

'There are lots of therapeutic benefits,' Angelica assured her.

'Very commendable,' Anise snorted.

'There's nothing fishy about it.'

'I've seen halibut that are less fishy,' Anise sneered. 'And I suppose she told you all this clap-trap about aromatherapy.'

'She did. Her name is Rose and she's very nice. And,' Angelica stared pointedly at her sister, 'she should be here.'

'Yes, yes, all right. Perhaps I should have invited her. But we don't want that sort getting involved with the affairs of the village.'

'She isn't a sort. She's a perfectly nice young lady.'

'I think you're looking at the world through your *rose*-coloured spectacles again.' Anise allowed herself a little tinkling laugh. 'You don't know what we're dealing with here.'

'Neither do you, Anise. You just think you do. I might be wearing *rose*-coloured spectacles, but at least they're not blinkers.'

Anise stiffened. 'I didn't want to bring this up at the meeting. We have matters of greater import to discuss. But you have forced my hand, Angelica. You have forced my hand.' She adjusted her glasses on her nose and checked carefully over either shoulder before speaking. 'Mr Patel informed me that she gets a magazine – this . . . this . . . *aromatherapist* – about sado-masochism.' She sat back in her chair and watched this pearl of wisdom drop before the swine, a sardonic smile at her lips. There was a gasp from Mrs Brockett, the gills of Mrs Devises had gone decidedly green, while Mrs Took fanned herself vigorously with a copy of the parish magazine, *Good Neighbours*. Melissa's lips held the glimmer of a smile.

'He said nothing of the sort, Anise.' Angelica raised her eyes to the ceiling in supplication. 'I was there. He said she gets the M&S magazine. M&S, not S&M. Marks & Spencer, Anise. I think you'll find that's totally different.'

A titter went round the room and Mrs Took recovered sufficiently to restore the parish magazine to its former resting place on the table. Anise's face suffused with a shade of purple not dissimilar to the cashmere twinset she was wearing. 'Anyway, she's not here for whatever reason. And neither are a good deal of other people who ought to be – and who *were* invited.' She bristled with indignation. 'There's no one here from the Toddlers Group, or the Cubs or Brownies. Even the Tummies, Bottoms and Thighs haven't turned up.' Anise refused to say Tums and Bums – even Thighs was a struggle. It was such a lascivious word.

'Perhaps it's because they're happy with the fact that we're going to get a new village hall,' Angelica voiced. 'That is part of the plan.'

'It's a sop,' Anise said crisply. 'Offered up in the vain hope that we will turn a blind eye to the ruination of our village.'

'Dan only wants to build a few retirement flats,' Angelica said. 'He showed me the drawings. I must say they looked rather nice. Each one had a little wrought-iron balcony.'

Mrs Took nodded in agreement and opened her mouth

to speak until she saw the black look she was getting from the self-elected chairperson.

'Yes, it might just be a few harmless flats this time, Angelica, but if we start letting standards slip in the village, we'll simply open the floodgates. Next it will be a new Tesco's or a late-night petrol station or, heaven forfend, a Spud-u-Like. How would you like that?' She remembered she had a notepad and with a flourish wrote Spud-u-Like on the blank page in front of her. 'And why on earth do they need balconies? This isn't the Costa del Sol.'

'This place is an eyesore, Anise.' Angelica surveyed the decrepit hall distastefully. 'It looks like something Pontin's would have built in the 1950s.' There was a lot to look distasteful about. 'Corrugated iron and breeze block isn't exactly in keeping with the village image – if there is one. It's a health hazard, too. A visit by Dyno-Rod seems long overdue. Wouldn't it be nice to have somewhere brand, spanking new for the toddlers? It can't be very nice prancing round in a leotard in sub-zero temperatures and we wouldn't all have to wear thermal underwear just to come to the whist drives either.' Mrs Took looked in serious danger of nodding again. 'Or sit with our legs crossed all night because we're too terrified of what we might find in the lavatory.' Mrs Took could hardly contain her urge to nod. The unpleasant incident with the tramp was obviously still firmly planted in her mind.

'If we're not very vigilant, this rural slice of England will be turned into a gateaux.'

'I think you mean ghetto, Anise.'

She ignored her sister's comment and continued, 'If you don't want to save the old village hall, why are you here?' she asked tartly.

'I thought it was supposed to be a discussion, not a foregone conclusion. And I'm not altogether sure that it is worth saving.'

'You're being very vociferous today, Angelica.' It wasn't

like her sister to disagree with her. Especially not in public. 'Are you sure you haven't been trying this aromatherapy?'

Angelica flushed. How could Anise make innocent words like aromatherapy take on connotations of dancing naked in the moonlight and satanic worship?

Melissa came to her rescue. 'Why don't we have a social evening? The village hasn't had a get-together for ages. We could see what money we raised, then either use it to do up this place or perhaps buy stuff to kit out the new place.'

'That sounds like a jolly good idea,' Angelica enthused.

Anise didn't look the least bit enthused.

Melissa continued, addressing her comments to the other ladies present, who hadn't so far dared to speak. 'I've had a word with Dave and he thinks it's a goer. He suggested a Viking evening. You know, fancy dress and all that.'

'What's wrong with a nice harvest supper?' Anise was affronted.

'You can't have a harvest supper in March,' Angelica observed reasonably.

'You've got to move with the times, Anise,' Melissa advised. 'People like theme evenings. I went to a dinner party the other week and we all dressed up like people out of the war and ate boiled mutton with mashed potatoes and spotted dick. We had to guess which one was a murderer.'

'I'd plump for the caterer,' Anise said.

'It was a real laugh.'

'It sounds ghastly,' Anise retorted.

'That's because you remember the war and boiled mutton the first time round,' Angelica suggested sweetly.

Anise slammed down her redundant pencil. 'This is what you get when you have a vicar that wears an Aran sweater. The last vicar would never have stood for a Viking supper. It was always a barn dance or a harvest supper, no argument. Those were the main features on the church calendar.'

'Perhaps that's why the church was always empty,' Melissa said. 'At least Dave's got some new ideas. And at the end of the day, it's up to the church whether they want to sell the land to Dan or not. There's not much we can do about it.'

'You may be able to dress up in wartime clothes, young lady, but that wasn't the spirit that defended this country from the Hun. You youngsters have no backbone these days.'

'Perhaps we should put it to the vote?' Mel suggested.

'I'm the chairperson, Melissa. I'll say when we vote.' Anise picked up her pencil again with deliberate slowness. She would make them all wait. The gingham curtains fluttered in the breeze. 'Shall we vote then?'

Everyone at the table nodded. 'The motion is that the village should hold a Viking evening,' Anise said with a sneer. 'All those in favour raise their hands.'

Mrs Devises bravely shot her hand in the air, followed by the other ladies on her side of the table, most of them members of the church flower committee. Mrs Took, emboldened by this display of overt rebelliousness, edged her hand skyward, until Anise noticed and fixed her with a withering stare. The hand was returned under the table from whence it came. Anise made a show of counting their hands. She wrote the number of dissenters on her pad, next to the Spud-u-Like. She put on her Betty Boothroyd voice. 'I think, unfortunately, the ayes have it. Lord help us all!'

'It will be rather fun,' Angelica said, putting her hand in the air rather belatedly.

'I think I would rather spend three hours locked in a shed with Roy Hattersley and a Rottweiler,' her sister replied.

The ladies pushed away from the table and formed an

excited little huddle. Anise clapped her hands. 'We will reconvene next week to discuss the catering arrangements, ladies,' she instructed. 'Perhaps then the vicar will grace us with his presence.'

Anise watched the cosy huddle of ladies, tittering and giggling together like silly schoolgirls, and felt curiously isolated. Angelica was in the middle of them and was clearly enjoying the attention. Her sister had been deliberately non-compliant today and it wasn't a trend Anise was keen to encourage. Someone would have to be on her side for this battle. She had the sneaking feeling that she was not only the spearhead of this campaign but, at the moment, also the sole reinforcements – apart from Mrs Took who could always be relied on to do as she was told.

Mrs Devises sidled up to Angelica. 'I've heard that the nice young lady at number five does Sasha Distel.'

'So have I,' Angelica said with a nod.

'And Cliff Richard,' added Mrs Took, not wanting to be outdone.

'And Mick Hucknall from Simply Red,' Melissa said.

'And Michael Ball,' came a joint offering from the ladies of the church flower committee.

'Have you seen any of them yet, Angelica?' Melissa asked.

'No,' Angelica mused. It didn't seem appropriate to mention that they logged all of Rose's visitors and there hadn't been even a minor celebrity in sight yet, apart from the man that looked suspiciously like Melvyn Bragg. 'I expect they arrive incognito.'

Melissa gave an unconvinced shrug. 'I would have thought they'd arrive in chauffeur-driven limos,' she said.

A small silence fell over the group as everyone wondered whether Melissa had a point.

Chapter Fourteen

STOPPING SLEEPLESSNESS
Lavender, Marjoram, Vetiver, Valerian.
When pressure of work or some more specific anxiety
won't let you rest, this potent mixture of essential oils can
help to lull you to a sound and refreshing sleep when all
else has failed.
  from: *The Complete Encyclopaedia of Aromatherapy Oils*
by Jessamine Lovage

Rose, very much awake, flung her arm across the pillow
and stared at the luminous green numbers on her alarm
clock. It was exactly midnight. She hated looking at the
clock at exactly midnight. Normally, she wasn't a superstitious person; she could walk on cracks in the pavement,
under ladders, forget to say 'white rabbits' on the first of
the month, all of those things, without a second thought.
But there was something that made her flesh creep if she
saw the hand of the clock brush past the witching hour.

It was one thing living in a quaint detached cottage
down a lonely country lane surrounded by rolling fields
during the day, at night, it was a different beast altogether.
Nasty things might lurk in the hedges and neighbours
couldn't hear you scream. Melissa had told her that when
she was first married to Frank she could never sleep
when he was on night shift and had always kept the radio

on low so that she couldn't hear the pings and creaks of the house settling down for the cold of night. Anything was worth a go.

She had a full appointment book tomorrow and had deliberately come to bed two hours ago to get a good night's sleep. What a waste of time that was; she might as well have stayed up and watched *Prisoner Cell Block H* until her eyes were gritty and she was totally exhausted. She switched the radio on. It was tuned to Bucks County FM in the hope of catching the Cassia Wales' chat show which had, so far, eluded her. There was the exaggerated sound of a creaking door and the maniacal laugh of Vincent Price. '*Murder at Midnight,*' the DJ announced in Hammer House of Horror tones. Rose slammed the radio off and slammed her hand into her pillow.

It was a spooky night. The moon was bright and clear and bathed the room in a chill, pale light that bleached the colour from the walls and the furniture. Even her cheerful Laura Ashley duvet looked wan and ghostly. The wind whistled emptily in the eaves and she wondered whether there was enough insulation in the loft. Clouds scudded across the sky and were thrown into shadow relief on her walls. There were no curtains at her windows. They were a really awkward shape because they were tiny dormer windows that jutted out into the roof. Aesthetically, very pleasing. Practically, downright impossible for curtain hanging.

Icy, stabbing rain hurled itself at the leaded panes – mock ones, not real ones. A lone tendril of ivy had curled itself along the window ledge and, with the rhythm of the wind, it tapped against the glass with a thin skeletal finger, a hollow, insistent, nerve-shredding noise. She would have to get Basil up there to cut it down. He had already told her, with some disgust, that it was growing into her gutters. Such misdemeanours could make you public enemy number one in Great Brayford.

Basil, all things considered, had been a great success. She didn't know exactly what he did for his five pounds an hour, but there always seemed to be bonfires smouldering damply at the bottom of the garden and the lawn now looked like real grass, green grass rather than a combination of brown wet leaf mulch and moss. The door of the potting shed was always open and rows of tools – hoes, spades, rakes – leaned expectantly against it. As Angelica had warned her, it did take some getting used to talking to a man wearing a trilby and Nike trainers without laughing.

Another scrape on the window from the ivy brought her back from her mental meanderings about Basil and the nonexistent curtains. The clock was reading twelve fifteen and the wind was just winding itself up to full throttle. It was the sort of night that no one in their right mind ventured out in, thus making it ideal for rapists, murderers, serial killers and Freddy Kruger.

This is a wonderful train of thought, she chided herself. Just the sort of thing to keep you wide-eyed and buzzing until dawn. She turned up the heat setting on her aromatherapy oil diffuser. Even her trusty oils were determined to be untrustworthy tonight. To start with she had burned lavender oil – its gentle clinical fragrance was perfect for soothing and calming anxieties. It had failed miserably. She had simply lain there getting more and more uncalm and anxious. Then she had upped it a gear to marjoram – warming, comforting. Nothing. So she had added a few drops of vetiver – heavily sedative and good for releasing deep-felt tension. Her deep-felt tension went even deeper when, after another half an hour of tossing and turning, vetiver failed to do its stuff.

In desperation she turned to valerian. It wasn't her favourite oil. Not these days, anyway. Perhaps it was because Hugh's surname happened to be Valerian. It had a smell like ripe dog pooh, which reminded her of Hugh because he was a complete shit too. But for the terminally wide awake, valerian could succeed where all else failed.

She could hardly blame the oils, though. It was the telephone call that had unsettled her. There hadn't been one for over a week and she had hoped, fervently, that whoever it was had got bored with terrorising her and had gone on to pick on someone less vulnerable who would give him a flea in his ear and not sit there whimpering pathetically, pandering to his sick power kick. Who could it be? One of her clients would be the most likely. They knew she lived alone and that she was new to the area. Perhaps one of them thought it would be fun to give her a personal welcome. Rose considered each of them in turn. They all seemed perfectly sober and respectable. Not one of them groaned in that certain way that made you realise they were enjoying being massaged just a bit too much. She couldn't think of anyone who had erected a telltale tent in the nether regions of his towel while she was effleuraging their spleen.

She had always been very lucky in her dealings with clients in the past. At the last clinic she had worked in, they had regularly endured phone calls from men looking for 'extras'. On the whole, though, they were very polite and when they were told, equally politely, that the only 'extra' they were likely to get was a cup of herbal tea or decaffeinated coffee, they usually apologised profusely and hung up.

If it wasn't one of her clients, perhaps it was someone closer to home. Maybe someone had started taking seriously the allegations of wild goings-on and blatant prostitution that Anise Weston had been bandying about the village. Her bedroom certainly smelled like a busy night at a brothel with all the different oils she had been burning.

It was a problem. She couldn't go ex-directory because she needed her number in the book for business and yet, as Dan pointed out, it left her at the mercy of strangers. Maybe she shouldn't be working from home. Maybe she shouldn't have bought this house at all. She didn't need anywhere this size. In the day it was fine. Perfectly proportioned. At night it grew, so that she rattled around its emptiness like a frozen pea in a tin can. Maybe she shouldn't have left Hugh at all.

The shrill ringing next to her ear made her jump. Her heart pounded double-time and her mouth went as dry as dirt. The pervert obviously couldn't sleep either. Rose switched on the bedside light. It seemed better to talk to the pervert in the light rather than in the dark. On the other hand, if he was one of the nasty things lurking in the hedges he would have seen the light go on. She wondered if perverts had embraced twentieth-century technology and now used mobile phones. Reluctantly, she picked up the phone. 'Hello,' she said, dismayed at the quiver in her voice. There were jellies that would kill for a wobble like that. There was no reply, just an empty threatening silence that stretched into the night. She took a deep, unsteady breath. 'I know who this is,' she said bravely. 'If you don't stop hassling me, I'll go to the police. Stay out of my life!' she shouted and slammed the receiver down.

It felt good having stood up to her pervert. If only her body would agree and stop shaking. She got out of bed with trembly legs and grabbed the teddy from the rattan chair in the corner of the room. Taking him back to bed with her, they snuggled beneath the duvet, Rose shivering slightly against his fat, furry body. He had been a Valentine's Day present from Hugh last year. The teddy and a set of red sexy underwear. Not the harloty kind. Tasteful red sexy underwear. There were no peephole nipples and the crotch was definitely where it should be. The teddy was a Forever Friends bear. He was cute, smiley, and sported a blue bow tie with large pink spots.

There was a faint blush to his cheeks and his nose was round and coloured a rich burgundy-brown, like an overripe morello cherry. It just begged to be kissed. His tummy was rotund and comforting and it made her think of Hugh – simply because Hugh's tummy wasn't rotund at all. There were days when she still missed its concrete concave contours desperately. She called him Casanova. The teddy, not Hugh.

Rose stared at the ceiling. It was steeply sloped and a cobweb of hairline cracks ran across the faded white paint. There were three beams in the room which gave it a homely, cottagey feel. They looked genuine enough, solid, dependable, take-me-as-you-find-me beams. But they were false. False, false, false. Hollow, weak, insubstantial compared to solid oak. They had been chipped and scarred and painted as black as coal and disguised as real beams. But they were false. Like her.

Rose hugged Casanova tightly to her. Thirty-two years old and still frightened to sleep alone. So much for wanting her independence. For wanting to stand alone. Could it really be classed as independence when somebody else had given her the money to pay for it – and under extreme duress at that? No wonder the villagers thought she was a hooker. All she had wanted was to be free of Hugh. To get off the dizzy roundabout of endless adultery.

She had chosen a strange way to do it. She had blackmailed Hugh. She had threatened to tell his wife, his kids, his colleagues. She had demanded a fee – a substantial fee – for her freedom and her silence. And he had paid her off, casually, coldly, without question, as though she was a taxi driver at the end of a particularly unpleasant ride in a cab stinking of vomit from last night's drunks. Except he hadn't given her a tip. Or a backward glance. Or even a 'thanks for the ride'. He had slammed the door on their relationship and walked out of her life.

Rose let out a long, unhappy sigh into the back of Casanova's head. She had slept with Hugh for two long years. Eager to be his plaything at the click of his smooth, well-manicured fingers. And he had settled her account in full with this house. But how could she ever be truly independent when the roof over her head, the curtainless windows and the too big, unruly garden was paid for by someone else? Someone who didn't, at the end of the day, love her.

Rose took the phone off the hook and suffocated the receiver with her spare pillow to blot out the droning disconnected tone. Turning the light off, she slid down into the depths of the bed with Casanova and pulled the duvet over her head. Hopefully, if the caller was watching from the hedge, he would take it as his cue to settle down for the night too. 'Goodnight,' she said to Casanova. It was when she shut her eyes that Rose realised how relieved she was that no one answered back.

Chapter Fifteen

Detective Constable Elecampane's bottom was smarting. He was tied to the bedposts of Melissa's Hänsel and Gretel pine bed while she set about his buttocks with the spatula that had come free with her Kenwood food processor. It was wonderful, she said, for getting that last little drop of cake mix out of the bottom of the bowl and also, it appeared, for smacking buttocks.

To be honest, DC Elecampane couldn't say that he was enjoying it as much as Melissa appeared to be. In fact, he couldn't say anything at all. Melissa had taped up his mouth with that horrible brown tape they used for parcels, the stuff that refuses to co-operate with even the sharpest scissors and you usually have to resort to ripping the package apart with your teeth. He wondered, with a vague sense of unease, what it was going to do to his lips when she eventually decided to pull it off.

They had fallen into a pattern of regular weekly meetings. He was still referred to as 'the ironing' in her diary and he still resented it. She still insisted that he had the Spanky Panky treatment each week and he still didn't have the heart to tell her that he wasn't keen to be beaten by the entire contents of the Argos catalogue. Melissa probably had more kitchen utensils than Mrs Beeton. And a great deal of them appeared to be sharp.

His mother had always warned him that women would only hurt him but until now he had never known one who charged him £69.99 for the privilege. Mel insisted that Spanky Panky wasn't her favourite and that she only did it to please him. For someone who wasn't keen, Melissa entered into it with a relish that he had previously only seen exhibited by women on a hockey pitch. She was all flying hair and flailing arms and he just had to lie there and brace himself for the next blow. And another thing, he was getting fed up with his bottom smelling of the Germolene that he was having to smear liberally on his rear end to prepare himself for next week's onslaught.

There was only one way to stop this. He groaned as enthusiastically as he could through his parcel tape and shuddered violently against the Garden of Romance sheets. Melissa smacked him soundly for the final time and then flopped off him with a heavy sigh. 'Was that nice?' she asked sweetly.

He nodded weakly. It was difficult for a man to fake an orgasm and he hoped that Melissa would be too preoccupied with packing away her spatula to notice. He didn't want to offend her, after all.

Melissa rolled off the bed and began to get dressed. There was a wistful, far away look in her eye as she pulled on her leggings and T-shirt and Bob Elecampane's heart lurched with love for her. What price would he pay to see her smiling sleepily with the contented flush of afterglow, hair across the pillow, her full rounded body curled against his? Certainly more than £69.99. Perhaps it was a gift so priceless that it couldn't be bought. A muffled sigh escaped from his lips. Melissa turned round. 'Sorry, I forgot about you.'

She peeled the tape from his lips, taking tiny shreds of skin as she went. He wished he had the courage to tell her to rip it quickly and get it over with, but he couldn't bring himself to voice it. 'You looked miles away,' he said rubbing his lips together to ease the pain.

'I was just thinking.' She smiled but it was a sad smile.

As she undid his bonds, he took her hand. '*Après l'amour, les animaux sont toujours triste.*'

Melissa looked blankly at him. 'What?'

'It's French,' Bob said earnestly. 'After love, the animals are always sad.'

'What animals?'

'Well,' he hesitated. 'I think it means us – we're the animals.'

Melissa was affronted. 'You might be an animal, but I'm bloody well not!'

'I was trying to be romantic.' Bob was deflated. 'Perhaps I didn't explain it right.'

'Oh,' she said uncertainly. He was encouraged to see that she looked somewhat placated. 'That's nice, then.' She still sounded cagey. 'I didn't know you spoke French.'

'I save it for special occasions.' He'd loved French ever since he heard Maurice Chevalier singing 'Sank'eavon fur leetle gels'. It gave the ordinary things in life a certain *je ne sais quoi* and sent a shiver down the rigid spine of the mundane. Let's face it, if a scrawny little git like Charles Aznavour could manage to pull gorgeous, sexy birds, then speaking French must count for something. And Robert Elecampane was at that stage in life where he was prepared to give anything a try.

Melissa pulled her hand away from his and began brushing her tousled hair. The brush had sharp spikes and made a rasping sound and he hoped that she would never be tempted to make the connection between it and his bottom. He fixed his bashful look to his face and tried to attract her attention again. 'There's a lot about me you don't know,' he said sincerely. 'I'm a man of many talents. Unfortunately, most of them are hidden. There have been very few women to whom I've revealed myself.'

'I should think so too,' Melissa said, putting her brush back on the dresser out of harm's way. 'There's a law against that sort of thing, as well you should know being a detective.'

'I don't mean like that.' It was hard not to become exasperated when Melissa was being obtuse. He sighed and tried again. 'I want to tell you things about myself.'

'But you're too shy?' Melissa ventured.

'Something like that.'

'Well, I also do mucky phone calls for some of my clients,' she said brightly. 'It's cheaper, only £29.99 an hour, but we have to have a fixed time so that Frank isn't here. And I like it to be when I do my ironing – it helps to pass the time.'

'But I thought I was "the ironing".'

'Silly,' she giggled. 'You're only the ironing in code. This is the ironing for real. I take in for three or four houses in the village, so I have a lot to do. It can get a bit tedious.'

Is that what their purpose in life was, Melissa's clients? To relieve the tedium of her ironing? 'How can I make a dirty phone call to you when I know you're doing the ironing? I wouldn't have your full attention.'

A flash of surprise crossed Melissa's child-like face. 'What do you expect for £29.99?'

'Nothing.' Bob was heavy of heart. 'You're right, it's very good value.' There was a chill spreading over his body, now that the numbness was disappearing from his limbs, and he started to get dressed. 'I didn't actually want to make a telephone call to you, I wanted to talk to you face to face.'

'But you said you were too shy,' Melissa said reasonably.

'That's just the way I am.' He paused with his trousers round his ankles. 'I might come across as a rough, tough, man of the world, but inside I'm nothing more than a lost little boy.'

Melissa didn't look convinced.

'Perhaps we could do next week a bit differently.' Bob

cleared his throat. 'I feel the enjoyment of being beaten by household objects has run its course somewhat,' he said hesitantly. 'Maybe we could have a quick, ordinary sort of session – you know, me on top, you underneath – without the compulsory use of corporal punishment and then we could spend some time just talking.'

Melissa laughed. 'I've never had anyone who wanted to pay just to sit and talk.'

'Well, I do, Melissa,' he said gently. 'And I don't want to talk about sex either. I want to talk about ordinary things. The things that make you cry. The things that make you laugh.'

'*You're* making me laugh,' she said in alarm. 'Why do you want to know about me?'

Bob took a deep breath and zipped up his flies. It was an intimate movement, zipping up one's flies in front of a woman. He felt it showed a trust and a willingness to be open that he had never been able to achieve before. In the past, he would have turned away fumbling, furtive, and the moment would have been lost. 'I am beginning to care for you, deeply,' he said. 'I don't simply want to share your body. I want to drink tea and eat custard creams or bourbon biscuits with you and discuss why, after years of being a treasured institution, *Coronation Street* has suddenly become so naff.'

A look of fear had settled on Melissa's face and he wondered whether perhaps he had gone too far. But there was no turning back. She must know how he felt. 'I don't want to talk to you merely as a client. Talk is cheap.' Although at £29.99 a go it wasn't exactly dirt cheap. 'Hopefully, you can think of me as more than a client, more than someone to share your body with, more than a pile of ironing in your little black book. I want you to consider me as a friend.'

Melissa swallowed deeply and he tried unsuccessfully to push all thoughts of Linda Lovelace and her obliging throat out of his mind. She sat on the edge of the bed. 'This has come as a bit of a shock to me,' she said. And, indeed, Bob felt she sounded slightly dazed. Although, he was beginning to realise, this it wasn't uncommon with Melissa.

He shrugged his shirt on to his shoulders and fastened his buttons as nonchalantly as he could with trembling fingers. 'I'll leave it with you till next week to think about.'

Melissa pulled her diary out of the bedside drawer.

'Same time?' he suggested.

She opened it at the relevant page.

Bob raked his hair nervously. In for a penny, in for a pound – or £69.99 in Melissa's case. He licked his tongue across his lips, which were still raw and peeling and would probably scab. 'Perhaps you could write me in as something nicer than the ironing? What about changing the sheets?' he offered tentatively. 'That would make me feel a lot better.' More desired. More wanted.

'Why changing the sheets?' She paused with her pencil, puzzled.

'Well, everyone likes nice clean sheets,' Bob explained. 'It's something to look forward to.'

Melissa looked up from her diary. 'You're asking a lot of me this week.' Her voice was harsh and it made him jump. It didn't suit her at all.

'I'm sorry.'

She slammed the page shut. 'I can't do you next week,' she said tightly.

'Why not?'

'I'm busy.' She threw the diary decisively into the bedside drawer.

'Doing what?' Bob was aghast.

'We're having a Viking supper to save the church hall. I've got some cooking to do.'

'What do Vikings eat?'

'A lot. It's going to take me ages,' she snapped in a tone that brooked no discussion.

'And that's more important than I am?'

'I don't know.' Her face was flushed and her lower lip was quivering and it looked suspiciously as if she was going to cry.

'I'd better go,' he said hastily, slipping with equal haste into his shoes and jacket. 'Perhaps you'll change your mind.'

'I might,' she sniffed.

'You know where I am. Just let me know if you can fit me in.' It was the sort of comment that he would normally have followed with a hearty guffaw, but it didn't seem appropriate in the circumstances. He moved to the door. 'I'll let myself out.'

Melissa stared, unmoving, at the wallpaper – Garden of Romance, again – except that the wallpaper bore only tiny tasteful sprigs of co-ordinating flowers rather than the profuse riot of blooms that covered the duvet, the curtains, the cushions and the lampshades.

Bob hurried to the front door. His radio was squawking, bringing him back to the sane, safe world of criminals. Mainly male criminals. Thankfully. Would he ever understand women? It had taken him long enough to understand French and look where that was getting him. Nowhere. Fast. It looked as if he was going to be hurt again. He should have been happy with the Spanky Panky, but it was too late now. Sensible men always listen to their mothers. He was in too deeply. The scars that he would bear from this would wound more cruelly than anything a spatula from a Kenwood food processor could ever inflict.

It was only when he was back in the safe cocoon of his car driving back to the concrete urban jungle of flat-roofed, flat-faced houses and bleak, straight, unpeopled roads that made up the south side of Milton Keynes that

DC Elecampane realised that in his haste to depart, the bill for services rendered hadn't been paid. A smile spread across his face. It was a thought that cheered his pained soul immensely.

Chapter Sixteen

Basil was trying to repair the damage Anise had done to the leylandii with the pinking shears. It was a frightful mess. Snipping neatly with the secateurs, he tried to blend in the great gaps that she had hacked in the luxuriant dark green foliage. Good heavens, she was wonderful when she was angry. The sap must have been rising forcibly within her when she set about this hedge. The thought made Basil shiver with pleasure.

Standing back to admire his handiwork, he suspected that Suzette of Suzette's salon never took so much trouble with her clients. Whenever he had availed himself of her services, he came out looking like one of Great Brayford's cornfields in the autumn, a quarter inch of chewed stubble sticking out unattractively from the surface after it had been slashed erratically by a combine harvester. He hadn't visited Suzette recently and, therefore, relied heavily on his trilby and the glossy accompaniment of Brylcreem to perform all of his hairdressing requisites.

Basil stacked the leylandii trimmings tidily in the ancient wheelbarrow and contemplated his role as gardener. He had always hated gardening but he had always done it because his mother insisted. This had, over the years, given him a certain reluctant knowledge of plants and lawns and bonfires that had allowed him to ingratiate himself with the Misses Weston, with the main aim of getting to know one of the Misses considerably better than the other. So at least he had something to thank his mother for there. Mind you, one didn't really have much choice with plants, throw a bit of water and fertiliser on them and they either grew or died. There was very little else you could do to influence them.

He wished it had been the same way with women. There seemed to be so much else to do in order to get relationships with them to grow into anything remotely resembling a healthy shrub. Only once or twice had there been anything like the promise of a green shoot of romance, but they had very quickly become sickly saplings and had withered and died despite his best efforts. Relationships, it appeared, had to be constantly nurtured like hothouse flowers and he wasn't sure he had the patience any more – or, indeed, the time. He was not green-fingered when it came to the girl department.

It was his mother's fault. She had lived far longer than was reasonable for a woman in her condition, enjoying, as she always had, a certain robust strain of ill health. Basil had never thought to leave her and, even though she had outstayed her welcome by at least twenty years, he had cared for her meticulously, alone. For most of his life he had viewed her as the prime cause of his enforced bachelorhood. What woman in their right mind would want to take her on? He had even tried a few that weren't entirely in their right mind, but still no joy. When she died he missed her bitterly. Perhaps that was what had brought him back to gardening, the need to care for something small, helpless and fragile again. Shooting squirrels had also proved very therapeutic.

Anise was coming through the front door bearing a silver tray with a mug of tea and some sort of stodgy-looking cake. She had taken to doing this for him on the days that he tended their garden and he had seen it as an encouraging sign. Normally, she didn't strike him as the type of woman to carry a tray for anyone, let alone a torch. He straightened up and massaged his lower back, thinking that the sympathy vote wouldn't go amiss either.

'Basil.' She nodded curtly as she approached with the tray. 'Fine weather.'

'Indubitably so, good lady.' He took the rake and leaned on it at what he calculated was a rakish angle.

'The weathermen said it would rain.'

'If I had my way, I'd hang the bastards,' he said pleasantly.

'They're so often wrong,' she agreed.

'Quite.'

'Tea?' She offered him the tray. 'Angelica has made the cake. It's barely edible. Mr Kipling makes a much better job of it, but she won't be told.'

Basil took the tray and balanced it precariously on the edge of the wheelbarrow.

'If you want to throw it on the compost heap, I shall understand perfectly. But do make sure that it's under the leylandii clippings. Angelica would fall apart if she saw you had discarded it.'

He wanted to say, she isn't strong like you, but felt it was too early in the scheme of social foreplay to offer such flattery. 'Will you be attending the Viking supper at the church hall, Anise?'

'Unfortunately so, Basil. I'm in complete opposition to the whole project and I feel I have to make my presence felt. There are so few of us left who are concerned with standards these days.'

'I trust I may be counted among them.'

Anise looked surprised. 'It hadn't occurred to me, Basil.' She twisted the string of pearls at her throat. 'A man that can wear a lilac shell suit with brogues doesn't strike me as being overly concerned with standards.'

Basil raised one eyebrow enigmatically. 'Standards, like still waters, run deep,' he informed her. 'Clothing is mere frippery for the flesh.' He leaned forward seductively on his rake. 'Unlike manners, dear lady, they do not maketh the man.' He resisted the urge to wink.

Anise licked her lips nervously and glanced back at the house. 'Well, yes,' she said, a modicum of fluster peeping through her bravado.

'I'd like to assure you of my utmost support,' Basil continued.

'Well, that's very nice to know.' Was he mistaken or was there a girlish flush to her cheek? 'Leadership is sometimes a very lonely place.'

'Margaret Thatcher said the very same thing,' he declared.

Anise was taken aback. 'Did she?'

'If she didn't, then I'm sure that on many an occasion it was merely a hair's breadth from her lips.' He tried an ingratiating smile, which seemed to hit the bullseye.

Anise looked coy. 'Chairperson of the steering committee for the Viking evening can hardly be classed as the same thing.'

'Nonsense. Two women trying to uphold standards against cruel odds. I'd call you kindred spirits.' And Thatcher was a right old battleaxe too, he thought.

'You're very kind, Basil.'

It was time to make his move. 'Perhaps you would permit me the honour of a dance at the Viking supper.'

There was a definite reddening of cheeks. 'I'm afraid the organisation of the entertainment is in the hands of the Reverend Allbright and Melissa. Goodness knows what we shall get. The word "discotheque" has featured. I fear there'll be no room for a foxtrot.'

'There's nothing that John Travolta can do that I can't.' He smiled beguilingly. 'I can assure you that you'll be in safe hands.'

'Well, that remains to be seen.' Anise fanned herself vigorously with her hand and he hoped that he hadn't leaned too close with garlic breath. 'I'm co-ordinating the food, so at least there'll be something to eat.' She turned round, checking either side of the garden before she spoke again. 'Tell me, Basil. How are you getting on with that young woman across the lane?'

'Rose?'

'Yes. I understand Angelica has cajoled you into a spot of gardening for her.'

'We get along perfectly well. She's very charming, if a little lax with her horticultural habits.'

Anise's face shaded with disappointment. 'Haven't you noticed anything unusual going on in her house?'

'Not that I can think of.' Basil pushed his trilby back and scratched the side of his head, acquiring some Brylcreem beneath his fingernail. 'Was there anything specific you were thinking of?'

'This is a very delicate subject.' Anise cleared her throat gently. 'I am concerned – extremely concerned – at the number of male visitors that Miss Stevens seems to entertain.'

'Men?'

She lowered her voice. 'They come out looking quite flushed and very pleased with themselves.'

'Oh, men!' Basil exclaimed. 'Now I know what you mean. Mr Patel said that you thought she was running a bawdy house.'

'Basil, please keep your voice down.' Anise spun round. 'Angelica is Rose's keenest champion. She will hear nothing said against her. If I didn't know better I would suspect that she was dabbling in this . . . this . . . *aromatherapy* herself.'

He pushed his trilby back further, until it perched with gravity-defying properties on the back of his head. 'Can't say I've seen anything funny. She seems a busy little bee, but I've never seen what you might call "goings-on".'

'Well, Basil, I can assure you there are goings-on. Going on right under our noses.' Anise held her forehead and fluttered her eyes closed. 'She is brazen and shameless.'

Basil rubbed his chin. 'You do surprise me. Like everyone, I had my reservations, but she seems so nice.'

'That's what they said about Sarah Ferguson and look what happened to her!'

He tapped the side of his nose. 'I get your drift.'

'Perhaps I could prevail upon you to give this matter some attention during the course of your duties.'

'I don't see why not. If I stand on my tiptoes I can see straight into the room where she does this aromatherapy business. Tell me though –' Basil followed Anise's lead and also surveyed the garden to check that there was no one in earshot '– exactly what sort of thing am I looking for?'

'Basil! You are a man of the world, are you not?' Anise giggled coquettishly. 'I don't think you need me to tell you what you're looking for.'

'Don't I?' His eyebrows met in the middle.

'Look for anything out of the ordinary, Basil. Out of the ordinary.'

'Out of the ordinary.'

'*Out of the ordinary*.' She mouthed it silently. 'Well, I'll leave you to your tea,' she said loudly as if playing to an audience. Basil spun round but no one was there. 'Don't let it get cold.'

Winking theatrically at him, she turned and strode back to the house. Basil picked up his tea. It was cold and the barrow full of leylandii clippings looked more appetising than the cake. His eyes followed Anise's ramrod straight back, her sturdy calves and her severe snatched-up hair. Good grief, she was a formidable woman. If anything was out of the ordinary, it was her. Strange though – he allowed himself a little self-satisfied smile – he never had her down as a winker.

Chapter Seventeen

GIVING UP GUILT
Jasmine, Vetiver, Ylang-Ylang.
We all have things to be guilty about. But there are times when those feelings of guilt overwhelm us, giving rise to feelings of inadequacy and unworthiness. This powerful blend of oils will help you to gently let go of that guilt – if only you'll allow them to!

from: *The Complete Encyclopaedia of Aromatherapy Oils*
by Jessamine Lovage

In order to assuage the guilt she felt about her attraction to Dan, Rose looked up oils under the judgmental heading in *The Complete Encyclopaedia of Aromatherapy Oils* and settled for the 'Giving Up Guilt' remedy. She hoped it would be more successful than her giving-up-chocolate-for-Lent fiasco which had lasted about four days before she succumbed to the hedonistic delights of a Cadbury's Creme Egg.

So far, the riot of oils had done nothing to allay the butterflies in her stomach as she readied herself for the Viking evening ahead. Someone had once told her that all you had to do with butterflies was persuade them to fly in formation. Hers still seemed intent on Kamikaze missions. So she slipped a small bottle of lavender oil into her pocket for good measure.

Perhaps Dan wouldn't come tonight, she thought as she made her way to the village hall. He wasn't exactly Mr Popular as far as the hall was concerned and it hardly seemed like the kind of bash that Gardenia would be eager to be seen at.

Standing in what was euphemistically called the 'cloakroom' of the village hall, Rose surveyed the dank room with half a dozen rusting coat pegs clinging precariously to the wall. The water marks that trickled down from the ceiling would soon be in headlong collision with the rising damp, and she couldn't understand why Dan was being viewed as the big, bad wolf. It wouldn't take very much huffing and puffing at all to blow this particular house down.

Rose regarded herself critically in the cloakroom's chipped and grimy mirror. Brown hessian was not her colour. It drained her, making her look wan and tired and in need of a good night's sleep. She *was* in need of a good night's sleep, thanks to the pervert, but there was no need to accentuate it. It had encouraged her to be heavy-handed with the blusher and she tried to smooth the excess away with the back of her hand. Her hair had been expertly coiffured by Suzette for the princely sum of £10 but, she had decided to walk to the church hall and, in that short distance, the wind had added its own tousling, so that she now sported a more 'ravished' look. Or, more accurately, 'ravaged'. Viking was not a word that leapt to the front of the mind. She looked more like one of the cast of *Les Misérables*.

Trying to analyse her feelings about Dan had proved tricky. It was easy to be casual about him when she didn't have to see him. And she hadn't seen him since she had stormed out of his Discovery in a huff. Her fireplace remained steadfastly unfinished. Rose sighed at the mirror and braced herself to join the growing crowd of people, all in various states of Viking ensemble, in the main part of the hall.

She sidled into the room nervously, wishing that she hadn't, for the sake of authenticity, left her handbag at home. It meant that she had nothing to do with her hands and her money jingled uncomfortably against the bottle of lavender in the pocket of her brown hessian sack dress. Angelica swept towards her, greeting her with a kiss on both cheeks. She was wearing a long black dress, bound with rope at the waist which matched the rope-type band wound through her hair. Angelica had no qualms about authenticity and carried a black patent leather handbag over her arm. 'You look divine, dear,' she said enthusiastically. 'Let's go and get you a drink. I expect you'll need one. These things can be quite an ordeal if you're a newcomer.'

Reg from the pub was running the bar and had tried to enter into the theme of the evening by supplying copious quantities of Carlsberg lager and something called 'Pillager's Punch'. Feeling like a killjoy, Rose eschewed the lager and the punch – which appeared to be Ribena with a tin of fruit cocktail floating in it – and stuck to the safety of a glass of dry white wine.

'Come and say hello to Anise,' Angelica urged. 'She's in a good mood – relatively speaking. It might help matters if she gets to know you.'

Anise was busy turning her nose up at the buffet table, or the *smörgåsbord*, if you were a stickler for accuracy. 'Are you sure that Vikings ate pizza?' she asked Mrs Devises who seemed to be shaking with fear.

'Mrs Took was dispatched to the library to research it, Anise. She borrowed a book called *Dining With the Danes*. Some of the ingredients were terribly difficult to get hold of. They don't sell reindeer in Tesco's, so I think some largesse was allowed.'

'I think this amounts to the largest largesse I've ever

seen.' Anise held up a Plumrose pork chipolata wedged with a pineapple and some cheddar cheese on a stick and eyed it disdainfully. 'Hardly fodder for plundering primitive countries.'

'Can I introduce you to Rose Stevens?' Angelica interrupted the dissection of the buffet. 'The nice young lady from number five. I know you've been dying to meet her.'

Anise looked suspiciously at Angelica's innocent smile. 'Good evening,' she said through clenched teeth. 'We hope you'll be very happy in the village.'

'Thank you so much. The warm welcome I have received has made me feel very at home,' Rose replied sweetly.

'We're quite friendly – unless you upset us,' Anise said tightly.

Rose stood her ground. 'So am I.'

Anise looked thunderous, aware that she was being made to look a fool. At that moment, a small, dumpy woman wearing a sack and a metal helmet appeared at the door.

'I must have a word with Mrs Took about the eclectic nature of the provisions,' Anise said curtly and took her leave.

As Mrs Took made an unsuccessful attempt to dodge Anise's attention, Dan appeared in the doorway. It was a stunning entrance. He dwarfed the door and looked terribly menacing without even trying. So far, he was the only one in the place who could successfully carry off the Viking look. He wore tight black leather trousers bound to the knee with braiding, a billowing white shirt open to the waist and a furry cape slung round his shoulders. The spear on top of his broom handle looked frighteningly realistic and he carried a proper shield rather than the dustbin lid favoured by the other warrior men. His blond hair formed an unruly mane round his head and his face had a shaggy look that said he hadn't shaved for quite a few days. He looked magnificent and from the emotions that tugged inside her body, it was clear that Jessamine's best efforts with the 'Giving Up Guilt' oil hadn't a snowball's chance in hell against him.

She hoped, for one giddy moment, that he had come alone. It was then that the two siren sisters, Gardenia and Cassia Wales, sauntered up behind him. He stood aside for them to enter. They had spurned the traditional attire of Vikings, much as Mrs Took had taken liberties with their cuisine, except the effect on Gardenia and Cassia was more eye-catching. They both wore diaphanous chemises of white gossamer material, transparent to a degree that even Madonna would think twice about.

They were both bound about the waist and breasts with a fine gold cord that performed the duties of lifting and separating better than anything Playtex had ever designed. If they had worn these in Denmark, even in the summer, they would have gone blue with cold within minutes. In Great Brayford in March, Rose thought they ought to freeze to death. In fact, they both emitted a healthy glow, as if they had been reclining for an hour or two under the ultra-violet lights at Tans R Us in Milton Keynes. To top the look, elfin-face and smoke-voice wore immaculately applied Cleopatra-esque make-up and tiny tiaras of gold laurel leaves. It was the Danes go on holiday to ancient Greece.

Despite the fact they had both taken a somewhat liberal interpretation of the theme, there was no arguing with the fact that they looked wonderful. Rose knew that in a million years she could never compete with Gardenia, in or out of fancy dress. It wasn't guilt that she should be ladling the oils on against, it was a fast burgeoning inferiority complex. Every fibre in her being wished she wasn't wearing brown hessian. Her heart sank resolutely to the bottom of her espadrilles and refused point-blank to come back up.

It was proving a long evening. In deference to the Vikings, Rose had also left her wristwatch at home and, consequently, had no idea what time it was. She had drunk more wine than was sensible and, as a result, had a thumping headache. The clock in the hall had long since ground to a halt at ten past three – about two years ago – and it seemed rude to ask anyone else the time. Dan mouthed 'Hello' to her from across the room, and she managed to return what she hoped was a demure smile, before he was steered away towards the Carlsberg lager and Pillager's Punch by a thunderous looking Gardenia.

Solace was served up in the form of the buffet and Mrs Took nervously set to, removing clingfilm from the Viking sausage rolls, pizza squares and vol-au-vents. People made their usual charge to the table and by the time Rose reached the queue it was snaked down the hall and she was near the end, holding her paper plate forlornly. Dan was ahead of her, standing behind Gardenia, resting his hands on her shoulders. Rose could have quite happily grabbed one of the myriad fake spears that were propped against the wall and fallen on it.

Anise was ahead of her too, looking sniffily at the array of food spread before her. Mrs Took hovered anxiously, her hands visibly shaking as she gulped her Pillager's Punch.

'There's an awful lot of people here, Mrs Took,' Anise observed. 'Do you think there's going to be enough *Viking* fare to go around? It's a bit late in the day to run to Mr Patel's for some extra sausage rolls.'

'Oh well. Really. I'm not sure . . .' Mrs Took mopped her brow with her handkerchief. Her metal helmet had tilted to an alarming angle over her eye. Rose looked at her with concern.

Anise continued, 'We should be like John Lewis – their

motto is "Never Knowingly Undersold". As the ladies of the village hall committee, our adage should be "Never Knowingly Under-catered",' she said smugly.

'I think there'll be enough.' Mrs Took looked worriedly at the table, which seemed to be groaning under the weight of food, as far as Rose could tell. Mrs Took was pink with panic. She tugged uncomfortably at the neck of her sack dress. 'It's always so difficult to . . .'

Rose saw the woman's knees sag and dashed forward to catch her before she hit the floor. Dan also rushed from the queue and they were able to support her weight together and lay her down gently without her harming herself.

'Oh dear,' Mrs Took said, trying to push herself up. 'I don't know what came over me. I could feel myself swooning.'

Rose looked over the top of her to Dan, who was still supporting Mrs Took's head. Their eyes met and lingered on each other for a fraction too long. Rose knew exactly how Mrs Took felt. She broke away from Dan's gaze and rummaged in her pocket.

'Here,' she said, producing her bottle of lavender oil. 'Just breathe gently and inhale this. It'll make you feel better in no time.'

After a few moments, they helped her to sit up. 'Doesn't this smell lovely, dear,' she said to Rose.

'It's lavender. I'll put a couple of drops on your temple. It'll help you to relax.' Rose smoothed the oil on Mrs Took's forehead. 'Shall we sit you in a quiet corner for a little while? I'll bring you a glass of water.'

'Thank you, dears,' she said. 'I don't like to cause a fuss. This has all been a bit too much for me.'

'You're not causing a fuss,' Rose reassured her. 'Can I get you something from the buffet? You've probably been so busy making all this lovely food, you haven't had time to eat.'

A worried look crossed her face. 'I don't know if there'll be enough to go round.'

'Mrs Took,' Rose said kindly, 'if the five thousand arrived, there'd be enough salmon sandwiches for them. Don't worry.'

'It's not very Viking, either,' she said apologetically.

Rose ignored Anise, who was skulking in the background. 'I think it all looks perfectly wonderful. And anyway I'm not sure that elk or beaver would go down a storm in Great Brayford.'

Mrs Took giggled girlishly.

'Are you feeling better?' Rose asked.

'Much.' Mrs Took squeezed her hand.

Rose turned round to smile at Dan, but he had gone. He was back at the buffet table, passing a chicken drumstick to Gardenia. Before she put her lavender oil in her pocket, she put it under her own nose and gave a determined snort.

Apart from the brief excitement caused by Mrs Took's faint, the evening continued to drag. Melissa, who still managed to look mind-bogglingly voluptuous in her hessian creation, was intent on ensuring that Rose enjoyed herself. She was a good friend – her only friend – and Rose didn't know how she would have managed without her. She was a good customer too. Rose didn't think the Chippendales got through as much body oil as Melissa managed to. Still, what Melissa and Frank did in the privacy of their own bedroom was their affair. Mel chatted animatedly to her and asked her to dance with her and Frank. She lasted about three numbers with them – it was patent for all to see that Frank couldn't keep his hands off his wife. There was a good chance it was going to be a body oil night. Rose, feeling enough of a gooseberry as it was, excused herself as soon as it was politely possible. Everyone else had pretty much ignored her, apart from Angelica who had done her utmost to see that she was kept regularly supplied with wine, and a few people who had congratulated her on ministering to Mrs Took so well that she was now sitting splay-legged on the floor doing the rowing motions to 'Oops Upside Your Head'. Rose wasn't sure whether the rest of them were wary of her because of the rumours that Anise had been spreading or if it genuinely took five years before you could even begin to be thought of as a 'villager'.

Dan had abandoned his spear and shield and was dancing with Gardenia. He was quite a mover. Fred Astaire to Gardenia's Ginger Rogers. Was there nothing this woman couldn't do? Apart from work. She shimmied and sashayed seductively enough to slot seamlessly into any of the Spice Girls' routines. Anise was dancing with Basil, whose idea of Viking costume was his lilac shell suit worn with a shiny metal helmet with cow horns sticking out at jaunty angles. It appeared to make no difference to Anise, who was giggling maniacally and even went as far as rotating her hips in front of him. Rose tutted to herself with amusement. And she was supposed to be the one who had no shame!

She caught Dan's eye over Gardenia's shoulder and he gave her a look that said he wished he was somewhere else. The feeling was mutual. She couldn't bear this a minute longer. Gardenia was thrusting rhythmically towards Dan's groin and Rose thought she was going to be sick if she watched it any more. Primarily because she wished she was doing it herself. She was going to go home and look up 'Jealousy' in the Jessamine Lovage bible and order whatever the woman recommended by the gallon.

Pushing her way through several men in smelly costumes, she fought her way to the door. She would go outside, have a few minutes of fresh air and check the time on the church clock to see if it could be considered late enough to leave.

The night was crisp and chill, and brown hessian, she discovered, was no barrier against the cold. A strong wind was still gusting and a full moon shone over the church-yard, casting a phosphorescent glow over the broken teeth of the tombstones. It also illuminated the clock tower which, to Rose's dismay, informed her that it was not yet ten o'clock.

She leaned against one of the tombstones and con-sidered her predicament. She could go back in and feign some dreaded illness that required her to beat a hasty retreat to her bed or she could hang around playing the village wallflower for another hour until it could be considered a more suitable time to depart without giving them something to talk about. Or she could go back in, get steaming drunk, stay until midnight and even indulge in a little dancing on the tables.

Rose decided to pay a visit to the outside loo while she contemplated her options further. There normally wasn't light inside but, considerately, someone had rigged up some redundant Christmas fairy lights to a battery especially for the occasion. It gave a certain surreal quality to sitting on the toilet. With time on her hands, she took the opportunity to examine her fingernails carefully, which hadn't really changed much since last time she'd examined them. She also pulled aimlessly at a few split ends in her fringe and reminded herself that she needed to book a trim in the next week or two.

'Are you ever going to come out of there?' said a voice close to the slatted wooden door. It was a voice she recognised.

'Grief, Dan, you made me jump out of my skin.' Rose sprang up and started rearranging the brown hessian. 'Wait a minute.'

He was laughing when she came out. 'I thought you'd died in there.'

She was glad that it was dark, because he couldn't see

her blush. 'I wasn't going to the loo,' she protested. 'I was just sitting in there out of the wind.'

Dan stopped laughing abruptly. 'Is it really that bad in there?' He flicked his head towards the village hall.

'Yes.' Rose flopped down on the ancient crooked stones of the church wall. 'I'm such an outsider.'

'That bad?'

She nodded forlornly. 'They make me feel like something out of *The X Files*. Or like something they've stepped in.'

'Over,' he corrected. 'People in the village aren't crass enough to step *in* things.'

She smiled reluctantly.

'That's better,' he said, then he sighed heavily. 'You realise that we're both village outcasts, you and I? They think you're a hooker and I'm Ghenghis Khan's brother-in-law.'

'They're not all against you.'

'No,' he said thoughtfully. 'Just the influential ones. The Anise Westons of this world.' He gave her a wry smile.

'Yes, but you're only unpopular because of the village hall thing. Generally, you're very well liked. Respected.' She smoothed her hair back from her face as the wind insisted on whipping it forward. People speak very highly of you. All they do is snigger and sneer when I'm around.'

'You shouldn't let it worry you.'

'I can't help it. It's making me feel so isolated.'

'I do know how you feel.'

'Do you?' She turned to him. 'Do you really?' Their faces were close together. If it hadn't been so windy, she would have felt his hot breath on her cheek.

'You do have friends here, Rose. Don't ever think otherwise.' He had been drinking. His breath held the sweet tangy aroma of hops. Reg's Carlsberg was obviously going down well. 'There are people in the village that like you a lot.'

'Who?' She sounded like a petulant child and she hated herself for it.

Dan thought for a moment. 'Angelica Weston.'

'Angelica!' Rose tutted. 'Angelica doesn't have a malicious bone in her body. Anise took them all.'

'Melissa's always singing your praises,' he continued. 'So is Mr Patel. Mrs Reg says you're the best aromatherapist in the village.'

Rose narrowed her eyes. 'I'm the *only* aromatherapist in the village.'

Dan ignored her. 'And you've certainly won Basil over.'

'Basil's more than likely insane!'

'Well, you don't *have* to be mad to be your friend—'

'But it probably helps,' she finished for him with a wry smile.

'You'll have also won some fans for the way you looked after poor Mrs Took.'

'I suppose so,' she admitted reluctantly.

He was silent for a moment. The only sound was the wind gusting through the trees and the ominous creaking of the pines that towered on the fringe of the churchyard. He took a deep, shuddering breath and said, 'I like you.' Dan took a strand of her hair and twined it round his finger.

She shivered and it was nothing to do with the chill factor.

'You look very beautiful tonight.' His eyes twinkled mischievously in the moonlight. 'I must say the brown hessian is particularly fetching.'

'Oh, it's just something I threw on.' It would be stupid to admit that it had taken her hours to look this ridiculous. Her voice was so breathless, she sounded as if she had just run the London marathon. 'I like your cape.'

He fingered the fur round his shoulders tentatively.

'It's a rug. Yak,' he explained. 'I brought it back from the Himalayas – years ago.' His eyes never left her face. 'I went trekking there when I was young and stupid and didn't know about the Maldives. Fluffy peed on it once and now Gardi won't allow it in the house.'

She shuddered at the mention of Gardenia's name. How could he say she was beautiful when Gardenia was in there looking as if she'd missed her way from some Paris catwalk and ended up at the village hop by mistake. She searched for something witty to say to impress him. 'It looks nice,' was the best offering her brain could produce.

'You have impeccable taste,' he said.

'I didn't, somehow, imagine you as a leather trousers man, I have to say.'

'I borrowed them from a mate on the building site. He's a Gary Glitter fan who won't grow up.'

'They look nice,' she repeated. It was about time she threw those aluminium pans away, they were starting to deplete her brain cells.

'I don't really know much about Vikings,' Dan admitted. 'Expect that they raped and pillaged.'

'I was never quite sure what pillaging was,' she confessed.

'Well, whatever it is, it doesn't sound as much fun as . . . you know.'

'I know.' The words lodged in her throat. He leaned towards her, his arms either side of her. The wind was tugging at his hair and his yak rug and, in the moonlight, he could quite easily have been taken for a Norse warrior. Or even, if she was feeling really complimentary, a Norse god. It was warm in the circle of his arms and, suddenly, the brown hessian felt like a fur coat. He lowered his head towards her.

'Dan,' she croaked. 'We can't . . . What about Gardenia?' Her lips were parting and she instructed her brain to snap them shut. The old grey matter didn't comply. 'I don't want to hurt anyone,' she pleaded. 'I've been here before and I can't do it again.'

'I don't believe you,' he said softly. His hand twisted in her hair and he tilted her face towards him. 'Say it like you mean it.' He pressed against her, the smooth leather of his trousers pushing the brown hessian creation up her thighs in a manner that didn't entirely befit a church social. 'I want to kiss you,' he breathed.

He was coming very close to squashing her.

'I've wanted to since the first time I saw you.' Towering over her, his eyes glittered darkly. He crushed her to him and his hand moved to cup her face, lifting her mouth to his. Their lips met and Dan's were warm, inviting, seductive, sweet and very insistent. Her head swam and it wasn't just because she was balanced precariously on the wall.

'That flaming DJ is stuck in the seventies,' Basil complained loudly to Anise as they came round the corner from the hall into the churchyard. 'Why can't we have a bit of Oasis? I'd hang the bastard, if I had any say.'

'Damn,' whispered Dan. He released her so quickly that Rose nearly fell backwards off the church wall.

'I think he's doing quite a nice job, Basil. It's much better than I expected,' Anise replied. 'I didn't know I liked modern music. But then I didn't know you could cha-cha-cha to Take That.' Anise sounded as if she'd been at the Pillager's Punch.

'Hello, young lovers,' Basil crooned as he spotted Dan and Rose on the wall.

'Evening, Basil,' Dan said casually. Rose scrambled to rearrange her hessian and her hair.

'Isn't it a bit cold out here for you, Gardenia?' Anise asked.

Dan tried to stand in front of Rose to shield her and failed miserably.

'That isn't Gardenia, is it?' Anise said suspiciously. 'She's much too fat.'

Rose cringed miserably.

'No,' Dan said emphatically. 'I, er we . . . we were just having a chat. It's . . .'

Anise's face turned as stony as the church wall. 'Oh,' she said tartly. 'It's you!'

'My word!' Basil said.

'You certainly get about, young lady, don't you?' Anise said.

'Now then, Anise, don't go jumping to conclusions.' Dan's tone was placating. He put his hand over Rose's mouth as she tried to speak.

'We'll pretend that we haven't seen you,' Anise said magnanimously. 'Far be it from me to spread gossip.'

'That's very kind, Anise,' Dan said levelly. 'There seems to be enough malicious tittle-tattle flying about the village with the sole aim of tarnishing Rose's reputation. We don't need any more being added to it.'

'I hope you're not insinuating that it has anything to do with me.'

'Like you, Anise,' he said calmly, 'I'm not one to jump to conclusions.'

'I came out here with the sole purpose of using the facilities.' She turned to her companion, who seemed to have lost interest in the proceedings and appeared to be practising his dance steps instead. 'Didn't we, Basil?'

He stopped abruptly. 'I should say so.'

'Then don't let us stop you,' Dan stood aside. 'Mind you, wouldn't it be nice if you didn't have to go outside on a cold March night, simply to go to the loo? That's just one of the many benefits of having a new church hall, Anise.' He gave her a wry look that may, or may not, have been lost on her in the darkness.

'Despite my appearance, I am not the frail, genteel old lady that people take me for,' she replied coldly.

Even Basil's eyes widened in disbelief at that one.

'I am made of much sterner stuff than you think.' Anise sniffed majestically and threw her head back, regarding them coolly through narrowed eyes. 'In fact, if one were being cruel, one could say that I'm as tough as an old boot.'

One didn't appear to dispute it.

'A modicum of nastiness on the sanitary front is of little concern to me,' she said. Her voice had taken on a distinctly regal note. 'Come, Basil,' she ordered.

Basil obediently fell into step after her, but it didn't stop him pulling a disgruntled face at Dan and Rose behind her back.

Dropping his hand from Rose's mouth, Dan gave a heartfelt sigh. He stared after Anise with unconcealed hostility. 'I really, really hope that a bloody great tarantula, the size of my fist, comes out of the bog and bites her bloody bum.'

Rose thought she couldn't have said it better herself.

Chapter Eighteen

'Why did you put your hand over my mouth?' Rose asked, jumping down from the wall. 'You were lucky I didn't bite it!'

A grin spread across Dan's face. 'I bet you a pound you weren't going to say anything nice.'

Rose looked at him under her lashes with a reluctant half smile. 'I might have done.'

'I know Anise,' he continued. 'It was better to try and calm her down rather than rile her. You would have called her a nosey old cow, and it wouldn't have helped matters.'

'But you *did* call her a nosey old cow,' Rose pointed out.

Dan looked hurt. 'Not in so many words.'

'How many words does it take?' she laughed. 'It was as clear as crystal. I've never seen anyone, or anything, look so riled.'

He was close to her again and she could feel the heat from his yak rug. 'So you don't think I should quit building and become a diplomat?'

Laughter bubbled in Rose's throat. 'I don't even think you should quit building and become a beer mat.'

'Thank you for your faith in me,' he said morosely.

'And speaking of building,' Rose raised her eyebrows, 'I have only one word to say to you, Dan Spikenard.'

Dan looked puzzled. 'What's that?

'Fireplace!'

'Oh, hell!' His hands raked his hair. 'I know. I know. I

didn't think you'd want to see me after our little discussion last month.'

'I would sacrifice anything for some plaster.' She gave him a rueful smile. 'Besides, I overreacted and I'm sorry.' She gave him a neat little bow.

'No, it was entirely my fault.' He held up his hands in apology. 'It's none of my business what goes on between you and Hugh.'

'I told you there is no me and Hugh,' she said quietly. Her eyes met his squarely. 'It's over.' She lowered her eyes and her voice. 'You didn't seem to be too worried about Hugh a few minutes ago.'

'Blame it on the moonlight, the music and the Carlsberg.' Dan's mouth twisted into a smile. 'I'm sorry.'

Rose forced down a gulp. 'There's no need to be.'

'Are you sure?'

'Yes.' She nodded.

'It won't happen again,' he assured her.

Rose wasn't entirely sure that was what she wanted to hear, but it didn't seem the right time to mention it.

'Come on, let's get you back inside before you freeze,' he said. 'And before our friends come back.' He stole a furtive glance at the loo, where Basil waited patiently outside.

Rose shook her head forcefully. 'I'm not going back in there.'

Dan looked concerned. 'Why not?'

'I can't face any more Abba or the Bee Gees,' she said with an overwhelming weariness. 'There's only so much "Come on, Eileen" a person can take in one lifetime and I have reached that limit. I'm going home.'

'I'll escort you,' he said quickly.

'No you won't. People will notice we're missing.'

'No they won't.'

'Yes they will.'

'They won't,' he insisted. 'Trust me, I'm a builder.'

'Gardi will notice you're missing,' she said firmly, desperately longing for him to come with her.

'Don't ever call her Gardi to her face,' Dan warned.

'Thanks for that advice,' she said wryly. 'But I don't need walking home.'

'It's dangerous to wander around on your own at night.'

'In Great Brayford?' She looked at him incredulously. 'It's not exactly the crime centre of the world.'

'You could get mugged.'

'I'm hardly a promising target,' she observed. 'If I wasn't wearing brown hessian and was dripping in gold, I might be more concerned. I only came out with a tenner and I've spent most of that on Reg's plonk. It is possible to get mugged for less than a pound, but not very likely in Great Brayford.'

For a moment he looked deflated. 'What about your pervert?' he piped up cheerfully. 'He could be waiting for you in a bush.'

'Thanks for those reassuring words, Dan.'

'Well, you never know,' he said sheepishly. 'It could be someone from round here.'

'It could be you,' she pointed out.

'That's charming! Is that really what you think of me?'

'No.' Her face was full of longing. 'No, it's not.'

He placed his hands gently on her waist. 'Then I insist you let me walk you home, to prove that you do indeed trust me and aren't just saying that to make me feel better.'

Rose sighed. 'And Gardenia?'

'We're not on speaking terms at the moment. That little demonstration was for everyone else's benefit, not mine. Besides, I've had enough of "Come on, Eileen" too.'

'Okay,' Rose relented, unable to resist him a moment longer.

'I knew you'd see sense in the end,' Dan grinned. He laid his arm casually across her shoulders and guided her carefully through the higgledy-piggledy tombstones.

Gardenia pressed her back against a patched-up section of breeze block on the church hall. The wind was billowing the diaphanous dress and whipping her long hair across her face. Gripping the flimsy material in tight, clenched fists, she tried to hold it flat to her legs so that it wouldn't balloon out and give her away. She watched with tearful eyes as Dan and Rose meandered out of the churchyard and up towards Lavender Hill.

'What about a quick nightcap?' Dan turned Rose to face him.

'Dan!' she exclaimed. 'You're incorrigible!' He was also irresistibly close and getting closer. His yak rug smelled of dog pee but, unlike Gardenia, Rose didn't care.

'Just one little drink,' he pleaded, pouting his lip as his mouth turned down at the corners.

Rose sighed and fished for her doorkey in her pocket. 'Why are all men so pathetic!' She turned and unlocked the door.

'Why do women always fall for it?' Dan grinned mischievously as he followed her inside.

She wagged a finger at him. 'One drink. That's all.'

He took his yak rug off and threw it on the floor in the lounge, before he collapsed on to the sofa.

'I think you've had more of Reg's Carlsberg than you're letting on.' Rose gave him a rueful glance.

Closing his eyes, Dan rubbed his temples. 'I think you might be right.'

'Do you still want a drink?'

He opened one eye. 'Just a small one.'

'I haven't got much in the way of spirits. All I've got is tequila, or brandy.'

'I'm a single malt man, myself. But brandy's fine.'

Rose poured a small measure of brandy and handed it to him. She flicked the CD player on and *The Number One Love Album* blared out. There was a fault on the player which made it start at track four – Take That, 'Why Can't I Wake Up With You?' She wondered if Dan would notice and stole a surreptitious glance at him. His eyebrows lifted quizzically in the centre, but his eyes remained closed.

What was she doing? 'I'm going to put some coffee on,' she said, beating a hasty retreat to the safety of the kitchen.

'Fine,' he said sleepily.

After the cold of the churchyard, it was warm and stuffy in the house. Years of keeping the heating on at full blast in deference to her naked clients had turned her into a hothouse flower. Her body didn't seem to operate in less than eighty degrees these days. Whether it was the contrast in temperatures or the nearness of Dan she wasn't sure, but something was making her feel unusually warm. As she set out the cups and spooned coffee into the cafetière, her hessian creation which had prickled and chafed against her skin all evening became suddenly unbearable. She decided to slip upstairs and change while the kettle was boiling.

In her bedroom, Rose stood in her underwear and stared at her reflection in the full-length mirror. What, if anything, could Dan see in her rather than Gardenia? She pulled jeans and an old sweatshirt out of her wardrobe and struggled into them, then checked the mirror again. The figure that looked back at her screamed gardener, not seductress. She had seen Gardenia dressed in faded jeans and a plain white shirt and she had still managed to look like a complete glamour puss. Maybe it was the lack of Gucci loafers and Ray-Ban sunglasses that failed to give the desired effect. Certainly the Marks and Spencer navy velour slippers didn't help. What did it matter, anyway?

Who was she trying to kid? There was nothing she wanted more than to go downstairs, knock Dan's eyeballs out with her nonchalant sexiness and render him powerless to resist her. This was ridiculous. Why had she let Dan in here if it wasn't for a spot of rape and pillage? She was going to have to make a decision whether she wanted to be a femme fatale or Mother Teresa.

Shutting the wardrobe door with more determination than was necessary, Rose made her way back downstairs. Her mind was made up. She was going to give Dan one quick coffee and send him home. It was cruel of her to have let it go this far. And he should know better than to want to deceive Gardenia. But perhaps it was her fault that men wanted to cheat on their other halves with her. Maybe something in her make-up coerced them into duplicitous behaviour. Or was it just her make-up? Why couldn't men commit fully to her? Was it something in her genes? Or was it something in *these* jeans?

Rose took a deep breath before she opened the lounge door. As the door opened, so did her mouth. Dan was laid full length on the sofa, shirt completely unbuttoned, cuddling a cushion to his bare chest and snoring gently. His glass of brandy was empty and the bottle which had miraculously appeared next to it was looking considerably less full than it had.

She sighed wearily and gave his arm a gentle shake. 'Dan,' she said firmly. 'Dan, wake up!'

He smiled contentedly, muttered incoherently and nestled the lucky cushion closer to him.

'Dan!' she tried again. He was dead to the world. Putting her head in her hands, she massaged her eye sockets, which were beginning to throb ominously. She needed this like Imelda Marcos needed a new pair of shoes.

Coffee could be the answer. The kettle had boiled and gone cold again. She flicked it on and tapped her foot impatiently, thinking about the old adage that a watched kettle never boils and pretending to study the rack of herbs above it instead. This kettle obviously wasn't superstitious – it boiled in an instant and she poured the steaming water into the cafetière.

Dan had curled on to his side by the time she carried the tray through to the lounge. She set the tray on the table with as loud a crash as she could manage without smashing the cups. No reaction. 'Dan.' She shook his shoulder roughly. 'I've brought some coffee. Why don't you try to sit up and then you can have a drink.'

'Where've you been?' he muttered half-consciously. 'I missed you.'

'I was gone five minutes, Dan. Five minutes.'

'You were ages and I love you so much.'

'No you don't,' she said sadly. 'You're thinking of someone else. Sit up and have some coffee.' She tried to pull him up by his shirt and failed unequivocally.

'I love you, Rose.'

'No you don't!' She was perilously close to crying. 'Dan, you have to go home to Gardenia. That's who you love. She'll be getting worried.'

His face was the picture of misery. 'I don't love her any more, Rose. I love you.'

'Dan, don't do this to me. You don't know what you're saying. You'll regret it in the morning.' She plunged the cafetière and poured a cup of coffee. 'Wait here,' she instructed him. 'I'll be back in a minute.' It was a stupid thing to say. Dan wasn't going anywhere in a hurry.

Rose returned armed with a flannel soaked in cold water. 'Look, I'm going to rub your face to wake you up. It'll be a bit cold.' Understatement of the year, she thought grimly. She braced herself and put the flannel to Dan's face.

'Ooo, hoo, hoo,' he said and started to giggle.

'Dan.' She started to smile herself. 'Be serious. This is to wake you up. I'm doing it for your own good.'

He was laughing uproariously and trying in vain to grab her arms. 'Don't struggle!' she shouted, her grin spreading from ear to ear. 'Just bloody well wake up, you bastard!'

He made a lunge at her and pulled her down on to his chest. The flannel sailed harmlessly across the lounge and landed in the cup of coffee. 'Now look what you've done.'

'Sssh,' he whispered tenderly in her ear and sank back into sleep.

Rose collapsed against him. This was ridiculous. There had to be a way to get him up and out of here. Gardenia might not have missed him at the Viking evening, but she would certainly notice if he wasn't in her bed. Rose looked at the clock. It was still reasonably early. Half past eleven. The dance didn't finish until twelve. Then say quarter of an hour for Gardenia to say goodbye and wander home. Perhaps the best thing to do was let Dan sleep for half an hour and then try again to wake him up. There was a remote chance that he might have got over the worst of it by then.

She was completely exhausted too. No wonder Sumo wrestlers had to stuff themselves with food to keep their strength up. Mrs Took's Viking vol-au-vents had been inadequate preparation for grappling with Dan. Prising herself from his embrace, she picked up the brandy bottle and took a healthy swig. She coughed, burped, and took another swig. Flopping back on the sofa, she nursed the bottle to her chest. Dan looked so peaceful. He had dropped into a deep slumber, a boyish half-smile on his lips. She dragged at the brandy bottle again, before tiredness overwhelmed her. Who said that village life wasn't interesting? She'd had enough interest tonight to fill her monthly quota. The last track of *The Number One Love Album* finished playing – Meat Loaf, 'I'd Do Anything For Love, But I Won't Do That'. Taking another swig of brandy, she smiled to herself. Life was full of its own little ironies.

Rose let her eyes close. She would just have a few minutes' rest herself before trying to wake Dan again.

Chapter Nineteen

HELLISH HANGOVER REMEDY
Rosemary, Fennel, Juniper.

It's very easy to over-indulge during the festive season or at a special celebration. In the party mood the inclination to have 'one more drink' is all too tempting. And it's usually only when we wake up in the morning that we regret the night before – by which time the damage is well and truly done! This highly effective remedy will help to ease the discomfort of the punishment that will be exacted upon you!

from: *The Complete Encyclopaedia of Aromatherapy Oils*
by Jessamine Lovage

It was nine o'clock. Rose lay frozen to the spot as the church bells dolefully informed her with slow, relentless chimes that echoed painfully in her head, calling the upright citizens of Great Brayford to Sunday worship.

She wasn't one of them. She was a slumped citizen. Slumped on the sofa, her head on a cushion, the empty bottle of brandy beside her. Reluctantly, she followed the line of her body to check that this wasn't a dreadful nightmare. Dan, unfortunately, was still there, as large as life. Or as large as lifeless in this particular case.

His mouth had flopped open and his face bore a greenish-grey tinge. On a Martian it might have been appealing; on a builder it was a definite no-no. At some point she had obviously removed her slippers, for which she was grateful, because her legs were sprawled across Dan's chest and she had a bare foot resting either side of his stubbly chin.

As she looked at him, he opened his eyes and looked back at her.

'Good morning,' she said flatly.

He jumped and pushed her feet ungraciously out of the way while he rubbed his eyes. 'What time is it?' he croaked.

'Time you weren't here,' Rose said sagely.

'What hit me?' He sat up gingerly, only to fall back against the cushions as the effort proved too great.

'I would hazard a guess at Reg's Carlsberg and half a bottle of brandy.'

'I think I'm going to die.'

Rose removed her legs from his chest and curled up at a safe distance at the other end of the sofa. 'Not in my lounge, you're not,' she warned him. 'We're in enough trouble as it is.' She gave him a sideways glance. 'Though it might be easier to explain a corpse . . .'

Dan looked at her through half-closed lids. 'Forget what I said. I think I'm going to live after all.'

'Do I forget the other things you said?' she asked softly.

'Oh my word.' He rubbed his hands over his stubble. 'Would you like to remind me of them?'

'Do you need reminding?'

'No.' He shook his head and looked as if he regretted such a rash movement. 'I don't think I do.' He eased himself upright again. 'I'm really sorry, Rose. I shouldn't have done this. Or not done this.' Wincing as he moved, he continued tentatively, 'I don't know what I should apologise for first.'

'How do you intend to explain this to Gardenia?'

'Preferably not with a carving knife at my balls,' he said succinctly.

'I think that may be wishful thinking.'

'Do you mind if I use the bathroom?' He massaged his hands over his face as if to pre-warn it of the impending onslaught of cold water.

'No. I think you'd better get tidied up.'

'What is worse?' he said thoughtfully. 'To look like I haven't slept all night or to look like I have?'

'I don't know, Dan.' Rose hung her head and not just because of the effort it was taking to keep it upright. 'It's going to take some pretty nifty digging for us to get out of this hole.' As far as showing her face in the village again was concerned, she was dead and buried anyway.

'Do you think Gardenia will believe me?'

'I don't think I would.' Rose's heart twisted at the hangdog expression on his face. She pushed herself up from the sofa. She was stiff from spending the night curled up against Dan. 'Would you like some coffee?'

They both looked over at the wreckage of the tray – two cups of stone-cold, scummy coffee, one with what used to be a fluffy peach flannel soaking in it. They looked at each other and simultaneously said, 'No.'

Dan also forced himself from the sofa and stretched his back, groaning loudly.

'I'll make up some aromatherapy oils to help you recover while you go and freshen up. The bathroom's straight ahead at the top of the stairs.'

She found her slippers and padded through to her treatment room – complete with half-finished fireplace – and put her brain on auto-pilot as she mixed the blend of oils in a small brown bottle.

Dan came downstairs a few minutes later looking no better than he had before. Without the complete Viking ensemble he looked vaguely silly in his large shirt and leather trousers. Well, not even vaguely silly, just silly. It was definitely not a cold light of day outfit. She was relieved she had changed out of the brown hessian. But then if she hadn't changed out of the brown hessian, perhaps he wouldn't have fallen asleep on her sofa. And if she had stayed with him on the sofa, awake, who knows what might have happened. Last night they had been more 'In The Mood' than Glen Miller.

'You don't look a lot better,' Rose observed.

'Thanks,' Dan said. 'I don't feel a lot better either. In fact, I think being vertical feels a lot worse.'

'Do you want a drink of water?'

He nodded gingerly and followed her into the kitchen.

'I'll stir a spoonful of honey into it.'

Dan grimaced.

'It'll do you good,' she assured him. 'Try to drink plenty throughout the day. You need to flush your system out.'

'Yes, nurse.' With a sigh of resignation, he drained the glass of water. 'I feel better already,' he said miserably.

'This is your hangover remedy,' Rose said with forced brightness. 'Especially recommended by Jessamine Lovage.'

'Who?'

'It doesn't matter. Suffice to say, it's a reviving blend of oils to help detoxify the body.'

He looked suspiciously at the label which read baldly in big letters, 'HELLISH HANGOVER REMEDY'. 'What's in it?'

'Rosemary, fennel and juniper.' She took the cap off the bottle and wafted it under his nose. 'It's quite stimulating.'

'Stimulating?' Dan recoiled in horror. 'It stinks!'

'Well, yes.' Rose smiled. 'Perhaps not one of the most attractive blends. But it'll do you good.'

'I hate medicine,' he complained.

'It's not medicine. You bathe in it – just a few drops. Or rub it on.' Rose raised her eyebrows. 'Perhaps you could get Gardenia to give you a nice soothing massage.'

He narrowed his eyes and gave her a look that was as black and as ugly as his leather trousers.

'It also has a diuretic effect.'

'Marvellous,' he said. 'I'll look forward to that.' He took the bottle from her and sniffed the oil again. 'Are you sure this will do me good? Just the smell of it is making me heave.'

'It'll either kill or cure. If it kills you, it might save Gardenia a job.' Rose smiled sympathetically. 'Either way, you'll never want to drink Carlsberg or brandy again.'

Dan managed a feeble laugh.

The phone rang. Its shrill, clinical tone seemed threatening and angry. The sound froze them both to the spot.

'Shit,' Dan said unhelpfully. They stared at the phone.

'What shall I do?' Rose touched his arm and instantly wished she hadn't.

'You'd better answer it.'

Now it was her turn for the black look. 'I can't!'

'It's your house,' he said.

'And this is *your* doing,' Rose said as she walked to the phone.

'*Our* doing,' Dan insisted.

Rose looked at him reluctantly. Her face softened. 'I suppose it does take two to tango.'

'Oh no!' Dan put his head in his hands. He peered at her through his fingers. 'We did the tango?'

She grinned at him. 'I was speaking metaphorically.'

The phone continued to ring.

'One of us should answer it,' Dan suggested.

'We have nothing to feel guilty about,' Rose reasoned. 'Nothing happened. It was all a terrible misunderstanding.'

'You don't sound very convinced.'

'I'm not.'

'Was it?' Dan cocked his head to one side.

'What?'

'A terrible misunderstanding?' He chewed his lip nervously.

'No.' Rose could feel her heart beating in her mouth. 'It was a moment of madness brought on, as you yourself said, by an excess of moonlight, music and Carlsberg. Or white wine in my case. And brandy,' she added as an afterthought. 'We shouldn't have done it.'

'But we did.'

'Gardenia doesn't deserve this.'

'And what do we deserve?' he asked candidly.

'The sort of hangovers that we've both got?'

The phone continued to ring. They both looked mournfully at it. Dan nudged her elbow.

'Answer the phone, Rose.'

For once, she wished desperately it was her pervert. How delighted she would be to hear nothing but his empty, threatening silence at the other end of the line. She hoped vehemently he had been lurking in the hedge with his mobile phone and was picking a very opportune moment to terrorise her.

'Hello, Rose speaking,' she said brightly, keeping her voice as steady as she could manage.

It was Gardenia. 'I'll have him back when you're sure you're quite finished with him,' she spat into the phone.

'I can explain everything, Gardenia,' Rose said.

The line went dead. Forcefully.

'Well?' said Dan hopefully. 'That was short.'

'But not exactly sweet.' She looked at him ruefully. 'She wants you back when I've finished with you.'

'And have you?' he asked.

'What?'

'Finished with me?' He took her hands.

'Well and truly, Dan.' She pulled her fingers away from his. They were slightly too warm, slightly too rough and slightly too strong for her peace of mind.

'This is all my fault and I feel absolutely terrible about it.' He massaged his temples. 'Your name's mud in the village already. Just wait till they hear about this.'

'You have such a reassuring way with you, Dan.'

'Can I at least pop by and finish your fireplace?' he pleaded.

'I think the less popping in the direction of Rose Cottage you do, the better for all concerned.'

'Rose Cottage?' His face twisted into a grimace.

'That's what I'm going to call it.'

'That's a bit naff, isn't it? Rose Cottage, Lavender Hill.'

'For a man whose taste in house names runs to Builder's Bottom, I would have thought that you'd be the last person in a position to criticise.'

'Yes, but at least Builder's Bottom has character.'

'Rose,' she said firmly, 'happens to be my name. And this, unless I'm very much mistaken, is my cottage. I would have thought it was quite appropriate.'

Dan looked unconvinced. 'It's a bit big for a cottage.'

'It's got lead windows.'

'And the church has a lead roof – or it used to have – but that's not a cottage.'

Rose put her hands on her hips. 'Why, exactly, are we standing here arguing about the relative merits of my choice of house name?'

Dan put his hands on his hips and squared up to her. He cleared his throat with a cough. 'Because, quite frankly,' he mimicked her tone, 'I'm too frightened to go home.'

Rose's face broke into a smile and Dan smiled back. He picked a lock of her uncombed hair and twisted it in his fingers.

'Try to sort this out with Gardenia,' she said softly. 'You owe her that.'

'I know.' He let her hair fall back to her shoulder and turned towards the door.

'Who knows, she may be more understanding than you think.'

'I think Ronnie Kray was probably more understanding than Gardenia.'

'Well, just go and get it over with.' Rose opened the front door for him. 'Good luck,' she said.

'I'm going to need it.'

'Quite probably,' she agreed.

'Just one thing.' He turned back to her. 'You said on the phone to Gardenia that you could explain it all. What exactly were you going to say?'

'Are you looking for a crumb of hope?'

'A whole loaf.'

She shook her head. 'I haven't the faintest idea.'

'Thanks.' Dan smiled. 'You're a great help.'

'Go on, she'll be worried,' Rose said.

He leaned on her doorframe. 'Would you think I was awful if I said I wanted to kiss you?'

Rose flushed. 'I'd think you were stupid.'

'I'm a builder. I have a perfect excuse.' He stepped towards her and slid his arms round her waist.

'Dan, this isn't very sensible. What about the Westons? The spy station that never sleeps.'

'It's Sunday morning. They'll be at church. You know Anise, she never misses a chance to show everyone how righteous she is.'

He kissed her cheek, along the line of her jaw and her nose, with light, flitting kisses before his mouth found hers and settled there. She was melting quicker than a bar of Galaxy left on a radiator. 'Dan,' she said breathlessly as she broke away from him.

'I know.' He gave her a wry smile. 'It's time I was going.'

He turned and walked up her path, waving casually in the air, but without looking back. There was less of the Norse god about him this morning, more of an ageing beatnik, but that didn't make him any less attractive. Rose closed the door and went to clear last night's debris from the lounge.

There was a strange smell in there. Rose sniffed the

air. Stale coffee, stale booze and something else she couldn't quite place. She would have to get her aroma-therapy burner going with something nice and fresh, like lime or grapefruit oil, to take this terrible pong away.

She smoothed the cushions on the sofa, patting the one which bore the indentation of Dan's head with more tenderness than was strictly necessary. When she bent to lift the tray from the coffee table, she found the cause of the smell. It was Fluffy's yak rug, the discarded Viking cloak, lying on the floor by the sofa. Holding it at arm's length, she carried it out to the garage and deposited the reeking rug on top of the work bench. How on earth Dan had managed to spend the evening with this disgusting thing draped round his shoulders, she could not imagine. It probably wouldn't be appropriate to ring him now and tell him that he'd forgotten it.

Returning to the house, she carried the tray into the kitchen and washed the cups. The coffee-stained flannel was way beyond recovery. With a sigh of regret, Rose consigned it to the bin.

Debris cleared, the lounge was returned to normal. Rose surveyed the room sadly. Dan seemed to fit into it so comfortably, yet after a bit of cushion-plumping and the washing of a few dirty dishes – and the disposal of Fluffy's urine sample – there was no trace that he had ever been here. She touched her face, tracing her fingers softly over her jawline, her neck, her lips, thinking back to Dan's kiss on the doorstep. The room might be back to normal, but she certainly wasn't. She knew it wasn't going to be as easy and as quick to clear the feel of Dan's kisses from her skin. Like the coffee-stained flannel, she felt permanently and irretrievably marked.

Anise Weston wasn't at church. It was the first time she had missed the morning service since Lent last year, when she had been struck down with a severe bout of Chinese influenza. Those foreign bugs never agreed with her, just like foreign food. It was mercifully rare that Angelica produced spaghetti bolognese, which looked like dog food on a skein of undyed wool. And tasted much the same.

She had woken, in the early hours, feeling particularly unwell and was convinced it was one of Mrs Took's 'Viking' sausage rolls. They were frozen, she could tell, and there was a certain unpleasant sogginess to the bottom and a telltale singeing of the top that denoted a careless cook. It would be the last time she would ask Mrs Took to cater for a church social. The woman simply hadn't got what it took, buckling under the pressure like that. It was shameful for a woman of her age. Years of living with Angelica's culinary disasters should have given her a keen eye for those with a disposition for cooking. It had been a mistake to ignore her misgivings and now she was paying for it. She had a throbbing headache and was feeling nauseous deep in the pit of her stomach. And dizzy. But that was probably due to the fact that she was at the top of the stepladder.

She had seen Builder's Bottom leaving the house of ill repute across the road. Snogging – that was the term these days – with that 'nice young lady' in full view of Lavender Hill in the same clothes that he wore at the Viking evening. Anise smiled smugly to herself. Now find Miss Butter-wouldn't-melt-in-my-mouth trying to deny her licentious associations with the male gender.

Anise reluctantly let the binoculars hang round her aching neck like a lead weight, while she scribbled the details of the assignation she had witnessed across the leylandii in her notebook. If only Angelica had been here to witness it. If she saw the evidence with her own eyes, she wouldn't be so quick to act as counsel for the defence.

She was in cahoots with the girl, Anise could tell. Only the other day, when she had been tidying Angelica's drawers for her while she was out shopping, she had come across some aromatherapy oils. Clearly, that woman was starting to have a corrupting influence on her sister, whose first and foremost fault was that she had always been as pliable as putty. Their parents had gone through a terrible time trying to retain some sort of control over her. Yo-yo knickers, she was called in the village. It was no wonder Angelica felt an affinity with the harlot on the other side of the lane. Then there was that awful business with the married man. That had taken some living down and Anise always took the opportunity to remind her of it.

Saints preserve us, aromatherapy at her age! Whatever next? She would be taking Ecstasy next and going to raves with a baseball cap on back to front. Could it be that Angelica was having another menopause? Was there such a thing as a senile menopause? There was reputed to be a male menopause, even though they didn't have the necessary equipment. And there was certainly senile dementia. It could just be that. There might be nothing to worry about at all. Angelica could simply be going senile. It was a comforting thought. She would have to have words with her about it.

Chapter Twenty

SALVE FOR INTENSE SADNESS
Chamomile Roman, Lavender, Sandalwood, Geranium.
There are times when intense sadness can pierce deep
into our souls, leaving us bereft and breathless, bound in
our pain. The end of an affair can often leave us unable to
move forward, with our emotions mentally handcuffing
us to the past. This oil will prove the perfect salve. Its
gentle, healing properties will provide comfort for the
raw and wounded.
   from: *The Complete Encyclopaedia of Aromatherapy Oils*
                                    by Jessamine Lovage

Melissa didn't want to have tea with DC Elecampane. Or
custard creams. Or bourbons which, if she had allowed
him to talk to her, he would have discovered she didn't
like anyway. They had a habit of leaving slimy brown bits
in your teeth which you didn't discover until hours later.

   She didn't think she wanted to have sex with him again
either. He was starting to want more than she was
prepared to give for £69.99. It wasn't that she didn't like
him. In some ways that was the trouble. She had actually
started to look forward to his visits, and looking forward
to doing 'the ironing' was a very sad way to live.

   Melissa didn't think she had ever liked one of her
clients before, not *really* liked. It was worrying that she

had started to look on him with some sort of affection –
not affection like she had for her husband Frank. Not
solid, dependable, tea and toast in bed every morning
type of affection. More sort of squiggly in the tummy
affection that she'd never experienced before. But then,
she'd never considered her clients as real people before.
Not that she'd thought of them as cardboard cutouts or
anything stupid like that. It was hard to pinpoint what
exactly she did think of them. But Bob Elecampane
wanted to make himself too real to her and she wasn't
sure that she liked it.

He was due in a few minutes and Melissa was dreading
it. She, like him, had begun to tire of beating him with
household objects. There were only so many variations
on a wooden spoon, a spatula and a steak mallet that one
could use without inflicting serious injury. And she didn't
want to hurt him – although sometimes just thinking that
made her beat him more vigorously. The overriding
temptation was to clasp him to her ample bosom and let
him nestle there in her womanly harbour safe from the
buffeting storms of Milton Keynes' criminal classes.

Frank talked about Bob a lot too, which didn't help.
He said that no one liked him at work. He was a pariah.
And a git. And he never bought his round of tea in the
canteen. Which, in police terms, was real lowlife behaviour. Perhaps that was why she felt the way she did
about him. She had a soft spot for hard-luck cases. She
had always been a champion of the underdog and the
unloved. A sucker for the runt of the litter. And Frank
had called Bob Elecampane something very similar to a
runt several times.

At school, while the other kids had made a grab for the
best gingerbread man at the playtime tuck shop, Melissa
had been more than happy to rescue the one with only
one leg, or a crummy arm, or one of its Smartie eyes
missing. She couldn't bear the thought of the misshapen

one being left abandoned on the cold counter with no one caring enough to eat it. She had consumed more Jammy Dodgers that were light on their quota of jam to last her a lifetime.

It wasn't that Bob was unattractive or misshapen. He was quite presentable. Nearly all of the other detectives she had met had been gnarled and careworn, with greasy, straggly hair and ripped jeans and battered leather jackets that even Oxfam would have thrown in the bin. Sometimes they looked so hardened and villainous, it was difficult to tell them from the criminals. Bob Elecampane wore jeans, but they were as neat as a new pin, endlessly washed until they were as pale as a summer sky, and meticulously ironed with a sharp white crease down the front of the legs. His important little places were all clean, and for Melissa that was very desirable in a man.

The doorbell rang. It was one of those that could give a plain, ordinary ring and play a selection of twenty-four catchy little jingles, depending on the mood of the householder. Today, it was set to a halting version of 'You Are My Sunshine.' She wished she'd had the sense to change it before Bob arrived. 'You Are My Sunshine' didn't sum up the mood of the householder today. Hopefully, Bob wouldn't take any notice of it or he might get the wrong impression.

The doorbell rang again. Decisions had to be made, however painful, and some couldn't be put off for ever. After all, she wasn't getting any younger. An intense sadness swept over Melissa and she stared into the mirror with an air of abject melancholy. Perhaps Rose could blend one of her wonderful whiffy oils to help her get over this feeling of loss in her life. She sighed with supreme weariness and rearranged her minimalist Lycra creations into some semblance of decency while she went to let Bob in. She hadn't forgotten that he had departed from their previous encounter without paying her. But she was prepared to overlook that in the circumstances. Even when buying petrol you got a free gift every now and again. What he didn't yet know was that there would be no more free gifts. Detective Constable Bob Elecampane was about to spend his last hour and his last £69.99 with her.

'You don't seem yourself today,' Bob said. They were wrapped in the Garden of Romance duvet, illuminated by the weak, watery sun that had weaved its way into the room through a chink in the matching curtains. He tilted her face towards him and looked deep into her eyes.

'I'm fine,' Melissa said flatly.

'Is there something worrying you?' he persisted. 'Perhaps I can help.'

'I'm fine,' she repeated. 'I don't need your help.'

Bob shrugged and pulled her closer to him. 'It's just that I got the sneaking suspicion that something was wrong today. You didn't seem as, well, as . . . as *enthusiastic*, I suppose.'

'I'm sorry about that,' Melissa snapped, 'but it was you that wanted to do it this way.'

The handcuffs hung bereft of hands on the ornate posts of the bed. She hadn't beaten him, she hadn't tied him up, she hadn't physically abused him in any way. She had made love to him, tenderly, and had enjoyed it. And, consequently, she was feeling very unnerved.

'And wasn't it nice?' he whispered softly.

'Yes,' she admitted reluctantly.

'So why the long face?' Bob chucked her gently under the chin.

'You know what you were saying about the animals always being *triste après l'amour*.'

He smiled with delight. 'You remembered, *ma chérie*.'

'Yes.' She studied the Garden of Romance wallpaper intently. 'Well, today I'm very *triste*.'

'But why, *mon petit chou-fleur*?' His voice sounded concerned.

She looked away from him. 'I don't think I want to do this any more.'

'Do you want to go back to the handcuffs and spatulas?' he said gruffly.

'It's nothing to do with the handcuffs.' Melissa turned to face him again. 'Or the spatulas.'

'Then what is it?' There was an element of panic creeping in.

'It's not just you.' She tried to be reassuring.

'What isn't?' Bob sat up in alarm.

She pulled the duvet round her for security. 'It's the whole thing. I'm giving it up.' Melissa looked at him for understanding. 'I'm not going to do . . . *this* any more.'

'Why not?' There was a paleness about his face, which she was sure wasn't just because the duvet and the wallpaper contrasted so brightly against it. 'You're very good at it.'

'That's not the point.' Melissa felt terrible and gnawed absently at a piece of hard skin on her finger. 'It's gone too far,' she said plainly. 'I've got to stop before Frank finds out. I don't think he'd like it.'

'You don't *think* he'd *like* it?'

Melissa had the grace to look sheepish. 'Well, I'm *sure* he wouldn't like it, then.'

Bob narrowed his eyes. 'What if I told him?'

'He wouldn't believe you,' she said without emotion. 'He'd have to see it with his own eyes. Frank trusts me implicitly.'

'Then he's a bloody fool.' Bob threw the duvet aside and sat on the edge of the bed, head in his hands, his back towards her. 'I'm a bloody fool too. I trusted you!'

'I never promised you anything,' she appealed to his tensed spine.

'I love you,' he wailed. It was a painful sound, as if he

had stood on a nail or a drawing pin or a hedgehog while wearing only flip-flops.

'How can you say that? You don't know me!' Melissa pushed herself up in the bed. Her voice was rising and there was a sob lurking dangerously in her throat. 'I'm a cheap tart that you pay sixty-nine quid once a week to screw. Nothing more. Don't forget that.'

'But I tried so very hard to forget that.' He spun round and grabbed her wrist. 'I wanted it to be so much more than that.'

'It was a business arrangement,' she said coldly. 'And now it's over.'

He yanked her from the bed towards him – rather ungraciously for one who was professing love not a moment ago, she thought.

'Is that all I am to you?' he said through clenched teeth. 'A business arrangement?'

His eyes were glittering wildly – it was the sort of thing she had read in *Scarlet* romances, but she had never seen it manifested until now. Frank's eyes never glittered wildly. It was the sort of glittering wildly that was normally attributed to the baddy, just before he hissed, 'If I can't have you, no one else will!' and then proceeded to tie the heroine to the rail track in front of an oncoming train. The thought sent a little shiver of fear down her back and she suddenly wished that Frank was here.

Melissa swallowed nervously. 'This was a business deal. And I am a—'

'Business woman.' Bob laughed hollowly.

'I didn't want it to end like this,' she said placatingly.

'Don't tell me,' he scratched his chin thoughtfully. 'You wanted us to be friends.'

'Yes,' she agreed quickly.

He slammed his fist on the stripped pine bedside cabinet and Melissa hoped he hadn't dented it. She'd bought them from *Grattons* too and they had cost a small fortune.

'You really are a silly little cow, aren't you?' He pushed his face close to hers. 'I don't want to be your friend any more,' he said menacingly. 'I want to be your worst nightmare.'

This was it. The 'if I can't have you, no one else will' syndrome. It was a good job there wasn't a handy rail track around, she thought.

'Now don't go all nasty on me, Bob, and spoil everything.' She was aware that she sounded like her primary school teacher, Mrs Bates, who had been a stickler in her day. 'We've had a lot of fun and now you should find yourself a nice girl to settle down with. Someone young and pretty, and *not married*, who'll love you for yourself.'

Bob's shoulders sagged and his face softened. 'You're right,' he said. 'I should remember this fondly for what it was.' The angry glitter went out of his eyes to be replaced by a welling tear.

Melissa patted his knee. 'There's a good boy,' she said kindly. 'You know it makes sense.'

Bob smiled weakly. 'Do you think we could have one last cuddle before I go?' He looked up shyly. 'For old time's sake?'

Melissa tutted. 'You are an old softy at heart, aren't you?'

He nodded silently. She opened her arms and he squeezed her to him tightly.

It was when she heard the familiar click of the handcuffs that Melissa realised that all was not well. When Bob let go of her she was cuffed firmly to the ornately carved bedpost and he was looking at her with a self-satisfied and altogether unpleasant smile on his face.

Her forehead creased to a frown. 'That's not very nice, is it?' she said sternly, trying to keep a tremor from her voice and bring back a full-blown Mrs Bates.

'No,' he answered with a sigh. 'But then you haven't been very nice to me either, have you?'

He seized her other wrist and wrestled her to the post on the far side of the bed. Melissa struggled and kicked against him. Click.

'You'll regret this,' she said vehemently.

'I don't think so.'

'I'm an asthmatic,' Melissa informed him. 'I could have an attack.'

He opened the top drawer of her bedside cabinet and pulled out her inhaler. 'Good guess,' he said, brandishing the blue plastic tube. 'Open wide.'

'I will not!'

He stuffed the inhaler in her mouth while it was open. Holding it there with one hand, he reached for one of her stockings – Marks and Spencer's 'Barely There' – and wound it once round the inhaler and then took the two ends over her ears and tied them in a knot at the back of her head.

He sat back on the bed and admired his handiwork. Melissa glowered at him as darkly as she could manage and shouted muffled obscenities through the inhaler.

'Don't go away,' he said brightly. 'Oh sorry, you can't, can you?'

He dressed slowly and leisurely, whistling while he buttoned his shirt, smoothing his over-washed jeans over his hips and putting his feet up on the bed – on her Garden of Romance duvet! – to tie his shoelaces.

He glanced at his watch. 'I must be going. It's nearly time for Frank to come home from his shift.'

Melissa twisted her head and looked with panic at the clock.

'You said Frank wouldn't believe it unless he saw it with his own eyes.' His voice was cheerful and light. 'You're going to have fun explaining this.'

'Ith muth thith thwat shuff nuff mith bothath,' Melissa

said, kicking her heels into the bed.

'Didn't quite catch that.' Bob shook his head. 'Though I'm pretty sure one of the words was bastard. Am I right?'

Melissa nodded violently.

He reached into his pocket and pulled out his own set of handcuffs. 'Here's one for good luck.'

Clasping her flailing ankle, he secured it with a resounding thunk to the heart-shaped cut-out at the foot of the bed. 'One other piece of advice, Melissa. Never so much as park on a double yellow line in Milton Keynes. I'll be right behind you and I'll do everything within my power to make damn sure the judge puts his black cap on before he sentences you.' Bob winked at her. '*Hasta la vista*, baby!'

'FITH UFF!' Melissa replied with as much force as she could manage with an inhaler in her mouth.

She listened as he stomped down the stairs whistling. There was a smash, which didn't interrupt his whistle and which she judged to be the wall-mounted box containing the twenty-four selections of popular doorbell tunes. As the door slammed, 'You Are My Sunshine' started to play. Understandably, every other note was missing. So DC Elecampane had noticed and it seemed he had taken it rather badly.

Chapter Twenty-One

MASSAGE RUB FOR STIFF MUSCLES
Black Pepper, Marjoram, Rosemary, Chamomile
German.
When we are over-stretched, our bodies can react by
rendering us unable to let go of the rigid tension that
builds up in our muscles. Gentle massage with this
restorative blend of nature's essential oils can really help
by stimulating the blood circulation that gives relief to
aching spasm.

from: *The Complete Encyclopaedia of Aromatherapy Oils*
by Jessamine Lovage

Rose opened the door with a mixture of surprise and
pleasure on her face. A sympathetic smile twisted her
lips.

'Richard the Third, I presume?' she said.

Dan was bent double, clutching his lower back. He
raised his head to look at her miserably. 'A massage, a
massage, my kingdom for a massage.' His gritted teeth
wouldn't allow him to smile.

'I don't want your kingdom. Forty quid will do.'

'A king's ransom then.'

Her smile widened and she held the door open. 'Come
on in and let me see what I can do. You're lucky, I've got
a gap.'

He hobbled past her gingerly. 'I have to say I hold you partly responsible for this.'

'Oh?' She gave him an inquiring look.

'My back hasn't been the same since I spent the night on your sofa.'

'And that's *my* fault?'

'You were definitely a contributory factor.'

'I would have thought the seventeen pints of Carlsberg and half a bottle of brandy contributed most.'

'You could have a point,' he muttered.

Rose led him, hobbling, into her treatment room.

'It's nice and warm in here,' he remarked.

'Yes, despite the obvious lack of open fire.'

'Ah.' Dan felt himself colour.

'Yes,' Rose said. 'Ah.'

'I can explain . . .'

That fateful morning he had eventually returned home after the Viking evening, he had rashly promised Gardenia that he wouldn't come near Rose again. This was mainly to ensure that he wasn't de-testiculated as he feared he might otherwise have been. Gardenia had threatened that all manner of unspeakable acts would befall his person if he so much as ventured in this direction of Lavender Hill for the remainder of his lifetime.

Dan, who had the mother of all hangovers, was in no fit state to form a cohesive argument and simply longed to smother himself in Rose's foul-smelling Hellish Hangover Remedy. The words 'quiet life' were at the forefront of his brain, so instead of remonstrating with Gardenia, or even voicing his innocence, he had tucked his tail between his legs and it had stayed there firmly ever since, out of harm's way.

It was all going quite well. Gardenia had restored verbal communication and he only thought of Rose once every hour or whenever he caught a whiff of the hangover remedy, which was quite often since he had taken to smearing it on his twingeing back, once the hangover had gone. Then he tried to pick up a paving slab this morning.

The pain had been unbearable – red-hot needles shooting down his back and his legs. He'd dropped the paving slab, narrowly missing his big toe. His brother, Alan brought him back to Builder's Bottom in the van. And, although Alan tried to drive carefully through the rutted country lanes to Great Brayford, ten years of vehicular abuse weighed heavily on his motoring style and every twist and turn and bump sent Dan almost through the roof with pain.

Gardenia laughed when she saw him shuffling up to the house, leaning on Alan like a six-foot-two hulk of walking stick. She laughed again when Alan had gone and Dan was alone in the house with her, so he knew she hadn't put on the laugh for his brother's benefit. And she called him Quasimodo. It was probably because she'd never heard of Richard the Third. When he complained of the pain, she told him to go and find something in the bathroom cabinet to rub on it. It took ten minutes for him to hobble upstairs one step at a time and all he could find in the first-aid box in the bathroom was a tattered packet of dog-eared plasters, honey-flavoured Strepsils, Night Nurse and an out-of-date bottle of Benylin Expectorant. Rose's Hellish Hangover Remedy was there too and that was what made him think of her – not that he needed much prompting. It was TLC that he needed, not TCP. And there wasn't even any of that.

The decision made, he had hobbled out of Builder's Bottom – without telling Gardenia where he was going – and down the hill to Rose's house, using for support as many obliging garden walls as he could along the way.

He looked at Rose, who was waiting expectantly. 'Forget I said that. I can't explain,' he said. 'It's a very long story.'

Rose shrugged. 'Tell me another time then.' She

pointed at a hook bearing two smart coat hangers on the back of the treatment room door. 'I'll leave you to take your clothes off.'

Dan looked startled.

'Do you think you can manage by yourself?' Rose asked.

'Oh yes,' he said too quickly. He hadn't thought about removing his clothes. If he'd thought, he would have taken a shower.

'Are you sure?' Her forehead creased with concern.

'Oh yes,' he repeated. He cleared his throat. 'Do you want me to take *all* my clothes off?'

'If you feel comfortable,' she said. 'I want to massage all round your lower back and your buttocks, just to make sure you haven't trapped your sciatic nerve or anything.'

'And that's where my sciatic nerve is?' Dan queried.

'Yes.'

'And you want me to take off *everything*? Even my, er, my shorts?'

Rose nodded in response. 'Even your, er, shorts,' she mimicked.

'Oh.'

She folded her arms before she spoke again. 'Mr Spikenard, I am a professional therapist trained in Swedish remedial massage as well as the ancient art of aromatherapy. You are in very safe hands.'

A look of terror crossed Dan's face. 'Swedish massage?'

'It has nothing to do with being beaten by birch twigs so there's no need to look so panic-stricken, I'm not asking you to get your kit off simply to have a glimpse of your bum.'

'I didn't for one moment suggest that, Ms Stevens,' he protested.

Rose smiled. 'No, but your face did.'

'Am I so transparent?'

'As a pane of glass. Now,' she pointed sternly at him, 'get undressed! I won't bite you.'

'That was the bit I was looking forward to.'

'Here, put this round you.' She laid a towel on the treatment couch. 'I'm going to wash my hands. I'll be back in a few minutes.'

Rose let the cold water from the sink in the downstairs loo trickle over her wrists. Her palms were hot and sweaty. She did want to look at Dan's bum, despite what she said. It was a terrible thing to have to admit. In all her years of practice and all the bottoms that had passed under her therapeutic hands – big ones, small ones, hairy ones, spotty ones and even a few nice ones – she had never felt hot and bothered about looking at one of them before. Not even Hugh's, as far as she could remember.

She smoothed her uniform over her hips and counted slowly to ten, before going back into the treatment room. Dan was perched on the edge of her work bench where she had been mixing oils earlier in the day. He was sniffing at the tiny brown bottles, his nose wrinkled in concentration – or disgust, she wasn't sure which.

'I'll mix you some oils for muscular spasm. That'll help,' she said as she crossed the room towards him. It was disconcerting having him sitting in her treatment room clad in nothing but a towel. His shoulders were broad and muscular, his body tanned to a rugged nutbrown. His chest was covered with a fine curling of dark blond hair and he looked as if he worked out, but he probably didn't need to.

'Will it smell any better than the hangover stuff?'

'Probably not,' Rose laughed. 'I'll use some marjoram and black pepper and some blue chamomile which is good for reducing inflammation. And perhaps some rosemary.'

Dan pulled a face. 'Are you sure you're not making a curry?'

'If you want to leave here smelling nice, you'll have to

come for one of my relaxing treatments,' she said brightly.

'I might do that.' Dan held her eyes and there was a catch in his voice.

'Well, yes. One day,' she said, flustered. 'But now, first things first.'

He leaned across her and picked up another bottle from the bench. 'What does rose oil smell like?' he asked, slowly unscrewing the lid.

'It's beautiful,' she answered, her voice higher than she would have liked. He was close to her and the heady smell of the rose oil drifted between them, filling the room with its delicious perfume.

He held the bottle to his nose and inhaled deeply. 'You're right,' he said softly.

'That's damask rose or otto of rose, one of the most precious oils in the world. You can pay hundreds of pounds for a teaspoon of high-quality oil. Which works out at about a pound a drop.'

'And worth every penny – or every pound – I should think.' Dan closed his eyes and inhaled again. 'Do you know that the rose is a symbol of Venus, the goddess of love?'

Her mouth was dry, her heart beating high in her chest. 'You suddenly know an awful lot about aroma-therapy oils.'

'Not really,' he said earnestly. 'I've been reading the back of Gardenia's underarm deodorant.'

Rose frowned. 'Dan Spikenard, you're taking the mickey!'

'No. I'm not.' He was smiling, but his eyes were serious, sombre.

'Come on. Let's get you on to my couch. For a man who was in abject pain not ten minutes ago you seem to be making a remarkable recovery.'

'Can't I have some of this?' He held up the bottle of rose oil.

'It's not really suitable for your back,' she said.

Dan made a petulant face.

'It's for nervous tension,' Rose explained.

'I've got loads of that,' he insisted.

'And impotence.'

Dan looked affronted. 'I haven't got that!'

Rose smiled kindly. 'Will it persuade you finally to get on my couch if I promise to do a little bit of facial massage for you? You can have some rose oil in that.'

'Promise?'

'Just get on my couch, Dan.'

He put the rose oil down and hobbled across the room.

'I'll lower this so you don't do yourself another injury,' she said. She reduced the height of her hydraulic treatment couch – a wise but pricey piece of equipment that she had invested in when she moved to Great Brayford to protect her own back for the future. She wished it was as easy to invest in something to protect her against Dan.

He sat down and swung his legs on to the couch, grimacing slightly as he did so.

'Now I need you on your front.' He turned over obediently, a groan joining the grimace. 'Take it easy,' she advised him.

'I don't think I can take it any other way.'

'I'll just raise this back to the right height,' she said, operating the control with her foot. Dan heaved a sigh of relief.

'Unhook your towel,' she instructed. 'I want to lay it on top of you.'

He looked at her suspiciously.

'Dan!' Her voice held a threat.

He reached round to his stomach and undid the towel. Rose spread it over his legs, exposing the top of his buttocks, and tucked it tightly under his hips. She was starting to feel very warm. He had a body shaped like a Dairylea cheese triangle. His broad shoulders tapered to a narrow waist and tight slim hips. He had the nicest buttocks she had ever seen. They looked like two hard-boiled eggs peeping out of a handkerchief.

'I'll make your oil,' she said nervously, glad of the chance to escape temporarily to the sanctuary of the other side of the room. With shaking hands, she poured the drops of oil into a clean glass bottle and then rolled it between her palms, warming the blend with the heat of her hands – which was not inconsiderable. As promised, she also blended a few drops of otto of rose with some peach oil for a facial massage.

She returned to Dan and, pouring the oils into her hand, took a deep, steadying breath before gently laying her hands on his lower back. He flinched slightly. 'Just let me know if anything is uncomfortable,' Rose said. Apart from me, she added as a silent afterthought.

Sliding her hands up his back, she tried very hard to concentrate on what she was doing and not on the fact that the body beneath her was strong and lithe and supple and fit.

The movement was called *effleurage*. A fine stroking motion, to help relax the body – the client's body. Clearly, it wasn't the therapist's in this particular case. All the massage movements had French names – *effluerage, pétrissage, tapotement* – which was strange considering it was supposed to be Swedish remedial massage. Perhaps rubbing, kneading and hitting didn't sound quite as aesthetically appealing in Swedish.

Her hands moved over Dan's shoulders and she swallowed hard. In her panic, she had used too much oil and it squeezed from under her palms through her fingers, warm and sensual. Dan let out a contented groan beneath her. This was sheer torture and at the moment she wasn't sure who was suffering most. She worked her slippery hands over his body, moulding them to him, feeling the hard tendons and sinews easing and releasing beneath her firm touch. Her thumbs circled alongside the deep hollow of his spine.

'You're very tense,' she croaked.

'Wouldn't you be?' Dan's voice was muffled from lying face downwards. He tried to turn round and speak to her.

'Lie down!' she instructed.

'I've never had a massage before, Rose. And, I must say, that contrary to my expectations, it's proving to be one of the most pleasant experiences I've ever had. I'm just not sure it's my back that it's having the most effect on.'

'It will in a minute. I'm getting to that bit now,' she said slightly breathlessly. The two boiled eggs seemed to be throwing out a challenge to her. TOUCH US AT YOUR PERIL, they said.

Rose put off the terrible moment and massaged over the back of his hips, as close to the buttocks as she could without actually touching them. *She* knew she was stalling and *they* knew she was stalling. IT'S ONLY A MATTER OF TIME, they said.

'Your sacroiliac is very tight.'

'I'll take your word for it,' Dan moaned.

'This is the problem area,' she said in as professional a tone as she could manage, considering her legs had turned to Slinkies and there were *things* doing cartwheels in her stomach.

'Oh, yes,' Dan said with a sigh. 'Oh, yes.'

Rose glared at the back of his head. As if sensing it, he turned and said, 'Sorry. I mean, that's where it hurts. You're on just the right spot.'

She was afraid of that. This would mean that the buttocks would have to be worked on. There was no avoiding it. She looked accusingly at them. Now they seemed to be winking at her. Suggestively. Everyone else's bottom just lay there patiently and waited its turn. But not Dan's bottom. It demanded attention.

Rose braced herself and then swept her hands over the tight curve of his buttocks. The muscles were both soft and firm at the same time. The skin smooth and yet rough with a down of coarse, barely visible hair. They were the most sensation-laden buttocks she had ever met.

Dan groaned with what was definitely bordering on pleasure. Right, Rose thought, she would knock the smile off the face of his bottom. She sank her thumbs deep into his flesh, *effleuraging* and *pétrissaging* with a ferocity that she didn't know she possessed until they yielded underneath her, begging for mercy.

Rose was panting heavily, her hands smoothing the buttocks she had so mercilessly battered. They were tamed, subdued and malleable – and quite probably bruised. It might make Dan's back feel better, but he probably wouldn't be able to sit down for a week.

He turned his head to look at her. 'Are you normally quite so enthusiastic about your work?'

'Of course,' Rose answered breathlessly. 'I'm a professional massage therapist. I told you so.'

'Far be it for me to argue with that.' Dan pushed himself up on his elbows. 'May I say, without risk of further punishment, that you've got very strong thumbs for such a little person.'

Rose smiled. 'How does your back feel now?'

'Wonderful.

'Has the pain eased?'

'What pain?' There was a smirk on his face and there was plenty of colour in his cheeks. The cheeks of his face.

'Well, give it a few days' rest,' she advised. 'If you must go to work, don't, for goodness sake, do any lifting or heavy work. Just walk round with a pencil behind your ear and look busy. You are the boss, after all. And if you do get any more twinges, I'd go to an osteopath and get it looked at properly. You need to nip any potential back problems in the bud, particularly in your job.'

'Thanks, Rose.' Dan turned over to lie on his back. 'I really appreciate it.'

'You can get up now,' she said. 'Do it carefully, though.'

'What about your promise?'

'What promise?' Rose looked puzzled.

'You haven't forgotten already?' Dan tutted. 'My face. The rose oil. You said you'd do it for me.'

'Oh, that,' she said lightly. Not more torture, she groaned inwardly. 'Just a few minutes then.'

Pulling her footstool to the head of the couch, she lowered Dan until his head was nestled comfortably in her hands. Smoothing his unruly hair back from his brow, she poured the rose oil on to her warm hands. Dan's chest was exposed, the towel pushed down provocatively low on his hips. His stomach was hard, flat and reminded her of driving through Milton Keynes – for the simple reason that the majority of housing estates in the city were plagued with a series of traffic-calming humps. Except, unlike Milton Keynes, Dan's stomach was row after row of tight-packed humps of muscle. And there was nothing calming about these humps.

'Close your eyes,' she said softly.

Dan obliged and she smoothed the oil over his shoulders and up on to his neck where her hands grazed against the bristle of stubble. She covered his face with her fingertips, trailing them delicately over his mouth, his cheeks, his nose and the frown lines of his forehead. The scent of the oil was heady, rich, erotic, floral sweet with a hint of exotic spice and almost, almost, overpowering. A thousand Valentine's Day bouquets rolled into one heady concoction.

'No one has ever touched my face like this,' Dan murmured contentedly. 'It is the most blissful thing I've ever felt. I feel like I'm floating on a cloud.'

Tears sprang to Rose's eyes. She brushed them away with the back of her hand, admonishing herself for being hormonal. So what if she was the first person in the world to touch Dan's face? What did that matter? But why hadn't Gardenia touched his face in all the years they had been together? Did familiarity really breed contempt? If Dan's face had belonged to her, she wouldn't have been able to stop herself from touching it. Like his bottom, his face was very, very touchable.

Her hands followed the contours of his full sensual lips, his long, strong nose. She swept her fingers over his chiselled cheekbones and up around his hairline. Working her thumbs lightly over the acupressure points on his forehead, she could feel him relaxing under her touch, sinking deeper into that peaceful half-trance between wakefulness and sleeping.

As she circled her fingers gently over the white creases of crow's feet by his eyes, she could see the years falling away from him. She could see the boy in Dan – soft-skinned, carefree, a fresh open face – and she wished that things could be different between them. Had he really meant the half-spoken words he said after the Viking night or was it simply Reg's Carlsberg talking? Why was he still with Gardenia when all they seemed to share, apart from Builder's Bottom, was a deep and abiding loathing for each other? Why did men always seem keen to expound how much they disliked their spouses while, at the same time, being curiously reluctant to do anything either to sever the ties or to work to make things better? Having an affair seemed to be the easy remedy these days. But, in reality, it forced so many people to live in abject misery. Surely not all relationships ended in acrimony. There were still some good ones left. Weren't there?

'Rose.' Dan caught her hand as it slid back down his neck towards his shoulders. 'I think you better stop there.' His voice was husky.

Rose glanced down the length of the treatment couch. She had seen the boy in Dan and now she was very definitely seeing the man, albeit still modestly covered with a towel. She could feel a scalding rush of blood flow from her toes up to her face. The sort of rush that would make her neck red and blotchy for hours.

'I'm really embarrassed,' he said.

'There's no need to be,' she reassured him.

He looked unconvinced.

'It happens sometimes,' Rose continued. 'Men aren't used to having their faces stroked by strange women. It can be a very sensual experience. It's not a big deal.' She cleared her throat. 'Honestly.' She pressed a button on the couch which raised him to a semi-sitting position.

Dan linked his hands behind his head. 'How do you normally handle it?' He gave her a sideways glance. 'I think I'll rephrase that.'

Rose laughed. 'I think you better had.'

'What do you usually do in this sort of situation?'

'It depends,' she said with a shrug. 'Either I ignore it and hope it will go away. Or, if they start to get too frisky, whack them with a cold spoon.'

'A cold spoon?'

'It was a trick my mother taught me for dampening the ardour of unwanted suitors.'

'I see.' Dan looked suitably impressed. 'And what are you planning to do with me?'

'I think you're the "ignore it and hope it will go away" variety.' Rose smiled kindly. 'I don't think you're some kind of pervert. There's no need to be embarrassed.'

'I feel like a pervert –' he said.

'– but where could I find one at this time of day?' they both joked in unison.

He sighed. 'But I do feel embarrassed, Rose. Here you are being all professional and clinical, and my mind – and my body – are behaving like a horny schoolboy and there's nothing I'd like more than to unbutton that crisp, starched little white uniform and fling it with wild abandon to the

211

other side of the room, pull you down on top of me and then,' he looked dangerously at the bottle of rose massage oil, 'smear that wonderful, sexy oil all over your wonderful, sexy body.'

'I see,' Rose said calmly, feeling anything but calm inside.

'Isn't that just cause for the cold spoon treatment?' Dan asked.

'I don't know,' she replied.

'Can I ask what's giving rise to your uncertainty?'

There was a long silence, during which birds twittered wildly in the garden. They were her favourites, chubby redwing thrushes, that swooped in and gorged themselves, eating all the berries on her bright orange pyracantha. But Rose didn't notice them now. A golden eagle could have been doing handstands on the bird table and it was unlikely that she'd have noticed that either.

Rose let out a long, shuddering exhalation of breath. Her shoulders sagged with relief – she hadn't realised how close to her ears they had become. Without speaking, she sat on the edge of the treatment couch, her thigh resting against Dan's. She looked squarely at him. 'I haven't whacked you with a cold spoon,' her voice wavered unsteadily, 'for the simple reason that I have been wanting you to do exactly the same thing.'

'I see.' It was Dan's turn to sound calm.

They sat there looking at each other, neither of them moving.

'Now what happens?' Dan asked eventually.

'You've got a bad back,' she reminded him.

Reaching out, he took her hand. His grip was firm, warm and confident. He pulled her towards him. 'Then you'd better be gentle with me.'

Chapter Twenty-Two

CASSIA

A brownish-yellow oil with a sweet tenacious aroma. Cassia is used mainly for digestive ailments such as flatulence, diarrhoea and nausea. It is little used in perfumes and cosmetics due to its unattractive dark colour. Cassia should never be used on the skin.

from: *The Complete Encyclopaedia of Aromatherapy Oils*
by Jessamine Lovage

'A pint of best, please, Reg.' Bob Elecampane leaned on the bar in the Black Horse. He didn't like the pubs in Milton Keynes, which were all disco music and tasteless designer beer at extortionate prices. 'And a packet of your finest pork scratchings.'

The trendy pubs in Milton Keynes made him feel old, which, at the end of the day, was the real reason he didn't like going in them.

Melissa had made him feel old, too. Old, unloved, abandoned. Consigned for ever to the Tidy Tip of romance. She had seen the sign that said 'DUMP RUBBISH HERE – NO BLACK BAGS, NO HOT ASHES, NO COMMERCIAL WASTE' and had done just that. Except that she had been mistaken – he was commercial waste. A business arrangement, she had said. Cold, hard, cruel.

It was strange, really, because only last week she had made him feel young and loved and cared for. Okay, so there was that slight disagreement about being referred to as 'the ironing', but what had he done to deserve this?

Nothing, as far as he could tell. She was the hooker and he was the client, and yet he had tried every way he knew how to please her. He had cared for her and catered for her every need – as far as the handcuffs and the spatulas had allowed. He had spoken French to her. All to no avail. Despite his best efforts, here he was – as Gilbert O'Sullivan so poignantly observed – alone again (naturally). That was him, Detective Constable Robert Horatio Elecampane, loser in love and life.

He would never get over Melissa. He had been cut to the quick by her cruelty. No other woman would ever get so close to him again. From now on he would take no prisoners – in the emotional sense; he hoped to take lots of prisoners in the law enforcement sense. That was all there was in his life now. He would have 'CAUTION – HANDLE WITH CARE' tattooed across his back.

Reg placed his pint of best bitter on the sodden beer mat in front of him. Bitter – what an appropriate drink to drown his sorrows with.

'You looked like you've found a pound and lost a fiver, mate,' Reg commented.

Bob shook his head ruefully. 'Bad day, Reg.'

'Are the criminals behaving themselves?'

'I wish.' He shook his head. 'I wish.'

Reg tossed the pork scratchings on the bar. The packet he pulled off the advertising card exposed the bare breast of a vacant-looking blonde in a white string bikini.

'Have these on me,' he said generously.

'Cheers, mate.' Bob was touched. Perhaps the world wasn't such a bad place after all. The bird at the end of the bar wasn't too bad either. She was a bit old, more of a mother goose than a spring chicken but reasonably well assembled.

Assembled was the right word, come to think of it. She was glamorous and sassy-looking, in an overdone way. But the general impression was that she had been put together by numbers from a kit. Everything looked as if it was made of plastic, even more so than the bimbo with the pork scratchings – face, tits, bum. It'd be like having sex with a Barclaycard.

She put her glass on the bar and regarded him coolly. 'Do you have a light?'

Her voice took him by surprise. It was rough and gravelly, as if she was just getting over laryngitis. If anyone could make money out of dirty phone calls, this one could.

Bob surveyed the bar, but there was no one else in close proximity that she could be addressing. 'Me?' he said, not so coolly.

She nodded.

Bob patted his pockets pathetically. He held up his hands in embarrassment. 'I don't smoke,' he said with an apologetic laugh.

The woman didn't smile back, she just held his gaze. 'Neither do I.'

Bob's heart skipped a beat. If Melissa was the fiver he'd lost, this could be the pound he'd just found. 'Can I buy you a drink?'

She downed the contents of her glass. 'Gin and tonic,' she said.

That's what he would have guessed. She looked like a gin and tonic sort of woman. No 'please', he noted, but then you can't have everything.

He ordered the drink from Reg, who winked lecherously at him, which he took as a good sign.

'I've seen you in here before,' she said when he gave her the gin and tonic. No 'thank you' either. 'Are you local?'

'Milton Keynes.'

'What brings you up here?' she asked. 'Surely Reg's beer isn't that well kept.'

'I'm with the local CID. I've been up here on a case.'

Her eyes widened – nearly at the same time. 'Anything interesting?'

He once thought so. Swallowing the lump that had come to his throat, he said, 'No. Routine inquiries.' If he could bloody well be 'the ironing', that's what Melissa would be in the future, 'routine inquiries'. He was beginning to feel better already. Even when he noticed that the pork scratchings were past their sell-by date, it did nothing to dent his rising mood of optimism.

'Married?'

Blimey, she didn't beat about the bush. He shook his head.

'A nice boy like you, who still hasn't found Miss Right?'

'I've just been having fun with the wrong ones,' he replied smoothly. Why on earth hadn't he chatted up old birds before! They were an absolute doddle. All that time he'd wasted trying to impress young slips of girls when there were oldies like this one who were desperate for it!

'Stiffener,' she said as she took a swig from her gin.

'Pardon?'

'Stiffener,' she repeated. 'Before going home to an empty house. Alone.'

'You single, then?' he asked.

'Might as well be,' she said with a bitter laugh. 'My husband's a plastic surgeon. He's at a conference in the Bahamas at the moment. He goes to a lot of conferences in the Bahamas. Very fond of dusky maidens, my husband.'

Bob smiled as the penny dropped. 'That explains why you're in such good nick,' he said, stopping short of adding 'for your age'. 'He's been doing a little private work on you.'

'I have to look nice because I'm a celebrity,' she told him.

'Are you?' Bob's interest quickened. 'I've never scre— met a celebrity before. Are you on television?'

'No. I have my own programme on the radio.'

'Radio One?'

She shook her head. Not surprising, she was probably a bit old.

'Radio Four?'

She shook her head again, more vigorously.

'Virgin?'

The gin stopped halfway to her mouth. 'I beg your pardon?'

'FM,' he added quickly.

'Oh, I see.' She laughed and it was quite a nice sound when it was sincere. 'No, I'll put you out of your misery. Bucks County FM.'

'Right.' Bob elongated the word. Never heard of it, he added to himself.

'Do you know *The Cassia Wales Show*?' she asked hopefully.

'No, but I do know the way to San Jose,' he quipped. She looked crestfallen. It was a shame to disappoint her. 'I'm sure my mum listens to it,' he said earnestly.

She smiled shyly. 'Well, I'm *the* Cassia Wales of *The Cassia Wales Show*.'

'No! She *loves* it. She thinks you're brilliant.'

'Does she?' Her face brightened.

Bob's personal radio crackled into life. 'Excuse me.' He turned away from Cassia and lowered his voice to a whisper. 'Elecampane,' he said briskly.

'Where are you Elecampane?' The voice from the station crackled over the radio like the rustling of paper bags.

'In Great Brayford.'

'Oh, wink, wink. Say no more.'

'I'm in the bloody pub. Making inquiries,' he added hastily.

'You won't be too busy to go to a call in Lavender Hill then.'

'Lavender Hill? Isn't this a uniform's job?'

'Just go, for pity's sake. You're only round the corner, you idle bastard.'

'Okay,' he looked longingly at Cassia, who was currently absorbed by her gin and tonic. 'What's up then?'

'Lady thinks her neighbour is running a house of ill repute.'

'You've got to be joking!' Bob lowered his voice. 'Not another one.'

'Apparently so. Thought that would make you smile.'

'Are you sure it's not the one we all know and love?'

'No, mate. Lady lives right across the road. She's been eyeballing them through a pair of binoculars.'

'What is it up here? Is there something in the water?'

'I don't know, but whatever it is, mine's a pint.'

'Is this really that urgent?'

'If you get round there now you'll catch him with his trousers round his ankles.'

The line crackled and Bob held it away from his ear. 'Poor bastard,' he muttered sympathetically.

'If you need any back-up, Frank Cox will be home soon. I can send him round if you need support.'

'Don't bother, I can handle it.' If anyone was going to be in need of support, it was Frank Cox when he got home. 'I'll report back, later.' Bob put his radio back in his pocket. He turned to Cassia. 'I've got to go,' he said flatly. 'Important police work.'

It was a shame he had to leave, all this undercover stuff usually got the women panting – except Melissa who had been bored to tears by it all. Melissa! Now there was a thought; perhaps she was starting a chain of village knocking shops. A light bulb lit up in his brain.

He could have her for pimping, too, then.

'I overheard you say Lavender Hill,' Cassia said. 'It's only across the road. I live further up the hill from there. I could take you up there. It isn't dangerous, is it?'

Pant, pant! 'You can never tell in this line of work, ma'am.'

'I'd like to do all I can for an officer of the law,' she insisted.

I bet you would, Bob thought.

'I could show you where my home is.' Cassia smiled sexily. 'Perhaps you'd like to join me for a nightcap – if your work doesn't prove to be too time-consuming. Did I mention that my husband was in the Bahamas?'

'It should only be a five-minute job,' Bob assured her. He would make damn sure it was.

Chapter Twenty-Three

Dan was fumbling feverishly with the buttons of Rose's uniform when the doorbell rang. 'Leave it,' he said, breathing heavily.

Rose glanced guiltily at the clock. 'I can't.' She broke away from his passionate embrace. 'It'll be my next client.'

'Is he due now?'

'*She*,' Rose corrected. 'Not yet. But she's often early.'

'Tell her to wait in her car.'

'That could hardly be considered the height of professionalism.' But then, neither could this, she reminded herself.

'Pretend you're not here,' he muttered urgently, his mouth working against her neck.

'I can't,' she said. 'It's not in my nature. I'm the sort of person that opens the door to Jehovah's Witnesses.' Reluctantly she extricated herself from his grasp. 'I can't bear to let people down.'

'You're letting me down!' He looked forlornly at his nether regions.

'I'm sorry, Dan,' she said, buttoning up her dress. 'I want this as much as you. It's just bad timing. *Awful* timing.' Her eyes begged him to understand.

'I've only just managed to get that undone,' Dan complained.

'Please, don't give me a hard time, Dan.'

He sat back on the treatment couch and folded his

arms in frustration over the teepee that was protruding from his lap. 'It doesn't look like I've got much choice.'

She smiled and blew him a kiss. 'Get dressed. I'll be back in two minutes.'

'Good evening, miss,' the man said when Rose opened the door. She could tell he was a policeman instantly, even without the giveaway of a uniform. It was a certain intonation of voice that earmarked them all – they must practise it for hours, like doctors must practise illegible handwriting. 'DC Elecampane from Milton Keynes police station.' He flashed his warrant card under her nose.

'Good evening, officer,' Rose replied, smoothing her tousled hair. 'How can I help?'

'Can I have a few words with you, miss? I think it would be best if I stepped inside.'

'Certainly.' She moved aside. 'Come in.'

'I won't beat about the bush, miss . . .'

'Stevens. Rose Stevens.'

'Miss Stevens.' Bob folded his arms. 'Can you tell me the exact nature of business that you're conducting on these premises?'

'I'm an aromatherapist.' Rose's voice wavered uncertainly. Why did policemen automatically make you feel guilty? It was like customs officers, they did exactly the same thing.

'An aromatherapist?' DC Elecampane looked unimpressed. His eyes travelled suspiciously over her uniform.

It was then that she realised her buttons weren't done up properly. In her haste, she had buttoned the top one to the next one down, so that she had an excess of collar on one side and, on the other, an abundance of fabric bunched round her waist. She hoped to God her lipstick wasn't smudged down her chin.

Bob purposefully took a notebook and pencil out of his top pocket. He licked the end of the pencil. 'An *aromatherapist,*' he repeated while writing it down.

Rose could feel a vibrant crimson flush spreading from her cleavage to the roots of her hair.

'And do you have a gentlemen with you at the moment?' he asked.

'Yes,' Rose said, her voice breaking up like a bad mobile phone line. 'Yes. I have a client with me.'

He nodded pensively. 'A *client.*'

'A client and a friend,' Rose added.

'There are two people here?'

'No. They're both the same person,' she explained. She was going redder by the minute and she could tell the fact hadn't gone unnoticed by DC Elecampane.

'So this gentleman is a *client* and a *friend.*'

'That's right.'

'And you're giving him *aromatherapy?*'

'He has a bad back.' Her voice was sounding more and more feeble.

'*A bad back.*' He wrote it down, then scrutinised her again. 'May I have a word with him – your *client.*'

'Is that necessary?' Rose looked puzzled.

'I'd like him to confirm what you've told me. If that wouldn't be putting you to too much trouble.' He cast a nasty, sneering glance at her dishevelled uniform.

'What *is* this all about, officer?' Rose was starting to get worried. 'Have I done something wrong?'

DC Elecampane took a hearty inhalation of breath. The sort of breath that said he meant business. 'I have to inform you, Miss Stevens, that we've had certain complaints from the neighbours about your *aromatherapy* business.'

Rose's mouth set in a tight line and a fresh surge of colour flooded her face. 'It's that poisonous bloody dragon, Anise Weston, isn't it?' she fumed. 'She's behind this!'

'I'm afraid I can't confirm our source, Miss Stevens.'

'You don't need to.' Rose was dangerously close to stamping her foot. 'I know full well who it is. It's the interfering old busybody who lives across the road from me. That's who it is!'

The door opened behind her and she whirled round to see Dan emerging from her treatment room. He was fully dressed again and looking considerably less crumpled than she did. 'Good evening, officer,' he said. 'Dan Spikenard.'

Bob nodded in acknowledgement. 'Mr Spikenard.'

'I suspect that Rose is right,' Dan said, his voice neutral. 'It was probably Anise Weston who telephoned the police. But I'm afraid Rose is an innocent pawn here. Anise is using her – and you – to make life difficult for me.'

Bob regarded him carefully. 'And why would she want to do that, Mr Spikenard?'

'I want to build retirement flats on the site of the old village hall. Miss Weston is *violently* opposed to it.' His voice and his face were both earnest. 'She hasn't got much support in the village. I'm going to build a new village hall as part of the deal, so most people are in favour.' Dan smiled sympathetically. 'I think Miss Weston is feeling a bit desperate. I'm sure she doesn't mean any harm. I'm afraid she hasn't anything better to do with her time.'

Rose could feel her jaw going slack as she looked at Dan in amazement. Anyone would think he was Anise's social worker rather than her arch-enemy.

DC Elecampane looked appeased. 'Do you mind if I take a quick look in here, Miss Stevens?'

'No, not at all,' she said, feeling slightly dazed. Dan winked at her behind the detective's back and she scowled in return.

Elecampane opened the door to her treatment room. It was spotless. Dan had folded all his towels neatly and the array of brown glass bottles blinked innocently from the shelf. Even the reflexology poster was looking particularly guileless.

Elecampane sniffed. 'Well, that all seems to be in order.'

'I can't apologise enough, officer,' Dan said. 'It seems that you've been brought up here on a wild-goose chase.'

Elecampane smiled knowingly. 'Unfortunately, that's part of the job, Mr Spikenard.' He folded his notebook and slipped it back into his pocket. 'Would you like me to go and have a word with Miss Weston? Caution her about wasting police time?'

'I don't think that will be necessary, officer. She's just a lonely old soul. It's unlikely that she'll do it again. But, if she does, we'll be sure to let you know.'

'I'll be on my way then.' Nodding curtly at Rose, Detective Elecampane said, 'Sorry to have disturbed your evening, Miss Stevens.' He looked squarely at Dan and there was a shrewd glint in his eye. 'And your *aromatherapy*, sir.'

Rose collapsed against the door when DC Elecampane had gone.

Dan's face turned black. 'I'm going over there to give that nosey old cow a piece of my mind, and if she was a bloke she'd get a piece of my fist too. She's nothing but trouble!'

'That was a quick change of tune.' Rose's face was grim. 'What happened to poor Anise, old and lonely and misunderstood?'

'She's a vicious old bat!'

'You made yourself sound like Great Brayford's number one citizen.'

'The good detective might not have left so quickly if he'd thought I was going straight over there to murder her,' Dan grumbled.

Rose twisted her hands together anxiously. 'I can't believe she could be so venomous.'

'This is one of the joys of living in a myopic little village,' he said, tugging his hand through his hair. 'There's precious little to do, so the locals have to make their own entertainment.'

Rose felt some of the tension leave her body. 'A bit like we were doing?'

Dan's shoulders sagged and he smiled a weary smile at her. 'It's spoilt the mood somewhat, hasn't it?'

'I'd never give Anise the satisfaction of knowing it, but her timing was perfect.'

They both laughed. Dan took her hands and pulled her towards him. 'Haven't you got an oil to get us back in the mood?'

Rose shook her head, unable to meet his eyes. 'It was wrong, Dan. I shouldn't have got carried away like that.' She stared at the treads on the stairs, which needed painting. 'When someone comes to you with a bad back, you shouldn't end up jumping their bones. It's not professional. Or ethical. Or even sensible.'

'You *were* encouraged,' he pointed out.

'I know, and that was wrong of you,' she admonished him. 'I should have hit you with the cold spoon while I had the chance.'

Dan smiled ruefully at her. 'There's still time.'

'There isn't,' Rose said. 'My client really will be here in a minute now.'

'Well, I'll go and give Anise Weston a good talking to then.'

Rose wrinkled her nose. 'Don't be too hard on her. She is an old lady.'

'Now who's going soft?' Dan chuckled. 'She's a vindictive old witch who delights in making other people's lives a misery.'

'That's because she's got no one to love her,' she said softly.

'Unlike you,' Dan replied. 'Who has someone who *adores* her.' He lifted her chin and kissed her on the tip of her nose. 'Can I see you later?' His voice was husky.

'I don't know.' Rose looked away.

'Why?' Dan sounded confused.

'What about Gardenia?'

Dan sighed heavily. 'I *will* sort things out.' The doorbell rang again. 'If that's her, I'm not here,' he said wryly.

'It should be my client,' Rose said. 'But if it's the rest of the Milton Keynes police force, then I'm not here either.'

Dan smiled. 'Whoever it is, I think I'd better go.' He kissed her lightly on the lips. 'I'll have to come back because I still owe you for my massage,' he said as an afterthought.

Rose pulled a face. 'I can't charge you after this! Then I really would feel like a prostitute.'

'Who said I was going to pay you in cash?'

Chapter Twenty-Four

FRANKINCENSE
A dark oil with a fresh top note and a warm rich tone
underpinning it. It modifies the scent of citrus oils,
particularly, Melissa. Frankincense is valued for healing
blemishes, wounds and old scars. It is a buffer for anxiety
and helps to bring spiritual enlightenment, unlock deep-
seated stress and release the battle-weary spirit.

from: *The Complete Encyclopaedia of Aromatherapy Oils*
by Jessamine Lovage

'What the hell's happened here?' Frank Cox said as he
came in the front door. Presumably he had noticed that
the twenty-four-tune doorbell was lying smashed to
smithereens on the hall floor. 'Mel!' he shouted.

She heard him check the lounge and the kitchen.
'Melissa!' he shouted again and she heard him race up
the stairs two at a time. The bedroom door was flung
open and Melissa flinched as it rebounded on the Garden
of Romance wallpaper. Her soft furnishings were certainly
taking some punishment today.

The blood drained from Frank's face when he finally
registered that she was tied to the bed with standard issue
police handcuffs, wearing nothing but her birthday suit,
with a Ventolin asthma inhaler held in her mouth with a
stocking. As he stared at her, his face ashen, she thought

she had never loved him more than at this moment.

'Are you all right?' he gasped faintly when he finally managed to speak.

Melissa nodded pleasantly.

'Have we had burglars or something?'

'SUFFTHIFF,' Melissa said enigmatically.

He came to the bed and with trembling fingers untied the stocking. The inhaler fell into her lap. Clasping her to him roughly, he said, 'Did they hurt you?' His voice was cracking with emotion.

'Er, no,' Melissa admitted. Although, to be fair, it had been jolly uncomfortable waiting for Frank to come home. She'd started to get cramp in her big toe on the foot that was handcuffed to the bed. 'And it wasn't a *them*, either,' she said sheepishly.

'*One* man did this?'

'Er, yes,' Melissa conceded.

'Didn't you struggle?'

'Er, a bit.'

'*A bit?*'

'I suppose.'

Frank closed his eyes and took a steadying breath. 'Did he threaten you with a knife?'

'A knife?' Explaining this was proving harder than Melissa had expected. Perhaps it was because of the shock of finding her like this. If she had been able to break it gently to him over a cottage pie, it might have been easier. But then, if she'd been able to tell him over a cottage pie, she wouldn't have told him at all.

'A knife,' Frank repeated. 'Did he have a knife?'

'Er, not *exactly*.'

'My poor love.' Frank squeezed her to him again, which was also uncomfortable as she was still handcuffed to the bed. He looked at her earnestly. 'This is what they call post-traumatic shock syndrome. Policemen get it all the time. It makes you unable to think or speak properly.'

'Oh, I see.' Melissa nodded sagely. 'That's nice.'

'I'm going to phone the police.' He spoke slowly and loudly to her, like you do when you're speaking to a Frenchman and you can't speak French.

'Frank, you are the police,' she pointed out.

'I know, but I have to report this – this hideous crime.' His slow, loud voice was quivering with tears.

Melissa cleared her throat. 'There's something I need to tell you, Frank. You must listen carefully.' She wriggled to make herself more comfortable. 'There hasn't actually been a crime.'

'Oh, my darling.' He stroked her hair. 'You're more deranged than I thought.'

'I've been meaning to tell you,' she lied. 'I've been doing a little part-time job for some time now.'

'Cleaning for Dave at the vicarage?' Frank looked puzzled. 'I know about that.'

'No,' she replied. 'In addition to cleaning for Dave at the vicarage.'

'What?' Frank looked even more puzzled.

'Er, I don't quite know how to put this,' Melissa said hesitantly. 'I've been doing some work from home.'

'Work from home?' Frank now looked completely lost. 'What sort of work from home?'

Melissa could feel her breasts turning pink. 'Er, this sort of work,' she said bluntly.

'*This* sort of work?' Frank repeated.

'Er, yes.'

It took a few moments for it to sink in. He looked at her incredulously. 'You're a hooker!' His voice had lost its quiver and had gone up an octave.

A frown crossed Melissa's face. 'There's no need to be like that!'

'You're a hooker! And you tell me there's no need to be like this?'

'I like to think of myself as a social service,' she said. 'A sort of recreational therapist for the unhappy and the inadequate.'

'And presumably one of your unhappy and inadequate basket cases did this to you?'

Melissa looked sullenly at him and she hung limply from her handcuffs.

Frank put his head in his hands, massaging his fingertips through his thinning hair. 'Why do you need to do it, Mel?' He looked at her pleadingly. 'Don't I . . . don't I *satisfy* you?'

'It's nothing to do with that!' she protested. 'Don't think that. This is totally separate. I've only been doing it so that I could put some money away for a rainy day.'

He stared at her with open-mouthed astonishment. 'You buy an umbrella for a rainy day, Melissa, not become a hooker.' He shook his head as if it would help him to understand. 'Especially not when your husband's a policeman.'

'Don't be difficult, Frank,' she appealed. 'It's not like you.'

'Don't be difficult!' Frank slammed his palm against his forehead. 'I come home from a hard day at work to find you've been handcuffed to the bed wearing nothing but a Ventolin inhaler in your mouth. I have visions of rape, pillage and burglary on a scale never previously seen in Great Brayford and then you tell me calmly that you're a hooker – sorry, recreational therapist – and that it was one of your cranky customers who tied you up like an oven-ready turkey for fun.' Frank sighed – a sigh that contained extreme sorrow. 'I don't think I'm being difficult, Mel. I think I'm exhibiting the type of patience any self-respecting saint would be proud of.'

'They don't do it for fun, they do it for £69.99,' Melissa said tetchily. 'And it wasn't a cranky customer, as you so nastily put it. It was Detective Constable Elecampane.'

'Elephant's brain!' Franks eyes went round like saucers.

'What in heaven's name was he doing here?'

'He's one of my nice regulars.'

'Nice!' he exclaimed. 'I suppose I should be grateful your inhaler was only stuck in your mouth and not in any other orifice. He's not nice, he's a sadistic bastard!'

'No, he's not,' she protested. 'Quite the opposite, in fact.' He had seen the sharp end of her Kenwood food processor spatula often enough for her to know.

Frank wouldn't be placated. 'Next you'll be telling me that he helps children and old ladies across the street,' he said.

'Now you're just being an old crosspatch.' If she could have, Melissa would have folded her arms.

'And you're being unbelievably naive, Mel.' He got off the bed and began to pace the floor. 'Have any more of my colleagues from the Milton Keynes constabulary tied you to the bed while I've been working afternoon shift?'

'Speaking of which.' She nodded her head towards her handcuffs.

Frank crossed the room and, with an unhappy huffing noise, fumbled in his pocket for his handcuff key and started to undo them.

'Our little secret's safe,' Melissa assured him. 'There was only DC Elecampane.' She paused hesitantly. 'And, of course, one or two others.'

Franks face suffused with a blood-red hue.

'They speak very highly of you,' she added quickly.

'What am I going to do with you, Melissa?' her husband wailed. 'You've ruined me!'

'Don't take on so,' she said. 'I haven't ruined you. I love you.' Melissa snuggled against his stiff body. She wanted to rub her wrists and her ankles, they were throbbing like mad, but she thought it best to leave it until later. It made you wonder whatever possessed her clients to want to pay £69.99 a week for it. She couldn't see the attraction herself at all.

'I wanted us to have a baby.' She softened her voice and fiddled with the buttons on Frank's shirt. 'I thought if I could do a bit of work on the side, it would help us to buy nice things. I've got quite a nest egg put by.'

'I don't think I want to know this,' Frank said. 'I couldn't cope with being married to a hooker *and* a tax fraud.'

Melissa ignored him and continued, 'You want our baby to have nice things, don't you? And the work I do for Dave doesn't pay very much. I wanted to help.'

Frank gripped her hands and held her away from him. He looked squarely at her. 'Let me see if I've got this right,' he said in a well-modulated voice. 'You set yourself up as a hooker because you wanted to save up for us to have a baby. That's what you're saying?'

Melissa nodded and smiled.

'Melissa, are you on the same planet as the rest of us?' he asked sincerely.

She pouted petulantly. 'I didn't want you to worry about money.'

'Don't you think that knowing my wife is a hooker will cause me even more worry?'

Melissa looked downcast. 'Probably.'

'*Probably*,' Frank repeated softly. 'At last we're getting somewhere.'

'I won't do it again, Frank,' she said earnestly. 'I was going to give it up anyway.'

'That's comforting to know,' he said.

'I'll be a good little housewife from now on,' she promised.

'Are you sure?' he asked. 'Wouldn't you be better off with someone your own age, who could give you a bit more excitement?'

'No.' She shook her head, tears filling her eyes. 'I've only ever wanted you.' Pushing thoughts of one mad moment of lust for Bob Elecampane to the back of her mind, she resolved to love her husband more. And to prove it she would make him cottage pie every night of the week, and she wouldn't complain if he came home late and it was burnt. 'I love you, Frank,' she sniffed. 'Do you love me?'

He shook his head, looking more than slightly bewildered. 'Surprisingly, I do,' he said.

'Then we won't mention this again,' Melissa said firmly.

'I guess not,' Frank agreed.

Melissa flung her arms round him. 'I love you!'

'So you've said,' Frank replied. 'Look,' he disentangled himself from her. 'I've got a lot to think about. Today couldn't really be classed as one of the best days of my life.' He rubbed his thumb along his eyebrows. 'Why don't you get yourself dressed while I go down to the Black Horse for a contemplatory pint with Reg?'

'There's one thing you haven't said,' Melissa pressed. She thought Frank looked older, more tired and more burdened. Perhaps this wasn't the best time to mention it.

'I can't imagine what.' His tone was resigned.

'You didn't say whether we could have a baby or not,' she said coyly.

He smiled, but it was a tired smile – a mouth smile, not an eyes smile. 'Yes,' he said. 'We can. But only if it's a boy. I don't think I could survive with two women like you in the house.'

Chapter Twenty-Five

'Would you like your Geonese apple cake up the ladder or are you going to come down for it?' Angelica asked.

Anise peered at her over the top of the binoculars and turned up her nose. 'You've been making cakes out of old and rotten apples again,' she said in an accusing tone.

'They're not old and rotten. Their skins are just wrinkled. Inside they're perfectly all right.' She sliced the Geonese apple cake and arranged it on the plate with a napkin. 'A bit like us really,' she said wistfully.

Anise tutted. 'Blow your blessed cake. I want to stay here and see what's going on. That policeman's still in there.' She gesticulated at Rose's cottage with the binoculars.

'How do you know he's a policeman?' Angelica inquired politely, nibbling the end of her cake.

'You can tell them a mile away,' Anise informed her. 'It's true what they say – they're all flat-footed.'

'And looking younger every year.' Angelica sighed regretfully. She sank into one of the faded chintz armchairs and regarded her sister who was balanced, rather precariously she thought, at the top of the ladder.

'Besides,' Anise continued. 'I saw him speaking into his walkie-talkie.'

'It could have been a mobile phone – everyone has them these days.'

'I don't have one,' Anise reminded her. 'And you don't have one either.'

'Everyone apart from us,' Angelica conceded. She picked crumbs from the arm of the chair. 'He could just be another client.' She looked up. 'She could be taking group bookings and having a gang bang.'

'A *gang bang*!' Anise's interest quickened and she fiddled with the focus on her binoculars. After a moment of intense focusing, she turned and stared at her sister through eyes narrowed to suspicious slits. 'What do you know about *gang bangs*?'

'Very little, I'm afraid. They never did seem to catch on in Great Brayford.'

Anise huffed through her nose and turned back to the window, flicking the curtain aside to improve her view. 'Oh, here we go. The door's opening.'

'I don't know how you can see anything, it must be pitch dark out there now.'

'It's never dark up the lane any more with all her security lights flashing on and off every five seconds. It's like living next door to a lighthouse.'

'You can get infrared binoculars these days – built into a helmet. The baddies used them in *Patriot Games* to catch Harrison Ford in the dark.' Angelica dabbed at the corners of her mouth with her napkin, folded it and put it back on her plate. 'I think you'd look rather fetching in one of those. And it would take the strain off your arms.'

Anise wheeled round and glared at her. 'For a woman of your mature years, Angelica, you do talk a lot of tommyrot!'

'Perhaps I could borrow them from you on Sundays. I wouldn't mind having a go at catching Harrison Ford in the dark. He's well on his way to drawing his pension, but you would never think it, would you?'

'The policeman's leaving. I wonder what he had to say to them. Whatever it was, I bet it's managed to knock the smiles of their impudent young faces.'

'I don't know why you don't just leave them in peace,' her sister said. 'What harm are they doing to anyone?'

'Harm? *Harm?*' Anise roared. 'You need to ask what harm?'

Anise's face had turned puce and Angelica was glad she had moved the Geonese apple cake from the coffee table, otherwise Anise might have inadvertently sprayed it with spittle.

'You talk about that *girl* as if she's the Virgin Mary. When, as far as I can see – which is pretty far with these little beauties,' Anise patted her binoculars affectionately, 'they are both lowering the moral tone of Great Brayford. Her with her blasted *aromatherapy* and him with his tower block.' Anise leaned heavily on the top rung of her ladder. 'The very fabric of village life is at stake here.'

'And do you really think that standing up a ladder, spying on them through binoculars, is the best way to perpetuate the finest traditions of country living?'

'I like to do my part,' Anise retorted.

Angelica stood up and briskly brushed the remnants of Geonese apple cake from her skirt. 'Great Brayford has always had couples living together without being married and husbands sleeping with their wives' best friends. And how many vicars in the past few years have been caught with one of the congregation with their cassocks hitched up round their waists?' She clashed the china tea plates together as she tidied them away. 'More than I care to remember, that's how many. There isn't a day that goes by when there isn't some whiff of scandal. I'm surprised we haven't had a knocking shop up till now – we're probably long overdue for one.'

Anise's face had darkened to a rich burgundy hue. 'If I was your mother, I'd wash your mouth out with soap,' she spat.

'Well, you're not,' Angelica said, heading for the kitchen.

'You're just my cantankerous older sister.' She turned and glared at her. 'And if *I* were *your* mother, I'd wash your *mind* out with soap.'

Anise was about to speak, but snapped her mouth shut instead. 'Wait a minute,' she said, raising her binoculars. 'The front door's just banged. Just as I thought, it's him.' She sniggered triumphantly. 'And the smile certainly looks like it's been knocked off his face.'

'I hope you're satisfied with yourself,' Angelica said with disgust.

'Oh, my.' Anise craned her head at an unnatural angle. 'The smile *has* been knocked off his face.' There was a note of anxiety in her voice. 'He looks very unhappy indeed.' The anxiety increased to panic. 'Oh my word. Angelica!' She turned to her sister, spinning round on the ladder; the binoculars slipped from her grasp and she reached out to catch them, losing her footing. In a flurry of cashmere, chiffon and pearls, Anise fell to the floor, landing with a sickening, unhealthy crack.

'Heavens above.' Angelica abandoned the plates and rushed to Anise's side. 'Are you hurt?' she asked her sister, who very much looked as if she was.

'Ohh, ohh,' Anise groaned. Her face had taken on a ghostly pallor as she nursed her leg which was bent at an angle not normally associated with the range of human legs. 'I don't know how I will live with the shame,' she lamented.

'Come now, Anise. Don't take on so.' Angelica patted her hand. 'I'll telephone for the doctor, he'll be here as soon as he can. Just lie still.' She smiled kindly at her sister. 'Everyone's entitled to be a little clumsy sometimes.'

'It's not that, you idiot!' Anise snarled. 'Builder's Bottom is heading this way, looking absolutely ferocious. He waved his fist at me – right down my binoculars.' She turned fearful eyes to her sister and clutched at her hand. 'I'm afraid, Angelica, that I've been rumbled.'

Chapter Twenty-Six

'It's broken,' Dan said flatly, kneeling at Anise's side. 'At least, I think so.' He looked at Anise with a sympathetic smile. Her face was grey with pain and the fine, tight lines seemed to be etched that bit deeper. 'The ambulance won't be long now. Try to relax, if you can.'

Anise leaned back against the velvet fringed cushions he had propped against the stepladder behind her and began to weep gently.

Angelica touched his arm. 'Thank you, Dan. You've been very kind, when I'm sure she doesn't deserve it.'

Anise wept a little louder.

'That's okay,' he assured her. He gave her a guilty look. 'I do feel partly responsible.'

'That's nonsense,' Angelica retorted. 'She's no one to blame but herself. If you go poking your nose into other people's business, it sometimes has a habit of poking you back.'

'Maybe you're right,' he agreed.

'I know I am,' she said firmly. 'Now, I'm going to go into the garden to tell Basil. He'll only go into a panic if he see's an ambulance coming. I can't believe he's still here. Goodness only knows what he's doing in the shed at this time of night. I think I'd better make a lot of noise as I approach him, don't you?' She gave Dan a rueful smile.

'When you've seen Basil, can you pop across and tell Rose too?' Dan lowered his voice. 'I came over here threatening to kill Anise. I wouldn't want her to think that I'd actually done it.'

'I would normally say what a shame, but it somehow seems churlish under the circumstances,' Angelica whispered back. 'Though why she hasn't been assassinated before now is beyond me. She's managed to make enough enemies.'

Dan suppressed a smile. 'We shouldn't speak ill of the broken-legged,' he said. 'Go and tell the others, I'll stay with her until the ambulance arrives.'

Angelica did as instructed, coughing loudly as she approached the garden shed and clicking her heels on the concrete path. Anise always said she shouldn't wear high heels at her age, that they would stunt her growth and give her osteoporosis or she'd fall over and break her leg. Ironic really. And if, at seventy years old, despite decades of squashing her feet into stilettos, she still hadn't succumbed to bunions or corns or fungus-thickened in-growing toenails, she was damned if she was going to start wearing Clark's sensible footwear now. Heels gave a woman a shapely turn of leg, no matter what age.

It was a balmy evening, the damp warmness of spring in the air. The garden was looking a picture. Even in the gloom she could tell that there was no superfluous grass growing in the path, and Basil seemed to be making a career out of edging the lawn. It looked considerably smarter than he did. Perhaps it would be fit for the Great Brayford Open Gardens Day, but it was doubtful that Anise would want hordes of sightseers with ice creams paying a pound to wander among the petunias.

Angelica paused and coughed again outside the shed door. What old men did in sheds was one of life's mysteries that had never revealed itself to Angelica. And she didn't want it to reveal itself now in the form of Basil.

She was relieved, when she did open the door, to see

that Basil was browsing through a Suttons seed catalogue rather than the *Playboy* or *Penthouse* she had feared. He hurried his seed catalogue away just as guiltily though.

'Angelica,' he said, peering at her like a startled bird through his monocle. 'What brings you to the shed at this hour?'

She folded her arms protectively across her chest. 'A little domestic crisis, I'm afraid, Basil.'

'Crisis?'

She perched on the edge of the potting shelf. 'Now, I don't want you to panic,' she said, touching his arm reassuringly. 'But I'm afraid the love of your life has had a nasty accident.'

'Anise?' Basil's eyebrows shot into his hairline, merging his facial hair into one unruly mess. He looked remarkably like a rat peeping through an untidy hedge.

'Yes, Anise.'

'Accident?'

'Dan's looking after her until the ambulance arrives. Very capably, I might add.'

'Anise? Accident?' Basil repeated in a dazed way.

Perhaps he had believed Anise was invincible, Angelica thought. Perhaps they all did. A shiver of fear ran through her. It was the first time she had seen her sister vulnerable. She sent a quick prayer to God that he spare her sister. And if he did spare her, could he also make her nicer.

'Yes,' Angelica said. 'We think she's broken her leg. Help is on its way.'

'Accident? Anise?' Pennies obviously took a long time to drop into Basil's slot. He looked blankly at Angelica. 'I must go to her side,' he said.

'Come on, then.' Angelica held her arm out for him. 'I'll help you.' She levered him out of the folding deck chair by his lilac shell suit. 'Perhaps we'll find you a little snifter of brandy, Basil. You look like you could do with it.' But then he always did, she thought.

* * *

Rose appeared in the driveway at the same time as the ambulance did. Her jacket was slung round her shoulders and she was huddling into it like a hibernating doormouse. The blue light rotated with a languid rhythm, illuminating her face with a pale, translucent sheen. She looked flushed and fraught and very fanciable, Dan thought miserably. He stood watching helplessly as the ambulance men loaded the still-whimpering Anise into the back of the ambulance. Crossing to where Rose stood, he laid his arm across her shoulders and squeezed gently. 'I'm going to drive Angelica and Basil to the hospital and wait with them. I don't know how long I'll be.'

She looked up at him and there were dark smudges under her eyes. 'Do you want me to come too?'

'No.' He shook his head. 'You look tired. Besides, three is a crowd, four would probably count as a mob. Have you finished your client?'

'Yes.'

'Why don't you put your feet up and relax. I'll call by later and let you know how she is.'

'Was it our fault, Dan?'

'Ladies of a certain age shouldn't climb stepladders to spy on their neighbours.' He looked at her ruefully. 'And I shouldn't have charged over there like a raging bull. I'll apologise to her when she's *compos mentis* again. Though it's doubtful she'll forgive me.'

Angelica came to join them. 'The ambulance is about to leave. Are you ready, Dan?'

'I'll go and get the car.'

'Should you really be driving?' Rose asked. 'What about your back?'

'You must be a miracle worker,' Dan said. 'I can't feel a thing.'

'Be careful.' Rose looked at him tenderly and touched his arm.

He wanted to kiss her – on her nose, on her mouth, on her throat, on her . . .

Angelica shuffled impatiently next to him.

'I'm coming,' he said. The ambulance started to reverse. He looked at Rose. 'I'll see you later.'

Their eyes locked and they exchanged '*a look*'. It was the only way Dan could describe it. It was a look that signalled a shift in their relationship, the subtle movement to a deeper, more intimate understanding of each other. A look that said, I need you as you need me. A look that said, the future is for us. The knowledge of it thrilled through his veins.

'Possibly a lot later,' he added.

'I'll be waiting,' she said.

Chapter Twenty-Seven

'You don't look your normal self, Frank.' Reg finished pulling his pint and placed it on the bar in front of him. It was a quiet night in the Black Horse. A few locals who had nursed the same half-pint of bitter for the last hour played dominoes in the corner of the snug. Despite the fact that the dominoes were almost devoid of spots, they shunned the brand new old-fashioned pub games that Reg had bought in to keep the lawyers and the oil men entertained – classics such as shove-ha'penny, draughts and cribbage. They went down a storm with Perrier water and Lollo Rosso.

Frank pulled the glass to him and regarded its contents coolly. 'Got a lot on my mind, Reg.'

'Would some pork scratchings help to take some of it away?' Reg waved one of the last three dozen remaining packets at him. 'On the house?'

Frank shook his head. 'No thanks, Reg. I'd probably break a tooth on one and then I'd have even more to worry about. It's been one of those days.'

Reg opened the packet himself. After regarding one of the pork scratchings disdainfully, he popped it into his mouth with a grimace. 'It's not like you to worry, Frank. You're the one that normally sorts out other people's problems.'

Frank took a gulp of beer and wiped the froth from his lips. 'Well, this time I've got problems of my own.'

'Anything I can help with?' Reg leaned on the bar, his elbows oblivious of the damp beer towel beneath them.

'No,' Frank said seriously. 'But thanks for asking, mate.'

'What are mates for?' Reg said stoutly. He took a swig of his whisky – the first one of the night. Or maybe the second. And smacked his lips in appreciation. 'One of your boys was in here earlier. That Detective Constable Elecampane. Is he a friend of yours?' Reg inquired.

'He's no friend of mine,' Frank answered grimly.

'Funny bugger,' Reg said directly. 'Can't say I'm over-fond of him myself. He was making up to Cassia Wales. Or she was making up to him, it was hard to tell which.'

Frank's interest quickened. 'Was he now?'

'Anyway,' Reg carried on, 'they left together, snug as two bugs in a rug, and her old man's away in the Bahamas.' He gave Frank a knowing look.

Frank put his pint down. 'Is he now?'

'I think she's a bit of a one on the quiet,' Reg said sagely. 'She comes in here full of airs and graces but she certainly looked like she was up for a bit of rough. No offence meant, Frank.'

'None taken, Reg.' Frank pursed his lips. 'And what time did you say that was?'

Reg glanced at the clock. It was shaped like a pint of Guinness and the second hand moved round stealthily with a glob of imitation froth on the end. 'An hour or so ago at a guess. Not that long.'

Frank drained his pint. 'Fill that up for me again, Reg. I'll be back in a minute.'

He strode purposefully out of the door, leaving an open-mouthed Reg trying to work out what exactly he had said.

DC Elecampane's car was parked outside the pub. Frank hadn't noticed it when he came in and he wondered why. It was a flashy motor, arrogant and showy. All go-faster stripes and fur trimmings. The lads at the station jokingly called it the 'Crumpet Catcher', which didn't seem quite so funny now. Had Melissa been caught in it? The thought of it made him feel sick. Sicker than the thought of Elecampane in his bed.

The car had a sticker in the back window saying 'COPPERS DO IT IN HANDCUFFS'. Frank didn't realise just how appropriate that statement was, but the thought of Melissa handcuffed to the bed – their bed – in the buff, gave him the red mist of rage that he needed to complete his task.

Frank had never experienced cold fury before. He had always been a reasonable man. Calm, collected, conservative. He was known for it. Now reason deserted him. Well, not entirely all reason. He wanted to smash Elecampane's car into a pulp. He wanted to shatter its smug little windscreen, punch it on its pugnacious little nose and kick the chrome off its shiny pristine hubcaps. But that would be criminal damage and Frank Cox had never done anything criminal in his life. What little reason he had left told him that criminally damaging Elecampane would be infinitely more rewarding than a futile skirmish with a clapped-out Ford Scorpio.

He turned his attention to Lavender Hill, striding up to the Wales's house, determination written in bold capitals across his face. It was a large house. Palatial compared to his own neat terraced cottage. It had been built in the late seventies and, typical of properties of that era, offered precious little that was aesthetically pleasing. Frank scanned the glass-panelled front door. There appeared to be no bell, just a brass door knocker that was fashioned in the shape of a deformed fox with a rigid brush. It was as tasteless as Melissa's choice of a twenty-four-tune doorbell had been. Or what remained of it. Whatever they replaced it with, it wouldn't be one of these things.

Frank rapped at the door with the paws of the unlikely looking fox. 'Cassia,' he shouted through the letter box – also brass. 'Get that bastard Elecampane out here. Now!'

He paced the length of the front porch until with much clinking and clunking of brass door locks, Cassia Wales appeared furtively at the front door. Her hair made Basil's look as if it was styled by Nicky Clarke. She was flushed and florid and wore a short cotton kimono with a fierce red dragon embroidered over the fullness of her siliconed breast. Presumably a gift from one of Greg's conferences in the Far East. 'What do you want, Frank?' she asked timidly.

'Get him out here!' Frank snarled.

'He won't come,' she said.

'Then I'll come in and make him.' He pushed Cassia to one side.

'There's no need for that.' Bob appeared behind her in the hall. He sauntered to the front door wearing only his Dennis the Menace boxer shorts and leaned casually on the frame. A smarmy grin spread across his face. 'How's Melissa?' he said smugly.

Frank grabbed him by the arm, shocking the smile from his face, and pulled him into the drive. 'People like you give the force a bad name,' he said tightly. He drew back his arm and before Bob knew what had hit him, Frank had – cannoning him to the ground with a powerful right hook to the jaw.

Bob lay dazed on the block-paved drive, his eyes spinning erratically like a row of plums in a fruit machine. He licked his lip, which was split, a bloody line trickling from his mouth. His hand lifted tentatively and touched his jaw.

Frank wagged his finger at him aggressively. 'Don't you come near my wife again, elephant's brain,' he said darkly. He showed him the fist that had just made such fine contact with his chin, waving it with menace for good measure. '*That* was just a taster.' He turned, brushing his hands together as if to remove some unwanted dirt, and walked calmly away down Lavender Hill.

Bob sprang to his feet. 'I don't need her any more anyway!' he shouted after Frank. He flicked his thumb towards Cassia. 'This one only cost me two gin and tonics. She may not have been as good, but she was a darn sight cheaper!'

Frank carried on walking steadily down the hill. Bob snorted unhappily and turned back towards the house. Cassia's face was blacker than thunder. There was as much steam coming out of her nostrils as there was from the dragon at her breast, which was now heaving with indignant rage.

'You cheeky jumped-up bastard!' she spat. 'I don't know exactly what's been going on, but I don't like the sound of it.'

A thrill of panic ran through Bob. 'That was for his benefit,' he said ingratiatingly. 'I didn't mean it.' He put on his best wheedling tone. 'You were well worth two gin and tonics.'

The steam from Cassia's flaring nostrils was joined by steam from her ears. She stepped towards him. 'Say that again!' she ordered.

'I just said—'

'No.' Cassia held up her hand. 'Don't bother.' She struck a pose inspired by the late Bruce Lee and with a punch that rivalled Frank's. Bob Elecampane was sent sprawling, once again, to the ground.

She disappeared into the house and a moment later returned with a bundle of clothes. Bob lay inert on the block paving, all vital signs having temporarily ceased. Dennis the Menace grinned maniacally from his boxer shorts. It was a chill night and, if she was lucky, he might die of hypothermia. With a humourless smile, Cassia tossed the clothes on top of him and closed the door.

★ ★ ★

'You took your time,' Reg said as Frank sat down on his bar stool again. He placed his pint in front of him.

'I had a small errand to run, Reg,' he replied. 'A very small errand.'

'Well, it's certainly cheered you up, mate.'

Frank rubbed his knuckles and with a slow smile picked up his pint. 'You know, I think it has,' he said, his grin widening. 'I think I might have a packet of your finest pork scratchings after all, Reg. Suddenly, I'm feeling much, much better.'

Chapter Twenty-Eight

A five-hour wait in casualty wasn't unusual, the nurse assured Dan pleasantly when he complained for the twentieth time. He returned to his seat, crestfallen. It was the nature of the NHS in the 1990s – under-paid, under-staffed and under threat of closure.

They all sat in silence on hard orange plastic chairs, Angelica fussing around bringing them, at regular intervals, cups of disgusting grey fluid from a vending machine that purported to be tea, while Anise groaned unnervingly with pain. Around them people bled quietly from various slashes, bashes and gashes into grubby handkerchiefs and wished for death to come upon them rather than suffer the interminable wait for a proper bandage. Only those that vomited brought prompt attention for themselves. They were whisked briskly into one of the cubicles populated by white-coated, white-faced youthful doctors, where people went in but curiously never seemed to come out again. Dan looked up from his three-year-old copy of *Woman's Own* and the joys of using a loofah to eradicate stubborn cellulite, checked his watch yet again and thought about trying to persuade Anise to vomit so that he could go home and see Rose.

It was gone one o'clock in the morning by the time he eventually steered the Discovery up Lavender Hill and along the mud-gouged ruts of the dark lane. Basil sat next to him in the front seat, while Angelica rocked rhythmically in the back. They were all bleary-eyed and bone-weary. Anise's leg had been x-rayed and then she was wheeled off to the wards.

Dan glanced at Rose's cottage as he passed. There was a light on in the hall but, other than that, it seemed to be in darkness and what was left of his spirit deflated like a leaky balloon. She had probably been tucked up in her bed for hours and who could blame her? He should have phoned her from the hospital, but at the time he felt it would negate his excuse for calling on her when he got back. And he desperately wanted an excuse to call on her.

'Can I offer you a cup of tea, Dan?' Angelica said as they pulled up outside her front door. 'One that actually tastes like tea.'

He turned in his seat. 'No thanks, Angelica. I'd better get back, Gardenia doesn't know where I am. She may be worried.' But it was unlikely, he added to himself.

She patted his arm. 'Thank you for all you've done.'

'I feel awful about the whole thing,' he admitted.

'You shouldn't,' she reassured him. 'Anyway, she's in good hands now. *Finally.*' She turned to their companion. 'Basil, may I tempt you?'

'Would it be too much trouble, dear lady?'

'Not at all. I'd be glad of the company for a few minutes. This is the first time I've ever come home to an empty house. Anise has always been there before, waiting up for me.' She sighed thoughtfully. 'A bit like a jailer really.'

'Then let me do the honours.' Basil swung out of his seat and opened the door for Angelica. With an unexpected display of chivalry, he took her arm and helped her from the car. She giggled girlishly and Dan watched them as he escorted her gallantly to the front door, his lilac shell suit fluorescing vividly in the moonlight. Wasn't it supposed to be Anise that Basil had the hots for? Basil stood by attentively as Angelica dug in her handbag for her key and for once in his life he didn't look stark staring mad.

Angelica turned and waved. Dan took his cue and swung the car out of the drive, taking a final forlorn, longing glance towards the sleeping Rose who had said she would wait – but hadn't.

Builder's Bottom was also in darkness, but this time he felt a wave of relief. It meant that Gardenia wouldn't be standing behind the door brandishing a rolling pin. Not that she'd ever done that, but there was always a first time.

He unlocked the door quietly and tiptoed into the kitchen, grateful for once that Fluffy had lost the urge to bark at anyone who invaded his home and instead tried to beat them to death with the enthusiastic wagging of his tail. It was an unusual ploy for a guard dog and one that Dan was rarely pleased to encourage. Fortunately, the burglary rate in Great Brayford was minimal and Fluffy had not been called upon to put the method of defence by over-affection into practice.

Dan fed him – because Gardenia hadn't – and then sat nursing a scalding cup of tea between his hands, wishing that Fluffy would make less noise chasing his metal bowl round the York stone floor. It was ridiculous, this was his home, built by the sweat of his brow – and his brother Alan's – paid for by the toil of his hands, yet increasingly he was dreading coming home and being made to feel unwanted and uncomfortable. An interloper in his own lounge. This couldn't go on. He had said it before, but now it was time for action.

Something had to be done about the situation. Rose wouldn't wait for him for ever. What would they be doing now if she had still been awake? He closed his eyes and images of her silken skin, the intoxicating smell of the elusive perfumes that enveloped her, and the firm, gentle, strong, stroke of her hands tingled his tired senses. His mouth would be travelling the delicious curves of her body, their limbs entwined like wrestling octopuses, their bodies on fire with heat, desire and lust. Then he would have to contend with her bra.

Dan sighed and took a sip of his tea. He put his finger to his lips, encouraging Fluffy to eat less boisterously. He had never been good at bras. It was a lack of practical experience. Gardenia was the only woman whose underwear he had intimate knowledge of and after some youthful fumbling, Gardenia had decided it was easier and considerably quicker to take off her bra herself.

Sex was never like it was in films. A whole scene could be dedicated to peeling off each other's clothes. Five minutes to tempt one reluctant, confining button to freedom. Not a pot belly or a saggy breast in sight either.

In reality, it was hopping round the bedroom floor with one foot stuck in your boxer shorts and a quick dive under the duvet because you'd come back from the pub fancying a quickie and the central heating had gone off hours ago. It must be something to do with living in the warmth of California that made Hollywood producers think everyone spent hours making love.

He must have been such a disappointment to Gardenia over the years. He had never wanted Hollywood with her. If their love-making had been a film, it would have been a video nasty. A very short one. He didn't want reality with Rose. He wanted fantasy, stimulation of every sense, a journey of limitless imagination and a climax that would leave them breathless, weeping and reaching for their handkerchiefs. He wanted to spend hours uncurling the tight budded petals of her before him. He wanted to undo her bra himself.

It would hurt him to ask Gardenia to leave, they had been together a long time. Too long. Far too long. But that didn't make it any easier. He hated spiders, but he still couldn't kill them. There was something that turned his stomach about squashing them. Every time he found one in the house, he had to endure this self-inflicted performance of coaxing the wretched multi-legged thing into a glass with a newspaper, before bracing himself to carry it to the garden and depositing it on the grass to live another day.

So. How exactly was he going to coax Gardenia into a glass so that he could deposit her outside Builder's Bottom without any bloodshed? She might not have as many legs as a spider, but she could certainly be twice as scary if she put her mind to it.

Chapter Twenty-Nine

Basil was contemplating the building of a compost heap. It was a pleasant preoccupation that didn't, at the moment, involve any work other than leaning on the rake and looking determinedly at the ground. A compost heap was a necessary addition to any eco-friendly garden. Not that Basil was overly concerned with eco-friendliness. There was probably nothing green about shooting squirrels. But without a compost heap where else could you dump the grass cuttings?

It was to be situated at the far corner of the garden, underneath the branches of the hawthorn hedge that bordered the field behind, well out of view of the house. Basil stood and surveyed the site, silhouetted by the early snowy-white blossom on the hedge. Not that there would be any grass cuttings to put on it just yet. Someone had been blessed with the good sense to plant swathes of daffodil bulbs under the large specimen trees which graced the end of the garden, thus providing a wonderful excuse for not mowing the lawn until all the daffs had died.

They were out in flower now and would have looked splendid if it had not been raining persistently since first light. Their heads were bowed, sheltering from the weight of water that stooped their fragile stems. He had thought about not coming to do Rose's garden today. After all, it had been a very late night, what with the trip to hospital with Anise and then the nightcap with Angelica. It had been way past the witching hour when he had finally retired up the stairs to Bedfordshire. And then he hadn't gone straight to sleep. He had lain awake thinking not of Anise – the poor old bat, laid up in hospital with a gammy leg – as might have seemed appropriate, but very definitely of Angelica.

She was a fine woman and he wondered why he had not noticed it before. Her style was elegant and under-stated, well-suited to a woman of her advancing years. There was a strength of character to her that belied her gentle exterior packaging, a softness to her demeanour that had passed her elder sister by at full gallop. Her calm in the face of a crisis was something to be admired. Plus she made damn good tea, a fine strong brew, not overdone with milk so that it tasted like rice pudding. One could ask for little more in a woman.

Besides, he was getting nowhere with Anise. The Viking evening had shown him that she was simply toying with his affections. She had been singularly unimpressed with his fleet-footedness on the dance floor. Her ulterior motive in courting his suit had simply been to get him to spy on Rose. He could see that now. Basil looked up at the house. She was outlined at the kitchen window in her white uniform, washing dishes at the sink.

It was late afternoon and the light was beginning to fade, but if he screwed up his eyes he could see her brushing her hair tiredly out of her eyes with her hand. She was a nice young thing. And, as far as he could tell, there had been no untoward comings and goings, no string of gentlemen being entertained as Anise had intimated. In fact, she could probably do with entertaining a few gentlemen to put a bit of colour back in her pasty cheeks. Despite his initial misgivings, Rose had turned out to be a breath of fresh air. A welcome addition to the village – a bit like mains gas.

Basil regarded the potential compost heap site again and adjusted his position on the rake before he got cramp. The rain had let up slightly, but showed no signs of stopping for the day as that complete no-hoper Michael Fish had promised. Whatever had happened to that soft-voiced, sex god Francis the weatherman? He and his mizzle were something that could always be relied on. If Francis said frost, you could be absolutely sure that you would wake up to frozen pansies and blackened magnolia buds.

With that thought nestling pleasantly in his mind, Basil decided to go home before he risked being called on to do some work. Not that Rose was one to crack the whip. She paid up happily without questioning what he did for his money, unlike Anise who had wanted every blade of grass accounted for. He vowed that he would work harder for Rose tomorrow. And he also vowed that he would no longer be Anise Weston's dupe. She could do her own dirty work from now on.

Basil glanced at the house again. Rose had gone from the window, but – Basil paused and peered through the relentless drizzle. That was odd! He removed his monocle briefly and polished the raindrops from its surface with his sleeve to give him a clearer view. There was a movement at the side of the house. A distinct rustling of the leylandii, caused by more than a stirring of the rain-soaked wind. He narrowed his eyes and stared intently as a man wearing a beige belted Mackintosh, collar up against the pelting rain, emerged from the shadowy recess of the hedge and stood surveying Rose's cottage with more than a passing interest. Wiping the rain from his eyes, Basil watched as the man walked to the door, glancing around him suspiciously. Here was a shifty-looking character if ever there was one. Could he be Rose's pervert? As a stalwart of the Neighbourhood Watch, there was only one thing to be done – he must follow him.

Basil dodged behind the *Thuja Plicata* 'Zebrina' to keep a watch on him unobserved. Fortunately he was wearing his tweed ensemble today as there was precious little in the garden that could camouflage a lilac shell suit. He looked again at the dark-haired stranger. A handsome sort of fellow he supposed. Particularly for a pervert. City-type, neatly knotted tie and highly-polished brogues. He glanced down at his own mud-caked Nikes with disdain and a seed of sartorial dissatisfaction lodged itself deeply in the complex convolutions of Basil's brain, twisting his mouth into a grimace. He crouched down and his keen eyes followed the slow progress of the stranger.

Basil, his Nikes sinking deeply into the soggy grass, lurked in the shelter of the leylandii as the man approached the front door, dodging the puddles that were forming in Rose's gravel path. The furtive visitor looked round, glancing back down the lane. He raked his wet hair from his forehead, adjusted his collar and hesitated, his hand held aloft, before rapping loudly on Rose's front door.

Basil strained to hear the sound of the door swinging open and he pressed himself against the hedge, ready to spring into action – should action be required. He risked a glance from his leafy hiding place and Rose's face looked ashen and troubled. A heavy, elongated rush of breath escaped from her lips which carried on the wind above the pitter-pattering of raindrops. She lifted a hand to her mouth and Basil noticed it was shaking. There was a distinctly uncomfortable silence before she spoke. 'What on earth are you doing here?'

The man smiled uncertainly and buried his hands deep into the pockets of his Mackintosh. 'I could ask you the same thing,' he said.

Chapter Thirty

'Where are you going?' Dan had arrived home from work to hear the sound of wardrobe doors being slammed with a vengeance. The large suitcases that they normally took on their increasingly exotic holidays were open on the bed and Gardenia was flinging clothes into them as though it was her last task on earth.

A black and threatening scowl marred her beautiful face. 'What do you care?'

Dan sank on to the edge of the bed, out of the direct firing line of clothes. 'Of course, I care.' He sounded bemused. 'Are you going on holiday?'

Gardenia's mouth was set in a thin tight line and she regarded him coldly. 'Give me a break!'

'I don't know what this is all about.'

Gardenia paused with a handful of frilly lingerie in mid-air. 'You may think I'm a little green around the edges, but I'm not a total cabbage, Dan.' She flung the frillies at the case. Impressively, she scored a direct hit. 'I don't even want to hear an explanation about where you were last night!'

'Oh, that!' he said with something bordering exasperation. 'I can explain *that*!'

'I said I didn't want to hear.' Gardenia put her hands over her ears to emphasise the point.

'If you care to look,' Dan carried on regardless, 'you'll see that I spent the night in the spare room. The crumpled duvet is a bit of a giveaway.'

'Any idiot can crumple a duvet! It's where you were before that I'd like to know.'

'I was at Milton Keynes hospital with Anise Weston,' he explained in a studiously calm voice. 'She fell off her stepladder and broke her leg. The tibia,' he added for good measure. 'It took five hours for her to be seen and I didn't think you'd appreciate being woken up in the wee small hours to hear about it.'

'What was a woman of her age doing up a stepladder?'

Dan toyed with the fringe of one of the myriad cushions that Gardenia piled high on the bed for artistic effect. They served no other purpose as far as Dan could tell, although at this moment they were proving quite useful for avoiding eye contact. 'It's a long story,' he said cagily.

'I bet it is,' she huffed. 'And why were you there to witness it?'

'I didn't witness it,' he protested. 'I arrived just after it happened.'

'From where?' Gardenia put her hands on her hips, an expectant look fixed rigidly to her face.

You had to get up early to put one over on Gardenia, Dan thought testily. Much earlier than he had. 'I thought you didn't want to hear,' he said flatly.

'This wouldn't have anything to do with *Rose*, would it?' She couldn't say her name without putting on a simpering voice.

'Why do you insist on blaming her for all of our domestic altercations?' Block a difficult question with another question – he had seen it done every week on *Question Time*. It was amazing what you could learn from politicians – the art of wriggling off the hook, for one thing.

'So this has nothing whatsoever to do with Rose?' Gardenia persisted.

'Er, not exactly.' It obviously didn't work so well for him. Damn!

'Not exactly?'

'Not in the biblical sense of the word,' he said feebly.

'You left here – no, – let's get this right. You *hobbled* out of here sometime during the afternoon without telling me where you were going and then reappear a day later, not hobbling, without a word of explanation.'

'I'm trying to tell you now!' Dan raised his voice in frustration. 'If only you'd listen.'

'I think I've done more than my fair share of listening to you, Dan.' There was a chill to Gardenia's voice that he hadn't previously detected. It made the hairs on the back of his neck stand up in alarm. 'And I've done my fair share of watching you.'

'What do you mean?' He wasn't at all sure that he wanted to hear this.

'I've seen the way you look at her.'

It was pointless to ask at who.

'You've never looked at me like that.' She started to slam her array of perfumes – all hideously expensive and all hideously smelly as far as Dan was concerned – into the waiting cavern of her vanity case.

'Like what?'

She stopped and narrowed her eyes at him. 'You lust after her like a Weight-Watcher lusts after a cream cake in a baker's window, your hot little breath steaming up the window, your grubby little hands dying to touch it, and your mouth watering with expectancy.'

Did he? It certainly wasn't the image he was hoping to project. He hoped Rose didn't think of him like that. 'I don't!' he said emphatically.

A momentary flash of sadness stole across Gardenia's harsh features and accusing eyes. 'You've never looked at me like that,' she repeated quietly.

It was true. He couldn't deny it. The last thing in the

world he would ever compare Gardenia to was a cream cake. A sick, guilty weariness washed over him. 'So where are you going?'

'Far enough.'

'Do you have to go now? Right at this minute?'

'There's no need to prolong this, is there?'

'But it's raining.'

'I won't shrink, Dan,' she said tersely. 'Besides, there's no point waiting around to be made a fool of. A laughing stock. You know what this place is like.' Gardenia shrugged tightly. 'They probably all know more than me already.'

'There's nothing *to* know,' Dan said softly.

'You can't fool me, Daniel Spikenard. I know you too well.' Gardenia gave a hollow laugh. It sounded pained and for the first time in a very long time, Dan wanted to hold her. 'Can you say that you don't love her?'

He looked away from her and stared out of the bedroom window. It *was* still raining. All day it had been wet and horrible, the sort of day that made you long for summer and calmer weather. The evenings were getting lighter and it would soon be the first day of spring. A new beginning. A fresh start.

'We can't just end it like this, Gardi,' he pleaded. 'How long have we been together now?'

'The riposte *too long* is very tempting,' Gardenia replied with less venom than she might have used.

'Don't just leave, Gardenia. We need to talk things through.'

'Why?' She sounded tired and weary.

'That's what people do. We've been through a lot together. You can't just walk out.'

She shut the lid of her vanity case. 'Talking is what they do on *EastEnders* and *Emmerdale* and *Home and Away*. I don't need to talk.'

'You should, it's the best therapy.'

'Who told you that?' she laughed. '*Rose?*'

Dan sighed. 'This has nothing to do with Rose.'

'It has everything to do with Rose.' She started to rearrange the clothes in the cases so that they would at least shut. 'She's been like a nasty little fly in the ointment since she arrived.'

'I think that's grossly unfair,' Dan said. 'Things were going wrong long before Rose arrived.'

'She just gave you an excuse to stop trying.'

'It takes two to hold a relationship together, Gardenia.'

'But it only takes one to break it up,' she shot back. She examined her fingernails, before looking at him again. 'I saw you leave together after the Viking supper. You spent the night with her.'

'That was entirely innocent! Nothing happened.'

'By design or by default?' She fixed him with a withering stare.

'By virtue of the fact that I'd drunk more of Reg's Carlsberg than was good for me.' Dan rose to his own defence by jumping from the bed and pacing the bedroom carpet. 'I passed out on her sofa, for heaven's sake. How do you think that makes me feel?'

'Like a prat.' Gardenia was obviously in no mood to commiserate. 'Particularly if you *were* trying to seduce her.'

'It did cross my mind,' he confessed miserably. There seemed little point in pretending otherwise now, either to himself or to Gardenia. He fell silent and leaned against Gardenia's now empty wardrobe, adopting a pose that looked suitably wretched.

'Anyway,' Gardenia continued, clipping the cases shut with a snap that spoke of finality. 'Whoever told you that talking was the best therapy obviously doesn't know much about shopping. Believe me, it beats talking, bingeing and hypnosis hands down every time.'

'There's one small snag with retail therapy, Gardi. Who's going to pay for it now?' Dan asked without malice.

'That's really no concern of yours any more, is it?' She manhandled her cases from the bed to the floor. 'I know you think you've been the great and wondrous provider, but I'm sure I'll manage without you.'

Strong words, but nevertheless Gardenia's face crumpled. Dan felt even more wretched than he looked.

Gardenia sniffed. 'I think it's time I was going.'

'Do you have to?' Dan stepped forward. 'I didn't want it to end like this.'

Gardenia tilted her chin and looked at him defiantly. 'But you did want it to end.'

Their eyes met and they looked at each other levelly and with more honesty than they had ever managed before. Dan nodded.

Gardenia shrugged and gave small sigh. 'Then I wasn't completely mistaken.'

He shook his head. There was a lump in his throat the size of a cricket ball. 'No,' he said softly.

She bent to pick up her cases. Dan stepped forward. 'Let me carry those for you.'

'Can I take the Merc?' she asked.

Dan nodded again. 'It's got a full tank,' he added when the cricket ball had shrunk and he was sure of his voice.

They walked to the Mercedes in silence. Partly because Gardenia's bags were so heavy that carrying them wasn't conducive to continuing a conversation. And partly because it seemed they had run out of things to say. Perhaps Gardi had been right about shopping being the best therapy. Talking had done them precious little good. Maybe it was just a case of too little, too late.

His hand brushed hers as he loaded her bags into the boot. They both jumped slightly at the contact. It was stupid, they had shared a bed, their bodies and their lives for the past ten years – even longer if you counted the bit pre-bed and pre-co-habitation – and now they couldn't even touch a harmless bit of skin without feeling awkward.

'Here,' she said to him. 'You'd better have this back.' Gardenia handed him her credit card.

'Won't you need it?'

'You always were too soft, Dan,' she said without unkindness.

'But you *might* need it,' he said.

'I'll manage.' She got in the car. 'Besides, I might wake up one morning in a foul mood and exact some horrendous financial revenge on you. It's better if I give it back. Clean break and all that.'

He thought he heard a catch in her voice. 'I've never begrudged you money, Gardi.' It was too late to be saying these things now. 'Not really.'

'I know.'

'I'll pay the bill when it comes.'

'That's nice.' She shut the door, but opened the electric window. Dan leaned one hand on the roof of the car. 'Perhaps you should give it to Rose.'

'Don't be like that.'

Gardenia started the engine. 'You're much better suited to her than you were to me.' She put the car into gear. 'Be happy, Dan.'

'You too.' He stood away from the car.

'I did love you,' she said without emotion. 'Once.' The window slid silently back into place, cocooning her in the jaded luxury of a Mercedes with too many miles on the clock.

Gardenia swung out of the drive and Dan watched the tail lights growing smaller as she drove away down Lavender Hill. She turned right towards Milton Keynes and the little red dots disappeared into the enveloping blackness of the night. It was still raining. Dan stared bleakly into the darkness and wondered when the once had been.

Chapter Thirty-One

Rose flicked on the carriage light by the front door and peered through the security peephole. Years of paranoid living in London were hard to undo. People said that villages were far, far safer than cities, but she had still managed to acquire a lurking pervert from somewhere so her insecurities weren't in a tearing hurry to be dashed.

Dan stood at the door. Even in the fish-eye lens she could tell he was white-faced. He looked more scruffy and bedraggled than she had ever seen him. His hair was flattened to his head with rain, making him look as if he'd had an uncontrolled frenzy with a tube of hair gel. Water dripped steadily from his strong aquiline nose and splashed on the coir mat that said 'WELCOME' in big black letters, which she had put there in a vain attempt to stop clients walking muddy shoes through the house.

She was wearing her comfy towelling dressing gown, her hair was wet too – from the shower rather than the rain – and her feet were bare. Which somehow made it worse. Dan had never seen her bare feet apart from the morning after the Viking supper when he had woken up with them wedged under his chin, but at the time he probably wasn't in a fit state to remember it.

Rose opened the door. Halfway. Like you would if it was a double glazing salesman or the milkman who was going to catch you in your dressing gown.

'Hi,' he said, sounding as feeble as he looked.

'Hi,' she replied, leaning on the doorframe and burying herself as deep in the towelling as she could.

His face was illuminated weakly in the 60 watt bulb from the lamp. 'Gardenia's gone.'

'Gone?'

'Gone,' he echoed.

'Where?'

'I don't know.'

'What do you mean you don't know.'

'I don't know where's she's gone.'

'Didn't she say?'

'No.'

'What, nothing?'

'No. She wouldn't talk at all.' He rubbed his hand over his wet hair. 'They say actions speak louder than words and Gardenia's action was to pack a suitcase. Well, two suitcases to be accurate.' He looked pathetically endearing as he looked at her. 'Two very full suitcases.'

'And she just went?'

He nodded and shrugged and raised his eyebrows and made as many other little uncomfortable gestures as one body could cope with in an emotional crisis.

'Why?' Rose persisted.

'She blamed you.'

Rose sighed. 'Why doesn't that surprise me?'

'I don't blame you,' Dan said with a faint smile.

'That's some consolation.' Rose returned his smile.

He stared up at the sky and held out his hand. Great splots of rain splashed on his palm. 'Look, would you mind if I came inside. I'm in serious danger of drowning if I stay out here much longer.'

Rose shifted uneasily against the doorframe, balancing one bare foot on top of the other. 'Er . . .' Her voice stuck in her throat and refused to come out. 'This isn't really a good time,' she said eventually.

Dan looked at her in distress. A drip dripped from his

nose to her doorstep. '*This isn't a good time?*'

She stared sheepishly at the floor. 'Not really.'

Dan laughed and it had an unpleasant hollow ring that scared her. 'I come to you when my life is crumbling round my ears looking for succour, solace and somewhere dry to talk, and you calmly stand there and tell me that this isn't a good time?' Dan shook his head in disbelief. 'When is?'

'I was expecting you to come back last night and you didn't.'

Dan's eyes widened. 'Would that have made a difference?'

She had never heard Dan sound annoyed before. Not *really* annoyed.

'It might have done.' Rose bit her lip nervously.

Primarily, because Hugh hadn't turned up on her doorstep out of the blue then. If Dan had been here to support her when the ex-love-of-her-life had arrived she might have had the courage to tell him to get lost. Hugh not Dan. As it was, she hadn't. And things had changed. They were confused and blurred at the edges and she could feel the panic of insecurity and uncertainty rising in her. Was it simply the jolt of seeing Hugh so unexpectedly that had scattered her emotions to the wind like a handful of Basil's lawn seed? She never thought that he would find her, or even come looking. And just when she thought she had finally got over Hugh he had pulled her back towards him, sucking her down under his charm as deadly as a riptide.

'I was at the hospital with Anise, as well you know,' Dan said. 'For five long hours. I couldn't just abandon ship and rush back to your arms.' A smile pushed through his anger. 'Much as I would have liked to.'

'Is there a problem here, Rosie?' Hugh's laid back drawl drifted from behind her.

Rose's eyes widened with panic.

Dan leaned past her and pushed the door open with a touch more brute force than was necessary outside of a Bruce Willis movie. It swung wide, straining on its hinges. Hugh was standing on the stairs wearing nothing but a peach fluffy towel round his waist and a smug smile.

Rose could feel a blush starting at her toes, which spread up her body until its fire burst out of the top of her dressing gown on to her face.

'No,' she stammered. 'Please leave us alone, we have something to discuss. Privately.'

'Okay.' Hugh winked at her and sauntered back up the stairs.

Dan's face was no longer white, it was black. 'So we've got something to discuss, have we?' he said tightly.

'You were telling me about Gardenia.'

'It doesn't matter now.' He glowered at the empty stair where Hugh had been standing.

Rose sighed and closed her eyes. If she wished very hard perhaps she could make all this go away. She opened her eyes and a very wet, very hurt Dan stared back at her.

'I don't need to ask who that is, do I?' He flicked his thumb towards the stairs.

'Probably not,' Rose said dejectedly. 'And this probably isn't what you think it is, either.'

'Well, I'm glad you're not a mind reader, Rose, because your ears wouldn't just burn if you knew what I was thinking now, they would more than likely explode into balls of flame.'

'Dan, please believe me, nothing's going on.' Tears were trembling on her eyelashes.

'I'm not blind, Rose. Or stupid.'

'He came to talk.'

'Couldn't he have "talked" with his clothes on?' He let his eyes travel disdainfully over her dressing gown. 'And what about you? Did you have to take your clothes off to listen to him?'

'It was an accident.' Rose rubbed the palm of her hands over her eyes. 'I was in my treatment room blending some oils. He leaned over to kiss me—'

'First he's talking, now he's kissing! I take it he didn't get the cold spoon treatment either.'

'*Tried* to kiss me,' Rose corrected bleakly. 'I moved away from him – too quickly – and we knocked over my huge container of almond oil. It went all over Hugh's trousers and I managed to get it all over my clothes when I was trying to mop it up.' She spread her hands in a pleading gesture. 'We were both covered in it. We had to take a shower.'

'Together?'

She turned despondent eyes to him. 'I'm not even going to answer that, Dan.'

He lowered his voice and spoke between gritted teeth. 'I really thought we had something special going. You disappoint me, Rose.'

The tears splashed on to Rose's cheeks. 'What gives you the right to judge me? I've done nothing to be ashamed of.'

That wasn't strictly true. She had done plenty she was ashamed of, but not tonight. It had been so difficult not to give in to Hugh. He had found her and was begging her to go back to him. He was offering her the moon and the stars. It was all she had wanted, longed for, throughout the years they were together. And it could have been hers, but she had turned it down. She had thought of Dan and that had given her the strength she needed to resist him.

'What can I do to make this right?' Rose pleaded.

'Let me in and throw him out,' Dan said starkly.

Rose closed her eyes and breathed heavily. 'I can't do that.'

'Then I might as well leave.' Dan turned to go.

'Please!' Rose tugged his arm and he wheeled back. She edged herself out into the pouring rain. 'He's left his wife for me. Things are all up in the air – I can't just throw him out now. We need to sort this out once and for all. Give me until tomorrow. Twenty-four hours, Dan. That's all I'm asking. I've told you a thousand times it's over with Hugh. Give me until tomorrow and he'll be gone.'

'Tomorrow will be too late.'

'A few hours then. That's all I need.'

Dan stared at her. 'No can do,' he said coldly. 'He goes now or I do.'

'I know you're angry and hurt and this looks really bad, but can't you understand my dilemma?'

'This is a *dilemma*, is it? Oh, I do beg your pardon.'

'You know what I mean, Dan. Don't be like this.' Rose rubbed her forehead. 'I'm not saying the right things because I'm upset and confused.' She sighed and tried to focus her scrambled thoughts. 'Hugh has left his wife *and* his children. Do you understand what that means?'

'Yes,' Dan answered tightly. 'It means he's finally offering you some measly crumb of hope after years of stringing you along. You've said as much yourself.'

Rose felt something snap inside her. She was fed up with being everyone's doormat. Her life was spent trying to please everyone else and she always seemed to end up pleasing no one. Especially herself. There was a blankness inside her and she knew she could take no more. She had tried so hard to become part of the village and still they treated her like an outsider. Dan had been her one true ally. Her one true love. And now even he had turned against her. Enough was enough.

'Were you any different?' Rose challenged him. 'The fact that you were living with Gardenia didn't stop you from wanting to get in my underwear, did it?'

'We weren't married!'

'You mean you didn't have a piece of paper that made

it legal. Emotionally, is it any different? You should have been committed to her.'

Dan's face hardened. 'I can hardly believe you're saying this! You did precious little to discourage me. And for your information, we were jogging along quite nicely until you came along!'

'Were you?' Rose looked astonished. 'Are you sure? Because from where I was standing it looked like you were on your last gasping breaths of an uphill struggle!'

Dan's face was stony and unflinching. 'I once said that I couldn't imagine you as the other woman, Rose. You've made it a lot easier tonight. Thanks for that.'

'Is there anything else you'd like to get off your chest? Or have you quite finished?'

'No, I haven't finished!' Dan was very wet now. His shirt was sticking to his body and his shoes were emitting a nasty little squelch as he paced up and down in front of her. If it hadn't been quite so pitiful, it would have been funny. 'You're right.' He pointed at Rose. 'I should have been committed! Committed to a loony bin for thinking that you could ever care about me when all you've ever cared about is yourself and that smooth, slimy American bastard.'

The tears welled in Rose's eyes once more. 'I think you've said more than enough, Dan.'

'I don't think I've said *nearly* enough!' he railed.

She hugged her arms across her chest protectively. The temperature had plummeted. If this rain ever stopped, there would be a hard frost, or maybe even snow. It summed up her mood perfectly – a drizzling, drenching, drowning deluge. She looked at Dan. A quiet calm settled over her and it was much more disquieting than the torrent of emotions she had been experiencing only moments ago.

'Go on, then,' she said with wearied resignation.

'I think . . .' he shouted. His feet squelched across the

gravel. 'I think . . .' he said more quietly. He came to a halt and stood in front of her, breathing heavily. Steam came in exasperated pants from his mouth and from his flared nostrils. His face was once more ashen and bleak. 'Er, I think I've said enough.'

'In that case,' Rose said softly. 'It would be nice if you would go now.'

A spark lit in Dan's eyes again. 'So that's it, is it?'

'It would seem so.'

'Just go?'

Rose nodded sadly.

'Fine.' Dan's mouth was set in a tight line.

There was a sadness, an emptiness in his eyes that made Rose's resolution waver. Why was she doing this? Dan had a right to be angry. She had given him every reason to think that there might be a future for them. It was what she wanted. What she had dreamed of. Wasn't it? And, not a day later, he had found her in what must look like a scene from a *Carry On* film. She had tried to explain honestly why Hugh was here and, more importantly, half-naked. But he hadn't been willing to listen to her side of the story.

He had come to her when she needed him and she had turned him away like an unwelcome gatecrasher at a private party. Which, essentially, he had been. Suddenly, the realisation of it didn't make her feel any better. Was she going mad? She had been so sure it was Dan that she wanted until now – not Hugh. How on earth had she got into this situation? Rose stared at Dan blankly, uncertain what to do for the best.

'That's fine,' he repeated tersely. 'If that's what you want, I will go.' He turned and walked away up the drive.

'Dan,' she called out to his back. 'Don't! We've both said things we don't mean. Come back. Please! We can sort this out.' She ran out into the rain after him. 'If you go like this, I'll never forgive you.'

He stopped stock still and turned towards her as the rain lashed around him. His hair was plastered to his head, the water was coursing down his face and Rose was sure she could see tears mingling with the driving rain. 'Never is a very long time, Rose.' His voice was as sharp and icy as the pelting rain. 'And besides, it isn't your forgiveness I want, it's you.'

'Dan!' A lump came to her throat and his name came out as a feeble plea that was cruelly snatched and tossed aside by the wind.

He gave her one last look and it was an expression of such pain and hurt that she never wanted to see it on anyone else's face as long as she lived. Dan turned from her and disappeared into the night.

Chapter Thirty-Two

DISCOVERING DECISIVENESS
Clary Sage, Cedarwood, Patchouli.
We are constantly faced with difficult choices. We can never be sure that the path we take will be better than the one we have turned our backs on. This intuitive blend will help you make that choice and give you the calm assurance that what you have decided is right for you!
from: *The Complete Encyclopaedia of Aromatherapy Oils*
by Jessamine Lovage

'What *am* I going to do with you?' Rose flopped on to the edge of the bed, her body and her mind as weary as each other. She had cried downstairs until she couldn't cry any more and then had climbed the stairs to find Hugh had made himself comfortable in her bed. 'Bastard,' she said without feeling.

'You know you don't mean that,' Hugh replied with an easy smile.

'Here.' She threw his trousers at him. 'They've come straight out of the tumble dryer. They're a bit creased, but they'll do.'

Laying the trousers next to him on the bed, Hugh rested his hands casually behind his head. He was bathed in the soft glow from the bedside lamp and looked lean, fit and healthy.

'May I ask who *he* was?'

'His name's Dan Spikenard and he's a local builder.'

'And local heart-throb?'

Rose didn't answer.

'He wasn't your type.' Her ex-lover smiled sardonically.

She pursed her lips miserably. 'He thought we'd been in the shower together.'

Hugh raised one eyebrow. 'That would've been nice.'

Rose ignored his comment and frowned. 'And probably a lot worse.'

'That would have been even nicer,' he said with a lazy grin.

Rose's eyes welled with fresh tears.

The grin subsided. 'Come here,' he said softly. 'Let me kiss all your memories of him away.' Taking her hand, he pulled her to him and his warm lips brushed hers with a light feathery kiss.

Heaven only knows she wished it could be so easy! 'Hugh!' She pulled away from him, but let her hand rest in his. 'I've spent months trying to get over you. You can't just march back in to my life and expect everything to be the same as it was. Things have changed.'

'They *have* changed,' he agreed. 'I'm a free agent!'

'I think you should leave.' She stared at the floor.

He snuggled down on the bed and gave her a heart-melting pout. 'It's bitterly cold. It's dark. It's wet. You wouldn't turn a dog out on a night like this.'

'I would.'

Hugh shook his head slowly. 'I know you too well.' He squeezed her hand and eased her towards him. 'I want you, Rosie. I love you. And you love me. This time I'm here to stay.'

It was frightening really, one more day and Hugh could have abandoned his wife and children for nothing. As it was, Rose wasn't sure what she wanted anymore. Should she have even contemplated a life in Dan's arms if she felt something for Hugh? Yet as soon as Dan had appeared on the scene, she had truly started to forget Hugh.

Could she really be so fickle? Didn't she at least owe it to Hugh to give him another chance? He had sacrificed everything for her. Okay, so it may well have been at the eleventh hour, but he had, *eventually*, left Ruth. Could she just turn her back on him? Especially when things seemed so hopeless with Dan. There was no doubt that she would have to leave the village now. She could never look Dan in the face again. Her eyes were drawn back to Hugh. What did she have to lose?

'Come here,' Hugh whispered urgently. His eyes held that come-to-bed look. Soft and dreamy.

'You've made yourself very much at home,' Rose tutted, running her eyes over his lean body. The last time she had entertained a man wearing only a towel in this house, it had got her into trouble too. Her heart squeezed painfully as she thought of Dan. If only he had listened to her when she had tried to explain what was really going on.

So Gardenia had left him. Rose wondered if he would ever have left Gardenia for her, or would their relationship have dragged on for years like it had with Hugh? Why did she seem to cause heartbreak wherever she went? She only wanted someone to love. Was that such a dreadful thing to ask for?

'Do you think we can pick up again where we left off?' Hugh murmured. He slid his hand up the sleeve of her dressing gown and his thumb travelled along the sensitive skin on the inside of her arm.

She shivered and Hugh took that as encouragement. 'This is like old times,' he said softly.

It wasn't like old times, she thought. Where's the tingle of excitement? There are goosebumps, but that's because I'm still cold. Cold right through to my bones. Where's the rush of heat to my throat? The churning, stirring, aching in my stomach? Instead there was nothing. Just a longing for Dan.

His hand reached inside the fold of her robe, cupping her firm breast with his warm, soft, architect's hand. It had no callouses like Dan's hand, no roughening of the skin on the fingertips that rasped delightfully against vulnerable bare skin. Hugh's fingers were as soft and as gossamer as silk. They outlined the mound of her breast and she could barely feel his caress at all. She closed her eyes, trying to recapture the fire that Hugh's touch used to inflame in her. All she could see was Dan's face. Dan with his dirty blond hair and his stubbly face and his Colgate smile. She squeezed her eyes tight shut until all she could see were blurry red splotches on the insides of her eyelids.

Hugh nuzzled his face into her neck, tasting, kissing, biting her skin and she remembered how good it once used to feel.

'I don't want this, Hugh,' she said huskily, her traitorous body arching towards him. You do want this, her brain said. You want to be held and loved and cared for.

Hugh pulled her down on the bed, flinging Casanova to the far corner of the room where he landed on his head in the wastepaper basket. Rose lay down next to him compliant, confused, her body fighting the desire to lose herself in love-making and her reluctance to admit she was giving herself to the wrong man. She couldn't even find it in her to protest about the abuse of her teddy bear. His hands undid her dressing gown, sliding it over her shoulders, exposing her to him and she did nothing to stop him. No protest came from her mouth. Feverish fingers travelled her body, tracing and teasing and tantalizing her numb, numb skin. Rose stared ahead with sad, tear-filled eyes, willing herself to forget Dan, while Hugh moved rhythmically above her, her body failing to respond to his heat deep within her. His Adam's apple jerked against his flushed, straining throat and then he sighed and flopped against her, nestling his head on her breast. Rose sighed too, but for different reasons. Her desolation marked only by a solitary tear which squeezed through her lashes and rolled silently over her cheek. It was dark. Pitch black. And the rain had ceased its beating against the windows. Hugh lay on his back beside her, his breathing rhythmic, contented.

Outside, the security light flicked on over the patio. Its harsh, glaring beam lit up the room. Normally, there would be a lurch of terror in her stomach as she imagined the pervert emerging from the leylandii to lurk beneath her window. The presence of another body made it so much less frightening. And for the first time since Hugh had arrived, Rose was truly glad that he was here. She pulled her dressing gown round her and padded to the window to investigate. It was cold and the central heating had long since gone off.

She peered out of the window, but not before the light had switched off again. The darkness and silence of Great Brayford at night still took some getting used to. It reminded her of one of those plain black postcards people sent from their holidays with 'Skegness at Night' written on the front. Great joke. They'd obviously never been to Great Brayford at night. In the distance there was the ever-present glow of tungsten from the streetlights of Milton Keynes, which looked a bit like a downmarket UFO landing in a far-off field.

The flat in London had been constantly noisy. It was at the junction of two main roads, so the sound of traffic was interminable. Add to that the sporadic succession of slamming doors as people arrived home at various unsocial hours during the night, car alarms, burglar alarms, singing drunks and the odd bout of road rage at the traffic lights, and it was amazing that they ever got any sleep at all. But then, in the early days of their affair, sleep hadn't been a top priority.

The strident arc of the security light flared over the patio once more, catching a hedgehog trundling across the patio in search of a juicy snail. It froze momentarily, looked up in her direction and then carried on unperturbed. Rose smiled to herself. The light clicked off. The flat had always been bright too, bombarded by lights from the street below. Tungsten, neon, halogen. They had been forced to buy dark curtains. Here it didn't matter whether there were curtains or not. The light switched on again. The hedgehog was heading back the other way. Rose frowned.

'What are you doing?' Hugh murmured. 'Come back to bed.'

She turned to look at him. He had curled into a contented ball, dark hair flopping over his face and a smile softened Rose's tight lips. Perhaps it could be like old times again? 'I was just checking why the patio light kept coming on,' she said.

'And why is it?' he asked, not sounding terribly interested.

'There's a hedgehog doing a cabaret,' Rose replied as she came back to the bed and slipped under the duvet next to Hugh. His arm curled round her waist, his body hot and comforting, moulding with easy familiarity to her contours.

Rose stared, wide-eyed at the cracked ceiling. 'It's nice to have someone here.'

'Just someone?' Hugh queried. 'Not me in particular?'

'It's nice to have you here then,' she corrected. 'I mentioned it to you earlier, I think – I've been having trouble with nuisance phone calls.'

'No wonder you always sounded so edgy when I called,' he mumbled sleepily.

Rose's body froze momentarily. When she had regained

movement, she pushed herself on to her elbow and turned to face him. 'Say that again.'

Hugh's eyes opened wide now and there was a distinctly cagey look to them. 'I said, no wonder you always sounded edgy.'

'When you called?'

'That's right.'

'How did you get my number? Come to think of it, you still haven't told me how you managed to find out where I lived.'

'Ah,' Hugh said lamely. He sat up in the bed.

'Come on, spit it out,' Rose said.

'It was Jerry.'

Rose frowned. 'Jerry Wright? From the office?'

Hugh nodded with some reluctance.

'*Jerry* gave *you* my phone number?' Rose set her mouth in a tight line. 'The bastard. He promised.'

'He didn't exactly *give* it to me,' Hugh said sheepishly. 'I sort of took it.'

'You *took* it?'

'Out of his Filofax while he was at lunch,' he admitted. 'It's very slapdash practice leaving your office unattended with personal possessions lying around. You never know who might go through them.'

'Quite!' Rose snapped.

'Well,' Hugh drawled defensively, 'I had to resort to sneak tactics. No one would tell me where you'd gone.'

'That was the whole idea!' Rose tugged at her hair in exasperation. She sat up next to Hugh and pulled her knees into her chest.

'So when exactly did you call?

'Oh, I don't know.' Hugh stared ahead of him. 'Once or twice.'

'Once or twice?'

'A few times.' He cleared his throat. 'Quite often.'

'And you didn't leave a message?'

'I couldn't!' Hugh stared fiercely at her.

'Why?'

'Because it wasn't your answerphone that answered.' He lowered his eyes. 'It was you.'

'I did?' Rose said incredulously.

'Yes,' Hugh said tersely. 'And you always sounded so tense, so aggressive that I lost my nerve!'

'So you sat at the other end of the phone and said nothing?' Rose's voice was, to her surprise, level and calm.

'Pretty much.'

'I don't believe this.' Rose shook her head in amazement. 'You realise what you've done, don't you?'

Hugh said nothing.

Her eyes challenged him. 'It was you all along, wasn't it? You're my pervert!'

'You said you knew it was me!' Hugh protested. 'You said you'd go to the police if I didn't stop hassling you.'

'I was bluffing!'

Hugh twisted his mouth hesitantly. 'Well, you certainly fooled me.'

Rose put her head in her hands. 'I've been terrified for months, thinking that I had a heavy breather and possibly an axe-wielding maniac hiding in my hedging. And all along it was you!

'*And*,' Rose continued when she had calmed down, 'it still doesn't explain how you found out my address. Jerry might have had my phone number, but he didn't know where I lived. I only gave him my number because he has a brother-in-law in Aylesbury who wanted an aromatherapy treatment. Mind you,' she paused for thought, 'his brother-in-law never phoned. So how *exactly* did you end up here today?'

'Cassia Wales gave me your address,' he said flatly.

'*Cassia Wales*? How on *earth* do you know her?'

'I don't.'

'How did she manage to give you my address then?'

'Well, I wasn't getting anywhere with the phone calls, especially after you'd threatened to call the police, so I decided to forget all about you.' He smiled disarmingly at her. 'I was going to become a monk and live a chaste and celibate life making smelly cheese and foul-tasting wine for charity.'

'And Cassia Wales changed that?'

'I was driving up the M1 earlier today on my way back from a site meeting in Northampton – new supermarket.' Hugh looked at her as if she should have been impressed. She wasn't. 'And the radio was tuned to the local station where this vacuous bimbo—'

'Cassia Wales,' Rose interjected.

'Cassia Wales,' Hugh confirmed, 'was wittering on about this brilliant aromatherapist who had moved into her village from some swanky London practice and had brought a string of celebrity clients with her.'

'Not Cliff, Sacha and Mick?' It was all becoming horribly clear.

'I think she mentioned Rod Stewart too.'

'Good grief.' Rose let out a long unhappy sigh.

'While she was playing a record, I rang the radio station from the car and asked to speak to her. She was very obliging.'

'She's known for it.'

'I told her that I thought she was talking about an old friend of mine and that I happened to be in the area. She confirmed that it was you and was quite happy to give me your address.'

'I bet she was!'

'Now, Rose. It was just a happy coincidence on my part.' He snuggled closer to her. 'Besides, she's done us a favour. She's brought us back together.' He stared earnestly at her. 'You do want us to be together?'

Rose sighed uncertainly. 'I don't know, Hugh.'

'Come back with me, Rosie.' Hugh stroked her arm,

wheedling and cajoling her. 'Back to London. You're not meant to be stuck out here in the sticks.'

'And what about this?' She gestured with her hands to encompass the house – every creaking door, every cracked ceiling, every chipped ceramic tile.

'Sell it and keep the money. Start another business with it.'

Perhaps she should go back to London, Rose thought. Set herself up in one of those swanky practices and get to grips with some of those pop stars she was already supposed to have manhandled.

'You and I used to be good together, Rose. This time, it'll be better.' Hugh squeezed her to him. 'No strings. No double life. No ghosts. What do you say?'

Rose exhaled wearily. In one way and another it had been a very long day. 'There's a lot to think about, Hugh.' She smiled gently at him. 'Let me sleep on it.'

She slid down inside the bed, aware of Hugh next to her, his breathing steady and soothing, slowing down to sleeping speed. It would be wonderful if hers would do the same. Instead her breath snatched erratic little gasps at the top of her lungs. How she wished she could go downstairs and get some essential oils to burn to help her sleep. All the bottles by her bedside were empty – that's what you get for mainlining insomnia oils. She wondered what Jessamine Lovage would advise for decisiveness. Perhaps clary sage or cedarwood or patchouli. Rose couldn't decide.

What was keeping her in Great Brayford anyway? They had hardly clasped her to their bosoms with open arms. Well, Dan had been keen to yesterday. Yesterday. When all her troubles seemed so far away. It wasn't even a choice between Dan and Hugh anymore. Dan would want nothing to do with her now, whether Gardenia was around or not. He had nailed his colours to the mast using a very substantial nail. Her throat constricted painfully and she dug her nails into her palms so that she wouldn't cry. What would he think of her now?

Hugh said there would be no ghosts this time. Presumably he meant Ruth. But what about Dan? Would he haunt her for the rest of her life? Should she try to forget him? Did she really owe it to Hugh to give their relationship another chance? After years of promising, he had finally turned his cosy little duplicitous life upside down for her. He had left Ruth. For her.

Rose turned off the bedside light and stared into the darkness. She would consult Jessamine Lovage first thing in the morning. Decision time was fast approaching. It was like an express train looming towards her and she was powerless to move behind the comparative safety of the yellow line and let it rush past her. There was a choice to be made and she would need all the help she could get.

Chapter Thirty-Three

BASIL (TRUE)

True sweet basil has a light fresh scent with spicy undertones. It is an excellent essential oil for those with nervous dispositions. Known to clear the head, relieve fatigue, strengthen the weary mind and improve clarity of thought.

from: *The Complete Encyclopaedia of Aromatherapy Oils*
by Jessamine Lovage

'My, you look rather dashing, Basil,' Angelica said. Barely recognisable was more accurate. He had turned up on her doorstep minus his usual startling array of facial hair and sporting a black roll neck, black slacks and dark grey cashmere jacket – as opposed to the usual tweed and Nikes or the lilac shell suit. Rather than his usual faintly unwashed aroma, he was swathed in a cloud of aftershave that smelt suspiciously like Old Spice. He had a distinct look of Donald Sutherland about him. It was a startling transformation.

'No. I haven't dashed, dear lady,' Basil replied casually. 'I've sauntered up here slowly, taking in the delights of this fresh spring day.'

'And all because the lady loves Milk Tray.' Angelica nodded towards the box of chocolates tucked under his arm. It appeared to be Dairy Box, but who was she to argue over detail.

'It's Dairy Box,' Basil confirmed, proffering the said chocolates. 'Mr Patel had run out of Milk Tray – due to the recent Mother's Day celebration, I presume. Neither did I have to jump from a helicopter or swim through shark-infested waters to get here,' he added jovially.

Angelica took the box from him. 'Unfortunately, Anise is still confined to her bed in Milton Keynes General. They insisted on her staying as they said she was ranting deliriously. The doctor said it was probably brought on by the shock. I tried to explain that she's always like that, but they wouldn't listen.'

Basil looked bashful and blushed. Angelica had never seen him blush before, but then she had never really seen his face before either. It was quite a handsome face without the grey and wiry untamed Brillo pad that normally obscured it.

'They're not actually for Anise,' he said hesitantly. 'They're for you.'

Her hands fluttered anxiously over her hair and her heart cartwheeled with unexpected delight. 'Then don't underestimate yourself, Basil,' she said coyly. 'You're risking Anise's wrath by coming to court me and that's far worse than anything whirling rotor blades or Jaws ever had to offer.' She giggled with nerves and kissed him affectionately on his cheek. His smooth cheek. 'Thank you.'

She led him into the lounge, fanning her face to cool the redness that was flaming her cheeks. Nursing the Dairy Box to her she sat down and motioned to the chair opposite her. Basil obediently sat down, smoothing his nonexistent hair as if he was still trying to get used to it himself.

'I take it you *are* coming to court me, Basil,' she said directly, the tremble that she felt inside thankfully not translating itself to her voice.

'I had rather hoped to,' he said shyly.

Angelica smiled. 'We did get on rather well the other night, didn't we?' They had, over several cups of Earl Grey, discovered a mutual appreciation for the music of Cole Porter, the paintings of Cézanne and the taste of Italian food.

'I should say so.'

'It was unfortunate that Anise's accident had to bring us together, but every cloud has a silver lining, so they say.' She crossed her legs and hoped that she wasn't showing too much stocking. 'You were here for nearly two hours, Basil, and you didn't say "I'd hang the bastards" once. That has to be a good sign.' Angelica smoothed her hair away from her forehead with practised elegance, hoping that perhaps she had finally found someone who would appreciate it.

'I find that all anger seems to dissipate in your presence.' His voice was earnest. 'You're a fine woman, Angelica.' Basil looked at something invisible in his lap. 'I was full of admiration for the way you handled the crisis. It was a side of you that I hadn't seen before. Calm and resilient. I like that in a woman.'

'I've had years of practice, Basil. Anise invariably creates the crisis and I come along with the emotional mop and bucket afterwards. It's always been the same.'

'Do you think you could look upon me as a suitor?'

'I'd be delighted to, Basil.' She gave him a sideways glance. 'Though we both always thought that you had eyes only for Anise, and I'm afraid it won't be the first time I've snatched a young man from under her nose. She isn't likely to take kindly to it.'

'Anise was using my affections as a tiramisu.'

'I think you mean as a trifle, Basil.'

'I was trying to update myself for the nineties,' he explained. 'You can do an awful lot more with sponge fingers now than you could in my day.'

'How true,' Angelica sympathised.

'Anyway, Anise was using me purely to spy on poor Rose.' Basil sniffed in an offended manner. 'I may be a lot of things, Angelica, but nosy isn't one of them.'

'Poor Rose,' Angelica echoed. 'Anise has had it in for her since the day she arrived in Great Brayford and, as far as I know, she hasn't put a foot out of place.'

'Actually,' Basil rubbed at his stubble less chin. 'One of the reasons I'm here is because of something that happened at Rose's yesterday.'

'Oh?'

'She had a visitor. At first I thought it might be her pervert, but he was far too smart.' He glanced up at Angelica. 'I'm almost certain it was the chap that she'd left behind in London. He looked that sort.'

'But what has that got to do with us?'

He was fidgeting with his hands and looked like he wished he had brought his security-blanket trilby with him. Basil sighed. 'He reminded me of myself when I was younger. I used to be quite a spiv back then.' He smiled winsomely.

'I'm sure you did.'

'It made me realise that I'd let myself go.' Basil studied his fingernails. 'For the first time, I saw myself as I really am – a sad old man. With no one to care for, I'd also stopped caring for myself. I decided that it was time to stop the rot.' He fixed her with an intense stare from his blue eyes. They were quite clear and sparkling, not rheumy like most old men's eyes were. Not too long ago she would have call them mad eyes, now they were just mischievous. Basil took a deep breath. 'To use modern parlance, I want to get a life before it's too late.'

'Basil! There's plenty of life in the old dog yet.'

'With you I feel like a frisky young pup.'

'Oh, Basil!' Angelica coloured. 'If you're not careful you're going to make me blush.'

He wrung his hands like a dishcloth. 'Your face is like poetry in motion, Angelica.'

'What do you mean, Basil? Composed of uneven lines and heading south?'

'*Dear lady!*'

'You haven't been drinking, have you?'

Basil's crest looked in danger of falling. 'I only popped into the Black Horse for a swift one before I came here – a spot of Dutch courage. Nothing more.'

'Not Advocaat on an empty stomach, surely, Basil.' Angelica shook her head. 'I think I'd better put the kettle on.'

Basil struggled from the chair and, with some effort, fell to his knees at her feet. 'Angelica, I'm here to plight my troth.'

Angelica looked disconcerted. 'What exactly is a troth, Basil? And how can you be sure you want to plight it?'

'I'd like to ask for your hand,' Basil persisted.

'My hand?' she said with surprise. 'What about the rest of me?'

'I want you to marry me,' he announced in a rush.

'*Marry you?*'

'Does that seem so outrageous?' Basil looked pained. It could have been because he was kneeling on the carpet. The underlay had been past its best for years.

'But what will Anise say?' Angelica said.

'Does it matter what Anise says?'

'No.' Angelica was firm. Firmer than she had ever sounded before.

'No, you won't marry me?'

'No!' Angelica repeated. 'No, I don't give a damn what Anise says! We're both old enough and wise enough to do exactly as we please. We should make hay while the sun shines, Basil.' Angelica gazed at him with mischief glinting in her eyes. 'But wouldn't you prefer to live in sin? It sounds so much more exciting.'

'I'd rather make an honest woman of you, if you don't mind,' Basil said apologetically.

'I've been an honest woman all my life. I've found it's very much overrated.'

'Marry me,' he implored earnestly, the discomfort of the carpet etched into his face – and probably his knees.

Angelica's heart went out to him and a smile spread over her face. 'I'd be delighted to marry you.'

Basil struggled to his feet. He might be dressed like the man in the Milk Tray advertisement, but he certainly wasn't as athletic. With trembling fingers, he took Angelica's hands. 'I'm not a sad old man any more. You, my dear, dear lady, have made me a very happy one.'

'Well,' Angelica patted her hair self-consciously. 'I think that a cup of tea is definitely called for.'

'Surely this warrants more of a celebration!' Basil boomed.

'You're absolutely right. Wait here. I have a bottle of champagne in the fridge that I won on the tombola at the Christmas fête.'

'That sounds more like it!'

'We should start as we mean to go on.' Angelica's voice drifted from the kitchen. She reappeared brandishing the bottle and two glasses. 'Would you like to drink this upstairs, Basil?'

'Dear lady!' Basil's eyes widened and he looked decidedly flustered.

'I'm no lady, Basil,' she said. 'Don't let my appearance as an elegant old has-been fool you.'

'I'm embarrassed to admit that I'm terribly out of practice in the ways of courtship.' He cast his eyes towards the Axminster with the worn underlay. 'Particularly in the bedroom,' he mumbled. 'It's a long time since I . . .' His voice faded to nothing.

'Basil,' she said softly. 'The last time I was horizontal in bed with a man, Bill Hailey and his Comets were at the top of the pop charts with "Rock Around the Clock". There's nothing to worry about. It's about time we had some fun.' She took his hand and led him towards the bedroom, waving the champagne bottle. 'We'll have some French courage first. It should sit very nicely on top of your Advocaat.'

Chapter Thirty-Four

BUILDING UP BREAKS AND FRACTURES
Ginger, Lavender.
Once a break or fracture has taken place, it is often difficult for the broken parts to knit together again in the same way. Rubbed regularly over the damaged area, this blend of warming, healing oils will help to strengthen that which was torn apart.

from: *The Complete Encyclopaedia of Aromatherapy Oils*
by Jessamine Lovage

'I hear that you're leaving.' Angelica smiled sadly.

'Mr Patel?' Rose said, raising her eyebrows quizzically.

'Who else, my dear.' Angelica took her hand and patted it. 'We shall all miss you terribly.'

'Perhaps some people will.' She gave Angelica a rueful smile. 'But in other quarters I certainly won't be considered Great Brayford's biggest loss.' They both looked through the half-open door to the lounge where Anise reclined in a garden lounger which had been pressed into service because the armchairs were too low for her to sit in. Her bare toes were sticking out from the end of her plaster cast which was resting on a cushion on the coffee table. They glanced knowingly at each other.

'Well, *I* shall miss you,' Angelica assured her.

Rose lowered her voice. 'Talking of people who *won't*

miss me,' she put a small brown bottle of essential oil on the kitchen work surface, clearly labelled 'Building Up Breaks and Fractures', 'I've brought a peace offering for the invalid.'

'Oh, how sweet of you.' Angelica peered at the label. 'What's in it?

'It's a blend of mainly ginger and lavender.'

'How lovely.'

'Nothing too sinister,' Rose added.

'Shame,' Angelica said, eyeing the inoffensive bottle with longing. 'Still, it's so much more useful than flowers. The house is beginning to look like a florist's and there are only so many chipped and dusty old vases that one can drag out from the under stairs cupboard without too much shame. It's amazing really, I never thought Anise was so popular.' Her mouth turned down in thought. 'Perhaps they were all hoping she'd died.'

'She should rub the oil into her leg every day, once the plaster has been removed.' Rose toyed absently with the bottle. 'Do you think she'll use it?'

'I'll encourage her to. But you know what they say,' Angelica shook her head. 'You can lead a cow to water, but you can't make it drink.'

'I think it's actually lead a horse to water.'

'I'll stick with cow,' Angelica replied with a twinkle in her eye. 'It seems more appropriate in this case.'

Rose smiled. 'How's she coping?'

'Not very well. Whoever invented the word patient didn't take Anise into account. She's still behaving very badly.'

Rose clicked her tongue behind her teeth in sympathy. 'You deserve a medal!'

'Not really.' Angelica's voice wavered. 'I haven't been very kind to her. And, despite my scathing comments, I'm trying to be nicer.'

'It must be very difficult to see her so incapacitated.'

'Yes.' Angelica nodded with feeling. 'It's so much more difficult for her to be intimidating when she's forced to sit down.' She laughed weakly. 'And it's surprising how much I miss it.'

Rose's face creased with concern. 'More importantly, how are *you* coping?'

'In truth,' Angelica sighed, 'I'm not coping terribly well. I'm getting far too old to look after this big house and, quite frankly, I've got better things to do with my time.'

Rose sat down opposite her. 'So I'd heard!'

'Mr Patel?' Angelica ventured.

'Of course.'

'Well, they say that good news travels fast.'

'And this is very good news, Angelica.' She took the old lady's hands and squeezed them affectionately.

'That's another reason I'm trying to be nice to Anise. It's very unfair of me to have stolen her beau. She's not going to be frightfully pleased.'

'I wouldn't have thought that Anise would have requited Basil's love.'

'Possibly not, but that won't stop her from making a meal out of the fact that he's deserted her.' She pulled out a chair and sat at the kitchen table. 'Or continuing to make my life a misery.'

Rose clapped her hands together excitedly. 'Who'd have thought, you and Basil! I hope you'll be very happy together.'

'I'm sure we will.'

It was a fine spring day and a warm breeze blew in through the open back door. The fresh green expanse of lawn was punctuated by the vibrant pink and white blossoms of the burgeoning cherry trees. The spindly hedge at the bottom of the garden was laced with the bright yellow splash of forsythia, a showy statement that belied the dullness of the plain green shrub that followed.

A vase of daffodils stood in the middle of the table, echoing the swathes of pale lemony blooms that nodded gently in the garden – except the ones on the table were from Tesco's. Two bunches bound by elastic bands, courtesy of the Reverend Allbright.

'Are you going to move out of here?' Rose asked as she admired the garden.

Angelica glanced cautiously towards the lounge door. The bare toes wiggled. She lowered her voice to a whisper. 'I expect so. I can't see that Anise would welcome Basil here with open arms.'

'That might be expecting too much,' Rose agreed with a grin.

'I wanted her to consider moving to one of Builder's Bottom's retirement flats. We don't need a house this size. Half the rooms are beginning to smell musty because they're unused. I thought it was a very good idea.'

'Did Anise?'

'She said I was asking her to live in penury.' Angelica tutted forcefully. 'Penury. I ask you. Whatever gave her that impression? All I wanted her to do was to move across the road to somewhere that won't be damp in the winter. I don't even know where penury is!'

Rose smiled to herself and chose not to trouble Angelica with directions.

'In the meantime, while we discuss the pros and cons of our domestic arrangements, we're going to get a new gardener and a cleaner.'

'Basil's retiring?'

'It's too much for the poor dear lamb and he had an ulterior motive. This sudden love for gardening was a ruse to get closer to Anise.' Angelica smiled wickedly. 'And look where that got him.'

Rose linked her hands under her chin. 'I suppose I'll have to find someone else too.'

'That's hardly going to be your problem, is it?'

'Oh.' The smile dropped from Rose's face with the realisation of what lay in store for her. 'Of course. I'd forgotten. Just for a moment.'

Angelica leaned forward conspiratorially and whispered, 'I'm going to get a couple of surly young things who'll give Anise as good as they get.'

'Make sure that you get someone who can vacuum properly!' Anise's voice came stridently from the lounge.

Angelica raised her eyebrows, nodded in the direction of the lounge and then gave Rose a perplexed shrug. 'And this from a woman who has never handled the dirty end of a vacuum cleaner!'

'I thought you were going to be nicer to her,' Rose reminded Angelica.

'I'll start tomorrow,' she promised earnestly, patting Rose's hand. 'Anyway, that's enough of us, now you must tell me all about you. I believe your man from London has come back – your *grande passion*.'

'Mr Patel really should get an OBE for services to broadcasting'

'Ah, now that's where you're wrong, my dear. Our Mr Patel must have been having an off day. Basil beat him to it.'

'Basil?'

'He saw your young man arriving.' Angelica gave a tinkling laugh. 'I believe he mistook him for your pervert.'

Rose's eyes darkened. 'Actually, Basil wasn't a million miles away,' she said. 'For an intelligent man, Hugh can be such an idiot at times.'

Angelica's eyebrows drew together in a frown. 'That doesn't sound like the sort of thing one should be saying about the love of one's life.'

Rose looked down self-consciously at her fingers. Half of her nails had disappeared already and she'd only moved a couple of the tea chests that the removal firm had delivered. 'No,' she said quietly. 'It doesn't.'

Angelica heaved a weary sigh and covered Rose's smooth, unlined hand with her age-flecked, papery one. 'Are you sure you're doing the right thing, my dear? I thought you were getting on so well with Builder's Bottom. You seemed so perfectly suited.' She paused, waiting for Rose to answer. When she didn't, Angelica continued, 'I take it you know that Gardenia has gone.'

Rose nodded mutely.

'Mr Patel again,' Angelica added as an afterthought. 'Dan seems so very unhappy. Even more unhappy than when he was with her. And that's very unhappy.' She tilted her head sideways, forcing contact with Rose's lowered eyes. 'The only time I've seen him look truly happy in recent years was when he was with you.'

Rose looked up, an expression of abject misery on her face. 'Don't say that, Angelica. Please. It's the last thing I want to hear.'

The old lady looked kindly at her. 'The truth sometimes is.'

'It was awful. We had a terrible fight.' Rose's eyes had started to water and it was much too early to be blamed on hay fever. 'He came to see me after Gardenia had left him. He was in a terrible state when he arrived and was in an even worse state by the time he left.' Rose put her elbows on the table and began to pick viciously at a tiny patch of dry skin next to her thumb. She grimaced at Angelica. 'After he discovered Hugh was there.'

'Did he catch you *in flagrante delicto*?' she asked.

'Not exactly.' Rose looked away, ashamed of herself. 'But it was obvious that was what he thought.'

Angelica looked at her sympathetically. 'And do you care what he thought?'

Tears spilled over Rose's lashes and streamed down her face. 'Yes,' she cried.

Angelica spoke to her softly. 'Then I must ask you,

once again. Are you sure you're doing the right thing?'

'No,' Rose admitted truthfully. 'It's just that things are so complicated now.' She looked balefully at Angelica. 'Hugh has given up everything for me.'

'Everything?'

Rose exhaled an unhappy, shuddering breath. 'He's left his wife. And children.'

'Ah.'

'I keep thinking back to what you were saying about your lover. The man who . . .' She saw the sadness steal over Angelica's face, deepening the lines that time had etched there.

Angelica cleared her throat before speaking. 'History very rarely repeats itself, no matter what people might have us believe.' Her voice was thick with emotion. 'There is one other thing I didn't tell you about my *grande passion*.' Angelica fluttered her hands over her hair and stared out into the garden where the vibrant colours were more suited to a hot summer's day in the Mediterranean than a clear spring one in Buckinghamshire and made Angelica look all the more pale. She turned back to Rose. 'He was a terrible philanderer. A flirt, a womaniser and a scoundrel.' She swallowed with a deliberate slowness before she continued. 'I wasn't the first, you see. And I wasn't the only one, even at the time. In reality he made my life a misery. Everyone knew that he'd had a string of mistresses, most of them young and gullible. Like me. That's why he was hounded so much. I'm afraid most of my romantic notions about him are purely flights of fancy. The feeble ramblings from the ageing brain of a woman who has, by all accounts, led a terribly dull life.' She looked at Rose wistfully.

'Oh, Angelica,' Rose said sadly. 'At least, you have Basil now.'

Angelica forced a bright smile. 'Yes,' she said emotionally. 'And now that I've found him, I'm going to grab him with both hands and hang on for the ride. If you'll pardon the expression.'

'I think it's Basil that will have his hands full with you!'

The elegant elderly lady winked decorously and then said, 'I want to be serious now, Rose, and you must listen to me.' She leaned forward in her chair and spoke urgently. 'Don't waste your life like I did. You must do what your heart tells you. One thing I did say that was totally and absolutely true when we spoke before, you must think only of yourself. Your own happiness is paramount.'

Rose gave a weak laugh. 'I suppose you're right,' she said. 'Anyway, it all seems irrelevant now. The house is on the market, the removal van's booked for Friday and Hugh is waiting in London for me with open arms.'

'It sounds like your decision is final.'

If only it felt the same as it sounded, Rose thought.

'And have you told Dan?' Angelica asked succinctly.

Rose avoided her gaze. 'Not, yet.'

'I think you owe him that much.'

Rose folded her arms on the table and stared unseeing out into the garden. 'I don't know if I can bear to tell him.'

'Then that sounds, unless I'm very much mistaken, as though you have unfinished business, my dear,' Angelica observed. 'Hugh may have given up everything for you, but you must now ask yourself the question: are you prepared to give up everything for Hugh?'

Chapter Thirty-Five

SECRET PASSIONS
Rose, Jasmine, Ylang-Ylang.

All of us harbour secret passions. Little things that only we know can stir our blood, warm the dark corners of our hearts and make us feel like we're walking on air. This highly fragrant and extravagant blend of luxurious natural oils will help to unlock the secret passions deep within you – so that your secret love will be no secret any more!

from: *The Complete Encyclopaedia of Aromatherapy Oils*
by Jessamine Lovage

She would have no fingernails left at all at this rate. Another three had snapped as Rose reluctantly packed the dinner plates, first wrapping them in newspaper before stacking them in a tea chest with brutally jagged edges. No doubt she would slash her hands to ribbons, too, by the end of the day.

It was stupid to pack most of her things as she wouldn't be taking them back to the flat in London. It was too small, too cramped, too plush for her belongings. Leaving them here in tea chests wasn't ideal either, but there was a finality about completely emptying the house that she was anxious to put off. If she allowed herself to think about it, there was a finality about leaving Great Brayford that she was anxious to put off too. In the end, packing these bits and pieces would only make it easier for burglars to load the entire contents of her life on to a Ford Transit. Pushing this thought aside, Rose packed on regardless.

She was taking only the small items, bedding, china and one or two of her better pieces of furniture. Most of the stuff was only fit for a bonfire and Basil had been eager to oblige there.

A blackbird was singing its heart out in the garden and Rose abandoned the plate she was wrapping and walked over to the back door. The door stood open and she leaned on the frame as she watched the bird perform its love song for the uninterested-looking lady blackbird that perched on the edge of the concrete bird bath shaped, for some inexplicable reason, like a cherub. The bird was a superb ventriloquist. From the high ground of the fence, it was trilling up and down its scales with a juicy fat worm wriggling in its beak – no doubt the bird world's courting equivalent of a dozen red roses. The poor creature was getting nowhere fast. Despite his best efforts, the haughty lady blackbird refused to acknowledge him. Perhaps she should have treated Hugh like that. Disdainfully. Refusing to let him worm his way back into her life with such ease.

There would be no more bird-watching back at the flat. Even sparrows were a rarity there and those that did appear had a scrawny, streetwise appearance that wasn't as endearing as the friendly, well-fed birds that graced her garden here. She looked further down the lawn, taking in the improvements that Basil had started to make. It was a constant battle to maintain a plot of land this size. Turn your back for ten minutes and nature started to steal back what was rightfully hers. It was all very well having *Wildlife On One* in your back garden, but there were disadvantages too. The badgers broke the flowers off the bergenia, the muntjacs munched the muscari and you couldn't go for a stroll without stepping in rabbit pooh.

She was starting to feel the pull of the pollution in her lungs. Her acclimatisation had begun in earnest. Who wanted clear fresh air laden with the foetid smell of ripe cow manure when you could just as easily be asphyxiated by diesel fumes and the smog of pollution? Hadn't she always been a city girl at heart? Perhaps that was why she had never really settled in the country. Being woken by a double-decker bus trundling past your window may not sound as romantic as the dawn chorus or, indeed, sheep baaing, but it was just as effective. And, after all, surely the romantic quality of your alarm call depended on *who* you were waking up to.

She was young and bright and sophisticated and still had so much living to do. Weekly attendance at line-dancing classes or Tums, Bums and Thighs didn't count as living. Village life was riddled with petty ways – the constant tittle-tattle and gossip, the fact that you couldn't change your underwear without everyone taking an interest. At least in London no one spoke to you at all. You could be dying on the pavement and people would just step over you. It was all very well having a village shop run by the fount of all knowledge, but if you went in for just a pint of milk you couldn't get out in under half an hour. Mr Patel who ran the corner shop at the other end of the road from the flat in London barely looked at you as he gave you your change; you could be back home and in front of *Brookside* before the commercial break was over. And Mr Patel of London didn't look at you as if you were barking mad when you asked if he stocked herbal tea.

When she came to think of it, there were a lot of things that she could well live without. But could she live without Dan?

Bleakly, she looked back at the jagged edge of the half-packed tea chest and struggled to resist the urge to saw her wrists back and forwards across it. Who was she kidding? She would miss the village like hell. And some of its occupants distinctly more than others.

Before she got too suicidal, Rose decided she would go and see Melissa. Pulling on a jumper over her scruffy 'packing up the house' T-shirt, she collected the small brown bottle of essential oils that she had blended for Mel and, banging the front door decisively behind her, headed for her friend's house.

Melissa, surprisingly, was baking a cake. There were smears of flour on her face, hair and T-shirt and the work surface was submerged beneath a liberal scattering of caster sugar. She was beating something that already looked within an inch of its life in a large brown bowl.

Rose knocked gingerly on the back door and let herself in. 'Hello!' she said with a cheerfulness she didn't feel.

Melissa's cheeks were flushed and she blew her fringe out of her eyes with an upwards curling of her lower lip. 'You'll have to put the kettle on yourself, if it's tea and sympathy you've come for,' she said over her shoulder to Rose. Her hands and arms up to the elbows were spattered with a pale grey substance. 'I'm baking a cake.'

'I would never have guessed,' Rose teased.

Her friend frowned at her and stopped punishing the cake mix.

'Don't let me stop you,' Rose said. 'It looks like a very serious business.'

'It's a bastard,' Melissa agreed.

Rose leaned on the kitchen table which, for the moment, was the only place which seemed to be a flour-free zone. 'I didn't know you were such an avid baker.'

Melissa regarded her with disdain. 'Do I look like one?'

'Perhaps not,' Rose conceded.

'I tried it once with the Kenwood food processor, but I ended up with even more mixture on the floor and ceiling than I've got now.'

It was difficult to see how.

'And then I sort of lost the spatula,' she said shiftily.

That was more understandable.

'This is "Chocolate Cake Made Easy" by Mary O'Hoorahan.' Melissa pointed at the recipe book and thus flicked a shower of cake mix at the hapless page. 'Lying bitch,' she muttered under her breath.

'Why are you doing this?' Rose ventured tentatively.

'It's a labour of love,' she snapped. 'I'm trying to be a better wife.'

'And baking a cake constitutes being a better wife?'

'It's a start.'

'Couldn't you just buy a nice ready-made cake from Mr Patel – he has an extensive selection. Or a packet mix might be less tortuous.'

'That would be cheating,' she said flatly. 'And I've been doing too much of that lately.'

'Oh. Anything that you want to share?'

'No,' Melissa said petulantly. 'I've been very stupid and I don't want to talk about it.'

'Does Frank know?'

'Yes.'

'And what does he say?'

'Oh, you know Frank.' Melissa paused momentarily from mugging the fledgling cake. She wiped the hair from her eyes with the back of her hand, smearing cake mix across her eyebrows. 'He just goes quiet – even quieter than usual – and keeps his feelings to himself.'

'Are things okay between you?' Rose held up her hand. 'Tell me to mind my own business if you want to.'

'No.' Melissa thrashed at the mixing bowl again. 'I don't mind. I hope we'll be all right. Fortunately, I came to my senses just in time. It's funny,' she stopped beating and turned to Rose, 'you never do realise what you've got until it's gone. Or almost gone in my case.' Mel absently sucked cake mix from one of her fingers. 'Why do we always take for granted the people that really love us?'

'Oh, I don't know, Melissa,' Rose said with a sigh. 'But you're going to push me deeper into my dark depression if you carry on like this.'

'I thought that you'd be happy now that you're going back to London.'

'So did I,' Rose admitted.

'I'm just surprised that you're going back to whatsit.'

'Hugh,' Rose filled in.

'Hugh. Especially after all you said about him. I thought you hated him.'

'So did I.'

Melissa abandoned her attempts at 'Chocolate Cake Made Easy' and leaned on the work surface, placing her cake-mixed hands in the sugar with a recklessness that was admirable. 'So what changed your mind?' she asked.

Rose scraped her hair back from her face. 'He finally left his wife and kids.'

'What a bastard!'

'No, that's good! It means he can commit fully to me now.'

'And you'd want a man that can heartlessly ditch his wife and kids to be committed fully to you?'

'Put like that, I don't really know,' Rose said, her face a picture of misery.

'Are you fully committed to him?'

'I don't know.' Rose buried her face in her hands. 'I just feel so *confused* about the whole thing.'

'What about Dan?' Mel flicked her hair back from her shoulders and the ends draped in the bowl of cake mix. 'I thought you two were about to become an item.'

'Were we *that* obvious?'

'No,' Mel said. 'You dark horse. I hadn't a clue until Mr Patel told me. You certainly kept that quiet. But then I have been rather preoccupied lately.'

Rose wrung a wry smile from her lips. 'If we kept it

quiet, how did Mr Patel know?'

'Mr Patel knows everything.' Melissa tapped the side of her nose. 'Well, *nearly* everything.'

'Does he know why Gardenia left?'

'He thought it was because of you. Apparently, Dan's been crazy about you since you arrived. Gardenia couldn't stand the competition.'

Rose tipped back on her chair. 'That is pure conjecture. I'm sure this village is the one that made the original molehill into a mountain.'

'Villages thrive on gossip,' Melissa informed her. 'There's nothing else to do. And, besides, you have given them rather a lot to talk about.' She smiled kindly.

Rose huffed unhappily. 'I suppose I have really,' she admitted.

'So you and Dan weren't getting it together?'

Rose hesitated. 'Not in the Luther Vandross sense of the word,' she said reluctantly.

'This is me you're talking to, Rose.' Melissa wagged a cake-mixed finger at her. 'Honesty is the best policy.'

'We weren't getting it together, as you so nicely put it,' Rose sighed, 'but not for the want of trying. We just seemed to have more than our fair share of near misses.'

'And then what happened?'

'Then Hugh happened.' Rose opened her hands and expressed hopelessness. 'Dan found out. He was mad. We had a fight.'

Mel's eyes widened with delight. 'You hit him?'

'Emotionally, right below the belt,' Rose said flatly.

'Wow,' Mel breathed. 'This really is true love!'

'Oh, Melissa, don't start that again. I know what your idea of true love is.'

Mel folded her arms, oblivious of the cake mix still caking her hands, and stared directly at her. 'And what's yours, Rose?'

'Are you going to do something with that cake before

it's too late?' Rose asked. 'If you're not going to put it in the oven, do you mind if I go and stick my head in there instead?'

'Just let me finish it and then I'll make us a cup of tea.' Melissa turned back to the mixing bowl and poured the watery beige liquid into two sandwich tins. 'Mary says it's supposed to be the consistency of double cream.' There was a worried look on her face. 'It looks a bit runny to me.'

'It doesn't look terribly chocolatey either for chocolate cake,' Rose pointed out.

'Oh, bum!' Melissa cried in dismay. 'I *knew* there was something I forgot.' She stared malevolently at the cake tins and slammed them in the oven anyway. 'Never mind,' she said. 'I've had enough of being domesticated for one day. Frank's so sweet, he'll eat it whatever it tastes like.'

'That's what I call true love, Melissa,' Rose said sagely. 'And now that you've found it, *don't* throw it away.'

Her friend turned and wiped a generous smearing of cake mix across her top lip. 'Perhaps it's time you took your own advice.'

They both sat at the table and nursed cups of tea. Melissa had scrubbed the cake mix off her hands and arms with a reasonable degree of success, but dried splotches of it still stuck to her face. Rose didn't have the heart to point them out.

'So there's no possibility of a reunion,' Melissa said as she sipped her tea.

'The words fat and chance have a certain ring to them,' Rose replied.

'You should go and see him.'

Rose sighed hopelessly. 'What good would it do?'

'I don't know,' Melissa said tartly. 'I'm not a bloody mind reader. I just don't think you should leave without talking to him.' She put her cup down firmly on the table.

'If what Mr Patel says is true – and there's no reason to doubt it, he's usually spot on – Dan is in a terrible state. He's not eating properly—'

'What's he doing in Mr Patel's shop then, if he's not eating properly?' Rose interrupted. 'It's a grocer's. You realise that this could prove to be a fatal flaw in your argument.'

'He went in to get some Chum for Fluffy.' Melissa was righteous in her indignation. 'It may disappoint you, but you haven't put the dog off its food as well. Just Dan.'

Rose hung her head. 'What shall I do, Mel?'

'When do you leave?'

'When did Mr Patel say?'

'Tomorrow.'

Rose nodded in confirmation. 'Tomorrow it is.'

'Then I suggest you finish your tea, get your butt out of that chair and go and find him.'

'You make it sound so easy.'

'I know,' Mel said encouragingly. 'It does sound easy. It's just a difficult thing to have to do.'

'Thanks.' Rose gave her a sideways glance and pushed herself slowly from the table. 'I brought this,' she said, producing the small brown bottle of essential oils from her pockets. 'It's a going-away present. I left the oils neat so they'd last longer. All you have to do is add some almond oil if you want to use them for massage. You can give me a ring when you want some more. I can either pop them in the post to you or you could come up for a girl's day out if you'd like to.'

' "Secret Passions"?' Melissa smiled sadly as she read the label. 'I think this should last me a long time. I won't be using as much as I used to. You see, my particular secret passion is, unfortunately, not a secret any more.'

Rose smiled in response but instinctively knew that somewhere along the way she was missing the point.

* * *

She could see Dan helping Fluffy into the back of the Discovery as she walked briskly up Lavender Hill.

'For heaven's sake, Fluff,' she heard him snap. 'Stop messing about and just get in the car!'

Rose slowed her stride. He didn't sound in the best of moods. In fact, he sounded like a man in serious need of some geranium oil. She stopped walking and stared up at Builder's Bottom. Dan swung himself into the driver's seat and slammed the door with a force that echoed down Lavender Hill and caused Mr Took to look up from weeding his lawn. That's how loud it was.

What was she going to say to him anyway? Did he really want to hear that she was leaving tomorrow? What did she expect him to do? Did she think he was going to prostrate himself at her feet and beg her to stay in Great Brayford? No, she didn't think so. Was that what she *wanted*? Probably.

A frown creased Rose's forehead. Did she have the nerve to confront what had been happening in their lives – the bit before Gardenia went and Hugh arrived? Could she admit to him her true feelings? Whatever they were. Could she even admit them to herself? And what about the longings that kept her awake when she should have been fast asleep? Could she confess those to Dan? Somehow, she doubted it.

The Discovery reversed out of the drive in an angry shower of gravel. Perhaps this wasn't the best day to clear the air between them. But then, if it wasn't today, there might not be another chance. With a surge of decisiveness Rose started to sprint up Lavender Hill at a pace that the Bionic Woman would have been proud of. 'Dan,' she shouted, her voice carrying away on the wind. 'Dan!'

There was a crunching of gears and a flashing of brake lights. Fluffy looked out of the rear window and barked, wagging his tail enthusiastically. Surely Dan would see her now. 'Dan!' she cried again.

The Discovery paused momentarily and Fluffy barked some more.

'Dan, wait!'

As she neared the back of the car, gasping hot air into her lungs, Dan pressed his foot on the accelerator and with a spin of wheels straight out of *The Sweeney* he sped away. Rose ground to a halt, her arm in the air silently hailing him. There was no discernible slowing down of the Discovery. Typical man! They never use their rear-view mirrors except for admiring their hair.

There were black streaks on the road where he had left an impressive amount of his tyre behind. A stitch twinged painfully in her side and she dropped her hands to her hips with the full realisation that the Bionic Woman would never have felt like this in the same situation. There was, at the same time, another realisation. Just as full and considerably more painful than the stitch.

Her breathing was returning to normal but her heart was thudding in her chest. It was like standing next to the speakers at an AC/DC concert. This was her last chance. Tomorrow she would be gone. 'Dan,' she shouted breathlessly. 'I love you, you stupid bastard!'

Rose watched bleakly as, at the top of the hill, the Discovery turned towards Woburn Woods with a screech of tyre and brakes. Rose stamped her foot and shook her fist after him. 'You stupid, stupid, stupid bastard!' she cried, kicking the brick gatepost that bore the wrought-iron sign entwined with pink roses that said Builder's Bottom. 'I LOVE YOU!' she shouted again.

She ran her hands over her face and tugged at her hair in sheer frustration before kicking the gatepost again. 'I love you,' she said to herself.

She turned and saw the startled face of Mr Took peering nervously over his garden wall. He had ceased weeding his lawn and stood with his mouth open.

'Good afternoon,' she said with dignity. 'It's a nice day for it, isn't it?'

Mr Took's mouth gaped a little wider, but no audible sound came out. With her chin held high and her back rigid, Rose marched stiffly down Lavender Hill, each footstep taking her further away from Builder's Bottom.

Chapter Thirty-Six

Rose unlocked the door of Rose Cottage and pushed it open. After two months without use, the door groaned in protest. Everything was all right in the house, generally – if you didn't mind scaling the mountain of junk mail behind the door. There was a slightly damp, musty smell from lack of use, but that would soon go once the new owners got the windows open and some fresh air flowing through.

She wandered through the rooms and let her hand trail fondly along the familiar walls. Her treatment room still smelled of essential oils. Ghosts of lavender, marjoram, black pepper, ginger, lemon, geranium lingered in the walls and the carpet. They would never get rid of that smell, and she hoped they wouldn't want to.

The fireplace was still only half-finished. You could never rely on British workmen these days and Dan had been no exception. Perhaps the new owners would have better luck. Rose looked up at the leaded windows and the tendrils of ivy that curled over the bricks and her heart twisted with sorrow. She would miss this place.

'It's only me!' Melissa's voice drifted through from the hall.

'In here,' Rose shouted.

Her friend popped her head round the door. 'I saw your car.' She smiled sadly. 'Come for a final look?'

Rose nodded, unable to coax her voice to say yes.

Melissa waddled into the room. She had abandoned her usual leggings and Lycra in favour of a voluminous flowery dress with a white lacy collar and a fussy little bow.

'What's all this?' Rose cried delightedly. 'You look like you've just walked straight out of Laura Ashley.'

'I'm going to make Frank a daddy!'

'That's great news!' She was genuinely thrilled for her friend, who she was sure would make a wonderful mother. Melissa was a natural earthy person, the sort that wouldn't care if the baby peed and puked all over her.

'I haven't got much of a bump yet, I just like wearing the floaty frocks,' she confessed with a blush.

'I'm so pleased for you!'

'Thanks.' Melissa's flush deepened.

'What else have I missed?' Rose asked.

Melissa shook her head. 'Nothing much. You know this place.' She rolled her eyes. 'The new people seem nice,' she said. 'Mr Patel's vetted them already. He's a bank manager. She's a teacher.'

'*So* much more respectable than a dodgy *aromatherapist*!'

Melissa gave her a rueful glance. 'They should fit in well.'

'Good,' Rose said without enthusiasm.

Mel wrinkled her nose. 'I wish you'd come back.'

'I can't.' Rose's voice wavered. 'You know that. Too much has happened. Too much has been said.'

'Lock up here and come to the pub,' Melissa urged. 'It's no good dwelling on things now. We can call into the new village hall on the way and you can admire Dan's handiwork.'

Rose's eyes filled with tears.

'Oh hell,' Melissa cursed. 'That was completely thoughtless. I'm such a silly cow.'

Rose laughed and sniffed back her tears. 'No, you're

right. What's done is done. We'll have a look at the village hall and then you can buy me a brandy.'

Melissa's eyes widened with surprise.

'That is what you give someone when they're suffering from trauma, isn't it?'

'Oh, Rose!' Melissa came to her and put her arms round her.

Rose slipped from her grasp and held her hand up. 'Don't, Mel. I'm just about holding this all together. One tiny little shove and I'll be over the edge.'

'Come on.' Melissa pulled her arm. 'We can't have you going all maudlin on your last day in the village.'

'You're right,' Rose smiled weakly.

'I may not be able to join you in a brandy,' she patted her stomach tenderly, 'but I can have an orange juice with you while you get suitably drunk.'

Where the old village hall had once been there was a great swath of mud, in the middle of which stood a small, attractive building with proper walls and a roof that didn't look in imminent danger of caving in. A neat little path led up to the front door. Presumably the new village hall. Rose had to admit that it was very smart. Compared to the old one, it was a veritable palace. Next to it was a taller building with French windows and neat wrought-iron balconies, but as yet only a lattice of timbers where the roof would eventually be. Definitely Dan's retirement flats. She gave a surreptitious glance towards the site, but there was no sign of him.

Melissa started up the path ahead of Rose and pushed the door open. The curtains were closed and it was dark inside.

'Wait a minute,' Melissa said. 'There's a light switch here somewhere.'

There was a click and the hall flooded with light.

A shout went up. 'Surprise! Surprise!'

Rose blinked her eyes to adjust to the brightness. The room was filled with balloons and streamers. Beneath them stood a party of villagers, twenty or more, headed by Angelica, Basil and Anise.

'Surprise, surprise,' Mel whispered in her ear.

Rose struggled to control the tears that sprang to her eyes. 'I can't move, Mel,' she hissed.

Melissa took her arm. 'Don't be a wimp,' she said and urged her forward.

'My dear, how lovely to see you again.' Angelica grasped her in a warm embrace. 'We have missed you so.'

Rose brushed away her tears. 'I don't know what to say.'

'There's no need to say anything.' She squeezed her tightly. 'Is there, Anise?'

Anise shook her head vigorously. She was leaning on a walking stick but was looking considerably more robust than when Rose last saw her. Just like her old self, in fact. Rose wasn't sure whether that was something to rejoice in or not. 'No,' Anise said gruffly. 'Why don't you come and have a piece of this lovely cake, my dear?'

Rose turned and looked at Melissa.

'*My dear*?' she mouthed.

Melissa shrugged.

'Melissa has baked it especially for you,' Anise continued.

Rose turned and looked at Melissa again, who stared impassively back.

'She's quite a rising star at the WI cake stall,' Anise said proudly.

'You're baking cakes for the WI?' Rose whispered to her friend.

'Don't ask!' Melissa whispered back, narrowing her eyes.

'I think you should cut it!' Angelica enthused, passing the knife to Rose.

'This isn't a wedding, Anglica,' Anise tutted. 'You're spending far too much time with your nose in *Brides* magazine. I'm perfectly capable of cutting a slice of cake.'

'I think Angelica is right,' Basil interjected. 'Rose is our honoured guest. It would be nice if she cut the cake.'

'All right, Basil,' Anise muttered, shuffling out of the way.

Rose was ushered forward and they all gathered round as she eased the knife effortlessly through the icing. Mrs Took swept forward and with a shy smile started to put the cake on to plates.

'Ten out of ten, Mel,' Rose said as she surveyed her piece of light, golden, sponge cake. 'Either your baking has improved or this is a Mary O'Hoorahan's chocolate frenzy gone seriously wrong.'

'I suppose you've guessed,' Melissa tutted. 'I buy my cakes from a little bakery in Leighton Buzzard.' She gave Rose a wry smile. 'No one's any the wiser.'

'You do sail close to the wind sometimes, Mel.'

'Only where cakes are concerned these days,' she said enigmatically.

Reg had provided a bar and was dishing out plastic cups of punch. Rose swallowed hard as she remembered the last social occasion at the old village hall. It was the night of the Viking supper when things had started to go horribly wrong. Her eyes roved over the party of villagers. They were all there – with one notable exception.

'We did ask him, dear.' Angelica had sidled up next to her.

'Who?' she asked innocently.

'I thought you were looking for Dan.'

'No, no, no!'

Angelica met her eyes.

Rose lowered her lashes sadly. 'Well,' she admitted, 'I did think there was an outside chance he *might* be here.' She looked at Angelica again. 'A *very* outside chance.'

'He's extremely busy.' Angelica touched her arm gently. 'But he did send his good wishes.'

Rose snorted miserably. 'I suppose I should be thankful for that.'

'It's not over yet,' Angelica advised. 'Swallow your pride, go to the site – it's only next door – and apologise.'

'He wouldn't listen.' Rose could feel her throat tightening.

'Try!' Angelica insisted. 'Don't get to my ripe old age and be sitting there churned up with resentment in your rocking chair regretting that you didn't try.'

'I don't know . . .'

'I do!' Angelica insisted. 'One other thing about this age is that I didn't get here without learning a thing or two.'

'I'll think about it,' Rose promised half-heartedly.

Anise limped towards them. She coughed delicately. 'I just wanted to thank you, my dear,' she said. 'For leaving that little bottle of oil for me. I've just started to use it and it's been absolutely marvellous.'

'Thank you,' Rose said, teetering on the verge of being rendered speechless.

'It's a shame that you're leaving us.' Anise lowered her head. 'I could do with a spot of that aromatherapy. I think it would be just the thing to get my leg in shape.'

'Yes,' Rose's brain replied – she wasn't altogether sure it came out of her mouth.

The villagers gathered round her again.

'We hope you've enjoyed your little farewell party.' Anise was clearly struggling to control her voice and Rose felt on the verge of tears again. 'We didn't have much time to say goodbye to you properly before you left.'

Cake had lodged in Rose's throat and was refusing to go down, but at least *she* knew she couldn't blame it on Melissa's baking.

'We hope you'll accept this little token of our good

wishes.' Anise handed her a small, neatly wrapped package. 'We persuaded one of our more talented members of the WI to fashion it for you. Hopefully, it will remind you of the good times you had in Great Brayford.'

Rose detected an apologetic note in Anise's voice. 'Shall I open it now?' she asked, biting on her quivering lip.

They all nodded. She fumbled with the packaging and layers of tissue, until eventually she was able to withdraw its contents.

'Thank you,' Rose said, genuinely moved.

It was the most beautiful and most perfect thing she had ever seen. She nestled the miniature ceramic replica of Rose Cottage in her palm. Her eyes misted over. It *was* beautiful, and she had never felt so sad in her life. Was this tiny china memento all that she was going to have to remember her time here by? As Angelica had said, would she look at it on her mantelpiece in years to come and regret that she had not tried harder?

She looked round at the friendly faces beaming beatifically at her. And why had the villagers chosen now to turn from the *Amityville Horror* into a Doris Day movie? It was going to make it harder than ever to leave.

'Thank you,' she stammered. 'It really is lovely.'

'And so are you, my dear,' said Basil, kissing her on the cheek. 'Now, let's charge our plastic cups and have a toast.'

There was a flurry of punch pouring. 'To Rose!' Basil suggested.

'To Rose,' they all echoed.

She looked at their smiling faces and had never felt so sad or so alone in all her life. The one person in all the world that she would have wanted to be here had failed her. He was too busy, was he? She would see about that.

Chapter Thirty-Seven

LOST LOVE CURE
Chamomile Roman, Lime, Neroli.
There is nothing so guaranteed to bring a deep and
abiding sense of unhappiness as parting from a lover.
This can be particularly difficult to overcome if we see
our own culpability as the reason for the failure of the
relationship. This exquisite blend can wrap its arms round
you, cushioning you against the storm and filling the void
that the loss of your loved one has left.
    from: *The Complete Encyclopaedia of Aromatherapy Oils*
    by Jessamine Lovage

It should be called 'Raining June' not 'Flaming June',
Rose thought as she ducked out of the village hall. When
had there last been a June that flamed? They always
seemed to be wet soggy affairs.

The last time she had spoken to Dan it had been
raining. It was the day Gardenia had left and Hugh had
arrived. Even though it was over two months ago, the
memory was still as fresh – or more accurately raw – as if
it had happened yesterday.

Rose put up her umbrella and walked briskly towards
the building site. It was a biting cold day and she was
inappropriately dressed. She was wearing beige suede
loafers, faded jeans, a white shirt and a navy wool jacket.

The sort of outfit she had sneered at Gardenia for wearing. But then perhaps that was the effect she wanted to create. It was pathetic. She didn't want Dan to think she was desperate, did she? Unfortunately, as well as being pathetic, it also meant she was freezing cold. She hadn't had nearly enough of Reg's punch to be feeling warm, or even courageous.

As she turned the corner she saw him. He was warmly dressed in a thick red jacket and a yellow hard hat. Somehow, he still managed to look as if he had just walked out of Austin Reed's. He was ticking off things on a clipboard, oblivious of the steady drizzle and of her. As he looked up, she tilted her umbrella away from her face, balancing it on her shoulder. There was a mixture of emotions on his face as he saw her – surprise, shock, pleasure and . . . What?

'Hi,' she said self-consciously.

'I didn't expect to see you here,' he said.

Rose detected an undisguised tremor in his tone. He looked thinner, more serious. She hoped that he had started to eat properly again.

'I can tell by your face,' she said lightly.

Dan smiled, took off his hard hat, smoothed his blond hair and replaced his hat.

'So,' Rose continued. 'You got what you wanted.'

He leant on the once-yellow dumper truck behind him and put his clipboard down on its snub nose. 'That depends on what we're talking about.'

Rose flushed. 'The church sold you the land,' she said, looking up at the half-finished flats.

'Ah, yes.' Dan nodded. 'They sold me the land.'

'That's great.'

'I thought so,' he said.

This was like pulling teeth without the benefit of anaesthetic. 'So how are things?' she persisted brightly.

'*Things?*' he said. He took off his hard hat again

and fiddled with it. '*Things* are fine.'

'I've seen Melissa,' she said, changing the subject. 'I take it you've heard her news.'

'About the baby?'

Rose nodded. 'I'm so happy for her,' she gushed.

'So am I,' he agreed.

Rose took a deep breath. There was no easy way to broach this. She might as well come straight out with it. 'And what about you, Dan? Are you happy?'

He looked at her steadily, but his jaw hardened like quick-drying cement. 'I'm not sure that you have the right to ask that question, Rose.'

She looked at her feet. Her beige suede loafers were sinking into the mud as fast as her heart was sinking into her loafers.

'No,' he said with a heartfelt sigh. 'I'm not happy, but I'm keeping very busy.'

'Angelica told me.'

'Isn't that what you're supposed to do?'

'Is that why you didn't come to my farewell party? Because you were busy?'

'Partly. I didn't think it was very appropriate for me to be raising a cheery glass to you and wishing you well in your new life.'

'I don't know why I came,' Rose stammered.

His lips parted in a slow, unhappy smile. 'Why did you come?'

'I wanted to talk to you. To clear the air between us.' She stared at him. 'I can see it's not going to work.'

'What do you expect from me? You come back after all this time and say you want to *talk*?' He banged his fist against the dumper truck. 'Shit!' he said with feeling.

'I wanted to say I was sorry,' Rose said past the constriction that had formed in her throat.

His eyes looked troubled, his handsome face pained. 'Don't you think we're past that stage?'

'I did try to tell you how I felt before I left,' she said. 'Remember?'

'No.' A puzzled look crossed his face.

'When I ran after your car. Did you think I was doing that for the good of my health?'

'When?' Dan's look of puzzlement grew to positively perplexed.

'Oh come on, Dan! You deliberately drove off just as I reached you.'

'I did no such thing!'

'It looked like it from where I was standing,' she insisted. 'You had Fluffy in the back and you were going to Woburn Woods.'

Dan's face cleared. 'And you think I'd be able to see you running behind the car with that fluffy-arsed hound in the back?'

'Don't you use your mirrors?'

'Only when I can persuade Fluff to sit down,' Dan said unemotionally.

'Oh,' Rose said, momentarily defeated. Then she pointed at him. 'What about your wing mirrors?'

'I have them positioned so that I can park the car, not watch pretty girls running up the road behind me.'

It seemed a reasonable thing to say. She particularly liked the pretty bit. Rose scratched her head. Her hair was going frizzy despite the protection of the umbrella. There were some days when Rain-Mates seemed a splendid idea.

'So what did you want to tell me?' Dan interrupted her thoughts.

'When?' she asked.

'When you went to all the trouble of chasing my car.'

Rose twirled her umbrella. 'I wanted to say . . .' She cleared her throat. 'I wanted to say I was sorry.'

'What for?'

'*What for?*' Rose echoed. 'For everything!' She felt

perilously close to tears. It had been a stupid idea to come. It had been a stupid idea to dress up like Gardenia. It had been stupid to expect Dan to forgive her. And it had been particularly stupid to walk on to a muddy building site wearing beige suede loafers.

'You're sorry for everything.' Dan looked intrigued.

'I am.' Rose hung her head. 'Because I'm still stupid enough to care,' she said quietly. As tears threatened, she turned to go. The route she had taken on to the site had become a mud bath and Rose hesitated, trying to work out where the least hazardous and most dignified exit for the beige loafers was.

'I'm moving out of Builder's Bottom,' he said to her back. There was an urgency to his voice.

Rose wheeled round. 'But you love it there!' she cried. 'It's your pride and joy.'

His hands were jammed in his pockets. 'Not my joy, Rose.' His eyes met hers. 'That was something else,' he said gruffly.

She shuffled uncomfortably in the mud. 'But why move?'

'Who knows? Too many memories, not enough of them good.' He paused. 'It just felt like the right time.'

'Where are you going to?'

'I'd like to tell you somewhere exotic. But it wouldn't be true.'

Rose forced a smile. A silence fell between them and she studied her feet – or what was left of them. The mud was seeping steadily over her loafers. 'Rose Cottage has been sold too. Apparently the new people are nice. I've just come up to collect a few things and sign the papers.'

'I see,' Dan said quietly.

'Well.' Rose sounded half-hearted. 'I'd better be off.'

'How are you finding life back in the big smoke?' he asked quickly.

She shrugged uncomfortably. 'Dirty. Busy. Expensive.'

She wrinkled her nose. 'Much the same as it was before.'

'Are you working?'

'I've rented rooms in a clinic again. They're pretty horrible.' She pulled a face.

'Still rubbing the shoulders of the rich and famous?'

'One or two rich,' she replied with a grin. 'But, despite the numerous rumours, not too many famous. But then you can't have everything.'

'So I've learnt,' Dan said. There was a sadness in his voice which turned Rose's insides to water.

She gave another shrug, this time so infinitesimal she wasn't sure if her shoulders had moved at all. 'You didn't say where you were moving to.'

'No, I didn't, did I?' His face softened perceptibly and a reluctant smile played at his lips. Some of the tension between them dissolved.

He leaned on the dumper truck and his body was more relaxed. But then his feet weren't getting as wet as hers were.

'I'm only going to the other side of Great Brayford,' he said. 'Old habits die hard. I've bought Basil's house. When he and Angelica get hitched, they're going to move into flat three.' He nodded at one of the balconied windows.

Rose followed his eyes. 'After all that fuss, the balconies look very nice.'

'I thought Angelica might be able to push Anise off one if she ever got really desperate.'

Rose laughed weakly, not knowing whether it was appropriate or not.

'What's Anise going to do?'

'Stay in the house on her own, I presume,' he said. 'No doubt getting steadily more cantankerous.' He looked up at the newly-constructed building. 'I'm going to call this Weston House.'

'I'm not sure whether that's a flattering gesture or a constant poke in the eye for Anise.' Rose gave him a searching look, relieved that conversation between them, though not entirely relaxed, was somewhat less stilted.

He raised his eyebrows enigmatically and made no reply.

'Basil's house is huge,' she said, changing the subject.

'Yes,' he agreed. 'It is. It also needs quite a bit of renovating. I think Basil's been working on the Quentin Crisp theory that if you don't clean a place, then after three years it doesn't get any dirtier. I think his mother before him followed the same rules.' He smiled wryly. 'I can't say it's a philosophy I agree with myself, but once we get the last sixty-odd years of gunge off the walls and open some windows, then we can start to get the place round a bit. It'll be fabulous when it's finished. And I'll be broke.'

'Is the "we" you and Gardenia?' Rose tightened the loop of her umbrella round her hand and avoided looking at him.

'No,' he answered without emotion. 'The "we" is me and Fluffy.'

'You didn't get back together then?'

'No.' He folded his arms and stared at her blankly. 'I found out she'd been having an affair for some time. When she left, it was to run off with an estate agent from Milton Keynes.'

'I'm sorry,' Rose said gently.

Dan shrugged. 'There's another property boom on the way. Apparently.'

There were things that she was desperate to say, but Rose couldn't make her brain direct them to her mouth. They stood looking at each other forlornly in the miserable, relentless drizzle.

Dan spoke to fill the discomfiting space, nodding at the man – a younger, stockier version of himself – who fussed in an unconvincing manner with some paving slabs just out of earshot. 'I'm hoping to persuade my little brother Alan that he'd really like to give up his evenings and all of his weekends to help me, but at the moment I'm failing miserably,' he said with a hearty attempt at jocularity. 'I did something heinous to his pet tortoise years ago and this is the time he has chosen to exact his revenge.'

'It must have been something pretty awful.'

'It was,' he said earnestly. 'I painted "Dan's tortoise" on its shell with a tin of white enamel paint that I found in an old Airfix kit. He never recovered.'

'The tortoise?'

'No, Alan. The tortoise was fine.' Dan's mouth curved into a smile and, for a moment, she didn't notice the rain. 'For another five years it roamed our back garden with "Dan's tortoise" on its back before it escaped. As far as I know there's still a tortoise out there somewhere marked indelibly with my name.'

'You are silly,' Rose chided with a soft laugh.

The silence hung between them again, as dampening as the rain. 'Still . . .' She swallowed. 'Aren't you going to be lonely in that big house all on your own?'

'I'll have Fluffy.'

'You know what I mean.'

'Are you frightened that I'll turn out slightly eccentric like Basil?'

'*Slightly?*'

Dan crossed one muddy boot over the other and stared at his feet. 'I'm hoping that one day someone will make an honest man out of me.'

Rose lowered her head. 'You're already an honest man, Daniel Spikenard.'

He stared at her and she met his gaze. 'Then perhaps I'll find someone that isn't too proud, too confused, too stubborn or too hung up on another man to realise it,' he remarked.

Silence again.

'How is *Hugh*, by the way?' There was a mocking tone to his voice when he spoke Hugh's name.

'I don't know,' she said.

Dan frowned. 'What do you mean?'

Rose pursed her lips. 'I mean I don't know,' she said again. 'It's finished. Over. Ended. Kaput. I only stayed with him for a few weeks after I moved back. And that was a few weeks too long.'

Dan ran his fingers through his wet hair. 'I don't believe this!' His voice was laced with concern. 'What happened?'

'When he said he'd left his wife, he was lying. Ruth turned up at the flat one day. She thought it would be a nice surprise.' Rose met Dan's gaze and felt a flood of colour rush to her face. 'She's very sweet. It was deeply, deeply upsetting.'

'Seeing people get hurt always is,' he said with feeling.

'I was such a fool,' she admitted.

'I could have told you that.'

'You did,' she said with a rueful smile.

'So now what happens?' There was a crack in Dan's voice.

'Time to start again.' It was a lot easier said than done.

'So why did you sell Rose Cottage? Can't you move back here?'

For a moment she thought his voice sounded hopeful. It was time for truth and she had really been hoping Dan wouldn't ask this. She wished the mud would swallow her up a bit quicker, but it was still only lapping the tops of her shoes. 'Starting again includes selling Rose Cottage. You see,' she sighed. 'Hugh owns the whole thing. Lock, stock and barrel. He paid me off with it when I threatened to tell his wife about our affair. I'm going to sell it and return the money. It's the only way I can ever be totally rid of him.'

There was a look of shock on Dan's face. He was glassy-eyed and staring. His body was frozen to the dumper truck.

'I blackmailed him.' Rose spelled it out just in case he wasn't exactly clear on the facts. 'So you see, Dan, I *was* the other woman, and then some.' She laughed, which was just as well, because if she hadn't she would have cried. 'You can say something derogatory if you want to. I'm sure I deserve it.'

Dan still hadn't moved. 'I think it's pretty safe to say that words fail me at this particular moment,' he said flatly.

'Then I think it's time to say goodbye.' Her eyes softened as she looked at him. It wasn't the perfect picture to remember him by, paralysed with shock propped up against a yellow dumper truck, a dazed and disbelieving expression immobilising his handsome features. 'Goodbye, Dan,' she said sadly and turned away.

A soft pat of mud hit her wetly on the side of the cheek. It adhered there as resolutely as if it had been stuck by Super Glue. She spun round to face Dan and lost her footing. Over-balancing in the mud, she stepped into a murky puddle and the water closed over her shoes. Flailing with her arms to right herself, she dropped her umbrella and it skittered away across the mud and the puddles in the wind until it lodged firmly in a pile of damp sand on the other side of the site.

Rose scraped the mud from her face. 'There was no need for that!'

Dan looked up, roused from his catatonic state. He stared at her as if he was seeing her for the first time. 'What?'

'You may not think a lot of me, Dan. But there was no need to throw mud at me.'

'What?' he repeated, his brow knitting together.

Another splattering of mud showered her face and she was glad that she had shut her mouth in the nick of time.

Rose bent down, her left leg sinking further into the mud until it reached halfway up her calf. She scooped a handful of squelching, icy mud. 'Take that!' she said and hurled the mud at Dan.

It missed him, sailing over his shoulder to land with a harmless thump on the seat of the dumper truck. His eyes flickered into life. 'What was that for?'

Rose scooped another handful of mud, this time taking aim more carefully. She had seen them playing darts in the Black Horse. In true Eric Bristow style she took two practice throws and then let the mud sail free from her hand, winging its way towards its target.

'Rose!' Dan shouted, lifting his arm to his face.

The mud pat hit him full in the mouth. 'One hundred and eighty!' Rose cried triumphantly.

Dan spluttered, spitting mud from his mouth. A white handkerchief, being waved hesitantly, appeared from behind the yellow dumper. Rose watched, breathing heavily, as Alan's face appeared from behind the makeshift flag of surrender. 'I come in peace,' he said tentatively.

'It was you! You threw the mud at Rose!' A lump of it fell from Dan's lip as he spoke. He wiped his mouth with the sleeve of his red jacket. 'Of all the stupid things to do!' he yelled.

'You were about to let her walk away!' Alan shouted back. 'So don't call me stupid!'

'I'm sorry, Rose.' Dan cast an anxious glance at her. 'Truly sorry.'

Alan had stopped waving the white flag but he continued to shout. 'You've been as miserable as bloody sin since Rose left and you're too proud to tell her! What else could I do? I had to do something! Besides,' he added petulantly, 'you were leaning on my dumper truck and I wanted to drive it.'

Dan spoke through gritted teeth. 'This is going to cost you dearly, Al. I want you at that house every night and every weekend for the rest of your life!'

'It'll be worth it if it puts a smile back on your miserable face,' he chirped. 'If you know what's good for you, take her home, Daniel!'

'Get out of here!' Dan said with a reluctant smile. He retrieved his clipboard from the front of the truck and tossed it in the footwell behind him.

Alan flashed him a grin. 'Sorry, Rose!' he shouted as he jumped into the seat of the dumper truck. His smile froze as he landed squarely on the mud pat that had missed Dan.

'Don't mention it, Alan,' she said with a slow smile.

'Touché!' He blew her a kiss and with the same hand wiped the mud from his bottom. Whirling the truck round he headed towards the pile of sand and the fugitive umbrella.

Dan walked towards her. 'I can't apologise enough,' he said, a suitable note of mortification in his voice.

Rose looked up at him. 'Neither can I,' she answered. Her lips quivered uncertainly. Hot stinging tears prickled her eyes, pooled on her eyelashes and then shamelessly spilled over on to her face. Her hair was plastered to her head and she could feel tracks of supposedly waterproof mascara making their way to greet the mud on her cheeks.

'Here, let me help,' he said with concern. He put his arms round her and tried to wriggle her out of the mud.

Her foot parted company with her shoe and her leg popped out of the mud like a cork out of a bottle.

'Oh shit!' Dan said, his hand flying to his mouth, unable to suppress a broad smile.

'Don't!' Rose sobbed, her mouth curling at the corners. She hopped in the mud. 'You're making me cry!'

'No, I'm not,' Dan protested. 'I'm making you laugh!'

Rose smiled and sobbed again. 'I don't know what to do!'

Dan's smiled died. He put his hands on her shoulders. 'Come home,' he said soberly.

'Home?'

'To Builder's Bottom,' he urged. 'Or at least for the next few months. Then, if you want to, you can move into Basil's house with me.'

'*Move in with you?*'

'Marry me, Rose. I love you. Say you'll stay and raise little builders with me.'

Rose smoothed the black tears from her cheeks, smearing on more mud from her hands. 'Yes,' she said. 'I will.'

Dan stood up and lifted her from the ground, twirling her in the air. He slid her slowly down his body until their lips met among the mud and mascara. A cheer went up and a chorus of wolf whistles penetrated the rain. They looked up and saw six workmen, including Alan, leaning over one of the wrought-iron balconies, grinning insanely.

Dan lowered Rose gently to the ground and slipping his hand round her waist, he guided her towards the little island of solid ground that remained.

'Does Basil's house have a name?' she asked, cuddling into his side.

Dan shook his head. 'Not yet.'

'Are you going to call it something as outrageous and colourful as Builder's Bottom?'

'Well, now that you've agreed to marry me, we ought to call it something to commemorate this momentous occasion.' His voice was thoughtful.

'Like what?' she asked warily.

'Well, it's at the top of a hill . . .'

'Yes,' she said suspiciously.

'We could call it Rose Mount.'

'Dan Spikenard!' Rose looked shocked.

'You don't like it?'

She smiled, stood on tiptoe and kissed the mud on the end of his nose. 'I love it,' she said.

'And I love you,' Dan replied.

He pulled her to him and kissed her again. It would

have been nice if the rain had stopped and the sun had come out. But it didn't. It would have been nice if Jessamine Lovage's 'Lost Love Cure' worked miracles. But it didn't. Rose knew that the only surefire cure for lost love was to go and find it again.

Let's Meet on Platform 8

Carole Matthews

In ten years of commuting, Teri had never had a conversation with anyone else on the train. She saw the same faces every day, year in, year out, rain, hail and snow – and never a word was spoken . . . So why was she sitting here in a rush-hour commuter train with a stranger, her foot resting just centimetres away from his groin, letting him know about the frustrations of her job? She was one step away from telling him her whole life story!

Could it be that she'd finally met Mr Right?

To Mum
for all we've been through together

And for Steve

With grateful thanks to Clare, Darley and Elizabeth for believing in me and to Pauline, a true and trusted friend.

Chapter One

It was the hole in her tights that made Teri start crying.
She looked at them in desperation as sheer as they were.
The tights were black with added Lycra 'For Working
Legs' and she'd paid £7.99 for them. Seven whole pounds
and ninety-nine pence for one pair of tights – and now
look at them! Perhaps they would have lasted longer if
she'd bought the ones for *non*-working legs.

Her knee was scraped and bright scarlet blood was
oozing through the grey grit-encrusted skin. She hadn't
had a scabby knee since she was ten, when she'd fallen off
the swings in the local playground in the unenlightened
days before the Council used knee-friendly landing areas
like squishy black rubber or shredded tree bark. It seemed
even more cruel when she had managed to negotiate the
icy pavements of Euston Road – which, at this moment,
were probably suitable for Torvill and Dean to practise on
– without an undignified incident.

To help matters along, her briefcase – seeking to exact
some minuscule revenge, as only briefcases can – had
decided to shed its contents, and her papers blew fussily
along the platform in the frantic funnelled breeze from
departing trains. *Including hers.*

'Oh hell, I'm really sorry. Here, let me help you.' His

1

voice was like being stroked with velvet. Okay, so it was a very romantic-novel type of thing to think in the circumstances. But it was true. The voice was soft and soothing and held the faint trace of a quiet, reassuring Scottish burr whose corners had been knocked off by too many years spent in the Home Counties. He looked sort of romantic hero-ish, too. Probably tall, though it was hard to tell as he was crouched over her briefcase carefully gathering its contents to his chest, while the last breathless stragglers hoping vainly to catch the 18.07 for all stations to Milton Keynes pushed heedlessly past them.

'I was rushing to catch the train,' he explained. 'I just didn't see you. I'm sorry.'

'Shit,' Teri said, fishing in her pocket for a tissue. There was one lurking in the corner but she could tell by its disconcertingly crispy feel that it was far too disgusting to pull out in public. 'I'd gathered that,' she said, summoning as much sarcasm as she could manage after having been savaged by such a cute-looking kitten.

'I feel terrible.' He put her papers inside her briefcase and clipped it shut. 'But probably not quite as terrible as you,' he added hastily.

'You'll miss your train.' She sniffed and wiped her eyes with the back of her hand. Although he had stooped to her level, she looked up at him. There was definite eye-contact. Lots of it. His eyes were greeny-gold and bordered with dark-brown rims – as if someone had carefully and lovingly outlined them with brown felt-pen to make the whites look Persil-white. They were soft and warm and she could tell he laughed often. At the moment, they positively oozed concern. Either he was genuinely mortified or he was the leading light in his local amateur dramatics group.

2

'It's already gone.' He produced a clean white handkerchief from inside his coat with the air of an accomplished magician. Somehow it looked more suave on him than it did on Paul Daniels. 'It was an all-stopper anyway. Here.'

Teri took it reluctantly. She had no idea that men under fifty carried handkerchiefs. It was the equivalent to wearing a string vest on chilly mornings or socks with garters or, even worse, those metal armbands that held shirtsleeves up that were otherwise too long. This hanky looked far too clean to wipe dirty things with. Hesitantly, she dried her eyes.

'Now fold it over and do your knee,' he instructed.

She looked at him to check that he was serious.

'Go on,' he urged.

It was a long time since she had been treated like a four-year-old – probably not since she was four, in fact. And it was even more mind-boggling that, for the moment, she didn't resent it.

Teri dabbed gingerly at the blood and grit, totally ruining the immaculate white linen. She winced. 'Ouch.'

He frowned. 'I think you need to get that properly cleaned up.' He offered her his arm. 'Here, let me help you to your feet.'

He slipped his arm under hers and lifted her easily to her feet. Teri's knees buckled. 'Oh God, I think I've sprained my ankle!' The tears sprang afresh to her eyes. 'That's just about a perfect *sodding* end to a perfect *sodding* day,' she said with feeling.

'Let me have a look.' She hopped round on her good leg, holding on to his back while he examined her ankle. 'No bones broken, but I think your diagnosis is right. Looks like you've twisted it.'

'Are you an expert then?'

He stood up and rubbed his hands together. 'No, but I've watched *Match of the Day* often enough to know when someone's really hurt and when they'll be running around the pitch the next minute as if nothing's happened,' he replied earnestly.

The fount of all useless knowledge straightened up and raked his fingers through his hair. It's amazing the details you notice when you're in pain, Teri thought. His hair was dark and wavy, slightly flecked with grey. Late-ish thirties, she guessed. It was receding slightly at the sides, giving a hint of the baldness that would rob him of his youthful looks later in life. But then nobody was perfect. She should know. She'd dated more men than she'd had low-calorie, low-fat dinners and still hadn't found Mr Right. She'd been through all of the other Mr Men though, in a short history of painful relationships – Mr Lazy, Mr Greedy, Mr Bump, Mr Completely Selfish, Mr Looking-for-Mother-Substitute and Mr Downright Pervert – but, as yet, no Mr Right.

'If I hold you under the arms, could you manage to hop to the public loos? They're not far – just at the end of the station.'

It was possibly the most original chat-up line she'd heard recently – if indeed that was what he was trying to do. And it was certainly better than the one all the double-glazing and space-age vacuum-cleaner salesmen used when she answered the door to them – the very original 'Is your mother at home?'

Perhaps other thirty-year-old women went all skittish and malleable when they were 'mistaken' for teenagers and instantly signed up for lorry-loads of UPVC windows they had no need of, and extortionately priced vacuum cleaners that would ruin your carpets within two years. In her book it earned them nothing more than a withering glare and a faceful of door sandwich.

'Can you manage this?' He passed her handbag to her and gripped her briefcase in the same hand as he held his own.

Teri nodded and hung on to him. 'It would help if you could just relax your grip a bit,' he said breathlessly, as he shifted her weight to his shoulder. 'I've nothing against blue, but I'd rather my face wasn't that colour just at the moment, thanks. Otherwise, we might not make it to the ladies' loos.'

'Sorry, sorry,' Teri said. God must have a really warped sense of humour to put her in this predicament with the most decent-looking man she had bumped into in ages – quite literally. 'You really don't need to do this, you know.' It was hard to hop and talk at the same time.

'Call it a salve to my guilty conscience. And anyway, there isn't another train for twenty minutes.'

'I'm glad to be able to fill in the time for you.'

'Oh sorry, I have the knack of saying the wrong thing.' He looked like a scolded schoolboy.

'Then let's just concentrate our efforts on getting me to the loo in one piece.' Hopping up the steep concrete slope from Platform Eight back on to the main concourse at Euston was an experience Teri wasn't keen to try again in a hurry. But, as usual, in the rush-hour no one gave her a second glance. All commuters worked on the same premise. If they simply looked the other way there was no chance that they could be called on to provide assistance which would delay their flight from the City to the relative sanity of the suburbs – for the few brief hours of respite before they turned round and did it all again.

She hopped to the turnstile at the entrance to the

ladies' loo and rummaged in her handbag for her purse.
'I've got a twenty-pence piece,' he said, and thrust it in
the slot before she could protest. He gently pushed her
towards the turnstile barrier. 'I'll wait here. Take your
time.'

The loos were not very clean – not enough to warrant
a twenty-pence entrance fee, anyway. Teri looked at her
face in the smeared mirror. Or more accurately, her
smeared face in the smeared mirror. Wiping the panda-
circles of mascara from under her eyes, she noted regretfully the decreasing amount of white on the borrowed
linen handkerchief that she still clutched like a security
blanket. She dragged her fingers through her hair and
fluffed it up hopefully. It fell flat to her head instantly. She
would bet a pound to a penny that Julia Carling didn't
have bad hair days. Especially when she had Mr Fanciable
of the millennium dancing attendance on her – even if it
was in slightly less than romantic circumstances.

'A nice young man asked me to give you these, dear.' A
white-haired old lady who looked incredibly like Barbara
Cartland – without the pink – thrust a packet of tights
into her hands.

'Thank you.' Teri raised her eyebrows appreciatively.
Thoughtful with a capital T. 'Wait.' Teri touched her arm.
'How did you know they were for me?'

'He told me to look for the dishevelled woman with a
scabby knee,' she replied sweetly. 'It had to be you, dear.'

'Thanks.' Teri smiled a tired smile. 'Yeah – thanks a
bunch,' she muttered under her breath to the old lady's
retreating back.

One attempt at trying to lift her foot into the wash
basin whilst balancing on her good leg told her that it was
far too acrobatic a manoeuvre to consider in a tight skirt,

considering the indignity she had already suffered. And the paper towels were too rough to bathe her knee with, so Sir Galahad's handkerchief was pressed into service again, then she dried her knee under the hot-air blower that was thankfully broken and was blowing cold. As an afterthought she gave the sodden stained handkerchief a cursory blast.

Teri nipped into one of the cubicles to change into the new tights and meditated on what kind of man would even think to go and buy her a replacement pair. Okay, they weren't anything flash, no Lycra, no Tactel for velvet softness, no satin sheen for enhanced elegance, no elastane for a perfect fit. But they were the right size – although with one size you couldn't go too far wrong – and the right colour – again with black you were pretty safe. At least he had noticed.

And so what if his description of her had been a little less than flattering; it was accurate. He could have said 'attractive, but *temporarily* dishevelled woman', it's true. But then Teri was a firm believer that actions speak louder than words. While she was there, and contemplating deeply, she made use of the facilities. If they were going to charge you twenty pee for a pee, the least you could do was make sure you got value for money.

He was still waiting outside. Which was just as well because he had her briefcase. But she wouldn't have been surprised if he'd disappeared. He could have just dumped it and cleared off. He could have just dumped *her* and cleared off, too. He'd done enough already really – despite the fact it was his fault she had been knocked down in the first place.

He was lounging against the glass wall of the sunbed

salon tucked incongruously into the corner opposite the toilets. How many people clamoured to top up their tans in the salubrious setting of Euston Station was another one of life's little mysteries that deserved further consideration at a later date.

She hopped towards him. 'Thanks for the tights.' She showed him her knee, which through thickish black nylon looked perfectly presentable.

'I hope they were okay. I didn't know if you wore tights or . . .' he blushed '. . . or well, the others, you know.'

It was years since she had seen a man blush. They didn't any more, did they? God, it was endearing. Carrying a handkerchief and blushing – this one was a prize. 'Well, you wouldn't, would you?' she teased.

'I got them in Knickerbox,' he said by way of explanation, gesturing towards the glass kiosk filled with pastel shades of frillies in every shape and size imaginable, marooned in the middle of the concourse. 'They have nice things in there.'

'Really?' Teri arched her eyebrows. His skin flushed to a deeper shade of beetroot. She wondered briefly if he was a pervert.

He cleared his throat. 'We'd better move it or we're going to miss this train, too. How's the ankle?'

'I'll live.'

'Come on then, take my arm again.' It had in fact improved to two limps and a hop and they struggled back to the platform for the next train. He paused to look at the display board.

'Which stop?' he asked.

'Leighton Buzzard. And you?'

'Milton Keynes. This one will do us. It leaves in five minutes on Platform Eight.'

They set off again. 'Look, you're helping me marvellously . . .' Teri paused for breath, '. . . with my Long John Silver impersonation.' Limp, limp, hop. 'And I don't even know your name.'

'Jamie,' he puffed. 'Jamie Duncan. I'd shake your hand but you don't seem to have one free.'

'I'm Teri Carter, that's T-E-R-I,' she said breathlessly, trying to co-ordinate breaths and hops to synchronised intervals. 'Pleased to meet you. I think.'

The train was sitting waiting patiently and already most of the seats were taken in the first few compartments. 'There are two together in here.' He opened the door.

'Look, I'll be fine. You've done enough.'

'I insist. My guilt complex still hasn't gone.'

They both sat down gratefully, opposite each other, and Jamie dropped the briefcases on the floor with an exaggerated sigh of relief. 'Thank goodness for that! I'm not sure which is heavier – you or your briefcase.' Several newspapers in the surrounding seats lowered to look briefly at the object of his derision.

'Well, next time you decide to knock a woman over, choose a smaller one!'

'Sorry.' He winced. 'Put your foot up here. It stops the swelling if you elevate it.' He indicated the seat beside him.

'More information gleaned from *Match of the Day*?'

'*Casualty.*'

'I didn't have you down for a *Casualty* watcher.'

'I'm not. My secretary tells me all about it – usually in its full Technicolor glory. She's obsessed with watching operations.'

'*Animal Hospital* is her favourite.' He gave Teri a sideways smile. 'If you'd been a pregnant rhinoceros I'd have known exactly what to do.'

'That's very encouraging, but it probably would have involved more than a pair of black tights and a strong shoulder.'

Jamie shrugged. 'Infinitely more.' Again, he patted the seat next to him. 'Foot.'

Obligingly, after adjusting her skirt to provide a modicum of modesty she raised her foot. He touched her ankle, stroking the swollen area gently. His fingers were cool against the hot skin that throbbed through her tights. Why was her mouth suddenly dry? It was probably delayed shock. She should have bought a drink from the End of the Line Buffet.

'I don't like the look of that.' He tutted and shook his head ponderously. 'I don't like the look of that at all.' His eyes travelled up to her knee. 'Does it hurt anywhere else?'

'Only when I laugh,' Teri said tartly and wriggled her skirt down.

The guard blew his whistle and there was a succession of slamming doors. Their carriage door was wrenched open and a sweating businessman with a florid face and a wet, bald pate squeezed himself on to the seat next to Jamie, smiling genially at him as he lowered his bulk, sandwiching her foot with his bottom. Casually, Jamie lifted her foot and put it on his lap as if it was something he did every day.

The businessman dabbed his face with a handkerchief that was considerably more grubby than Jamie's had previously been – although it was probably a good match for it now.

Teri didn't know which would be more embarrassing, to move her foot away or leave it there throbbing as acutely as her temples. The train jerked out of the station and she decided to leave it there for the time being until she could devise a way to extricate it without drawing too much attention to herself.

'So what do you do when you're not discussing *Casualty* or *Animal Hospital* with your secretary?' she asked, more in an attempt to deflect his eyes from her legs and the fact that one of them was resting ever so comfortably in his lap than out of sheer unadulterated interest.

'I'm a Database Manager for an insurance firm – the Mutual and Providential.'

'That's interesting.'

Jamie smiled. 'That's polite.' He had perfect white teeth, like the ones in a toothpaste advert. The sort of teeth that meant you needn't care less whether there was added fluoride or chloride or bromide – the sort of teeth that made you want to get your own teeth very, very close to them and have first-hand experience of that fresh-breath ring of confidence.

'It's actually the most boring job in the entire universe,' he went on. 'That's why I spend my days discussing the latest load of twaddle on television with my secretary.'

He wasn't touching her foot any more, which somehow made it worse. She couldn't relax, because it might flop and nestle somewhere more intimate than it was now. Hell, she was going to get cramp at this rate.

'What do you do?' he asked.

'I work in television.'

'Oh hell! Sorry.'

'That's all right.' Teri laughed as he flushed again. 'Most of it *is* a load of old twaddle. I work for City Television. And I can't claim any credit for the actual programmes. Like you, I'm at the boring end.'

'I didn't think there was a boring end in television. I

11

thought it was all glamour and luvvies and *dahlings* and free booze.'

'If you can make coffee and count you could do my job.' It hurt more than her ankle did to admit that, and she wondered why she'd told him. Why was she sitting here in a rush-hour commuter train with a stranger, her foot resting just centimetres away from his groin, letting him know about the frustrations of her job? She was one step away from telling him her whole life story!

In ten years of commuting, Teri had never had a conversation with anyone else. She saw the same faces every day, year in, year out, rain, hail and snow – and never a word was spoken. There might be the odd person with whom she was on nodding terms, and once, about three years ago, a woman who ran the Brides' Book at John Lewis in Oxford Street had accidentally prodded her with her knitting needle just outside Berkhamsted and they had chatted amicably for the rest of the journey. She had told Teri that she was knitting a matinée jacket for her new grandson and Teri had wondered if babies still wore white matinée jackets knitted by their grandmas. After that they had been on good nodding terms, which included a smile, but that was about it. She hadn't seen the woman recently and had assumed she'd retired – or died.

'You're probably underselling yourself.' His voice broke into her thoughts.

She shook her head. 'No, but I don't intend to be at the boring end for ever.'

They whistled through a tunnel, the wind buffeting against the windows making conversation impossible. The train was cold as they always are in winter – it's only in summer that hot air belches out relentlessly from beneath the seats – and Teri stared out of the window into the street-light-flecked darkness. The aroma of cooking biscuits from the McVities' factory hadn't twitched her nostrils tonight as it usually did. It normally started her taste buds tingling and her stomach rumbling so that the first thing she did when she got through the door was head for the jar where the Jaffa Cakes were kept and immediately eat three to sate her appetite until it was time for her calorie-counted meal. But not tonight. Tonight her stomach was churning but she certainly couldn't put it down to the enticing smell of biscuits. Perhaps it was Jamie. She hoped to God he wasn't a mind-reader.

He looked at her and winked. It was a reassuring kind of wink. A little shiver had travelled down her spine for a moment, but fortunately, this wasn't a wink that said, 'yes, I *am* a mind-reader'. It was just a wink. His face didn't move at all, just his eyelid squeezed languorously over his eye.

They were definitely feline, his eyes. They reminded her of one of her mother's cats – a long-haired white one with ginger ears called Sooty, which spoke volumes about her mother's state of mind. If anyone had winked at Teri on a train before, she would have hit them squarely on the head with the *Daily Telegraph*. Tonight, the *Telegraph* lay unopened in her traitorous briefcase and she just smiled back.

As the train slowed into Leighton Buzzard, she reluctantly removed her foot.

'Better?' Jamie asked.

'Much.' The puffed skin was swelling over the top of her shoe most attractively. 'Thanks for your concern.'

'It's the least I could do.' He stood up and picked up both briefcases.

'I can manage, thanks.'

'I want to see you safely home.'

'But you live in Milton Keynes! You'll have to wait for the next train.'

'You won't be able to drive.' It was a reasonable assumption. 'Is your car at the station? Or is someone meeting you?'

'No, neither. I walk.' She realised as she said it that walking home would be impossible. 'It's about fifteen minutes,' she added lamely.

'Then we need to get you into a taxi.' Jamie ushered her off the train, hand firmly under her elbow. Teri winced as she hit the platform awkwardly. He helped her towards the footbridge which led from Platform Four to the exit. The bridge looked as if it was made of Meccano and was painted bright red, which added considerably to the effect. They made slow progress. One limp, one hop. Was that an improvement or had it got worse?

'I'm not a mugger or a rapist,' he said thoughtfully as they inched their way along. 'There's no need to worry.'

'Thanks for that character reference,' Teri puffed. 'It hadn't crossed my mind until then.'

'Unless, of course,' he hesitated. 'If there's someone waiting for you and it would be difficult . . .'

'No, there's no one waiting,' Teri answered truthfully. 'Well, at least I don't think so. I'm sharing my house with a very close friend at the moment; I can never tell whether she's going to be there or not.'

'A *very* close friend?' A dark look crossed his face.

Teri laughed. 'Not *that* sort of close friend!'

'I'm sorry – for a moment I thought you meant—'

'I know what you thought! You don't need to spell it out. I might work in television but I'm not that trendy. Clare and I were at school together,' Teri explained. 'Her husband's just run off with some teenage bimbo and she's staying with me.' They took the steps one at a time, Teri clinging on to both Jamie and the handrail for support. 'Though how he found anyone more bimbo-ish than Clare it's hard to imagine. She's a trolley-dolly – sorry, *flight attendant* – at Luton, hence the irregular time-keeping.'

His arm was strong around her and his skin still held the faint scent of a citrus aftershave that said expensive. She was glad she'd agreed to let him take her home. Not that he actually gave her a lot of choice, but she could have invented some excuse for getting rid of him if he'd shown imminent signs of turning into a nerd. She'd had a lot of practice in the past.

It took ages to struggle over the bridge to the cheerful red station that looked as if it had been modelled on a pair of Christopher Biggins's glasses. To add to the bitter cold it had started to drizzle, but thankfully there was a solitary taxi still left at the rank when they emerged from the station. It was a Mercedes – one that had seen considerably better days, and its interior had been brightened by the touching adornment of nylon leopardskin seat covers. Instead of the ubiquitous fluffy dice hanging from the mirror, the driver had installed a yellow-and-black-striped fluffy bee with the legend BUZZ OFF stitched on its rotund stomach. They huddled inside, brushing a sprinkling of raindrops from their clothes.

'Bidefield Green,' she instructed the driver. 'Seven hundred and thirty-two.'

'Seven hundred and thirty-two?' Jamie repeated incredulously.

'I think the Council must have had a particularly heavy lunch the day that Bidefield Green came up for naming, and found it far too tiresome to think up individual and original road names – hence half of Leighton Buzzard is called Bidefield Green. It starts at number one and goes up to about four million and twenty-seven, I think.'

'Four million and twenty-seven?' Jamie echoed.

'At least,' she confirmed.

The driver swung out of the station road and headed up the hill towards the Linslade side of town and Bidefield Green. Leighton Buzzard and Linslade had once been two separate towns, but had grown together over the years to make one endless sprawl of commuter housing. Teri liked living in Linslade – until she had to order something over the phone and then it was a pain, because she had to spell out every line of her address to the operator.

She turned to Jamie again, who was peering out of the rain-streaked and steamed-up window trying to see where he was going in the darkness. 'The numbers follow no logical sequence either,' she said. 'Odds and evens meander randomly round the estate – it must have been a very good lunch. Still, looking on the bright side, it means that unwanted visitors haven't a hope in hell of ever finding you. Unfortunately, neither do the wanted ones.'

There was a grassy knoll as they approached Bidefield Green – halfway up the hill, separating the main road from the first of the houses. Well, it was more a sloping strip of land with a phone box and a post box on it and a couple of smallish oak trees. The post box was totally inadequate to cope with the amount of letters that spewed forth from the occupants of Bidefield Green. If you happened to want to post one yourself, you were invariably greeted by a smiling letter-slit that was crammed full and refused to take anything else – even the slimmest of overdue bill-payments.

Teri always thought of John F. Kennedy when she

passed the grassy knoll. They had learned all about his untimely death in History in the sixth form, and the teacher, Mr Seward, kept going on and on about 'the grassy knoll'. Teri couldn't remember exactly where the grassy knoll had come into it, but it had obviously played some deeply significant role in the assassination. This grassy knoll seemed pointless by comparison, except it was a good place for your dog to poo if you were too lazy to take it for a proper walk.

The taxi driver turned into the estate and threaded his way through the maze of roads. The leopardskin-lined Mercedes slowed to a halt. 'Taxi drivers are infallible though,' Teri said. 'We're here.'

Jamie helped her out. He turned to the taxi driver. 'Can you wait for me, please? I won't be long.'

Teri felt a flash of disappointment. Any thoughts that they might linger over a medicinal glass of Beaujolais had just gone straight out of the window.

'Give me your key,' he instructed. Teri obliged and Jamie opened the door. 'I'll resist the urge to carry you over the threshold, seeing as we've still to be formally introduced.' He ushered her inside.

The house was in darkness – which was a good sign. At least Clare wasn't around to poke her nose in. Jamie led her gently to the sofa and flicked on the light switch. 'Now let me make you a coffee or something.'

'Really, I'm fine. Your meter's running.'

'Black or white?' he insisted.

Teri gave a sigh of resignation. 'Black, no sugar.'

He disappeared into the kitchen and, following the banging of several cupboards, reappeared moments later carrying a tray which he placed beside her.

'Cheese and biscuits – a very fine Camembert – not

exactly a wholesome meal, but filling. One biscuit jar containing only Jaffa Cakes – Madam's weakness, it would appear.'

'Quite.' *That – and tall dark handsome strangers*, Teri added silently.

'One cup of hot coffee, black, no sugar. One large brandy, two painkillers and a bag of frozen peas for reducing the swelling in Madam's ankle.'

'Where did you learn your bedside manner from? Was it *Match of the Day*, *Casualty* or *Animal Hospital*?'

'From your first-aid book on the shelf next to the kettle – a very sensible place to keep it.'

He pulled the footstool towards her, lifted her foot, rolled the peas in a clean tea towel and balanced them on her ankle.

'Comfortable?'

She nodded.

He passed her the remote control for the television and crouched down before her. 'I'm sorry, but I have to go. Is there anything else you need first?'

A lump had risen in her throat. 'No, you've been very kind, thank you. I really appreciate it.'

'Well.' He stood up to go. He really was quite tall. 'Perhaps we'll bump into each other again on the 18.07. Just joking!' He made his way to the door. 'You probably need to stay off that ankle for a few days.' His face was suddenly serious and he looked embarrassed again. 'Are you sure you're going to be all right?'

'Yes, fine. Clare should be back tonight. Your taxi driver will be getting impatient.'

'I'll see you then.'

'Yes, thanks again.' The front door slammed behind him. She watched, stranded on the sofa, as he got into the taxi and it drove away. He really was the nicest man she'd ever met. There weren't many of them left any more, and he was the nicest of them all. No one had been that kind to her since she'd had her tonsils out and the doctor insisted she eat nothing but ice cream for days. So what if the resulting stomach ache had made her feel even worse than having her tonsils out. It was the thought that counted.

She flicked on the television – *Coronation Street*. Not another dose of emotional strain! She sipped her brandy and then, abandoning any sense of decorum, tipped the rest into her coffee and swilled it down with the two painkillers. It was when Jack Duckworth started to pull his first pint of the night in The Rovers Return that she started to cry again. His horn-rimmed glasses repaired with sticky tape always looked particularly pathetic, but never more so than tonight.

Sobbing on to the Camembert, Teri pulled Jamie's handkerchief out of her pocket. It was dirty, bloodied, mascaraed and wet, and still she had an overwhelming urge to use it to wipe away her tears. Damn the bloody man! Fancies himself as a knight in shining armour and he didn't even think to leave a box of man-sized Kleenex to hand. Then again, he might not have imagined her crying quite so uncontrollably when he left. *She* certainly hadn't.

Chapter Two

To hell with the expense. There was no way he was going back to the station to wait for another train now.

Jamie leaned into the taxi window and spoke to the driver. 'Can you take me to Fraughton-next-the-Green, Milton Keynes?'

He always felt stupid, asking for his address. It was like asking for *Poggleswood* or *Tickle-on-the-Tum*. Whoever named the estate in Milton Keynes had a more warped sense of humour than their counterparts in Leighton Buzzard. Mind you, with so many of them to name they must be running out of ideas by now.

The taxi driver looked blank.

'It's near the Open University,' Jamie said helpfully.

He swung into the back of the aging Merc, glad of the warmth after the penetrating dampness of the night. Gratefully, he sank into the worn seat for the drive home to Milton Keynes. He glanced at his watch. It would take about half an hour, providing the driver wasn't intent on breaking the world land-speed record as they so often seemed to be.

The driver turned at the bottom of Teri's road and headed back past her house. Jamie could just make out her outline through the slatted blinds on the window and thought that he should have closed them for her. With any luck, her friend Clare wouldn't be too long in coming home and she could look after her.

Why did he feel so ridiculously deflated, Jamie asked himself, walking away and leaving her like that? He'd done all he could. She wasn't his problem any more. So what *was* his problem? Why had he felt so ridiculously *elated* when she'd said that there was no one waiting at home for her? Why had he, for a brief and shocking moment, wished that he could have said the same thing?

Pamela would be furious. Again. He had promised that he would be home earlier tonight – and he had nearly made it. If he hadn't been rushing quite so much, he might never have rugby-tackled Teri at all. So really, this time, it was Pamela's fault he was late . . . although it wasn't an excuse he was keen to try on her.

Better to stick to the old faithful, he decided – signalling failures at Watford Junction. It was usually true. He certainly couldn't tell her the real truth. Pamela was not an understanding woman. Anyway, why did he feel so guilty about taking Teri back home? He was only doing the Good Samaritan bit, wasn't he? Anyone would have done the same, wouldn't they? Possibly not these days. There might have been a considerable amount of passing by on the other side.

Perhaps he was feeling guilty because it wasn't for entirely altruistic reasons that he had wanted to dally in her company. Hell, she had looked so sexy with her scabby little knee and her wobbly lower lip and her hair that looked as if she had been pulled through a particularly thick hedge backwards *and* forwards. He'd wanted to take her in his arms and cuddle her until all the nasty men went away – except that he had been the nasty man who had knocked her down in the first place. Well, he couldn't just abandon her after that. Could he?

He could hear the closing bars of *Coronation Street* as he turned his key in the lock and wondered briefly whether Pamela had lost her marbles completely while she was waiting for him to come home. She was not a *Coronation Street* person. *Dynasty* might be getting a bit closer, but certainly not the *Street*. Pamela had a terminal fear of all things working-class; she seemed to think that just by watching the programme, serious dropping of the aitches and a liking for black pudding might ensue.

'Hi, I'm home,' Jamie shouted tentatively. There was no reply. Not promising.

MacTavish was cowering under the radiator in the corner of the hall – this was not a good sign either. He wagged his tail tentatively and Jamie patted him. A brief 'Good boy' was all the encouragement he needed to be sent racing upstairs, tail battering the banisters as he went.

Jamie pushed open the lounge door. Next door's fourteen-year-old daughter Melanie was snogging – if that's what they still called it – with her boyfriend on the sofa. His hand was up her skirt and they both shot three feet in the air when Jamie peered over the sofa and said, 'Hello.'

Obviously, the efforts of the *Street*'s best scriptwriters had failed to capture their attention. Jamie rubbed his stubble. 'What *on earth* are you doing?'

They looked at each other for inspiration. Jamie moved up from his stubble and instead rubbed the frown lines on his forehead. 'Forget I said that,' he waved a hand dismissively. 'Where's Pamela?'

'She's gone to Francesca's school. It's parents' night.' 'Oh shit, shit!' Jamie banged the place he had just rubbed. 'I'd completely forgotten about it.' Pamela would do her pieces when she got home. 'Where are the kids?'

'In bed – about an hour ago,' Melanie said sheepishly. 'We're babysitting.'

'We had a different name for it in our day,' Jamie said caustically. They both looked puzzled.

He dropped his briefcase on the sofa. 'Go on, you can clear off home now I'm back.' They shuffled towards the door. 'Did Pamela pay you?'

They shook their heads. He pulled out his wallet and gave them a ten-pound note. 'Go and book yourself a motel room or something,' he muttered.

'Thanks, Mr Duncan.' They departed hastily – Melanie rearranging her Lycra as best she could – presumably before he could change his mind.

He took his coat off, shook the rain from it and hung it over the banister. Pamela hated that too. He would move it before she came home. Tiptoeing up the stairs, he peeped in the children's bedrooms. Jack was curled up with his thumb in his mouth, a tumble of blond hair curling over the duvet. He looked just like Pamela and, more unfortunately, had every sign of having inherited her temperament as well as her looks.

Francesca was stretched out fast asleep on top of her duvet with Barbie. She was like him – tall, the tallest in her class, dark and easygoing – lazy in school terms. He turned away from the doorway.

'Mummy's very cross with you.'

He suppressed a smile and turned back. 'I know. I was late home from work, when I said I wouldn't be. She's gone to see Mrs Rutherford.'

'I bet that'll make her cross too.'

He smoothed her hair and laughed. 'I hope not. Go to sleep.' He kissed her forehead.

'Mummy had to ring Kathy next door so that Melanie could come round to stay with us. She called you an inconsiderate bastard.' It sounded appealing with a faint lisp due to the absence of two front teeth.

'She's probably right. But those are grown-up words that aren't very nice. Don't try them in the playground or you'll upset Mrs Rutherford.'

'Goodnight, Daddy.'

'Goodnight, darling.'

'Daddy.'

'Yes, darling?'

'MacTavish is under the bed.'

'It's probably a good place for him at the moment.'

'Goodnight.'

Pamela had continued the illegitimate offspring theme in the kitchen. He opened the oven door and took out the well-cooked plate with a folded tea towel. On it were three fish fingers that definitely wouldn't have inspired Cap'n Birdseye to cry, 'Yo, ho, me hearties,' some sadly deflated livid green spheres that probably used to be peas, and some reconstituted potato Alphabites spelling the word BASTARD that were arranged in a neat semi-circle around the edge of the plate.

Jamie wondered whether his wife had got all the letters from one bag, or whether she had opened two bags specially. It seemed more vindictive to open two bags, but he fought the urge to search the freezer to check. Jamie popped the B into his mouth with his fingers. It burnt his tongue.

He took his plate through to the conservatory, taking the tomato ketchup from the cupboard on the way. It could be a bit on the chilly side in here in the winter, but at least looking at some of the exotic plants still thriving in there gave him an indication of the warmer days to come, and helped to dispel the misery he felt at spending six months of the year always leaving in the morning and returning home at night in the pitch dark.

It might also help him to digest this dried-up school dinner. His first inclination had been to scrape it into the bin – or into the dog – and make himself a sandwich, but that would have been ungrateful. It was his fault he was late and he would take Pamela's punishment like a man – or a mouse, depending on which way you looked at it.

Jamie spread ketchup over the rest of the -ASTARD and began to work his way through it letter by letter. It was a well-known fact of life that tomato ketchup made even the most unlikely thing edible. That was why the children smeared it on chips, cabbage, curries and cereal, even Coco Pops. It wasn't that Pamela couldn't cook, it was just that recently she had taken it into her head that everything in the house had to be educational. And that obviously included mealtimes.

These days, his wife wasn't happy unless the children could spell with their food, or at the very least make a funny face – which tended to prolong the time spent at the table. Jack could already spell DOG and CAT with Alphabites. Give him a book or a pencil and he was stuffed, but food, that was a different matter altogether. Jamie was under the impression that it was Pamela's aim for him to be the first three-year-old at the nursery to be able to read the baked-bean version of *War and Peace*. He had some way to go yet. But that didn't stop her from trying.

There had been one temporary moment of politically

incorrect madness when Pamela had returned pale-faced from Toys R Us, Francesca triumphantly clutching a Barbie doll – 'because she was the only girl in the entire school who didn't have one'. She omitted the fact that she had a computer complete with Pentium Processor, jigsaws too numerous to mention, a tool kit – non-sexist household – and all manner of mind-expanding playthings. But all had been forsaken in favour of Barbie – the anorexic blonde-haired bimbo who made Pamela Anderson look positively deflated. Pamela – Duncan, not Anderson – feared she was failing in motherhood and to make up for this brief aberration had turned all family meals into tutorials.

At least the awfulness of his meal had distracted him momentarily from thinking about Teri. He should have stayed and tucked into Camembert and cheap brandy with her – at least then he would have felt his punishment justified. Why did he feel so wretched about leaving her alone with nothing but a bag of frozen peas for solace? He pushed his few remaining peas round his plate in sympathy.

And her name – it slipped so casually off his tongue, as if he had been saying it for years. *Teri.* He wondered if it was short for something or whether her parents had been particularly trendy. He would ask her next time he saw her. Grief! What was he thinking of? There would *be* no next time. How many years had he travelled on that line without seeing her before? Still, he knew where she worked. He could casually orchestrate it so that he was walking by City Television offices just as she was going home for the evening – they were only just up the road from Euston Station. But perhaps she didn't go home at that time every night; perhaps she was leaving early to go to the dentist or something. But then she would have mentioned it . . .

He gripped the arms of his wicker chair. This was a train of thought that must stop – no pun intended. Why was he even thinking of wanting to meet her again? He was happily married – well, mostly – with two point two children, if you included Barbie. He and Teri had nothing in common with each other and no need to speak again. Commuting and communicating might begin with the same letters, but that was where the similarity ended. He had knocked her over – crass, but accidental – and he had done his bit and that was the end of it. And the sooner he convinced himself of that the better.

When he finally heard Pamela's key turn in the lock, Jamie let out a heartfelt sigh. With any luck, Francesca would have done the business and would have sucked up to Mrs Rutherford enough at the last minute to get straight gold stars for everything. That could come close to letting him off the hook.

The only thing that would massage Pamela's ego further was if Francesca's inspirational painting of 'My Mummy' looked vaguely like her rather than the abstract Picasso-style monster she usually managed to produce. Pamela would not be happy if she had green hair, white high-heeled shoes and was smoking a cigarette like she was last year.

'Hello, darling,' she shouted from the hall.

Jamie shrugged and raised his eyebrows. Things were looking up. Then he remembered that his coat was still draped over the banister rail. That could well mean the end of the *entente cordiale* as we know it and the start of another Cold War.

He heard his wife clip, clop across the parquet floor until she paused by the stairs. It was a technique the SS used in old films to menace prisoners of war who had thought to escape by rather overtly digging a tunnel while whistling loudly to cover the noise. The soldiers clicked along the corridors just before they were about to torture them without the benefit of modern anaesthetics.

After a sufficiently significant and nerve-wracking pause, Pamela clipped into the kitchen. 'I'm going to bed,' she announced in clipped tones and promptly clipped out again. She obviously needed time to think up a particularly hideous torture.

Jamie ate the last of his BASTARD with a heavy heart. It seemed he could look forward to facetious Alphabite messages for the rest of the week.

Chapter Three

'So what else did he say?'

'Nothing.' Teri lifted her hands in the air and gestured meaningfully. 'He just got in the taxi and went.'

'Just like that,' Clare said in disgust.

'Just like that.'

'I thought it was only Tommy Cooper who went "just like that!".' Clare did a passable impression. She waited for Teri to laugh.

Teri glared at her instead.

Clare carried on regardless. 'You must be losing your touch.' She flopped down on the sofa next to Teri, dislodging the carefully placed bag of once-frozen, now dripping peas. 'You, the same person who in her time has dated Billy Bunter and the Frog Prince – the one who turned from a prince into a *frog* – have freely admitted that you let the fittest man you have seen this century disappear in a taxi without so much as waving your Filofax at him!'

'He said he had to go.' Teri was getting irritable.

'He might have been waiting for you to ask him not to,' Clare pointed out. 'Men like that sort of thing these days.'

'He had me at a physical disadvantage. I wasn't thinking straight.' She kicked the peas off her ankle on to the floor.

'Besides – asking him not to go didn't keep your dearly beloved David in the marital bed.'

Clare looked stung. 'That was below the belt, Therese Carter.' She pronounced her name with the harshness of a scouser – rather than the softness her mother had sought to inject into it against all the Liverpudlian odds. To Clare, particularly in moments of sublime irritation such as this, she was Tereeza – a bit like *Malteser*. Teri had hated her name at school and wished desperately that she had been called Dawn – which was surprising considering how awful she was at getting up in the mornings.

'I know, I'm sorry.' Teri hugged a cushion forcefully. 'It's just that I could kick myself.'

'I could kick you too.'

Teri scowled. 'That's no consolation.'

'So you don't know where he lives or works or anything?'

'He said he was in insurance.'

'Riveting.' Clare rolled her eyes. 'You could crash your car,' she said helpfully, after giving it some thought.

'I think I'll just stick to hanging round Euston Station looking nonchalant.'

'Your intentions could be mistaken.' Clare picked at the remains of the Camembert. 'Still, you might earn a few bob while you're waiting.'

Teri thumped her with the cushion. 'He's not like all the others. He's nice.'

'Nice? Nice! *Nice* is a banned word! Surely you can't have forgotten the hours spent in Mrs Bagshaw's class discussing nice. "Nothing is *naice*, Clare".' She mimicked her teacher's cut-glass tones. 'She could reel off a thousand other adjectives that were better than dear old nice. And I still can't bring myself to write in red pen because of that woman.'

'He is nice. He's *very* nice! He's the only man I've met who doesn't act like Jean-Claude Van Damme on amphetamines. He's sensitive and intelligent.'

Clare continued unabashed, 'He can't be that intelligent if he walked out of here without fixing himself a hot date.'

'He may not have fancied me,' Teri mumbled.

'What does that matter? You were still panting after him like the Andrex puppy when I came home. Surely he was bright enough to know he was on to a sure thing?'

Teri glared at her. 'I'm glad you think so highly of my morals.'

'You never did know how to play hard to get, Therese. Look at Christopher Parry. You were all over him like a rash.'

'I only went out with him twice and I did have a rash!'

'It just goes to prove my point.' Clare smiled superciliously at her victory. 'So you didn't ask him anything else?'

Teri tutted. 'I couldn't really.'

'Why not?'

'I was embarrassed.' Teri flushed.

'Embarrassed!'

'He kept looking at me – like *looking*.'

'It's a good job you're not a private detective or an investigative journalist – you'd starve to death. You could learn a lot from paying attention to Kate Adie.' Clare wagged her finger. 'For goodness sake, you're a woman of the nineties! You carry rainbow-coloured condoms in your handbag! What are you planning to do with them – blow them up and twist them into cute little poodles or giraffes once they're past their sell-by date?'

'Be sympathetic! I'm supposed to be your best friend. I have opened my home to you in your hour of need; the least you could do is pretend to listen to me in mine.' Teri poured herself some more brandy from the bottle Clare had retrieved from the kitchen. 'And, anyway, you seem to have fewer admirers than Fergie at the moment, so don't give me a hard time.'

Clare groaned. 'Working for an airline isn't the best place for checking out talent. They're all either married or gay.'

'And what about David?'

'Still terminally ensconced with the nubile Anthea. Still declaring that it's me he really loves, but would I be prepared to accept the fact that he can love two women at the same time – and probably in the same bed, knowing David.'

'Bastard.' Teri threw back her brandy.

'Bastard.' Clare joined her.

Teri refilled their glasses. 'Here's to nice men!' The brandy was making her eyes water.

'To nice men,' Clare agreed. 'Wherever they are!'

They both drained their glasses. The brandy was giving Teri a warm glow that made her feel slightly blurred round the edges like a bad photocopy. Amazingly, she couldn't feel the pain in her ankle at all! It had gone clean away – just like Jamie.

The thought was enough to make her reach for the bottle again. She had found her nice man and she had let him go by mistake. Perhaps another drink would help. If she wasn't careful she could become very depressed about it.

Chapter Four

'I'm just amazed that you happened to be walking past the office exactly when I was leaving,' Teri said breathlessly. 'Isn't that amazing?'

'Yes, a coincidence,' Jamie shouted animatedly. 'How's the ankle?'

'What?'

'Ankle!' Jamie bawled, and pointed helpfully.

'Better!' she yelled back and gestured at her ear. 'It's the traffic.'

She pulled her coat around her and they leaned into the chill wind that gusted a few tired and dirty leaves across Euston Road, walking along in an uneasy silence enforced by the noise of the rush-hour.

Teri put her head down to stop the swirling dust blowing in her eyes. Her heart was pitter-pattering like stiletto heels clicking on a concrete pavement. She was keeping pace with Jamie – just about, he took long, easy strides that covered twice as much ground as she could. From the beat of her heart it sounded as if she was running a marathon.

She had been stunned to see him draped casually against the wall outside her office. In fact, she thought it was the closest she had come to suffering a cardiac arrest.

Despite trying to engineer it to bump into him at Euston she hadn't managed it at all and, apart from the physical evidence of a still green and purple ankle, was beginning to think that he had been a hallucination brought on by the stresses and strains of daily commuting. She had been about to give up hope of ever seeing him again. Clare had given up all hope on her unequivocally.

He was gorgeous. More gorgeous than she remembered – possibly because he didn't look quite so harried this time. She risked a sideways glance at him and he smiled in return. He looked suave and sophisticated. He was dark-suited under his light-coloured cashmere coat – brave for a commuter – and looked every inch the successful insurance company executive. His dress was immaculate – classic and traditional – but with a rakish cut to the clothes that spoke of a slight rebellious streak pushing against the bounds of staid conformity. The sort of man who wouldn't look out of place modelling designer clothes for *Esquire* magazine. Executives at City Television wore jeans with loud Hawaiian shirts and had bald heads and long ponytails.

They looked at each other and smiled occasionally along the route and did their best to ignore the entreaties of the hopeful homeless selling the *Big Issue* and the hopeless homeless already huddled down for the night in their sleeping bags.

The stark concourse of Euston Station always seemed relatively peaceful in comparison to Euston Road, despite the hordes of miserable-looking people. At least you could hear yourself speak in there. It was a functional station building – that was the best that could be said about it – square, austere, but functional. Its architecture made no effort to mimic the ornate, gothic romanticism of St Pancras or King's Cross. Euston, it appeared, had been styled along the lines of a Lego brick – seemingly a popular style of architecture in the early sixties.

Years ago it had been fronted by a small, scruffy park full of dossers and drunks and day-trippers. In its place there was now a bare plaza with half a dozen struggling trees, half a dozen concrete benches and a browning oblong of grass, banked on three sides by black-glassed office buildings.

In the centre was a modern sculpture – a sort of wigwam of crossed drainpipes bearing cheery colourful metal flags – which looked deep and meaningfully significant. There were two brass plaques at the bottom of the poles. One said: *Euston Banners 1994*, the other: *Smoke Extractor Basement Level Six*.

At the corner of the square next to William Hill bookies, stood a statue of Robert Stephenson, who died on 12 October 1859 – and who must be gyrating in his grave at the current state of the railways.

Once inside, Teri and Jamie crossed the main concourse dotted with small and colourful merchandise kiosks and stood beneath the black departure display board which towered above them. It was doing more clattering than a demented pinball machine.

'This looks ominous,' Jamie stated flatly.

Their train disappeared off the board – all stations to Milton Keynes being replaced by suspiciously permanent-looking blanks. A passenger announcement began in the usual mix of English, double Dutch and mumble. 'The late-running 18.07 for all stations to Milton Keynes has been cancelled. This will now become the late-running 19.07 for all stations to Milton Keynes, departing from

Platform Eight at approximately 19.37 for all stations to Milton Keynes. This unavoidable delay is due to signalling failures at Watford Junction.'

Jamie's shoulders sagged visibly and he looked at his watch. 'This is going to be another free-for-all fight. Do you fancy giving the scrum a miss and going for a drink instead?'

So what if she missed her 'Calligraphy for Beginners' at Vanwall Upper School? She'd long given up hope of ever needing it to write beautifully scripted wedding invitations. The best she could hope for now would be writing labels for jam jars when she eventually succumbed to her bath-chair and joined the WI.

Besides, Mrs Jessop made the ancient craft of illegible writing seem so utterly unenthralling and tedious that you could actually find yourself wishing for death during her lessons. The fact that the class had dwindled from a relatively healthy nineteen to start with, to a sickly four just after the start of the second term was possibly an indication that other students shared the same view.

Mrs Jessop had been teaching calligraphy for twenty-five years, she proudly told them every week. Perhaps twenty-five years ago she had made it sound interesting. Teri wondered how many hapless souls had in previous years signed their twenty-nine quid away to be subjected to torture by italics and half-uncials without any intervention from the local education authority – who were presumably supposed to monitor the standard of teaching. The stoic remaining students were all of the same if-you-start-something-you-see-it-out-to-the-end-no-matter-what-the-personal-cost school of thinking. It was now a matter of honour that she should keep this lifelong vow no matter how hard Mrs Jessop and her badly behaved waterproof ink bottle and interchangeable nibs tried to persuade her otherwise.

Teri was sure the other three stalwarts could manage without her for one week. Her low-fat chicken Tikka Masala for One wasn't going to come to any harm languishing in the fridge for a little bit longer either. The decision was made.

Teri nodded. 'I'd love a drink.'

The only pub at Euston hovered high over one corner of the concourse, jutting out over the bookshop and the burger bar beneath it. It was faced in the same flat grey-coloured tiles as the rest of the concourse and, as such, was virtually indistinguishable from the public toilets.

If you managed to get a window seat – a bit of a misnomer because there wasn't actually any glass, just a window-shaped hole through which a constant draught blew – you could watch the disappointed sagging of the shoulders as the swarming commuters ground to a halt beneath the display boards. This was the point where they recognised that it was going to be a long night and any hopes of an early dinner and a night in front of the telly were once again dashed.

The pub was called 'Steamers', presumably through some clever marketing man's bright idea of an allusion to the Golden Age of Railways, rather than to the fact that the only reason most people went to such an awful place was to get steaming drunk. Anyway, they could hardly call it 'Diesel Electrics' or 'Commuter Cattle Trucks', could they? Where was the romanticism in that?

The inside was an illusion of a bygone age, too. A sort of mock-Victorian fantasy had been forced to merge seamlessly with *Star Wars*. The stools were of the finest imitation tapestry, the lampshades crimson and fringed.

Even the toilet doors continued the theme, respectively adorned with silhouetted ladies in crinolines and gentlemen sporting top hats and canes. Somehow the bank of fruit machines, the juke box and the television screens detracted from the overall effect slightly. The prices made no attempt at nostalgia either – they were firmly fixed in the future.

Teri and Jamie joined the throng of other deflated commuters who had decided that battling against British Rail's best efforts to prevent them from getting home was something that couldn't be faced without a seriously topped-up alcohol reservoir. Sitting for two hours in a stone-cold carriage on a red signal while INTERCITY trains whistled past you wasn't something that was easy to endure while still entirely stone-cold sober.

'What would you like?' Jamie was already taking his wallet from his coat.

'A gin and tonic, please.' She really wanted a Beck's but that seemed so unsophisticated. A gin and tonic was so much more of a timeless classic – she didn't like it much, but nevertheless it was a timeless classic.

'Grab some seats,' he shouted over the noise as he pushed his way to the bar.

A table was just being vacated by two exceedingly blowsy women wearing particularly see-through blouses and ridiculously short skirts. As they pulled on their jackets and tottered out of the bar in totally unsuitable high-heeled shoes, giggling and patting overtly at their straw-blonde hair, probably wigs, no one else in the bar gave them a second glance. In the once-quaint market town of Leighton Buzzard they would have stuck out like Richard Branson in a dole queue, yet thirty-five minutes down the line in the great metropolis they were just two more weird-looking people having a drink. It was only slightly more weird that the drinks had been pints of bitter . . . That was feminism for you.

Teri pushed their abandoned glasses to one side, swept the puddles of spilt beer to the floor with the beer mat, and waited for Jamie.

He returned clutching two drinks and two bags of crisps, flushed-faced and obviously sweating inside his coat. He clanked the drinks on to the table and tossed the crisps after them. 'Thought these might keep us going.'

He took his coat off, rolled it into a ball and tossed it on the floor as casually as he had tossed the crisps on to the table. Teri didn't think it was a wise move but said nothing. She sipped gratefully at her drink. It was a dry Martini and lemonade, and the shock of the unexpected sweetness made her wrinkle her nose – but again she said nothing.

'Cheers.' Jamie held up his glass. Some sort of beer. 'I just wanted to apologise again for last week.'

'Were you waiting for me, then – outside work?' Teri swallowed the dry Martini again. It really wasn't so bad once you got used to it. Better than gin and tonic, actually.

Jamie shook his head vigorously and wiped a smear of froth from his top lip. 'Oh no, of course not.'

Teri's heart sank quicker than her vain attempts at making soufflés had.

'Well, when I say no, I mean not exactly,' he corrected. 'It was just that I thought I might see you – on the train – and when a few days had gone by and I didn't, well, I happened to remember where you said you worked and I just thought I'd see if you were around. Sort of.'

'Oh,' Teri said. Her throat had gone tight.

They both took a swig of their drinks. 'Yes, I actually

hung around outside your office waiting for you,' he admitted. 'Sorry.'

She smiled. 'No, that's okay. That's nice.'

'Well, I just wanted to check the ankle was okay, really.' He shrugged with a nonchalance that he didn't really feel. The sort of shrug that says, 'I won't lose any sleep over it' when in fact he had lost lots of sleep. The varying troubles of database management – which were the usual cause of his nocturnal insomnia – had paled into insignificance faced with the turned ankle of a fragile beauty on his conscience. He had been bleary-eyed and bad-tempered every morning after a night spent lying awake thinking about nothing but Teri Carter.

It was ridiculous; he felt like a fifteen-year-old sitting here, suddenly nervous and gawky again. Like a puppy still coming to terms with its oversize paws. She was just as he remembered her, though why he thought she would have changed in a week was uncertain. In fact, he wished she *had* changed, or that his memory of her had been too vivid and overblown, like a movie shown in Technicolor Cinemascope. But no, she was still beautiful. She was still elfin and dainty like one of the flower fairies in the book that Francesca was so keen on him reading at least three times every bedtime – when he was home in time.

Teri looked at him above her glass; her eyes were unnaturally blue and she had eyelashes like Daisy the Cow. He wasn't absolutely sure that she wasn't wearing coloured contact lenses. No one had eyes *that* blue . . . except possibly Paul Newman. Pamela always commented on Paul Newman's eyes. That was why she'd started to buy Paul Newman's Own Salad Dressing, because of his eyes. Teri's eyes could sell salad dressing. They could probably sell ice to Eskimos, too.

He was aware that she was speaking. 'Sorry?'

'I said it's fine, thanks.'

'The drink?'

'The ankle. You asked about my ankle.'

God, he wished she was ugly, he might be able to pay more attention to what she was saying. Her face kept distracting him. She had a tiny, rosebud mouth that pursed and pouted when she talked, and little perfect teeth that showed she wasn't one to neglect her dental appointments.

'Clare and I shared a medicinal bottle of brandy and got rather too carried away.'

Perhaps he should suggest putting a paper bag over her head, then he might listen to her rather than just wanting to sit and look at her. Then again, she could take it the wrong way.

'I had such a bad headache the next day, it made my ankle seem trivial by comparison. They say that the body can only cope with one type of pain at a time, don't they?'

Jamie snapped his attention back to her. 'Do they?'

'I don't know. Anyway, there'll be no more sherry trifle in our house for a while.' She abandoned her low-fat, healthfood kick and split the packet of Roast Beef-flavoured crisps open. All this talk of food, even if it was sherry trifle, was making her hungry.

'You put brandy in your sherry trifle?' he said inanely. 'Isn't there a hint there in the title somewhere?'

She hated sherry trifle and only made it when her mother came to stay. She used brandy in it to make her mother forget to ask her the usual irritating questions about the men in her life, the life in her men and the imminent possibility of grandchildren.

Sometimes the trifle was so strong that it resembled a

Madeira cake floating in half a bottle of Courvoisier, with a pint of Ambrosia ready-made custard precariously balanced on top. That was when it was getting towards the end of her mother's week-long visit. The dish might not be all that attractive or even that edible, but it kept Mrs Carter in a soporific state for a few hours so it certainly did the trick. Desperate times require desperate measures. 'I hate sherry,' she said, by way of simplified explanation.

It was Pamela's favourite drink, dry sherry – a small one on high days and holidays. That, and dry Martini and lemonade.

'Oh hell – I can't believe it! I bought you the wrong drink.' What was he doing? He was here on an illicit . . . an illicit *what*? An illicit drinking session with a girl he didn't know and he glibly bought her his wife's favourite drink. What a prize prat! 'You wanted a G and T, didn't you? Grief, you must think I'm an idiot.'

'I do, but it doesn't matter.'

'Let me get you another one.' He was already on his feet.

'No really, it doesn't matter.' Teri downed the Martini and lemonade in one. 'Oh, to hell with it, why not. Forget the gin, though. I'll have a Beck's and I'll drink it straight out of the bottle.' She smiled wanly at Jamie's startled face. 'Thanks.'

Two hours and several Beck's later they were finally jerking past the graffitied walls and out of Euston. Conversation had been difficult in the bar, partly due to the decibel level of the animated chatter of stranded commuters, and thanks also to the fruit machines, which bleeped and chimed above it all and then clank-clank-*clanked* their hoard of treasure out every few minutes. It was also partly due to the fact that Jamie seemed to go into a trance every time she spoke to him. Teri was beginning to wonder if she was boring him at one point, but he seemed to get over it as the evening wore on. Perhaps he was just tired.

It was difficult to talk now, too. The train was still crowded despite their diversionary delaying tactics of a dalliance in Steamers Bar. Jamie was sitting silently next to her and they exchanged the occasional smile, but neither of them seemed to think it appropriate either to chat or to get their newspapers out. The signals at Watford Junction, it appeared, still couldn't decide whether they wanted to function or not, so the train inched slowly from station to station while the evening sped rapidly by.

Although the term 'cry wolf' lodged itself firmly in Jamie's brain, he was feeling quite mellow. As mellow as a newt probably. But who cared? It only took him a moment to come up with the answer: Pamela would care. Pamela would care deeply. If you ate more than three wine gums in a row, Pamela thought you were on the rocky road to alcoholism. He would have to get a taxi back from the station and risk leaving the car to the tender mercies of the overnight car park. He would be lucky to have any wing mirrors or windows or stereo left by morning or, indeed, a car at all.

As soon as she saw the taxi turning into their drive she would know he'd been drinking. That in Pamela's vocabulary was drunk. As a skunk. Okay, so he'd had more than the local constabulary would find excusable, but he was still a long way off what George Best would consider a good night out. Still, it was worth it. He'd managed in his quest to bump into Teri again – even though it had meant leaving work early and hanging around the windswept wasteland of Euston Road until she appeared. But what had it achieved? he mused. They had spent a very pleasant couple of hours getting sociably inebriated with the perfectly viable excuse of signal failures at Watford Junction, and now what? The urge to see her again was stronger than ever before and she hadn't even got off the train yet! Teri wasn't just pretty, she was feisty and funny and could probably drink most rugby players under the table without looking even slightly the worse for wear.

Why did she seem to come right into the centre of him and fill a gap that he hadn't even realised was there? He wasn't unhappy with Pamela. Okay, they had their moments – sometimes it was like living with Princess Michael of Kent with the added bonus of premenstrual tension – but on the whole they had a reasonable marriage, certainly no worse than anyone else's these days.

All right, so he was bored utterly witless by his job; it was only the sheer volume of work and playing political pat-a-cake that gave him sleepless nights – the actual job he could do standing on his head and sometimes felt like doing so just to prove a point. Still, they paid him a barrow-load of cash just for turning up, so it could be considerably worse. He absolutely adored the kids – even when they vomited in the Volvo on long car journeys. They were the best thing that had ever happened to him. That, and winning the Club Championship at Melbrose Golf Club when he was eighteen . . .

So why was he doing this? Doing what? He wasn't *doing* anything! But if he wasn't doing anything, why did he feel so guilty about not doing it? Why couldn't he say to Pamela: 'I was late last week because I clumsily bumped into a woman and sprained her ankle for her in the process, and I'm late tonight because we happened to meet up at the display board' (slight alteration of the truth admittedly) 'and I took her for a drink to enquire about the well-being of the aforementioned ankle.'

Simple enough? Simple, but deadly. If there was one thing you had to understand about Pamela it was that she couldn't cope with glitches in her daily domestic harmony, and her husband taking a strange woman, however injured, for a drink would definitely be considered a glitch.

He could just see it now – it would mean tears, tantrums, a temporary but inconvenient banishment to the spare room, and an upgrading in the vile atrocities of Alphabite combat. So signal failures it was and signal failures it would remain and he would avoid the endearing charms of Teri Carter – named Therese after a genteel and elderly maiden aunt, but reappraised to Teri on account of the amount of time she spent shinning up trees and playing football as a wee schoolgirl rather than doing cross-stitch – as if they were a deadly plague.

'We're coming into Leighton Buzzard.' Teri stood up and smoothed her skirt, which didn't really need smoothing. He was aware that a few newspapers in the vicinity dipped noticeably.

'It's been great,' Jamie said lightly. She had picked up a thread of cotton on the arm of her jacket from the back of the train seat, which was split at the seam and oozing stuffing. He longed to reach out and take it from her, grooming her so that she looked perfect again. This was ridiculous. He locked his fingers together, just in case they had the urge to disobey his brain. 'Perhaps we'll bump into each other again.'

'I'd like that.'

The train stopped at the platform and the man in front of Teri jumped out. She hesitated, only slightly, but Jamie knew a hesitation when he saw one. Why couldn't she still have a sprained ankle, one that would keep her limping for months, then he could gallantly sweep her off the train and have a watertight excuse for escorting her home? He wanted to go with her to her little seventies box on the hideous sprawling housing estate and close the door behind them for ever.

'What time train do you catch in the morning?' she asked.

'The 6.25,' he answered, his heart pounding like a Bon Jovi bass line in his chest. 'It stops at Leighton Buzzard.'

She smiled. 'Perhaps I'll see you then.'

The door slammed behind her and he watched her picked out in the darkness by the platform lights as she ran nimbly up the stairs of the red metal footbridge. That was how it started. As simple as that.

Chapter Five

'Can't you come up with something more original than that?' Pamela clanged the spoon on the plate as she dished out some Alphabetti Spaghetti. 'Do the signals *ever* work at Watford Junction?'

'It would appear not,' Jamie said resignedly. 'Look, I've had a verra long day and I don't want to argue with you.' His accent always got stronger when he was cross – and he knew it annoyed Pamela. 'Would it make you happier if I told you it was vampire bats hanging from the overhead wires that had caused the delay?' And when Pamela snorted, 'I thought not.'

'British Rail have a much larger catalogue of excuses than the pathetic ones you resort to.' She banged the grill-pan into the dishwasher. 'Whatever happened to the wrong-type-of-snow or the feeble leaves-on-the-line routine?'

'Those are seasonal phenomena which can only be used for a paltry few weeks. The rest of the time they have to use more vague, catch-all excuses. There'd be no point in saying the wrong type of snow was causing delays when there'd been no snow at all.' Jamie rested his head in his hands. 'Commuters might be a pretty stupid bunch, but even we'd spot that one a mile off.'

Pamela tutted. It was an unconvinced *tut!* and she banged the drawer shut to underline it. He looked at his wife from between the hammock his hands made under his chin. She was tall, cool and classy, with great hair. It was long, straight and reddy-blonde like a lion's mane, although she had recently taken to having it surgically enhanced with highlights – unlike his own hair which was seeing the beginnings of genetically programmed highlights. Her eyes were the colour of chocolate buttons and she sort of blended in with autumn. The word which most suited her was 'aloof'. Definitely aloof – and perfect – and socially aware. Pamela was as different from Teri as *I Can't Believe It's Not Butter* is from, well, butter.

'You take no interest in the children.' She obviously had no intention of letting this drop.

'I take lots of interest in the children. It's just that it can't often be on a week night at the moment. They won't always be in bed by seven o'clock.'

'That's still not much use if you can't get home before nine o'clock.' The plate of Alphabetti Spaghetti and two burnt sausages was crashed down on the table in front of him. 'They could be eighteen by the time you get to see them on a Wednesday.'

Still surveying her he could see that Pamela was pale and her face looked strained. She must be tired because she had failed to spell anything vitriolic with the Alphabetti Spaghetti. That could also be because it was much more slippery to deal with than Alphabites. Creative caustic comments with unco-operative carbohydrates required a certain level of concentration – he knew this because he had tried it once to see how long it must take her. Admittedly, a novice at tinned-pasta abuse, he had spent ten minutes trying to find the right letters to spell bloody cow before he gave up. By which time the bright-orange-coloured tomato sauce had gone cold. There was definitely an art to it.

'You don't see them at the weekends either,' she went on tersely. 'You're always out on that damned golf course!'

Jamie put down the knife and fork he had just picked up. 'It's my only form of relaxation – and exercise, come to that. And it's certainly the only exercise MacTavish gets.' The dog slinked guiltily out of the kitchen before he was incriminated further.

Jamie picked up his knife and fork again. 'And despite getting up at five-thirty every morning to go to work, on Saturday I still get up at just after six so that I can play a few holes and be back here by lunchtime to see what word of the day is. Then we have all afternoon to do family things.'

'But we don't, do we? You usually fall asleep in front of the television in the afternoon while purporting to watch motor racing.'

'That's only if you haven't got anything specific planned – and besides, I'm so bloody exhausted at the weekends I can only just manage to sit upright after three o'clock.' He stuck his fork into a sausage and belligerently bit the end off it.

Pamela winced but didn't comment. Obviously, his eating habits would wait until another time.

'I take them to the playground at Willen Lake,' he munched. 'Occasionally.'

Pamela refused to be easily placated. 'It's not fair, Jamie. It's not fair on me, and it's not fair on the kids.'

'Look on the bright side, it's only a matter of time before they'll be big enough to play golf with me.'

Pamela's face darkened ominously.

'It was meant to be funny,' he said, putting his sausage down. 'It was a joke. Remember jokes? They come in Christmas crackers along with paper hats that don't fit and rubbishy bits of plastic that are broken by Boxing Day.'

'I don't think it's funny at all.'

'I don't think it's funny either. And if we're going to discuss not being fair – I hardly think you're being fair.' He pushed the plate away from him and massaged his temples. 'I work five long days each week in a mind-numbing job. I don't need this when I come home. I don't get in at this hour every night out of choice.'

It was horrifying to find out how easy lying became, once you started. The lies took on a life of their own and one little lie built on top of another until you had a huge shaky column of lies and you had to build another even bigger column next to it to support it. It was the same basic principle he was trying to teach Jack with Duplo and with considerably less success – except that with big, brightly coloured building bricks rather than people's lives it was infinitely more simple and didn't hurt so much when they all inevitably came tumbling down.

'Then leave your job.'

'You know I can't do that. I'm handcuffed there.' Jamie rubbed his eyes. 'They pay twice as much as anyone else would for the equivalent post.'

'You could take a pay cut. We could manage.'

'Don't be ridiculous. We certainly couldn't manage. There's the *Alien* mortgage on this house, the car, the *de rigueur* and consequently extortionate school that our offspring attend and are likely to for the foreseeable future.'

'You wouldn't want them to grow up to be vandals

with pierced noses and hair like hedgehogs?'

'No, I wouldn't – no more than you would want to drive round in a clapped-out Metro and shop at KwikSave.'

'And there are your golf-club fees to consider.' It was said in a tone that was sharper than was absolutely essential.

Jamie nodded hesitantly. 'Point taken.' It wasn't exactly the price of tee pegs to belong to the most prestigious golf club in the area. 'But then you wouldn't want me playing golf on a municipal course with apprentice electricians with pierced noses and hair like hedgehogs, would you?'

Jamie walked to the fridge and poured himself a beer. He saw Pamela stiffen and ignored it. 'Besides, there's no guarantee that another job would require any fewer hours or that the trains would be any more reliable. We're talking about something here that is totally out of my control.' More lies. See? Easy.

'Couldn't you drive in?'

'Is that what you want for me – spending two hours each way in a traffic jam? At least on the train I can read the paper.' *And see Teri.*

They had been meeting every morning for a few weeks now. He caught the 6.25 from Milton Keynes, stopping at Bletchley, Leighton Buzzard (6.37) and then only the briefest pause at Watford Junction before arriving at Euston at 7.16 – given a bit of luck and a following wind – and no signal failures at Watford Junction.

It got Teri into work far too early as she only had a five-minute walk from Euston, but she said she didn't mind because she enjoyed their chats together. Yes, they had actually broken the unwritten First Commandment of commuting – Thou Shalt Not Chatter Animatedly To Thy Fellow Commuter – particularly on trains before eight o'clock.

To prolong the agony of parting for a few extra minutes, they had a quick bland coffee together at the End of the Line Buffet before Jamie left to do battle with the Northern Line. Well, more precisely the Northern Line to Leicester Square and then change to the Piccadilly Line for Covent Garden.

The tube was a nightmare at the best of times, but after eight o'clock in the morning it was enough to make a grown man weep – hence the early start which some-times caught the larks on the hop. It didn't seem so bad to be squashed against sweaty bodies at the end of the day – besides, he didn't have much choice. But to start the morning like that was more than one human being should be asked to bear.

Jamie worked on the far side of Covent Garden, away from the tube, behind the trendy bijou shops and craft stalls that sold clothes no one would ever dream of wear-ing, scented candles in dubious shapes and clocks made out of scratched sixties records that had failed to become hits. The office was one of those impressive-looking Victorian buildings that are nothing more than glorified rabbit warrens in which you freeze from October to April and swelter from May through to September.

In the summer, the walk to the tube from the office involved doing battle with forty million Japanese tourists and sundry jugglers, fire-eaters, buskers of infinitely variable quality, break-dancing robots, living sculptures of Hollywood legends and Simon the Oracle – a pleasant chap who told you exactly what he thought of you for a small donation. At this time of the year it was relatively free from enterprising hazards and as a result the journey was five minutes shorter. These things matter when you are a commuter.

These things mattered more when he had started to arrange to meet Teri in the evenings too. Not every night. That would be ridiculous – and difficult to organise. Just a quick drink to fortify the heart and gird the loins before subjecting oneself to the mercy of British Rail. Nothing more. Perfectly innocent and understandable. Unless you were Pamela.

Jamie pushed back from the table. 'I'm going to bed.'

'What about MacTavish's walk?'

'I'm giving us both a night off. He can go and pee on the bushes in the garden. He does it when we're not looking anyway.'

'I'll be up soon. I'll just clear away first.'

She was quieter with the pans now that there was no one to make a point to. Which was just as well, because she had given herself a headache with all that purposeful clattering. If it had been the children making all that noise she would have shouted at them.

MacTavish skulked back in warily and, as Jamie suggested, she let him out into the garden. He took the opportunity to chew on his punctured ball and run round the garden with it clamped between his teeth like the frisky young puppy he wasn't. Pamela stood at the back door and watched him scampering carefree across the lawn, growling under his breath as the fronds of the pampas grass – an unwanted leftover from the last occupants that they hadn't got round to digging up – wafted in the gathering wind. It was times like these when she wished wholeheartedly that she was a dog. All you had to worry about was where the next Bonio was coming from and hope that someone would remember to give you your Bob Martin's conditioning tablets regularly.

She didn't know what was wrong with her just lately. The necessity to do the right thing weighed on her like the heavy constricting blankets of a bed that hadn't been updated to the liberating joy of duvets. It was such a hard job bringing up children the right way these days. When she was young, the pinnacle of creative stimulus was piano lessons. Now, if you wanted them to be socially rounded and properly integrated human beings, they had to have a fuller social programme than Ivana Trump.

Jack wasn't yet three and he attended two 'Mother and Toddler' swimming sessions per week at the local leisure centre, one session of 'Tumbling Terrors', two hours of 'Mini Musicians' – which was always a frightful experience resulting in severe Nurofen abuse – and three mornings a week at nursery. Add to that Francesca's dance classes, baton twirling, Brownies, horse-riding, ice-skating, music and swimming lessons, and there was precious little time left to do anything for herself.

And that was without all the birthday parties – 'jelly-flinging affairs' Jamie called them – of which there seemed to be at least one each week. Last Christmas he had bought her a sticker for the car saying *Mum's Taxi Service*, which showed a cartoon car slumped on its front end with its wheels falling off. She hadn't found that the slightest bit amusing, perhaps because it was she who was on her knees, rather than the car . . . and her wheels were in grave danger of falling off.

Taking a part-time job had been Pamela's way of reasserting herself as a human being with a life of her own. It was hardly demanding, but it gave her some extra money and she liked the work. Jamie had been all for it – but then he would be. It had meant not the slightest alteration to *his* daily routine. She was the one who raced around like Damon Hill on a good day, charging from one appointment to another with military precision. If she ever dared to complain, all he said was that if she was finding it too difficult to manage she should give up her job. This made her all the more determined to cope. Work was the only sanctuary she had. He just didn't understand.

She whistled to MacTavish, who came in reluctantly, looking back longingly at his ball and wearing the same expression Jamie did when he came through the door. She could be so hard on Jamie sometimes – it must seem as though she never had a good word for him. Which she rarely did. It was just that he was a typical man. He worked hard, but other than that he took his family responsibilities all too lightly. He didn't worry if Francesca only got silver stars instead of gold, although Mrs Rutherford could be very moody sometimes and had her favourites . . . Pamela sighed deeply. No, he left all the worrying to her.

Pamela spent a long time in the bathroom and when she got into bed she curled against him in a position of penitence. She was warm and soft and smelled of toothpaste and soap. It made him feel terribly guilty and ashamed.

'I don't mean for us to argue,' she said.

He patted her thigh the way men do when they've been married for ten years. 'I know.'

'Couldn't you look for a job locally? There are lots of big firms moving out of London to Milton Keynes.'

'I'll think about it.' He pecked her cheek. 'Goodnight.'

She pecked him back. 'Goodnight.' They turned off

their matching frilled Laura Ashley bedside lights in unison.

'Jamie.' Pamela spoke softly into the darkness.

'Mmm?'

'What is an *Alien* mortgage?'

Jamie sighed. 'It's a huge unseen monster that is completely indestructible and kills the occupants of the house very slowly from the inside out.'

He turned away from her and moulded his pillow to his face. 'In the building society no one can hear you scream,' he muttered under his breath.

Chapter Six

They had been on the train for nearly half an hour and the doors were still open. Jamie checked his watch for the third time in as many minutes. 'This isn't going anywhere in a hurry.'

It was a rather obvious statement, Teri thought, given the situation. 'A fire causing signals failure at Watford Junction' the muffled announcement had said. It was the third train they had been on so far, running from platform to platform like worried sheep, and none of them had moved. Because of the fire, the staff who were due to drive the trains were stuck on trains themselves – somewhere in that Never-Never land of 'further down the line'.

'Why don't we go and grab something to eat?' Jamie suggested.

Teri nodded her agreement, hiding her surprise. They'd only known each other a few weeks – a month or so at the most – but it was the first time he had suggested going to eat together. Most men she had known would have wanted you in bed within two days and then, equally quickly, would have dumped you. She hadn't had the slow smoulder build-up experience before; most of her exes had been from the crash-and-burn school of courtship. This was taking some getting used to.

Their relationship – and the term should be applied loosely – consisted so far of a quick coffee in the morning – nearly every morning – and an equally quick something more alcoholic at night. It wasn't nearly enough. Even the mornings probably wouldn't happen if she didn't make the supreme effort of getting a train nearly an hour earlier than she needed to, just to spend some time with him.

Clare told her that she was insane and that no man was worth missing an hour's precious beauty sleep for. Mind you, she was a fine one to talk; she was usually up in the middle of the night to get to the airport on time for an early-morning flight. She insisted that it was merely devotion to duty rather than mindless devotion to someone else which made all the difference. And she was probably right. The things we do for love!

Was it love, though? It was certainly deep and lustful infatuation, and that would do for starters! But were the feelings returned, or was this likely to be her forty-second bout of unrequited love since leaving The Sacred Heart of Jesus primary school? She had carried a torch for Michael Lacey that burned steadfastly despite his continued rejections and refused – until she was twenty-three and saw him again in Safeway's with a wife, two children and a not inconsiderable beer-belly – to be quenched.

Once she was in love it was hard for her to remain objective. This was a difficult one. He seemed keen to see her on the train etc., but that was about it. The only benefit to this dawn reveille – apart from the obvious one of seeing Jamie – was that it was gaining her an enormous amount of brownie points with her boss, the difficult-to-impress Richard Wellbeloved, who was stunned that she was not only in before him in the mornings now, but that she was also quite cheerful too.

'There's not a bad little pasta place just outside the station. I can't remember what it's called. It's next to the transvestite shop and that, well . . .' he paused. 'I suppose it tends to overshadow everything else.'

She wondered briefly for the second time whether he might not be a pervert. He had seemed very at home buying tights. Perhaps this would explain his reticence at becoming involved. Perhaps he was just using her as a cure? A bit of therapy as he decided whether to go through with a Gender Reassessment Programme. Both she and Clare had dated people with worse problems in the past.

In the event, the restaurant was imaginatively called 'The Pasta Place' – a nice little haven of minimalist monochrome, an oasis in a bleak and dirty street that had nothing else to offer but its proximity to Euston Station. Unless, of course, you were a transvestite – in which case next door with its array of size twelve stilettos, falsie bras festooned across the window like bunting and the promise of *He to She* transformations in under two hours, would be infinitely more appealing.

There were two men eating alone, faces buried alternately in pasta or the *Evening Standard*, and a young couple giggling and holding hands while they spooned food into each other's mouths. Jamie and Teri ordered quickly – Penne Carbonara for Jamie and Spaghetti Bolognese for her – less cream, less cheese, less fat, less than interesting. A cheapish, goodish bottle of Valpolicella and some garlic bread helped to stave off hunger pangs until the real food arrived.

They talked aimlessly of the weather and the state of the world in general before the waiter – a man with the strongest Italian accent she had ever heard, who had probably lived in Bethnal Green for the last twenty years

– placed two steaming bowls of pasta in front of them.

'Bliss.' Jamie inhaled deeply. He picked up his fork and lunged at his food.

'Enjoya!' the waiter instructed.

'This is wonderful.' He smacked his lips and spooned in some more.

Teri tried hers more daintily, but agreed that it was, indeed, wonderful.

'You don't know what it's like,' Jamie pushed some more Carbonara into his mouth appreciatively, 'to eat food that you can't spell your name with.'

Teri paused with her fork to her mouth and frowned. 'What?'

'I said,' Jamie repeated between chews, 'you don't know what it's like—' He stopped mid-sentence.

She put her fork back in her bowl. 'To eat food that you can't spell your name with,' she finished for him.

Jamie waved his hand. 'It's a long story. You had to be there to get it.' He drank his wine self-consciously.

'I bet you did.' Teri leaned across and pressed her face as close to his as two intervening bowls of pasta would allow. She tapped her fingernails on the table menacingly. 'Are you going to explain, or would you like me to guess?' she hissed.

Jamie's face had gone red, and it wasn't just the steam from the bowls of pasta. Guiltily, he looked round at the other diners, who were eating their pasta and pizzas blissfully unaware of their confrontation. He lowered his voice. 'Like I said – it's a long story.'

She took a swig of her wine and clanked the glass on the table. 'You're married, aren't you?'

Now they were aware. They all sat bolt upright and most of them turned so they could hear better.

'Yes,' said Jamie.

'I knew it! I bloody knew! Why didn't you tell me?'

'It never seemed to crop up.'

'We've been chatting away for the last few weeks discussing everything under the sun! We've even progressed from talking about the extortionate cost of our season tickets and the soul-destroying inequities of commuting with British Rail to black holes and EU directives on BSE – and all the time I've been the one with the mad cow disease.' She didn't know if it was the red wine or the anger, but something was making her cheeks feel very pink. 'Didn't it seem worthwhile mentioning somewhere along the line that you had a wife?'

The waiter from Bethnal Green leaned on the bar and started polishing a glass that already gleamed in the overhead spotlight.

'I didn't think I needed to.' Jamie raked his fringe back from his forehead. 'I just assumed I looked like a married man.'

'And what do married men look like? Do you think you've got *Keep Off – Married Man* stamped on your forehead in invisible ink that only single women can see?'

'I don't know,' Jamie admitted. 'It's not something I've thought about.'

Teri was in full flow now. She took a swig of wine to lubricate her throat. The man on the table next to them slunk down in his seat and raised his newspaper higher.

'I never go out with married men! It's an unwritten policy of mine. I'm a very principled woman.' She thought guiltily of her one illicit date with Clare's ex-husband Dave when he wasn't her ex-husband. It had been a disaster. He had tried to man-handle her in the car park at the isolated country pub he had taken her to before they had even got near the artificial beams and the horse brasses. It was shortly after that that she had become very principled. She vowed to be nicer to Clare when she got home.

'Well, I hate to be a stickler for the *actualité*, but we're not exactly going out, are we?' Jamie said, a mild expression of exasperation making him look even younger and even more appealing.

'What *are* we doing here then?' Teri jabbed meaningfully with her fork. 'Just filling in time until the next train comes along?'

'Well actually,' Jamie looked longingly at his Carbonara, 'that's exactly what we are doing.'

Teri opened her mouth and closed it again. He did have a point. 'So I'm just a better option than the *Daily Telegraph*, a can of lukewarm Coke and twiddling your thumbs for the next two hours while the fire brigade sort out Watford Junction?'

'You're a considerably better option than the *Daily Telegraph*, warm Coke and two hours of thumb twiddling.'

Teri smiled reluctantly. 'Well, I suppose I should be thankful for small mercies.'

'What would you rather I say? That I'm an incorrigible, habitual seducer who wants nothing more than to coerce you into an adulterous relationship?' By now the young couple had stopped spooning food into each other's mouths and were listening intently.

'Is that what you want?'

Jamie sagged visibly. 'I don't know.' He twiddled his fork in the middle of his penne, making a space in the sauce which showed the design on the bottom of his plate – a smiling stereotyped gondolier wearing his stripy jersey and obligatory red-ribboned boater inscribed with that old Italian saying *Hava Nisa Day!* When Teri had visited

Venice, all the gondoliers wore jeans and sulked and charged extortionate prices for the privilege of racing you round their dirty, stinking canals while screeching obscenities at anyone who got in their way. 'The truth is that I'm not an habitual seducer,' Jamie went on. 'And I've never been in this situation before. I just wanted to spend time with you.'

'Why? Why me?' Teri asked. The young couple exchanged a quick spoonful.

'For the last few weeks I've had something to look forward to, something to give my life at least a bit of purpose, rather than sitting on a train for nearly three hours a day and going home to an argument and food designed for five-year-olds. It's been months since anyone has taken an interest in *me*. I haven't talked to anyone for years like we've talked. I mean, *really* talked.'

'But we haven't *really* talked. We might have got on to the subject of your wife a bit earlier if we'd *really* talked.'

'I know. I was going to tell you.' Jamie dabbed at his sauceless mouth with his napkin. The man in the far corner of the restaurant folded his newspaper and the waiter was about to wear a hole in the glass he was still polishing intently. 'It just seemed easier to avoid it and pretend that you must know.'

'If you're a married man, why don't you wear a wedding ring? I'm a stickler for that – I always check.'

The man on the table next to them leaned closer to hear Jamie's reply. 'I lost it, months ago. I take Francesca swimming on Sunday mornings – "Parents and Pests". I haven't got round to replacing it yet. I did harbour the vain hope that someone might hand it in, but you just can't trust people these days.'

Teri narrowed her eyes at this, but her silent sarcasm

was lost on him. 'So Francesca is the five-year-old with educational food?' Teri found her throat had tightened.

'She's six.'

'No wonder you were at home buying tights. You're a regular family guy. I bet you don't baulk at buying Tampax either.'

Jamie shook his head. 'Or Pampers.'

Teri let out a heavy and unhappy breath, that said, 'I really don't want to hear this.'

'Jack's just three.'

'Are there any more?' she snapped. 'This isn't going to turn out to be the bloody Waltons, is it? There's no Jim-Bob, Mary Ellen, Fanny Anne and Uncle Tom Cobleigh as well, is there?'

'No, that's all. That's La Famille Duncan – Frankie, Jack and—'

Teri held up her hand. 'Don't! Don't tell me! I have no desire to know your wife's name. If she hasn't got a name then I can pretend she doesn't really exist.'

'Look.' Jamie lowered his voice further. The other diners in the restaurant and the waiter leaned closer. 'I didn't mean for this to happen – if anything *has* happened. I just wanted us to be friends.'

'And have you told your wife you've found a new friend – or are you leaving her to guess, too?'

'No, I haven't told her.' Jamie turned and glared at the diners who had abandoned all pretence of eating and were straining to hear. 'She wouldn't understand.'

'I don't believe it!' Teri's flabber had never been more gasted. 'My wife doesn't understand me. That's the oldest line in the book!'

Jamie bristled. 'It just so happens to be true. We've drifted apart recently. I can't tell her about you because she wouldn't understand that we can be just friends. Anyway, I'm a hopeless liar, it's best just to tell her nothing.' Admittedly, he was getting better at lying. Practice certainly does make imperfect.

'So that's what we are – just friends?'

Jamie shrugged. 'I don't know.'

'There's a lot you don't know, isn't there?'

Jamie smiled and showed his toothpaste smile. He'd got a piece of parsley from his Carbonara stuck between his teeth and his gum, and she had the most overwhelming urge to reach over and tenderly pick it out.

'From where I'm sitting, it looks like we've got a problem.' Her throat was dry and her voice was tight and even a swig of her rapidly dwindling Valpolicella didn't help. There was a virus going round at work and she hoped fervently that she hadn't got it. Sore throat, nausea, gippy tummy, chest pains, palpitations. Nasty. A lot like love really. 'We're more than friends, otherwise we wouldn't be meeting in secret, but we're not going out and we're definitely not having an affair. So what are we?'

'Hungry?' Jamie ventured.

'Starving,' Teri agreed.

Jamie reached out and laid his hand on top of hers. He chose the one in which she was holding her fork and it started to go sweaty in her palm. 'Besides,' his voice had suddenly gone all sincere and it worried her, 'if we are having an affair or simply going out or were even more than just friends, I could tell you that I thought you had the most beautiful eyes I had ever seen – that they're as striking as two lone cornflowers in a sea of golden wheat. If we were going out I could reach across the table and kiss your hand casually and think that later I could be kissing your neck and smelling your hair. And that for the last few weeks commuting with you has made me feel more alive than I ever thought possible.'

Teri pulled her hand away. 'Yes, yes. All right, I get the picture. So we're not going out and we're not having an affair. We're just friends. Let's get that clear. With no cornflowers and wheat and all that business about smelly hair and the joys of commuting. Well, fine, pour me another glass of wine and we'll continue not going out together and just being friends before our food gets cold.' Teri turned in her chair and gesticulated with her fork. 'And you lot can go back to your food, too!'

They finished their meal hurriedly, partly because they were now awkward with each other and partly because the pasta was unappetisingly lukewarm by the time they got round to eating it. Teri had baulked from asking them to reheat it in the microwave.

They sat on the train back from Euston in silence. Teri stared out of the window, pretending to be fascinated by the empty blackness and listening to the irritating squeak of her seat. How do you talk to a married man who has just declared undying friendship for you? What do you say? Would they be able to carry on meeting, now that things between them had irrevocably changed?

If she had thought only a tiny bit harder she would have realised he was married and would have said no thanks to the emotional Elastoplast he had been providing her with for the last few weeks. Perhaps she had chosen purposefully to ignore the nagging doubts that prodded her painfully in the ribs and pointed to the fact that he was unavailable.

It was like the two blowsy women she had seen in Steamers a few weeks before, swigging pints and wearing stilettos the size of boats. They were men; it was obvious when you looked at them – not even too closely. They must have been customers from the transvestite shop on a day out with the boys – or the girls – or whatever cross-dressers preferred to call themselves. All the clues were there – if only you wanted to see them.

But there is a certain blissfulness about ignorance, that only being hit round the face with the truth like a piece of wet fish can shatter.

Eventually, the train pulled into Leighton Buzzard. Teri stood up slowly. 'Thanks for the meal.'

Jamie was leaning against the window, his cashmere-covered elbow sitting in a puddle of condensation. 'I don't think we should part like this.' He didn't look at her, but stared out of the window at the empty platform. 'There's a lot more to say.'

'I don't know if I want to hear it, Jamie.' She swung the door open. The guard blew his whistle.

'Will I see you tomorrow?' His voice sounded husky.

'I don't know.' They spoke in unison and made each other laugh. It was a sad and strained sound.

'Take care,' Teri said, biting her lip, and slammed the carriage door.

Chapter Seven

'At Secure Home Limited we absolutely guarantee that all homes fitted with our advanced security systems are highly likely to be burgled within ten days of installation. Full stop. We carefully select a scurrilous – I think you'll find that's two r's – a scurrilous band of workmen with dubious criminal records as our employees to ensure that you have no peace of mind whatsoever. Yours, etc.' Tom Pearson sat back from his desk and leaned at a precarious angle in his favourite deep-buttoned leather swivel chair – the most expensive in the executive office furniture catalogue – arms resting behind his head. 'Did you get all that?'

'Yes, fine.' Pamela chewed the end of her pencil.

'I'd like four thousand copies sent out within the next half-hour,' he said with a smile. 'You weren't planning to go to lunch, were you?'

'Yes. I mean no,' she agreed.

'You're not actually listening to me at all, are you?' He sat back upright, elbows on his desk.

Pamela looked up, a frown creasing her brow. 'Oh, sorry, Tom.' She flicked her hair back from her face like a horse flicking an irritating fly away with its tail. 'What did you say?'

'Just read me back that last paragraph. If you'd be so kind.'

Pamela's finger trailed up her notebook. 'Er, from "At Secure Home"?'

Tom nodded.

Pamela continued. 'Er – "At Secure Home Limited we absolutely guarantee that all homes fitted with our advanced security systems are highly likely to be burgled within ten days of installation".' She looked up at him and winced. ' "We carefully select a scurrilous – two r's – band of workmen with dubious criminal records—" ' She let her notebook drop to her lap. 'Oh, Tom! I am sorry.'

'Please continue.' A smile spread across Tom's face and he cupped his chin.

Pamela cringed. 'Workmen with dubious criminal records as our employees to ensure that you have no peace of mind whatsoever. Yours, etc. Oh hell!'

'Your mind's not exactly on the job today, is it?'

'I'm sorry, I'm sorry!' She shook herself like a bird settling its ruffled feathers. 'I'm all right now – go back to where we left off.'

Tom walked from behind his desk and perched on the front edge directly in line with her. 'Give me that page.'

Pamela tore it out of her notebook. He shredded it like confetti and threw it in the air, scattering it on the brown shagpile carpet. Pamela looked horrified. 'Now close your book and tell me what's wrong.'

'There's nothing wrong.' She was perilously close to tears. It was ridiculous. Hot, spiking needles jabbed behind her eyeballs and threatened to shatter what little composure she could muster. 'I'm fine.'

'No, you're not fine. There is something terribly wrong when Secretary of the Year gives me a cup of black coffee with no sugar, when for the last eighteen months she has faultlessly brought me a cup of white with two sugars every morning.'

Pamela put her hands over her face. 'Gosh, did I? Why didn't you say something?'

'Because you looked exactly like you do now. As if you're about to burst into tears at any minute should anyone be cruel enough to say boo to you.'

One traitorous tear slid from under her eyelashes. 'Oh.'

'Come on, get your coat. We can leave the security of Milton Keynes hanging in the balance for a few more hours. I'm taking you to lunch.'

She allowed herself to be led quietly to the luxurious Mercedes that stood waiting in the car park. Tom whisked her at breakneck speed along the dual carriageway, while she stared out of the window at the featureless scenery that whizzed past too fast. If he was trying to impress her it didn't work. By the time they got there she simply felt sick.

They went to a pub aptly named The Windmill. It was at the end of the A5, a harsh new red-brick monstrosity. Its middle section had been constructed to look like an old windmill minus its sails, and it stuck up obtrusively from the barrack-like block of the rest of the building. Inside it didn't look like a windmill at all, but like every other brand-new, old-fashioned pub.

Tom ordered the food which they had chosen from glorious Technicolor replications on a huge laminated plastic menu – just in case anyone was unsure exactly what lasagne or steak pie and chips should look like. When Tom commented on this to the waitress she told them that they had exactly the same pictures hanging in the kitchens, so that the chefs knew exactly what they had to produce – even down to the quarter-slice of lemon, half a tomato and two sachets of tartare sauce that came with every plate of scampi and chips. Original flourishes were obviously not encouraged at The Windmill.

Tom and Pamela perched on uncomfortable stools in an alcove overlooking the artificial lake – which at least had real ducks – while they waited for their number to be called.

Pamela appraised her boss while she sipped her mineral water. Tom Pearson was swarthy-looking – a twinkly-eyed rogue, a gypsy out of place in a well-cut business suit. An Eastender by birth – a barrow-boy made good – he had found out at an early age that the streets of London weren't paved with gold, so at the inception of the new city, had tried his luck in Milton Keynes instead. It had proved to be a good move.

Tom had set up Secure Home Limited on a shoe-string, but with the burgeoning growth in crime that befits a new city cobbled together with the disillusioned from all walks of life, he was now making a not inconsiderable profit, and was living in the style that he always felt he should be accustomed to.

His hair was dark and wavy, and though there was no sign of thinning, there was a distinct snowstorm of grey. Pamela noticed that he still turned heads when he went to the bar to order some drinks, and wondered if her husband was viewed by more dispassionate females in the same light. It was hard to think of your own husband as a headturner, but there was no accounting for taste. And Jamie had managed to turn her head – once upon a time . . .

Tom was fifty-five but you would give him a good ten years off that, despite the greying hair. His figure was athletic, but with a definite softening of the waistline that spoke of too many business lunches under his belt. He dressed quite classily – a tribute to his wife Shirley rather than to his own sartorial tastes – and had a style that conjured up Ian McShane meets Man at Marks & Spencer – the shop where Shirley bought all his suits because someone had told her they were really made by Armani.

'So.' Tom looked at her levelly, one eyebrow raised in query. 'Are you going to tell me voluntarily what's wrong or am I going to have to drag it out of you?'

Her eyes welled up again and she stared sightlessly out of the window in the general direction of the ducks until she had the tears more or less under control. She cleared her throat. 'Things haven't been too good at home lately.'

'You've got two kids, what do you expect?' Tom teased.

She smiled and wiped her index finger under her eye, smearing a stray tear across her cheek. The food arrived, which did look every bit as Technicolor and as plastic as the photograph had suggested. They sat in silence until the waitress left. 'It's Jamie,' she continued. 'I think he's got a friend.'

Tom shrugged. 'We all need friends.'

Pamela tutted. 'I mean a *friend*. A special friend.'

Tom rubbed the side of his nose. 'Ah.'

'He's been singing in the shower.' Pamela held her throat as she felt it tighten. 'At five-thirty in the morning before he goes to work.'

'He might just be happy.'

'He's singing *Knock three times on the ceiling if you want me*.'

Tom stroked his chin thoughtfully. 'Then it's serious.'

Pamela pushed the plate of Technicolor food away from

her and fished a handkerchief out of her suit pocket. 'I don't know what to do.'

Tom swigged his beer and pushed the plate of food back towards her. 'Well, giving up eating won't help.'

Obediently, she picked up the fork.

'Does he know that you know?'

'I don't think so.' She sighed and pushed the plate of food away again. 'Oh damn,' she brushed across her eyes with the palms of her hands. 'I don't know if I'm imagining it all. There's nothing concrete for me to be suspicious about – apart from the uncharacteristic shower singing. It's just a feeling. He seems different. Eager to get out of the house in the morning and less than keen to come back at night.' She gave another heartfelt sigh. 'There's been no lipstick on his collars, no phones going dead when I answer them – nothing like that at all. And yet. And yet . . .' She spread her hands expansively. 'I just know. Don't ask me how.'

'How long has it been going on?'

Every sentence was accompanied by a sigh. 'A few weeks, a few months, a year. Or not at all. I have no idea. But I suppose I started sensing something a month or so ago.'

Tom folded his arms. 'Look, I'll be honest with you. I have to admit that over the years I haven't exactly been a role model for Mary Whitehouse. There have been times when, as a brash and callow youth, I've deviated from the straight and narrow course of marital constraints. But you know that Shirley and I have been married now for coming up thirty years. Only twenty of them happy, mind you.'

Pamela twisted her mouth in a reluctant smile.

'I mean that seriously,' he continued, wagging his fork. 'There have been a few distinctly unhappy years among

76

them too. Most of them my fault.' He took another drink of his beer. 'I don't know what it is with men, but we can't control what lurks in our underwear. One bit of glad eye from a pretty girl and we're off like a dog after a rabbit. It's pathetic really. I've had four affairs during my marriage.' Tom sucked at his lips. 'Four. You'd think I'd have learned before then.' He shook his head. 'Shirley knew about them all. I didn't let on that I knew she knew, and she didn't let on she knew either. She just waited patiently until I came home, tail between my legs. There were no accusations, no recriminations and life went on as normal, me vowing never to stray again – until the next time.'

'So that's what you think I should do? Just ignore it and hope that like a nasty little itch it will go away?'

'It worked for me and Shirl.'

'But it took four times before you came to your senses.'

Tom looked wounded. 'I didn't say it was a perfect solution.'

Pamela shook her head. 'I don't think it's what Relate would advise.'

'What do that bunch of interfering buggers know? A load of psychobabble and claptrap that blames everything on your parents.'

'But they encourage you to talk things through. Didn't you and Shirley ever talk about what had happened?'

'We didn't need to. I've spent the last ten years making it up to her. I treat her like a duchess now, not the duchess of York, of course – it's not good for anyone to be that spoilt. But Shirley only has to ask and she can have whatever she wants.'

Pamela looked uncertain. 'I don't know, Tom. I feel I ought to do something. I can't just sit there and wait to see if he comes back. I've got the children to think about.'

'Can I be really honest with you?' Tom drained his glass. 'Do you know what you should do?' He tilted his chin. 'You should loosen up a bit. You might be a brilliant secretary, Pamela, or assistant or whatever the hell the politically correct term is these days, but sometimes you look like you're chewing a toffee up your arse.' His brown eyes creased at the corners and they were twinkling mischievously. 'And do you know what I want to do?'

Pamela gulped and shook her head. He fixed her with his eyes and continued in a lowered voice that sounded distinctly threatening. 'I want to sweep you in my arms, push all the bloody paperwork on the floor and make love to you on my desk. I want to smear your flawless lipstick all over your face with kisses, tousle your immaculate hair and crease your perfect suit to hell.'

'Oh,' she said quietly, but it came out as a squeak. Her mouth had suddenly gone dry and her teeth were sticking to her lips. It had become very hot in the pub and her hand trembled as she sipped her mineral water. 'And you were just telling me you were a reformed character.' Her voice sounded considerably higher than it should have been.

'I *am* a reformed character.' He laughed easily and she could see why four women other than his wife had found him attractive enough to risk an affair with him. 'Fortunately, these days I not only have Shirley to consider, but also my back.'

'So you're a reformed character out of incapacity rather than inclination?' Her own vocal incapacity had, thankfully, been temporary.

'No. It's just that now I know which side my bread is buttered on. I still have the inclination, but I've also developed a bit of nous too.' He tapped the side of his head, showing that he did, indeed, know where nous was kept. 'Shirley comes first before everything else. It's about time she did.'

Pamela chewed her top lip. Hell, if she wasn't careful she was going to cry again.

'Besides,' Tom continued, unabashed, 'if I put my back out now I wouldn't be able to play in the medal on Saturday at the golf club. And although my urges are still governed by my balls, it's the small white variety rather than the other kind.'

'Your wife is a very long-suffering woman, Tom Pearson,' Pamela stated flatly.

'I know, I couldn't imagine life without her.' He was starting to get maudlin. 'But that's how it happens, Pamela. Men and women can't be just friends. Two minutes ago we were talking just like friends and the next minute I'd stepped over the boundary and we were discussing things that friends shouldn't. It's only another small step for mankind for us to be doing things that friends shouldn't either. And by tomorrow I'll have forgotten what I said and we'll be back to boss and secretary again. Yet you'll think of it every time you see my desk piled high with paperwork. That's the difference between men and women.'

'Well, let's hope that Jamie gets some sense into his head long before you did.'

'Don't be too harsh on him. If you're stand-offish you'll drive him away. Make him want to come home to you.'

'Haven't you ever heard of feminism, Tom?'

'It's bullshit. Why do women want to behave like blokes when we already make a bad-enough job of it ourselves?'

'Put like that it's hard to explain.'

'Act like a woman, not a wife – and least of all not like a mother.'

'If you ever get fed up of fitting burglar alarms, you could always go into counselling.'

'Now you're taking the piss – you must be feeling better.' He looked at his watch.

'Thanks.' She nodded and smiled gratefully. 'I am.'

He passed her coat to her. 'It's time for you to go and collect those angelic-looking brats of yours. Go home first and take that lovely suit off before Jack throws up on it.'

Pamela slipped her coat on. 'He's past that stage now.'

Tom smiled. 'They're never past that stage. My youngest son's just turned eighteen – he's tall, strapping and would make two of me. And he's still testing his limits with a bottle – only at his age it's with more interesting contents than milk. Shirley lies awake half the night until he deigns to come home and then after half an hour's kip she lies awake again for the rest of the night listening to him throw up in the bathroom.'

Pamela wrinkled her nose. 'What do you do?'

'I lie awake with her. The only difference is in the morning I shout at him and she gives him Alka-Seltzer.'

'That's another difference between men and women,' she said wryly.

'There are lots of them – not all of them good.'

'So you think I should take the Tom Pearson Route to Deeply Wedded Bliss and just sit at home like a good little wife, nurture his children and wait for him to realise that he's a complete bastard.'

'What's the other option? Confronting him while he may still be in the throes of passion, blasting off ultimatums like bullets? You might get him to wave a white flag, but he might wave it at you from the other trenches.

It could frighten him into thinking that he's actually in love with her.'

He took her arm and they headed towards the door. She could feel the heat of his hand even through her coat.

'You've said yourself you've got no evidence, that it's only a hunch – and look where that got Quasimodo.' Deep lines appeared at the corners of his eyes as he crinkled them.

Pamela looked at him sideways. 'You are silly.'

She ignored Tom's advice about going home and changing, and instead went straight to collect Jack from nursery. Would she ignore the rest of his advice just as easily? Tom might be a nice-enough man – and well-meaning – but he was hopelessly out of date with the way things were done these days.

People liked to talk, to discuss things openly, to air any problems and analyse them. But if they'd done that successfully, why were they in this situation now? Why was her husband doing strange and interesting things with another woman if talking had done any good?

Perhaps Tom was right. She was too uptight, too motherly and not womanly enough. She knew she had been neglecting Jamie recently, but then he was a grown man and perfectly capable of looking after himself. The children were small, vulnerable and totally dependent on her – it was only natural to put them first. Jamie should know that. He should appreciate how hard it was for her.

Then again, perhaps she should appreciate how hard it was for him, too. Was she the sort of woman who could stand at the door in a basque and stockings with the smell of *coq au vin* wafting from the kitchen? Was it the sort of thing that Jamie would want? She hadn't a clue. It seemed highly unlikely on both counts, but maybe she should give it a try. Perhaps it was asking too much for a man to live by char-grilled pork sausages and Alphabetti Spaghetti alone.

Chapter Eight

It was like *Wuthering Heights* meets *Brief Encounter*. Heathcliff and Cathy meet thingy and whatsit. She couldn't remember the exact details of *Brief Encounter* – except that it was black and white and her mother cried a lot at the end. But it was all about the train causing the strain rather than taking it. That much she knew. Something *she* could certainly empathise with. She was pretty sure that Trevor Howard was in it. After all, he seemed to be in most black and white films. Except she didn't think he was in *Wuthering Heights*. That was definitely Larry – but Trev might have had a bit-part.

The tension was twisting her stomach so much that it was almost like waiting to do her first bungee jump. In fact, it was very much the same situation – she was about to dive over the precipice into a deep and dangerous abyss with no idea what would be waiting for her when eventually she hit the bottom. If it all went horribly wrong, would she be able to bounce back – or would she simply splat in a broken heap and need a bigger budget than the Bionic Man to have any hope of ever being rebuilt?

At least with a bungee jump you had an elastic band for safety and the back-up of a gung-ho, spotty youth called Tarquin to tell you that everything would be all right, he had checked all the gear and they'd never had a fatality yet. *She* was going into this without the benefit of safety equipment. This could warrant a slot on *How Do They Do That?* – a programme featuring deeds of infinite danger enacted by death-defying daredevils – and a tribute to man's enduring stupidity. She always felt it should be more appropriately retitled *Why Do They Do That?*

As the train pulled in she was sure she was going to be sick. Was the mere thought of seeing Jamie again making her nauseous – or was it simply because she hadn't eaten any breakfast again? She had managed to stay away for two whole weeks. Every morning she'd got up early enough to catch the 6.37 and every morning she'd paced the lounge floor, like an addict talking herself out of her next fix, until it was too late – even if she had really rushed – to catch Jamie's train. Every morning she'd pushed her bowl of Weetabix and warm milk away from her untouched. And every morning she'd gone to work feeling unloved, unhappy and undernourished.

Sometimes she'd seen him in the evenings lingering by the End of the Line Buffet where they'd shared their putrid coffee each morning. She had waited outside the concourse, peering furtively through the grimy windows from behind a pillar until he finally got bored and headed for the train. It made her stomach ache watching him there alone with only his briefcase and a polystyrene cup for company, but she had resisted him.

Clare had helped too – not that she knew. There was no way that Teri could tell her in her present predicament that the new love of her life was actually a married man. It was listening to her on the phone with David – the tears, the begging, the pleading, the trying to fit together again the shreds of her life that made Teri feel incredibly guilty. Could she really even consider doing this to another woman? Another woman with children . . .

In other ways, Clare had been no help at all. To deflect attention from her own misery, she had pumped Teri constantly for updated information about this new mystery man. Teri had been reluctant to tell her anything, let alone *the* thing. Perhaps because she had this awful sense of foreboding that if she told her, she wouldn't be able to last out. It was a shame they didn't make patches that could break your addiction to men like they could to cigarettes. But then men were considerably more hazardous to your health than any carcinogenic substance was ever likely to be. And why was it when you finally met the man of your dreams you invariably found yourself in the middle of your worst nightmare?

Jamie always chose a seat in the front carriage – nearest the ticket barrier on arrival at Euston. It was a favourite habit of lazy commuters. She had waited on the platform at the exact spot. As soon as she got on the train she saw him. Her heart lurched at the same time as the train did. He was sitting in the middle section of the carriage, foot up on his knee – black lace-up brogue and fine-knit black sock – his newspaper strewn casually across his balanced leg. There was no one sitting in the seats around him – one of the few benefits of travelling so early.

'Hi, how are you?' she said, as the train pulled out of Leighton Buzzard.

He looked up, startled. 'Teri! It's you!'

'Still at our sparkling best first thing in the morning then?' She sat down opposite him.

He cast his newspaper aside. 'Have you been okay? I've been worried. I haven't seen you for weeks.'

The fact that he had worried about her was touching.

She didn't think she'd been worried about before. Except by her mother who worried about her, and everything else, constantly. 'I've been trying to avoid you.'

His face clouded over. 'Why?'

She looked round to see if they had an audience, but the few other people close to them in the carriage were either buried in their newspapers or asleep. 'You know perfectly well why.'

'I waited at the End of the Line nearly every night.'

'I know, I hung around outside until you'd gone. You made me miss two weeks' worth of calligraphy classes.' Teri put her briefcase on the seat next to her. 'I'll never be able to write jam-jar labels for the WI now.'

Jamie smiled ruefully. 'I'm sorry, I didn't realise my actions would have such far-reaching consequences. I only wanted to talk to you.'

'Why didn't you wait outside my office?' It had struck her over the last two weeks that he hadn't really tried very hard to see her at all. A bit of loitering round Euston Station hardly seemed the height of inventiveness. 'I seem to remember you engineered that quite successfully before.'

'I did wait one night, but it smacked of desperation. At least at the End of the Line, I could pretend I just wanted a cup of coffee.'

'You could have phoned.'

He fixed her with one of his deadly smiles. 'You'd have hung up on me.'

'True,' she said. 'But you could have tried.'

He had tried. Not *to* ring her, but to *not* ring her. How many times had he dialled the City Television number only to hang up when the switchboard answered? He had tried not to think about her, not to doodle her name on his telephone pad, not to see her face in his computer screen, not to loiter outside her office like a lovesick schoolboy. He had tried not to pursue her. If he had bumped into her accidentally then that would have been a different matter. He was a married man – it was too cruel, too calculating, too bloody unfair of him to pursue her in cold blood.

'You're here and that's all that matters.' He looked round to see that they weren't being listened to. 'I don't know why, but I need to touch you.'

He did know why. He wanted to make sure that she was real and that this wasn't just a dream and he wasn't still in bed with the alarm clock about to go crazy in his left ear. His dreams had consisted of nothing but this situation. It had played over and over in his head like a record stuck on a juke box and no one around with any loose change to put a different one on.

He had rehearsed this moment while he was awake, too. Waiting for his coffee to drop out of the vending machine at the office, he had thought up clever and witty things to say to impress her and to make her realise what a good guy he was, and to show her that he had taken her absence in his stride.

However, instead of taking it in his stride, he had stumbled around like a man lost in the empty wilderness without even an Ordnance Survey map to hand. And the clever, witty things? Of course, he had forgotten them all now that she was actually sitting here in front of him.

'Gosh, I've missed you so much.' His eyes were sincere and searching. 'Come and sit next to me.'

'Do you think this is a good idea?'

He shook his head. 'No.'

She slid on to the seat next to him and he took her

hand. 'This is ridiculous. I feel like a naughty sixteen-year-old,' she said.

'I don't think it's wise to try anything else on the train, the ticket collector might have us thrown off.'

'You mean the Revenue Protection Operative,' she corrected. 'Anyway,' she lowered her voice to a hiss, 'you're a *married* man!'

'I could have told you that!' he hissed back.

'But you didn't, did you – and now what are we going to do?'

'I don't know!' they said together.

In the event, it was decided for them. At Watford Junction the door swung open and several people shuffled reluctantly on to the train. They had that haunted, grey look reserved for prisoners awaiting execution on Death Row and Monday-morning commuters. Among them was Jamie's best friend, Charles Perry.

Charles was thirty-one going on forty with a mental age fast approaching nineteen. He was robust, roundish and cheekily attractive and had a more unkempt style of dress than Columbo. Despite these social setbacks he always managed to sport a pretty blonde, of distinctly uncertain age, on his arm when it came to company do's. It could have been the fact that there was old money lurking in the background, which Charles was unfortunately condemned to see only in dribs and drabs until the unhappy day his parents departed from this mortal coil and he copped for the entire wedge.

For this and other reasons that were fairly obvious to all after a few moments of partying in his company, his nickname was Champagne Charlie. He was Jamie's assistant manager at the Mutual and Providential – a job he did simply to fill in his days while he waited impatiently for his inheritance to arrive, whereupon he could dedicate himself totally to wine, women and a certain amount of song.

Charlie had a shock of fair, curly hair and a ruddy complexion that owed nothing to fresh air and clean living, but stated quite clearly that his favourite tipple was something stronger than lemonade. He stood out in a crowd like a Belisha Beacon in a cornfield, yet Jamie failed to notice him at all until he was standing right in front of them.

'Hello, hello, hello!' said Charlie.

Jamie dropped Teri's hand as if it had scalded him. 'For goodness sake, Charlie, what are you doing here? Sit down,' he snapped irritably. 'You sound like bloody Dixon of Dock Green.'

Charlie obediently sat down. 'Someone got out of the wrong side of bed this morning, dear boy – or was it just the wrong bed?' He winked theatrically.

'Don't be so damned rude, Charlie.' Jamie picked up his newspaper and shook it out crossly. Although he loved the bloke dearly, he'd picked a fine time to come barging in. 'This happens to be a good friend of mine, Miss Teri Carter.'

Charlie held out his hand and Teri shook it reluctantly. 'The pleasure's all mine,' he said breezily. That was something Teri could definitely empathise with.

'And this lazy good-for-nothing . . .' Jamie gestured at Charlie dismissively '. . . is supposed to be my assistant.'

Charlie looked suitably offended. 'Now who's being rude?'

'I didn't expect to see you here.' Jamie was still tetchy.

'You've made that quite plain, old thing.' Charlie went from offended to hurt.

'So, what *are* you doing on the train so early? Couldn't you sleep?'

'Haven't been to sleep, old boy. Came straight from the casino. Went home, had a bit of a wash and brush-up, and back out again. I've got lots to do in the office.'

'Don't make me laugh! No one has got *anything* to do in the office – it's like a morgue in there. I keep expecting to pull out one of the filing-cabinet drawers and find a dead body in there with a tag round its toe.'

'My, you are being spiteful today, James.' He sat forward and spoke conspiratorially. 'Look, there's no need to worry about me. Mum's the word.' He imitated a zip closing across his mouth and Teri fervently wished that there really was one there. 'Don't let me interrupt.' He opened his copy of the *Financial Times* and started to read. 'Just pretend I'm not here.' He waved his hand dismissively. It might have looked more convincing if the newspaper had been the right way up.

Jamie was flushed, either with anger or embarrassment or both – Teri wasn't sure. 'Sorry,' he mouthed to her silently.

She shrugged in return – there was little else she could do. It was a morose, mist-shrouded morning and she stared out of the window watching the McVities' factory whizz past just after Wembley Central, with its undeniable legend *You have to go a long, long way to bake a better biscuit* and an attractive, if slightly unnecessary, picture of a digestive biscuit. It failed to cheer her, particularly as you couldn't smell the biscuits baking in the morning. Did it mean that McVities' workers enjoyed a long lie-in, or was it just that her nose wasn't entirely functional until noon? Another question without an answer.

The three sat in uncomfortable silence – Jamie skulking

behind his newspaper. She stared at him and he failed to meet her eyes, so she focused instead on the electric blue and purple zig-zag fabric of the British Rail seats that matched nothing and was hard on the eyes at any time, let alone seven o'clock in the morning. In staring at the seats, she forgot to look for the man who lived in the soulless block of flats next to the sign that said *One Mile to Euston Station*, who vigorously towelled dry his important little places in front of the window each morning.

Another disappointment. Teri could feel the edges of her mouth settling into a downward pout. Three ornate pink lamp-posts loomed optimistically from the grime, and the tangle of tracks increased to spaghetti-like proportions, signalling their arrival at Euston. Whatever had happened to Heathcliff and Cathy and thingy and whatsit – she was pretty sure that a Charlie hadn't turned up in the middle to blight their reunion!

He left Teri awkwardly and reluctantly with a brisk goodbye at the mouth of the underground station and headed off with Charlie towards the Northern Line.

'I must say I'm disappointed in you, old chap,' Charlie said as they pushed through the automatic ticket barriers. Keeping up with the fast pace of seasoned commuters, they descended at a brisk walk down the escalator, which groaned in complaint, to the tube. 'I had you down for Mr Happily Married.'

In the subterranean tunnel, a young student-type played the love theme from *Dr Zhivago*, picking the strings of his battered guitar with the touch of a lover. On the floor next to him, his guitar case was filling steadily with coins. Further along the curving corridor of cracked tiles sat a young mother with a strong Irish accent and a toddler with an equally strong pair of lungs. She proffered the child in the face of passing commuters and said, 'Change, please!' The chipped china cup at her feet was empty.

'I *am* happily married,' Jamie snapped above the rushing noise of the wind on the platform. 'I told you, she's a good friend.'

'Do you always hold hands with your good friends on the train in the morning?'

'I hadn't seen her for ages and she was upset and needed comforting.' Lies, lies, lies. 'It was all going very well until you came along and put your size ten in.'

'I must say she didn't look very upset. She looked positively radiant to me.'

The train arrived and they got on, saving Jamie the need to explain himself further. All the seats were taken, but it wasn't overcrowded, so they stood with their backs against the side panels near the door facing each other.

'Does Pamela know that you meet good friends on the train and hold their hands?' Charlie continued as the train rattled its way to Leicester Square.

'I don't think that's any of your business, Charlie.'

'Look, I may be approaching the brink of alcoholism and the descent into early senility, but I'm not a complete idiot.' Charlie paused. 'You could disagree with me.'

'You *are* a complete idiot.'

'No, it's you, dear boy – *you* are the complete idiot,' Charlie said soberly, concern evident in his voice. 'This is a very dangerous game you're playing, Jamie.'

'It's not a game, Charlie.' Jamie was tight-lipped. 'Whatever you think this is, it's certainly not a game.'

'But it *is*! It's a game with people's lives. The rules aren't fair and I wouldn't mind betting that some of the players don't even know they're on the pitch.' He raised an eyebrow in query. Jamie looked the other way. 'That simply isn't cricket.'

They changed at Leicester Square – which was always heaving with bodies at any time of the day or night – to the Piccadilly Line for the one stop to Covent Garden. Hostility crackled between them like warning lightning before a thunderstorm breaks. A Japanese lady pushed on the train between them and they glared at each other openly. She shuffled uncomfortably and held the two cameras and the video recorder she had slung round her neck closer to her chest. When the train stopped she hurried off in front of them, casting wary glances over her shoulder, assuming that these were the pickpockets so many of her friends had told her to watch out for.

As they marched along behind her, Charlie continued, 'Finish it, Jamie, before people get hurt.'

'Nothing has started, Charlie.'

They waited for the lift to come to take them up to street level. 'You don't hold hands with people unless there's something going on.' He held his own hand up to stop Jamie's protests, which was a mistake. They crowded into the lift like very large sardines in a very small, very tight tin and Charlie's hand was trapped in a truncated wave against his chest.

Jamie glowered at him. 'If you're so ruddy disapproving, what was that camp, nudge nudge, wink wink, routine on the train for?'

'What could I say, dear chap? I was in an embarrassing predicament. I could see I was about as welcome as a fart in spacesuit – but I had to say something. It seemed apparent that polite conversation about Pamela and the kids was out of the question.'

'Okay,' Jamie said as they emerged into the grey drizzle that had started to fall. 'I'll come clean. There might have been the odd illicit drink and one meal. One meal, for goodness sake! That doesn't make me an adulterer. I haven't even given her so much as a peck on the cheek.' He turned and faced his old friend. 'I haven't seen her for two weeks and I've been like a lovesick teenager,' he confessed in a low voice. 'I can't eat, I can't sleep and I certainly can't make love to my wife. Today was the first time I'd held her hand – and look where that got me.' They continued walking. 'A bloody morality lecture from Oliver Reed's soulmate.'

'Nip it in the bud, Jamie,' Charlie said quietly.

He stopped and batted his palm against his forehead. 'You're like a broken record!'

'It's going nowhere, Jamie. Stop it now.'

He swallowed hard. His mouth was dry; he could have done with his usual cup of coffee with Teri at the End of the Line Buffet. He wished he could have talked to Teri properly, to have told her how he felt when he hadn't been able to see her. He wished Charlie hadn't turned up like the proverbial bad penny and spoilt their precious little time together. And most of all he wished he wasn't having this conversation.

The rain was heavier now and it was running down his forehead and on to his nose. He had an umbrella in his briefcase – a fold-up one that Pamela had bought him in Harrods. He deliberately didn't use it. He wanted to be wet and cold and miserable – and he didn't wish to be reminded of Pamela. Although he already had been.

'I don't know if I can stop it, Charlie,' he admitted at last. 'I feel like I'm on a runaway train that's gathering speed. It's out of my control.'

'That's complete bollocks, Jamie – and you know it. You can blow the whistle at any time you like. And the sooner you do it, the less painful it will be. Don't wait until you crash into the buffers and there's a mangled wreck around you.'

Chapter Nine

Clare held the soggy man-sized Kleenex to her nose again.
'If he crawled over broken glass to see me and arrived at
the door all nasty and bloody with bits of glass sticking
out of his knees I wouldn't have him back now.'

Teri handed her another tissue. 'Yes, you would.'

'No, I wouldn't.' Belligerent five-year-olds knew less
about sulking than Clare. She had done A-level sulk.

'Not even if he begged?'

Clare blew her nose heartily and cast the tissue on to
the ever-growing pile on the sofa. 'Well, I might.'

'I'm going to put these in the bin before they make a
damp patch on the Dralon.' Teri scooped the tissues up
with a shudder and went into the kitchen to dispose of
them.

'Women who go out with married men should be shot.'
Clare's voice drifted into the kitchen in between sniffs.
Teri stopped in her tracks, foot on the pedal bin, tissues
poised. There was a cold prickling feeling up the back of
her neck.

'They destroy lives.' Clare was in full swing. 'In fact,
shooting's far too good for them. It should be something
slow and torturous, like the Black Death. I know – the
Plague of Traitorous Women.' Clare was obviously feeling

better on this subject and the sniffing had nearly stopped. 'It should start with boils.'

Teri ditched the tissues and tiptoed across the room to stare into the pine-framed mirror over the kitchen-cum-dining-room table.

'Big black ones, all over their faces,' she said stridently.

Teri tentatively gave her skin an exploratory stroke.

'With a particularly big one on the end of their noses so that everyone could see what they had done.'

Teri examined her nose carefully.

'Then their fingernails should drop out.'

Teri swallowed hard. Hers were long and strong and more often than not, painted red. She was very fond of her nails.

'One by one,' Clare added as an afterthought. 'Then the skin on their necks should sag.'

Teri pulled down her polo neck and inspected her neck. There was a fairly deep crease-line across it, but no sagging.

'Mind you, that usually happens anyway,' Clare said philosophically.

Teri tore herself away from the mirror and rushed to the fridge to pull out the half-empty bottle of white wine. She braced herself to go back into the lounge.

'For goodness sake, Clare! I preferred you when you were suicidal to psychotic. Here,' she thrust the wine bottle at her friend, 'drink yourself into oblivion and then we can both have some peace.'

Clare tutted, but took the bottle anyway. 'You're not much of an Agony Aunt, are you? I would have expected a bit more sympathy. You know how upset I've been.'

'I know – I'm sorry. I've had a bad day.' Teri tugged her hair back from her forehead. 'It's just that you deserve better than David. He's always been a complete bastard and he always will be. I hate to see you wasting yourself on him.'

Clare refilled her glass. 'I need to lose some weight.'

'You've lost loads of weight! If you get any thinner you'll look like Kylie Minogue.'

'*She's* only a size eight.'

'Kylie Minogue?' Teri was puzzled.

'No! Her!' Clare tossed her hair back. '*Anthea!*'

'Is that what he rang up to tell you?'

'No. He's wanted me to know he's putting the flat on the market.' Her eyes filled with tears again and she reached for another tissue.

'Oh hell, I'm sorry, Clare.' Teri sat next to her on the sofa and put her arm round her friend's heaving shoulders. 'Look, it's probably for the best. A clean break and then you can get on with your life.'

'I'll never find another man,' Clare wailed.

'Of course you will.' Teri squeezed her shoulder. 'You've got so much going for you. You're young, you're pretty, you're slim – and getting slimmer. Who could resist you?'

'Everyone!' Clare wiped her eyes. 'My husband did. And everyone else over the age of twenty-one is married.'

'No, they're not.' Teri patted her arm.

'I don't want a toyboy. I want a mature man. A Tom Cruise look-alike, but taller with no emotional baggage and no ex-wives or kids.'

'It's a good job you're not picky,' Teri said lightly. She gave her another reassuring squeeze. 'Look, there are still some – a few – very nice men around.'

Clare turned on her. 'So how come it's taken you so long to find one?'

Teri shook her head and picked some imaginary fluff

from her jeans. 'Perhaps I just wasn't looking in the right place.'

'Still, you've found someone nice now and I'm really pleased for you.' She clutched Teri's hand, crushing it to her. 'I know I've been wrapped up in myself lately. I'm sorry. Come on then, tell me all about him. It'll take my mind off that bastard I'm married to.' She giggled and wiped her eyes. 'Dish the dirt, Tez. I could do with cheering up.'

'There's nothing to tell really.' Teri's voice sounded over-casual even to her. This was dangerous territory.

'Oh, don't be so mean. You know we've told each other everything since you confessed that you let Michael Lacey put his hand up your skirt under the coats in the cloakroom in Mrs Whittle's class.'

'Clare!'

Her friend was unperturbed. 'I know it's still on because you went to the Gossard factory shop and bought a load of new knickers last weekend.'

'What's that got to do with anything?'

'Well, it must be getting serious if you're lashing out on new undies.'

'The reason I bought new undies was because all my other knickers are grey.'

'Rubbish!' Clare elbowed her meaningfully in the ribs. 'I know you better than that.'

Teri's jaw tightened. 'The reason all my knickers are grey is that someone, who shall remain nameless, left a black sock in the bottom of the washing machine.'

'Oh.'

They sat in silence for a few moments and to cover the uneasiness Teri poured herself half a glass of wine, even though she didn't want it.

'So is it on or is it off?' Clare continued.

'Let it drop, Clare. Please,' Teri pleaded.

'We-e-ll,' she elongated the word, 'you're so cagey. One minute you're mad about this bloke – he's the best thing since the video shop started selling Häagen Dazs – and then next thing – *schtum*. What's the big secret?'

'There's no big secret.' The words nearly stuck in her throat. Clare was right – she *had* told her everything since the embarrassing and awakening Michael Lacey incident. They had confided in each other since the day they started at The Sacred Heart of Jesus primary school together. More often than not, this was because Clare did a superlative range of Chinese burns – Teri winced at the memory – and it was easier to tell her innermost secrets to her best friend than trying to explain away another bright red and bruised arm to her mother.

The only thing she had ever kept from Clare was her one moment of madness when she had, for reasons which still eluded her, agreed to a clandestine date with Clare's husband. And Jamie. He could still just about be classed as a secret. Mind you, with maturing years Clare had resorted to mental forms of torture rather than purely physical – and with equally profitable results.

'Then what's the latest state of play?' Clare was getting impatient, which was always a bad sign. 'Why does he never ring you or take you out? And more to the point, why haven't I met him yet?'

'It's just difficult, that's all.' Teri was trying to keep her temper. Her friend was under a lot of strain at the moment and the revelation about Jamie's circumstances wasn't likely to help.

'Why is it difficult?'

Clare could be very stupid and stubborn when she

wanted to be, and Teri was beginning to wonder why she had ever offered to share her home with her. They'd had a flat together once before, just after they finished university, and it had been an utter disaster. There was mould in the lounge, silverfish in the bathroom and a wide range of tropical diseases in the fridge. Clare had been blissfully unaware of all of them.

Within weeks, every plate and cup in the house was chipped, and there was more cutlery down the back of the cooker than there was in the kitchen drawer. A Pyrex dish that had been her mother's pride and joy for thirty-seven years had lasted one night with Clare. She had also taken an inordinate amount of interest in all of Teri's boyfriends. Why she thought it would be better second time around, goodness only knows.

'You've gone a very funny colour, Therese Carter. There must be something fishy going on.'

Teri shot her a filthy look. She could tell that somewhere in the convoluted recesses of Clare's brain, pennies were obviously dropping. Sure enough, Clare clapped a hand to her mouth. 'He's married! Oh God, he's married, isn't he!' She leapt off the sofa and began wearing a tormented path across the lounge carpet. 'Tell me, Therese, tell me that he isn't married.'

'He is married,' Teri said quietly.

'Tell me it's not true,' Clare wailed.

'It's true,' she said, equally quietly.

'What are you thinking of?' Clare wheeled on her. 'You've been cooking with that microwave door open again, haven't you? It's turned your brains to scrambled eggs.'

'I have not,' she said emphatically. Teri thought about sulking, but realised she would be competing with an expert.

'How can you do this to me?' Clare was starting to cry again. 'After all I've been through, how can you do this to me?'

Teri held out another man-sized Kleenex. If it looked like a flag of surrender it was meant to. Clare brushed it aside and wiped her nose on her sleeve.

'Clare, I'm not doing anything to you.' Teri spoke softly and calmly. 'Sit down and stop behaving like a drama queen. You were no good as the Virgin Mary in the school nativity play – a part which should rightly have gone to me . . .'

Clare shot her a withering look. Teri realised her mistake and corrected it, '. . . at the time. And theatrical histrionics don't suit you now either. If you want to discuss this like rational human beings then we can. If not, then I'm going to bed.'

Clare put her hands on her hips. 'You couldn't be the Virgin Mary because you were covered in chicken-pox scabs which didn't seem entirely fitting for the Mother of the Baby Jesus.' She could be very caustic when she tried. 'I seem to remember you crying hysterically until they made you one of the Wise Men – a part which doesn't seem highly appropriate now either.'

Teri slumped back on the sofa. 'I agree, it's very unwise, but I love him.' Her voice sounded matter-of-fact, but her heart was pounding uneasily like someone trying to play the bongos for the very first time. Why was she admitting this to Clare? She hadn't even admitted it to herself before now. And why was her pulse racing like this?

Clare snorted derisively. 'What makes you think that you love him?'

Teri twisted the bracelet on her arm distractedly. 'He's the nicest man I've ever met. He's kind, he's caring, he's—'

'Cheating on his wife,' Clare finished abrasively. They stared at each other. 'Does she know about this?'

'I don't know,' Teri admitted. 'We don't talk about her.'

Clare blew down her nose like an irritated horse. 'I bet!'

'He says they've drifted apart,' Teri explained feebly.

'Perhaps he's just been paddling in the wrong direction.' Her tone could be very scathing too. When Teri didn't answer Clare continued, 'Do you know what it feels like to find out that the man you love has been seeing another woman?'

'No,' Teri answered reluctantly.

'Then you are a very lucky person indeed, Therese Carter.' Clare jabbed emphatically at her stomach. 'It makes you feel sick – as if someone is pulling your insides out so that everyone can see them. Every miserable, broken-hearted, weepy, sentimental load of old pap that's played on the radio is aimed just at you. You can't think, you can't *stop* thinking; you can't sleep, you can't eat.' The tears were rolling silently down her face, which was more painful to watch than the dramatic sobs. 'I lost a stone in a week. A stone! Sod Rosemary Conley and her hips and thighs – the adultery diet beats it hands down every time.'

'I'm losing weight too!' Teri could hear herself whining and it was a very unpleasant sound.

'That's not emotional strain!' Clare wasn't in the mood for being swayed. 'There's nothing in the fridge that's over a hundred and fifty calories.' She pointed accusingly at the kitchen door. 'And that's because you want your bum to look like a firm young peach in your new lacy black thong.' Teri opened her mouth to speak. Clare glared at her through slitted eyes. 'Don't deny it – I've seen the Gossard box in the bin.'

'I resent that!' Teri said – mostly because it was true.

'She'll have no idea this is going on,' Clare said, changing tack. 'I didn't. I thought we were deliriously happy. One minute we were bonking away to our hearts' content, swinging from the chandeliers like Tarzan and Jane swinging through the jungle . . .'

'It was Tarzan and Cheetah who swung through the jungle,' Teri interrupted. 'Jane stayed at home and cooked.'

Clare turned on her. 'Now you're splitting hairs because you know you're in the wrong.'

'If you insist on moralising, at least get your story straight,' Teri said petulantly.

Clare continued unabashed. 'The next minute he was gone. No sooner had his feet hit the floor and the Durex was down the loo, than he turned and said: "I've fallen in love with someone else." Just like that!' She wagged her finger threateningly at Teri. 'And don't even think of doing a Tommy Cooper routine. *I* have the monopoly on bad jokes!' She paused for breath. 'Instead of basking in afterglow like *New Woman* says I should, it was "goodnight and thank you" for good.'

'But David *always* had wandering eyes – and hands!' Teri objected. Clare sagged into the chair opposite her. Teri felt horrible hurting her friend like this. It seemed an appropriate time to confess her own near-miss indiscretion with him to prove her point, but she didn't dare. No doubt it would come out in time, Chinese burns or no.

'Jamie isn't like that,' she went on, her voice softening. 'He's never done anything like this before. It's taken us both by surprise. We never intended it to happen. And besides, it's still purely platonic. How can I feel so guilty when we've done absolutely nothing?'

Clare made a strange strangled noise, which Teri took to mean that she doubted the validity of her statement.

'It's true!' she insisted. 'There's been nothing more than a few drinks and a bit of furtive hand-holding.'

It was true she was still a virgin adulterer, and even to her it was beginning to feel slightly as if it was verging on the ridiculous. She wasn't surprised Clare didn't believe her – she could hardly believe it herself.

'If that is true, then stay away from him, Teri. End it now before you ruin everyone's lives.'

'I don't know if I can, Clare.' They were both crying now. 'When I see him my heart lurches, I feel sick, my palms sweat and my tongue grows to twice its size so that I can hardly get my words out.'

'That's a virus – not love!'

They reached for the Kleenex box simultaneously. 'It seems so unfair. I've waited all my life to meet someone like him.'

'The minor snag is, Teri, that he's already got a wife. A small point, but not exactly insignificant.'

'And two children,' Teri sobbed. She waited for the backlash but it didn't come.

Clare rejoined her on the sofa and pulled the Kleenex box closer to them. She poured the dregs of the wine into their glasses. 'I could hit you on the head with this bottle, you know?'

Teri laughed and sobbed at the same time and it made a bubble come out of her nose. 'What am I going to do?'

'End it, Teri. Commute by coach. Change your job. Have facial reconstruction. Whatever the cost, avoid him.' Clare drained her glass and reached for another tissue. 'There'll be a price to pay for this, my love, and I'm not sure that you can afford it.'

'Just tell me one thing,' Teri looked at her squarely. 'How will I ever get over him?'

Clare sighed. 'Love *is* like a virus. It's totally debilitating and it takes a hell of a long time to recover from. And when you're low it'll hit you again.' She slammed her glass on the coffee table with a sobering finality. 'There's no damn medicine they can give you for it either.' She looked ruefully at Teri. 'If there was, I'd take a bloody great dose of it myself.'

Chapter Ten

Out and About had kept Teri constantly busy for the last two hours. It was a news-based programme, transmitted late afternoon just before they lost all their intended viewers to the BBC and the lure of Australian soaps.

Out and About – not exactly a 'totally crucial' title in her opinion – was produced with the emphasis very firmly on 'youff'. Most of the programme – over-enthusiastic reports from teenagers with obviously capped teeth and baseball caps on back to front – was pre-recorded on video tape, VTR, with live links provided in the studio by two odious brats in their early twenties pretending to be sixteen.

They were a total nightmare. Unreliable, unresponsive and unrepentant. Their idea of fun was to present the show sitting behind the desk with no trousers on and mooning to the crew while the VTR was being played. To their surprise, they were the only ones who found it amusing.

Despite the technological advantage of Autocue, they fluffed their lines constantly and the programme was on its third warning from the British Broadcasting Standards Authority about the repeated inadvertent use of the F-word.

The producer was a homosexual alcoholic with an ulcer and, for the latter complaint, Teri could lay the blame solely at the feet of these two individuals. He was called Richard Wellbeloved and was universally despised by everyone at City Television from the cleaning ladies up.

The main anchor man was an ex-art student with a ponytail and a suspicious habit of nipping to the toilet for lengthy periods during moments of stress. He insisted on being called 'Jez'. He was the main F-word offender, and similar F-words had filtered down from on high – television's equivalent to God, the Head of Programming – to let him know that he was on probation. Teri suspected that it wasn't the first time Jez had been on probation. One more deviation from 'Golly' or 'Wow!' and he would be sacked. It couldn't happen soon enough as far as she was concerned.

The producer, unfortunately, relied not on the educational content or on the skilful presentation of a quality programme to attract its rapidly dwindling audience, but on the fact that most kids watched because the whole thing was total chaos and you never knew when the next F-word might pop up. The entire programme needed a complete revamp, a mix of maturity and street cred to stop the programme from careering off the rails. Look at John Craven – what harm had he ever done to *Newsround*? Those were the days – lying on her stomach in front of the television pretending to do her homework while John intoned seriously about the dire state of the world. What would he have to say about it now? Back then, John was everybody's idea of a hero. Neat as a pin, clean cut, unsullied. All right, so the V-necked jumpers *à la* Val Doonican hadn't lent him the air of street credibility that might be deemed essential these days, but you knew where you were with John. No accidental F-words there.

In fact, what the programme *really* needed was Teri Carter at the helm. Her talents were wasted sitting in the dimly lit glass gallery that overlooked the studio, like some pathetic little fish in an aquarium, counting down the seconds to the links and trying to make sure that Richard Wellbeloved didn't tip his coffee – heavily laced with whisky – into the control panel.

She would add that necessary edge of common sense, sweetened by a girlish charm. And she wouldn't bare her bottom to the camera crew. Mind you, considering that her rear was infinitely more attractive than the pimply buttocks of the gormless presenters, this was something that might not go in her favour.

Teri picked up the producer's abandoned coffee cup and threw it in the bin, glaring at his back as he stamped out of the gallery. All she had to do was convince the inappropriately named Richard Wellbeloved.

She rubbed her eyes as she emerged from the gloom of the gallery into the fierce strip lighting of the office, and noticed that outside in the real world it was still snowing. The snow had been falling steadily all afternoon, inter-mittently distracting her from the programme schedule. Now great swirls of flakes like lacy doilies floated past her window and landed in drifts in Euston Road; if not trans-forming it instantly into a Winter Wonderland, it certainly made it look marginally less depressing than usual.

She had arranged to meet Jamie tonight too, which always brightened her day no end. If the weather was this atrocious in town, just think what it was going to be like, out in the sticks. The journey home would take an age. They would be stranded in the middle of nowhere for hours, listening to the futile slipping of the wheels on the line. And in the absence of any Boy Scouts to rub together, they would have to look to each other to provide bodily warmth.

It would be absolute hell. Her mouth curled into an involuntary smile.

It *was* hell. There may not have been fire and brimstone and little curly-tailed devils doing obscene things with toasting forks, but it was hell all right. On the departures board there were, predictably, a lot of blanks where once there used to be trains. The concourse was packed with commuters, ranging from the frankly bemused to the red-faced irate, who either stood and screamed into their mobile phones or at any hapless human who happened to pass wearing a British Rail uniform.

It was a perverse twist of fate, and an indication of the state of their relationship, that normally Jamie and Teri were the only ones who enjoyed delays. But this was the mother of all delays, one that made Eternity look like the brief and momentary blinking of an eye.

They stood holding hands. All fetters of embarrassment thrown off for the brief hour before they got home. Except that by the look of things, it was going to be ever-so slightly more than an hour before they reached their respective homes tonight. They listened to the announcement again, hoping that this time it would sound more like the Queen's English rather than one of the Queen's corgis.

'Bugger,' Jamie said. He translated for Teri. 'Stock excuse. Adverse weather causing signal failures at Watford Junction.'

'Typical!' Teri puffed. 'Is this what they call the wrong type of snow?'

'No, it's the right type of snow – there's just too much

of it.' There was a look of extreme exasperation on his face. 'We'll be lucky to get home at all tonight.'

Teri cleared her throat and said tentatively, 'We could try to get a room.'

'You know I can't do that.' His answer was more brisk than she thought was necessary.

'It was only a suggestion,' Teri said irritably. 'I was trying to be practical, not seductive.'

'Oh hell, I know. I'm sorry, I didn't mean to snap. I doubt there'll be any room at the inn tonight anyway. You know what it's like when one solitary flake falls in the capital, all the big companies phone round and block-book the rooms.'

'Ours doesn't,' she pointed out unhelpfully.

He sighed. 'Neither does ours.' He squeezed her hand. His hands were always warm. Always. Warm and soft. Hers were always like blocks of ice, winter or summer, but particularly in winter when she left her best thermal gloves at home next to the telephone on the one day when it decided to snow. That was another thing she could blame on Clare. It was she Teri had been speaking to on the phone. If you could call it speaking.

Clare was doing nothing to hide her disapproval of Teri's relationship with Jamie. To say that Clare wore her heart on her sleeve was an understatement of the third kind – she wore her spleen there, too. And vented it with a glory that was both Technicolor and alarmingly regular. In fact, she had taken spleen-venting lessons from Sister Mary Bernadette, former headmistress of The Sacred Heart of Jesus primary school.

Sister Mary Bernadette was known to be a strict disciplinarian with a temper that was never humbled or cowed by the constraints of her black flowing habit or her chosen faith. Today she would have been labelled a sadist, and been crushed under the weight of irate and indignant parents. Back then, no one had the gall to question her tactics or her motives. If she wanted to beat someone to within an inch of their lives for not eating their rice pudding, it was entirely her choice. There were times when Teri had been eternally grateful for a simple, if wholly undeserved, tanned backside, for if Sister Mary Bernadette chose to mentally scar you it was considerably worse.

It was sometimes difficult to have a best friend who still modelled herself on their former headmistress. At six o'clock that morning Clare had phoned to say – in curt, clipped tones – that she was snowbound with the airline in Ireland, and wasn't likely to be home tonight. It was even less likely now. Even if they managed to dig her out of Dublin, Luton International Airport would still be up to its ears in icicles. The weather, like their friendship, looked like remaining distinctly chilly for the foreseeable future.

'Come on.' Jamie broke into her thoughts. 'Let's go and get some food and give this another try later on.'

They went to their usual haunt – The Pasta Place. Tonight they were the only customers. Even the transvestites next door had been cowed by the weather conditions. The strings of coloured lights in the window of 'Terrific Transformations' had been turned off and the falsie bras hung forlornly. Perhaps they had all decided that it was one night when jeans and hobnail boots were decidedly more suitable attire than stilettos and pencil-slim skirts. And who could blame them?

Anyone with a modicum of sense had gone straight home and barricaded themselves in with a mug of hot, beefy Bovril. It would have been a good idea if she and Jamie had done the same. The restaurant was cold, the pasta was cold and, when they reluctantly headed back to Euston, the train they eventually boarded was cold, too. But at least they got a seat. And, after several false starts, they managed to find ones that didn't sound like Whoopee cushions when you sat on them.

It was another half-hour before the train moved, by which time every conceivable inch of floorspace had a disgruntled delayed commuter standing on it. Despite the fact that there was no tangible form of heat supplied by British Rail, the carriage started to steam with the warmth of damp and very squashed and very sweaty bodies trying to dry out.

'Good evening, ladies and gentlemen.' A strangulated voice came through the loudspeakers, sounding suspiciously like Charlie Drake. 'This is the late-running 19.07 to Milton Keynes, calling at Leighton Buzzard and Milton Keynes.' There was a flurry of consternation and several blanching faces before the cartoon-voiced announcer continued: 'This train will call additionally at Harrow and Wealdstone, Bushey, Watford Junction, Kings Langley, Apsley, Hemel Hempstead, Berkhamsted, Tring and Cheddington.'

There was an unappreciative groan from the occupants of the carriage. 'We'll be on here all night,' Jamie said under his breath.

Still the announcer droned on. 'British Rail would like to apologise for the late running of this train. This is due to adverse weather conditions affecting signalling equipment at Watford Junction. This train will terminate at Leighton Buzzard.' There was another louder and even more unappreciative groan from the carriage. 'This is due to adverse weather conditions affecting power lines at Bletchley. Transport in the form of buses will be provided for onward connections to Bletchley and Milton Keynes Stations. British Rail apologise for any inconvenience caused and wish you a pleasant journey.'

There were times when the use of the F-word was entirely justified, Teri felt. Perhaps she would look more kindly on Jez tomorrow. Then again, perhaps not.

Jamie flung himself back in his seat with a sigh. 'So the end of the line is sunny Leighton Buzzard and then buses to Bletchley and Milton Keynes.'

Teri twisted her hair round her finger. 'What chance do they have of getting buses through, if the trains can't make it?'

Jamie's brow furrowed and a look of resigned weariness settled heavily into his features. 'Trust you to spot the deliberate mistake.'

'They obviously have greater faith in the local councils than they do in Railtrack,' Teri observed.

'I think their faith might be somewhat misplaced.' He rubbed his chin thoughtfully. 'At this moment I think I have more faith in crystal therapy, divining rods, copper bracelets for rheumatism and Mystic Meg.'

Teri smiled sympathetically. At the end of the day he had quite a shadow of stubble on his face. In the morning, he was baby-faced and scrubbed. At night he looked paler and the stubble gave him a slightly down-but-not-out look. A bit like Bruce Willis in *Die Hard*. Handsome in an unwholesome sort of way . . . She wanted to reach up and stroke it to see if it was soft or scratchy, but so far she hadn't had either the nerve or the opportunity.

He was still muttering. 'And why do they always announce these things once they've got you trapped on the bloody train and it's already trundling out of the station? There's no way that you can make an impartial decision about whether you want to travel or not. Even if you want to get off, you can't.'

He lapsed into a deep and unhappy silence. It seemed somehow too churlish to point out that sometimes she felt exactly the same way about their relationship.

There was a queue outside Leighton Buzzard Station. A very long one. Made up of a lot of damp, dark people huddled together under dripping black umbrellas. It snaked along the front of the station and round past the empty taxi rank towards the snowbound car park. There was one very small and very full bus parked at the head of it. The driver was trying to start its engine. Unsuccessfully. The snow was still falling.

Teri could tell by the look on Jamie's face that his heart had just sunk to somewhere inside his shoes. 'You're going to be here for ever,' she remarked observantly.

Jamie fixed her with a withering glance. 'You could just be right, Ms Carter.'

'Look.' Teri lowered her lashes. 'I know you've turned me down once tonight, but I'll make the offer again. Why don't you come home with me? It's only up the hill.'

'I have to try and get home,' he stated flatly.

'It's madness to try to get home in this.' She fought an overwhelming urge to stamp her foot.

Jamie tilted her chin and forced her to look at him. 'It's madness not to.'

'Either way it's madness!' Her voice was rising, despite the fact that she was trying not to shout.

The bus driver tried his engine again. It reluctantly chug–chug-*chugged* into black, smoking life. Everyone in the queue shuffled forward one step, before the engine died once more into ominous silence.

'I don't know why you've suddenly turned into Mother Teresa of Calcutta on me,' she said vehemently. 'Are we going to spend the rest of our lives looking longingly at each other and holding hands? Tell me, for goodness sake, Jamie, exactly what are we doing?'

His face looked pained and jaundiced under the yellow glow of the street-lamp. He pulled her away from the stoic queue of ever-hopeful commuters. 'I've got a wife,' he said softly.

'And I've got bloody cold feet!' she said, and stamped off ankle-deep in snow away from the station. In the car park a few optimistic souls were trying to dig their cars out of snowdrifts using the scraper from the top of their de-icer can.

'Wait!' She heard Jamie call, but carried on walking, head down against the relentless flurries that were wet and stingingly cold and sharp on her cheeks. Not only did she have cold feet, but there was a hunger growing deep within her that had nothing to do with food. Two Big Macs, large fries and a thick chocolate milkshake wouldn't even begin to fill this space inside her.

He caught her arm and spun her round, flinging her off-balance on the slippery ground. In surprise, she let go of her briefcase and it sailed low over the snow, catching him squarely below the knees and taking his legs from under him as neatly as any of the Lion's full-backs could have done. He landed on the snow with an inelegant *oouf!*

'Oh, Jamie! I'm sorry.' She slithered towards him and reached out her hand to help him. He lay sprawled and lifeless in the snow. As she neared him she could hear him murmur.

'Speak to me, Jamie! What is it?' She crouched beside him, lowering her face to his lips, straining to hear what he said.

She heard a faint croak and leaned closer.

'That briefcase never liked me,' he whispered. His hand reached out and grabbed her ankle and, with an ear-piercing scream, she joined him in the snow.

'You complete bastard!' She kicked out at him, but only succeeded in sending an ineffective flurry of snow spraying into the air.

He was laughing now and pulling her close to him. The snow was seeping into her back, cold and wet where it had crept up inside her coat. It was in her hair and in her ears.

'I'll get you for this!' she spluttered, and grabbed a handful of snow and flung it towards him.

It scored a direct bulls' eye with his mouth, showering his face and hair with glittering shards of ice. He spat it out, laughing and writhing towards her, inching his face next to hers.

Pinning her to the snow with his arms, he raised himself above her. He shook the snow from his hair and the tiny flakes fluttered over her. She was surprised to find that hot tears were running down the chill of her cheeks despite the fact that she, too, was laughing.

He was still breathless when he started to speak. 'The reason I didn't want to come with you is that I'm terrified by what's happening.' He brushed her fringe back from her face. 'I wasn't looking for this. Do you understand that?'

She nodded silently, scared by the intensity of emotion on his face. His lips brushed hers, as lightly and elusively as the snowflakes that were falling in the darkness. 'So you don't need to tell me about cold feet, Ms Teri Carter.'

He parted her mouth with his tongue. It was hot and moist and disturbingly insistent, and despite the fact that she was soaked through to the skin and lying on a bed of freezing snow, she had never felt warmer.

'I know all about cold feet.' He held her away from him. There were snowflakes on his eyelashes. 'Because that's exactly what I've got, too.'

Chapter Eleven

He was an astonishingly good kisser for someone with cold feet. Teri gazed at her reflection in the bathroom mirror, wondering if she looked any different now that he had finally kissed her. Apart from soaking wet and completely bedraggled, that is. She decided that she probably didn't and set about rubbing her hair vigorously with the towel.

It had taken them ages to trudge back up to Bidefield Green. Normally it was a reasonably quick walk to the station – about fifteen minutes at a brisk pace – a bit longer going home as it was all uphill. With a good six inches of snow it was an entirely different matter. Sherpa Tensing and the odd oxygen canister on tap would have made the journey considerably easier.

There was a tentative knock on the door and Jamie peeped his head round. The Kiss hadn't been mentioned and they'd gone back to embarrassed shyness and tip-toeing round each other.

'I borrowed this,' he said.

'This' was her dressing gown. Navy-blue towelling, so nothing too girlie there. But those in the tailoring profession might have called it a neat fit. Its cross-over bit at the front didn't, and he was revealing a rather alarming amount of chest and thigh and there were bits of dark, curling hair that pointed dangerously to hidden bits of his anatomy.

Teri looked back at the mirror and hoped that Jamie realised it was just the steam in the bathroom that had made her cheeks go red. They had changed out of their wet clothes and had languished under the steaming hot shower separately. It was quite the most chaste love affair Teri had ever had. Well, at least since she was sixteen. It made Jamie seem all the more appealing, the fact that he didn't try to jump on her bones every five minutes. Although she did briefly harbour dark thoughts in the shower of him bursting in and taking her against the tiles . . .

'I hope you don't mind,' he said.

Teri cleared her throat. 'No. It's very fetching. I'll borrow Clare's. She won't be home.' Her voice wobbled. 'Her plane's stuck in a snowdrift in Dublin.' She made sure her towel was attached securely and then pulled a comb through her hair. 'It's pink and flowery and not really your colour.'

Jamie looked bashful and grimaced slightly. 'I need to phone home.'

Their eyes met, and there was an expression in his that obviously meant something deep and meaningful. But what? It didn't seem appropriate to ask. Instead she said, 'You sound like ET.'

'Sorry.'

'The phone's at the bottom of the stairs.'

'Thanks. I won't be long.'

She tried very hard not to listen, but it was impossible. Perhaps if she'd actually been able to make herself close the bathroom door and wrap her towel round her head it would have been easier, but with her ear pressed up against the cold, damp doorframe she could hear every word.

His wife must have answered the phone after the first ring. 'Hi, it's me,' he said. Not exactly lovey-dovey. 'I know, it's hell in town too.' Talking about the weather as the first topic of conversation – a sure sign that they'd been married for too long. 'I'm not going to make it home.' Not the slightest bit of hesitation there. 'I'm going to spend the night with Charlie.' Query by the wife? 'Why do you need his number? It should be by the phone.' Longer pause. 'Okay, okay. I'll get it.' Placating tone, but mild irritation creeping in? Rummaging in his briefcase. 'Watford 99246.' Briefcase clipped shut. Firmly. 'It's only for one night. I'll be home tomorrow.' Then: 'Perhaps Charlie will lend me some.' Underwear? 'Or I'll wear the same ones two days running.' Definitely underwear. 'How are the kids?' Lowered voice. 'Did they?' The first stab of pain. 'Give them a kiss from me.' Second stab. 'Me too.' I love you? Well, she's hardly likely to be saying 'I'm cold' and he's hardly likely to be answering 'me too'. 'Bye.' Phone clicks.

Teri poked her head out of the bathroom door. Jamie was sitting on the bottom step with his head cradled in his hands. She crept down quietly and sat next to him. 'I could rinse them through for you and put them on the radiator. They'd be dry in the morning.'

He turned towards her. His face was sad and tired. 'What?'

'Your underwear.'

'You've been eavesdropping.' A twinkle came back to his eyes.

'Only a little bit.'

'I'm finding this really difficult.' He reached out and took her hand and she could feel the tension in his fingers. 'It's not that I don't want to be here. It's just that I know that I *shouldn't* be here. I've never told so many lies in my life and it's not something I'm proud of.' He let go of her hands and scraped his hair back from his face. It was still damp and curled erratically at the base of his neck. 'I don't know if I can do this.'

'Look, let's get this straight. You don't have to *do* anything. I'm not pressuring you at all.' Teri nudged him in the arm encouragingly. 'This has more to do with survival than seduction. I didn't want you slithering home through Stoke Hammond on a suicide mission – although I don't think that particular bus was going to be slithering anywhere in a hurry.'

'No,' Jamie agreed thoughtfully.

'You could go back down to the station and join the queue if it would help your conscience.'

'No,' Jamie disagreed thoughtfully.

'So this is to do with common sense not sex?'

'Yes,' he admitted reluctantly.

'I think you'd better ring Charlie then and tell him where you really are,' Teri said. 'And give him my phone number – just in case. Will he mind?'

'Yes, but not as much as I do.' Jamie sighed heavily. 'If I feel this way about you – and I do – I should be sweeping you off your feet, throwing you over my shoulder and rushing you up the stairs to ravish you on the bed.'

'I'd be disappointed if you did.' *Liar.*

'I feel as though I'm letting you down. But if I don't let *you* down, then I let myself down.' He shook himself as if he was trying to clear his brain. 'I need to get my head together on this, Teri.'

'I know.' She wondered what would happen if she accidentally-on-purpose let her towel slip to the floor. 'You sort your head out while I go and sort your knickers out.'

'You shouldn't even be thinking of washing underwear for a man you barely know.'

'There are a lot of things I shouldn't be thinking about doing for a man I barely know, but I'm thinking them all the same.' She kissed him on the end of the nose. 'Ring Charlie.' She stood up and walked towards the kitchen.

'Hey!' He grabbed her hand and said softly, 'There's something I need to know.'

'What's that?' She hardly dared to ask.

'What *is* your telephone number?'

It was 01525 473663. Pamela knew because a female voice, which sounded like an old BBC announcer brought out of retirement, had broken the devastating news of her husband's adultery in well-modulated, robotic cut-glass tones: '*This tel-e-phone num-ber called to-day at twent-y-one, twent-y-five hours. To re-turn the call press three.*'

Quite an innocuous statement if you didn't realise the implications. She wondered how many more marriages would be destroyed by the invention of British Telecom's 1471 redial facility. She didn't have to be an idiot – despite the fact that her husband was taking her for one – to find out that 01525 was a Leighton Buzzard dialling code and that, wherever Jamie was, he wasn't in Watford with his alibi Charlie Perry.

Pamela stared out of the patio window into the darkness of the garden. The children had built a snowman when Francesca had come home from school. 'Frosty' had been given two charcoal briquettes, left over from last summer's barbecues, as eyes, and a traditional carrot nose. Jack had generously donated some Smarties, except for the blue ones which were his favourites, to provide his smile. He was also sporting a beige cashmere scarf, which seemed a trifle excessive for a snowman, but the children refused to come indoors for their tea until Frosty's comfort was fully catered for, and it was the only scarf Pamela could find.

At the moment, Frosty was being battered by the relentless snow which seemed even heavier than before; he looked as if he needed every inch of the expensive cashmere. He was a very small snowman, and already the fresh snow was drifting round where his knees would probably be, if snowmen had knees. His edges were becoming blurred and there was a mound of snow building up on his carrot nose that would soon make it drop off. He would probably be gone in the morning, or at the very least unrecognisable as the snowman he once was. Like their marriage. That too would never be the same again.

What would happen to Frosty? Would he melt into the ground, covered by fresh snow, so that no trace of him remained? Very soon, would it be forgotten that he had ever existed, what fun he had been and how he seemed so permanent at the time . . . or would they rebuild him? Perhaps make a bigger and better Frosty, more able to withstand the rigours of the elements.

It was the first time she had caught Jamie out in a lie. All the months of suspicion and wondering and she had finally been proved right by a robotic voice that innocently blurted out lovers' telephone numbers. Had she willed it into fruition? By concentrating all her thoughts and efforts into Jamie's supposed infidelity, had she made it come true? They say you should be careful what you wish for, because you might just get it. Had she wished this on herself?

There was nothing she could do now, either for Frosty or for her marriage. She was stuck here, marooned by the snow, caring for her children while her husband made love to his mistress not fifteen miles away in Leighton Buzzard.

Pamela pulled her cardigan more tightly round her and pressed her burning face against the cold glass. A mournful groan echoed down the chimney and the wind whipped the snow across the garden, splattering it spitefully against the window where it ran in slow, sad rivulets like tears down a frozen cheek.

Her husband wasn't making love to his mistress. He was in the kitchen making hot chocolate while she artistically arranged his washed underpants on the radiator.

'I may not be much good with a Black and Decker, but I'm a demon with a microwave,' he assured her. 'I know all there is to know. Primarily, because everything I've eaten in the last six years has, at some time, gone *ping!* Trust me.' He stirred the milk in the pan, having shunned the modern microwave method of milk heating – insisting that before you knew it, and ages before the thing went *ping!* the bottom of the microwave was invariably swimming in escaped over-boiled milk. He returned to his languid milk-stirring. 'Teri,' he said tentatively. 'Would you mind very much if we slept together?'

Teri put the finishing touches to the underpants and stood back and admired them. 'I thought that was the general idea when you were having an affair.'

'No, I mean actually *sleep* together – rather than, well, stay awake together.'

'Oh.' Teri tried to feel philosophical. 'I see.'

'It's just that I don't much feel up to it tonight. If you'll pardon the expression.' He stirred the hot-chocolate granules into the pan with the milk.

'Is it me?' Teri asked. 'Don't you find me attractive?' She leaned against the work surface behind him. The first person in the house after she had moved in had been the kitchen fitter. He had skilfully replaced the seventies orange melamine cupboards with tasteful limed oak – only affordable because the kitchen had so few cupboards.

'Don't think that, Teri. I wouldn't be here if I wasn't absolutely besotted with you.' He slid his arm round her waist and pulled her to him. 'I just don't think I'm a natural adulterer.'

Reaching behind him, she rescued the milk that was just about to bubble over the top of the pan and, moving away from him, she poured it into two mugs.

'Some people can dive headlong into irresponsible debauchery and hedonism. I think I'm the sort that has to put one toe in at a time until I'm accustomed to the temperature of the water.' Teri laughed. 'Does that make me sound terribly wet?' he asked.

'No, but it makes you sound terribly cautious. Little wonder you ended up in insurance.' Teri put the pan into the sink. 'Why on earth did I end up having an affair with the world's only conscientious objector?'

'Come here.' He pulled her to him again. 'I'm sorry, I really didn't mean for this to happen. You deserve someone far better than me. Someone who is free to give you what you want.'

'If you're going to start getting depressed I'll hit you with the milk pan.'

Jamie turned the tap on and let cold water run into the

pan. 'There's a nasty black mark on the bottom. I think I've burnt it.'

'It doesn't matter.'

'You'll need something abrasive to get it off with.'

Teri sighed. 'What a pity Clare isn't here, she'd do a great job.'

'Is she giving you a hard time?'

'Not as hard as Sister Mary Bernadette.'

'Who?' Jamie looked perplexed.

'It's a long story.' Teri picked up the two steaming mugs of chocolate. 'Come to bed and I'll tell you all about it.'

'I mustn't forget my undies in the morning.'

'Are you likely to?' Teri laughed.

He looked bashful. 'I suppose not.'

'Your hanky's there, too – the one you lent me when I fell over. I washed it *and* ironed it. You're very honoured.' She looked at the hanky distastefully. 'Though I have to say I couldn't get all of the stains out.' There were shadows of blood, and dirt-traces that formed random patterns on the cloth and reminded her of the ink-blot test.

'Perhaps I should frame it to remind us of what started it all?'

'Yes – we should frame it and sell it to the Tate,' Teri suggested. 'That grubby hanky could fetch thousands of pounds' worth of lottery money. It ranks up there alongside a pile of bricks or sheep pickled in formaldehyde any day. We could entitle it *Hankering After An Affair*.'

'We could,' Jamie agreed thoughtfully, then he took her hand and pulled her to him. 'Or we could be minimalist and simply call it *Hanky Panky*.'

While the whole country was covered by a blanket of snow, they huddled under a Laura Ashley duvet cover. They hugged it to their knees and clutched their mugs of hot chocolate which had been made marginally more romantic by the addition of a large slug of brandy and some aerosol whipped cream – half fat – that Teri found in the fridge.

Jamie was naked under the duvet, a fact which Teri found most disconcerting. He might feel inhibited about sharing his body with her, but he had no inhibitions about showing it to her, it seemed. He was long and lean. *All over.*

She had sneaked her pyjamas into the bathroom and had changed there – either as a barrier against temptation or frustration, she wasn't sure which. Torture by platonic adultery was probably worse than having your fingernails pulled out one by one. It wasn't an opinion she would voice too loudly though, as Clare would more than likely be keen to oblige if she ever wanted to carry out a real-life experiment.

Teri lay on her back and sighed. The barrier of Marks & Spencer's imitation silk was proving useless against the ache of desire that buzzed in her veins like caffeine drunk too late at night. Sod Trevor Howard and his *Brief Encounter*. She wanted this to be a distinctly brief*less* encounter – a full-blooded nineties fling, not some soppy, old, romantic movie where the undergarments stayed firmly in place and the nether regions well out of camera shot. They were all knowing eyes and puckering lips, but not one half-decent snog. She wanted to rummage in Jamie's under-wear, fling his knickers to the four corners of the earth, not just have them hanging limply on her radiator. He had a tighter bottom than any Lycra-clad *derrière* she'd ever seen pushed tautly at the television camera in the Tour de France. So often in her dreams her fingernails had fondled his firm bare flesh – leaving her breathless and sweating like someone in their first flush of early menopause. Usually, just as the alarm went off.

Why couldn't they just be like everyone else and get their togs off without all this ensuing guilt? Knowing her luck it would be just like *Brief Encounter* – not a bit of nooky in sight. But it would probably all end in tears just the same. This was one of the few sayings of her mother's that was invariably true. Why couldn't Jamie be playing the part of Michael Douglas in *Fatal Attraction*? The opening credits had barely finished before he had his kit off. She'd hardly had time to eat her Mexican Chilli Nachos and cheese sauce – which looked suspiciously like cold custard – before the woman with the blonde curly hair and the big nose was splashing about in the sink with her bottom bared to the full house at The Point multiplex cinema. Mind you that all ended in tears, slit wrists and boiled rabbit. Very nasty. It probably wasn't a comparison worth pursuing.

Jamie pulled her to him and she nestled into the crook of his arm. She had left the curtains open, and together they watched the snow fall soporifically through the dark window panes. His body was hot and comforting, and considerably more muscular than the Boots hot water bottle that she usually took to bed for warmth. He had a moustache of whipped cream on his lip and she hoped that she didn't.

'What are you thinking about?' Jamie whispered as he stroked her hair.

'Trevor Howard.'

He twisted his head to look at her. 'Who?'

'It doesn't matter.'

'If you won't tell me about Trevor, then tell me about your dreams.'

'My dreams?' she said wryly. 'They're all X-rated these days, Jamie, and you usually play the leading role.'

'Only usually?' He looked hurt. 'Is Trevor a rival for your affections?'

'No.' She nudged him with her elbow. 'It's you in my dreams. Mostly.' He challenged her with his eyebrows and she squirmed against him. 'Okay, then – always. It's always you. Satisfied now?'

He frowned at her, trying to hide the smile that twitched at his lips. 'Anyway, I didn't mean those kind of dreams. I meant *dreams* – life's ambitions, goals, hopes for the future.'

'I've got less hope these days than Bing Crosby has without Bob.' She shook her head. 'I don't know if I believe in dreams anymore. None of them ever come true.'

'What did you used to dream?' He squeezed her. 'Before you became a cynic.'

'I used to dream that one day I'd be a famous television presenter like Valerie Singleton or Angela Rippon.'

'Couldn't that still come true?'

'I still have some hope, but I'm reaching my sell-by date quicker than yesterday's milk. I'm the wrong side of thirty – only just – and I haven't had a single presenting job yet. I'd even be prepared to read the weather.' She tutted sadly. 'The programme I work on – *Out and About –*' she rolled her eyes and shrugged her dismay '– prefers spotty youths with attitude problems, and the producer is a homosexual alcoholic with a chronic ulcer so I can't even sleep my way to the top.'

'I think you're much more attractive than Valerie Singleton.'

'I'm eternally grateful for that compliment.' She sipped her chocolate. 'Although calling someone attractive generally means that they're plug ugly but with a great personality.'

'I think you're very beautiful.' He kissed the top of her head. 'And you've got better legs than Angela Rippon.'

'Wow, that's really saying something.' She snuggled further into him. 'What about you? Did you dream of working for an insurance company?'

'No,' he said pensively. 'I didn't dream it. I really do work for an insurance company.'

She kicked him in the leg. 'You know what I mean!'

'I wanted to be a racing driver. Formula One.'

'That's a little bit different from a database manager for the Mutual and Providential.'

'I'm haunted by unfulfilled dreams,' he said wistfully. Which was closer to the truth than he dared to admit.

'Why a racing driver?'

'Glamour, danger, thrills, chicks and huge pay-cheques.'

'So a lot like the insurance business?'

'Don't mock!' He tickled her rib. 'There are similarities between being a racing driver and working in insurance. I get a pay-cheque, possibly not huge, but not insubstantial. I also get the thrill of leaving the office every night – and there's always the danger of dropping a disk drive on my toe.' He rubbed his chin. 'Admittedly there's not much glamour and there are definitely no chicks. Two industrial tribunals have seen to that. Now we have an egalitarian policy of mutual respect and opportunity in the workplace irrespective of gender, creed, colour and whether you went to a comprehensive school. We have lots of that, but definitely no chicks.'

'What do you dream of now?'

'My dreams are simpler these days. I dream of paying

off my mortgage, of London Weighting keeping pace with the amount my season ticket costs and I dream that one day trains will run on time.'

'They're not very ambitious dreams.'

'No, but they're equally impossible to attain.'

'What do you think makes us such dreamers?' Teri asked dreamily.

'Too many hours spent sitting on trains with too much time to think.'

'Talking of which,' Teri said, 'in a few short hours, we'll be squaring up to do battle again with British Rail. I don't know about you but I need to get some sleep.'

'Do you think I could hold you?'

'Is this wise?'

'If we were talking about wise, I wouldn't be here at all.'

'True,' she agreed. They slid down into the bed together. Teri turned off the bedside lamp. Their bodies fitted together perfectly and Teri resisted the urge to rest her leg across his thighs. His mouth was moist against hers, anxious and searching. Her hand travelled over his chest to the hard lines of his stomach. Jamie let out a low groan.

'If you want to just sleep together and not stay awake together,' Teri reminded him, 'then we need to stop this now.'

'I don't know if I can.'

'You can.' She moved away from him. 'I don't want to be held responsible for leading you astray. If you're going to go astray, you must do it of your own volition.'

'You're a hard woman.'

'And at the moment you're a hard man.'

'It hadn't escaped my attention.' He sighed unhappily.

'Goodnight, Jamie.'

'Goodnight.' There was a pause, just long enough for three little words, which neither of them wanted to be the first to fill.

They lay awake on their backs, a foot apart, holding hands. 'Let's make a wish,' Jamie said into the snowlit blackness.

'We're too old to make wishes. They're like dreams. We know they'll never come true.'

'Well, I'm going to make a wish anyway.' He brought her hand to his lips and kissed it.

'Aren't you supposed to follow a ritual?'

'Not that I know of – unless you happen to have a wishing-well under your bed.'

'No.'

He lay perfectly still and she could hear his breathing shallow and uneven. 'I wish there was another way I could do this. I wish I didn't care about my wife and the kids. I wish I could walk away from you and not give you a second thought and I wish I'd left you sprawled on the platform with your scabby knee and tearstained face and had cold-heartedly caught the train. And more than anything, I wish I could forget who I am and make mad passionate love to you and damn the consequences.'

'That was actually five wishes,' Teri said with a lightness she didn't feel. 'And you had your eyes open, so I don't know if it counts.'

'I thought you weren't interested in wishes?' Jamie twisted on to his elbow to look at her, his face framed by the moonlight.

'It's a woman's prerogative to change her mind.'

'So you do want to make a wish?'

'Yes.'

'Go on then.'
'I wish you'd shut up and go to sleep.'
He flopped on to his back. 'Granted.'
'Goodnight, Jamie.'

Chapter Twelve

'He was out all night. He told me he was staying with a work colleague in Watford, but he wasn't – he was in Leighton Buzzard.' Pamela sat back in her chair.

'There are worse places to be,' Tom Pearson said laconically.

She shot him a withering glare, the one she usually reserved for Jamie. 'I phoned the 1471 redial thing and it gave me her number. Then I rang her house in the morning after I thought they would have left for work. It was her answerphone. She's called Teri.' Pamela wrinkled her nose. 'And she sounds terribly young and terribly beautiful.'

Tom clasped his hands behind his head. 'How does someone sound beautiful on an answerphone?'

'Just the same as you can tell when someone is smiling down the phone – or lying.'

'Any more singing in the shower?'

'*Torn between two lovers*.' They looked at each other and pulled the same face.

'Subtle,' Tom said.

'It was always Jamie's strong point,' she agreed.

'I must say, you're taking this very well.' Tom swung his legs off the desk.

'I'm not, I'm just a good actress. My mother always said I should have been on the stage. My time limit for pretending that everything's all right is two hours. If Jamie stays in the house any longer, I have to go up into the shower room and have a good cry and then I'm all right for another two.'

'Did you take my advice?'

'What – and prance round the house like something out of *Playboy*?'

'That's not what I said.'

'I know, but it's what you meant.'

Tom's face creased into a half-smile. 'Well did you?'

'If I didn't know that your philandering days were over I'd accuse you of being voyeuristic.' Pamela unconsciously pulled her skirt down towards her knees. 'And anyway, I haven't had time to be Playmate of the Month. Jack's had tonsillitis and Francesca's just gone down with a stinking cold.'

'So you're still playing at being a mother.'

'I *am* a bloody mother!'

'What you need is a revenge affair.' Tom stood up and paced the floor, slapping the palm of his hand with his pen. She could tell he had been watching too many American cop films again.

'I probably need a hole in the head more,' she said dismissively.

'I'm serious.' He certainly looked as if he was. 'A pretend revenge affair, that's what you need.'

Pamela's smile twisted sardonically. 'This pretend revenge affair . . . it wouldn't happen to be with *you*, Tom, would it?'

'Well, if you insist.'

'For heaven's sake, Tom, you're more transparent than

some of Liz Hurley's dresses.' She walked to the coffee machine and poured herself a cup from the constant supply.

'I bet it's a long time since you've been wined and dined by someone other than your husband.' He wagged his finger at her.

She held up a cup to Tom and he shook his head. 'It's a long time since I've been wined and dined by someone *including* my husband.'

'Give him a taste of his own medicine,' Tom said expansively. 'A few mysterious nights out, a few bits of frilly lingerie, a few phone calls that cut off when he answers.'

'I can't do that to him!'

'Why not? He's doing it to you.'

'I know, but he's a man. Men do this sort of thing. It comes naturally to them.'

'I'll take you for a couple of nice meals out, we'll stay a bit later than we should, you'll have a bit more to drink than a married woman ought to – and Bob's your uncle!'

'Bob might be your uncle, but I'm not sure he's related to me at all.'

'I'll take you to that new Thai restaurant, the one that's in the old James Hunt racing-school building.'

She could feel herself weakening, despite the fact that it was a ridiculous plan; however, no one else had come up with anything better. 'Can't we take Shirley with us?'

'Supposing he follows us? How can you be having an illicit night out with your boss if his wife is coming along too?'

'Jamie isn't the jealous type. He wouldn't suspect anything.' She circled the bottom of her cup thoughtfully with her spoon.

'Then make him suspicious!'

'Oh hell, Tom. I can't stand all this subterfuge. It's not in my nature. Can't I just have it out with him?'

'You'll force him into her arms.'

'He's there already!'

'Then you need to wheedle him out.'

'It's you that's trying to wheedle me out.' She pointed her teaspoon at him knowingly. 'What will Shirley think?'

'I'll explain it all to her. She'll understand.'

'She's a better woman than I am if she does.'

Tom looked hurt. 'It's entirely up to you.' He spread his hands. 'I'm only trying to help.'

'Not too many weeks ago you were advising me to sit there and do nothing but keep my mouth shut and my legs open.'

'You have a very coarse turn of phrase when you want to, Pamela Duncan,' he said accusingly. 'Anyway, that was when you merely suspected. Now you're sure and you need to take action.'

'I'm desperate, Tom!'

'Desperate times call for desperate measures.'

'You've said that before.'

'That's because it's true. I don't mind repeating myself when these things need saying.' He wagged his ballpoint. 'I said I don't mind repeating myself when these things need saying.'

Pamela tutted impatiently. 'I don't know if I should be listening to you. You're too damned persuasive by half.' She drained her coffee cup.

'Well,' he shrugged, 'my offer still stands. You only have to say the word.' He rested his arm along her chair and looked down at her.

Pamela swallowed hard. He really was quite muscular when he was at such close proximity.

'But right now. . .' His voice was so sweet and sugar-coated it should have come with a tooth-decay warning. He fixed her eyes with his and there was the suggestion of a contented smile on his face, like a cat which has just eaten a mouse with double cream on top of it. 'Right now I need to sell some impenetrable burglar alarms to some very vulnerable properties, otherwise their skimpy defences could be broken open just like – that!' He clicked his fingers.

She felt her skin flush; the room had suddenly gone very warm. All she needed now on top of everything else was to start an early menopause. How on earth did she think she could cope single-handedly with a night out with this man? He was a Lothario of the first order and always would be. She flicked open her notepad irritably. And why did he always manage to make even the most innocent sentence sound like the most tempting invitation to go to bed . . .?

Shortly before noon on that same day, Charlie came and sat on the edge of Jamie's desk. 'I've arranged for us to go to lunch with Gordy.'

'Charlie!'

'I know he's a crashing bore, but he's got a very salutary tale to tell.' Charlie rummaged aimlessly through the papers in Jamie's in-tray. 'One I think you should listen to very carefully, considering your current predicament.'

'What are you trying to do to me?'

Charlie, for once, lowered his voice. 'I'm trying to knock some sense into that very thick skull of yours before it's too late.'

'Look, I've apologised about the other night. I didn't mean to get you involved – it's just that the opportunity arose what with that business with the trains.' Jamie held up his hands. 'Anyway, I'm not going through that again. You know the story. I'm sorry. It's done. It won't happen again.'

'I can't just stand by and watch you do this. I like Pamela.'

'*I* like Pamela!' Jamie protested.

'You bloody ought to. She's your wife.' Charlie tugged fretfully at his unruly mop of curls. He looked as if he hadn't been to bed again and hadn't shaved. But then that was how he normally looked. 'If you still have any feelings for her at all, why are you doing this?'

'I don't have a choice any more.' Jamie looked round to check that no one else was listening. The worst thing about working in an office that was an ex-rabbit warren was that there were plenty of places for people with big ears to lurk. 'Being without Teri now would be like being without breath – a fairly vital component to human life, I think you'll agree.'

Charlie fished in Jamie's desk tidy and started joining all the paper clips together to form a chain. 'And what about Pamela – and the kids? What would life be like without them?'

'I'm not planning on leaving them.' Jamie's tone was becoming insistent.

'What exactly *are* you planning to do, then? Lead this double life for ever?' Charlie swung the paper-clip chain in front of him.

'I don't think that's any of your business.'

'You didn't go to boarding school, did you?' Charlie raised one eyebrow.

'You know I didn't.' Jamie looked puzzled. 'I am a product of Queen Elizabeth's Grammar School, Melbrose in the Borders of Sunny Scotland.'

'I went to boarding school,' Charlie said flatly. 'I was sent away by my parents when I was seven.'

'Now you're breaking my heart.' It came out more sarcastically than he had intended.

Charlie stared out of the office window. 'Did you go home every night to a loving family with your tea waiting on the table and your mother in her apron?'

Jamie frowned and said impatiently, 'Something like that. Why?'

'I cried myself to sleep every night for two years.' He looked back at Jamie. 'I know what it's like to be without parents. And mine thought they were doing the best for me – giving me a good start in life, making a man out of me.' Charlie pulled a wry face. 'If you can't think of Pamela, think of the kids.'

'I told you,' Jamie repeated tightly. 'I'm not about to abandon them.'

'Emotionally, you're already out of the door.'

'And when did you turn into Claire Rayner?' Jamie snapped. Teri was infiltrating his life so much he was even starting to use her phrases. But then she did have quite a good repertoire of cutting repartee.

Charlie ignored him. 'Supposing Pamela finds out?'

'She won't.' Jamie grabbed the paper-clip chain from Charlie's hands and flung it on to the desk.

'I bet Hugh Grant thought that too.'

'This is entirely different.'

'You're right, it is. You're not famous – you won't have an agent turning it into good publicity. It won't get you plum parts in new movies. And no one's going to pat you on the back and say what a good bloke you are, even though you're a bit laddish and ever so slightly careless.' Charlie stood up from Jamie's desk and stretched like a contented cat. 'Still, at least you're not paying for it like old Hugh.'

Charlie hadn't realised how strong Jamie was until his fist hit his face. It knocked him straight off his feet and on to the floor. But then the element of surprise probably had something to do with it as well. He realised he weighed a lot too, because he was sprawled on top of him punching at his body with a random ferocity that was quite alarming.

'You bastard!' hissed Jamie, showering spittle into Charlie's face. It sounded as if there were two secretaries screaming, but they only had one in the office so she must have been making that frightful din all by herself. Mercifully, someone hoisted Jamie off Charlie's inert and breathless body. He was holding Jamie by the scruff of the neck when Charlie recovered sufficiently to open his eyes. Unfortunately, it was Jamie's boss who had come to the rescue, the merciless Director of Information Technology, John 'Joyless' Lovejoy. Jamie's face was suffused purple with anger and he was still throwing half-hearted punches at the air.

'This isn't the flaming playground!' Joyless shouted. 'Get out of my sight and settle whatever this is about in an adult and dignified manner.' He pointed a finger at Charlie, who was still flat on his back and breathing heavily. 'I want you back in here by two o'clock acting like the best of friends, otherwise don't come back at all.'

Joyless released his hold on Jamie, who stopped flailing and straightened his tie. 'Help him up!' he ordered, and marched out of the room.

Jamie sat sullenly nursing his pint of lager. It was weak and flat and tasted of cleaning fluid. Charlie sat nursing a gin and tonic – a double – and his face. There was a bright red swollen splotch just under his right eye, which would eventually turn purple, and a slight cut – well, more of a slight graze really – along his cheekbone. He was gingerly holding an ice cube against it that he had fished out of his gin. All three of them were crowded round a beer-stained table that was only intended for two, and Gordy was holding court. Jamie and Charlie intermittently glowered at each other.

'We've been together two years, me and Tina,' Gordy said in response to Charlie's attempt at subtle questioning. 'It feels like a bloody lifetime.' His face sank deeper into its usual hangdog expression.

'What went wrong?' Charlie said. He sounded as if he had developed a slight lisp, but Jamie couldn't be sure that he wasn't putting it on in order to catch the sympathy vote. 'I thought she was a right little goer?'

Jamie narrowed his eyes at him menacingly. Charlie looked the other way.

' "Martini" they used to call her when she worked in the office. You know, "any time, any place, anywhere",' he sang tunelessly. 'And by God, she was, too. Over the desk, behind the filing cabinet, in the stationery cupboard – we tried 'em all.'

Charlie swallowed his gin and pursed his lips. 'What happened?'

Gordy raised his pint to his mouth and shrugged. 'She went teetotal on me as soon as we got married. Now it's "I haven't got the time", "we can't do it here" and "no way, Jose".'

'Surely it can't be all that bad.'

Gordy smacked his lips and returned his beer to the table. 'She hates my kids.' He had a line of froth settled on his top lip. '*I* hate my kids.' He sat back and folded his arms. 'I see them every other weekend and the only place they want to go – after McDonald's – is shopping. They've turned into Toys R Us vultures. They swoop in there and won't come out until they've picked the shelves clean. First it was Ninja Turtles, then poofy-looking Wrestlers and now they've got every Power Ranger in the frigging set. If their clothes haven't got a designer label on them, they've "Pocohontas" scrawled all over them instead. I'm dreading what comes next. I blame their mother,' he said sagely. 'She's encouraged them to see me as nothing but a bottomless bank account.'

'That's terrible.' Charlie looked pointedly at Jamie, who remained silent.

'No, Charlie, you know what's really terrible?' He was warming to his subject now. 'I pay for them all – the whole bloody shebang. One ex-wife and three ex-kids. Of course, she's got a lover. Surprising really, but she found one the minute I left. Young chap, too.' He stopped momentarily to contemplate the strange ways of the world. 'But will she marry him? Will she hell! She'd rather see me paying up until the day I die. It puts a terrible strain on our relationship, me and Tina. Of course, that's why she does it. And the courts back her up. There's no justice in this world. What can a chap do?'

Jamie thought that he looked as if he wasn't really open to suggestions.

'Absolute nightmare,' Charlie commiserated. He sat back in his chair, twirling the stem of his glass between his fingers. 'So really, you would say that having an affair was the worst mistake you ever made?' He sounded like the counsel for the prosecution summing up for the jury. Charlie smiled superciliously at Jamie.

'Having an affair? Bollocks!' Gordy said loudly. 'The worst mistake I ever made was marrying Tina. I should have left things as they were. Set her up in a little flat, saucy nooky on tap twice a week, no strings attached. Best thing I ever did was have an affair.'

There was a look of utmost consternation on Charlie's battered face. It was Jamie's turn to wear the supercilious smile.

'In fact,' Gordy leaned forward conspiratorially, 'I'm looking round for a nice young filly at the moment. If you know a good mount who wouldn't mind going over a few jumps with me, you give me the nod.' He winked theatrically.

Charlie's mouth was hanging open. 'You could park a bus in there,' Jamie observed lightly.

Charlie snapped it shut. He looked at his watch. 'We ought to be going, James. I have a mountain of work to be getting on with, even if you don't. We'd better go back together otherwise Joyless will want our resignations.'

Jamie stood up. 'So soon?' Gordy protested. 'I haven't even had a chance to ask you about that.' He nodded at Charlie's eye. 'What was it? Lovers' tiff?'

Charlie threw the rest of his gin down his throat. 'Naff off, Gordy,' he said shortly, and flounced out of the pub.

They walked to the end of the block in an uneasy silence. 'So what was the moral of that little tale?' Jamie said eventually.

Charlie shook his head. 'I'm buggered if I know.' They crossed over the road and then fell in step beside each other again. 'I suppose it just goes to show,' Charlie continued, 'that we never learn by our mistakes. We just keep on making them. And whatever anyone else says to persuade us otherwise counts for bugger all.'

Jamie touched the sleeve of his raincoat. 'Thanks for trying though, Charlie.'

His friend shrugged.

Jamie laughed and tried to lighten the mood. 'Do you think he sussed which one of us is having the affair, or is Gordy too wrapped up in his own troubles to notice anyone else's?'

'Was I that obvious?' Charlie looked concerned.

'Dolly Parton's breasts are less obvious than you, Charles.'

Charlie tutted. 'I thought I was being so discreet.' They walked along in silence again until Charlie said hesitantly, 'I'm sorry for saying what I did earlier, about, you know, about Hugh Grant and all that.'

'That's okay. I'm too touchy at the moment. I shouldn't have hit you.'

Charlie patted his face carefully. 'No, you shouldn't.'

'Not so hard anyway,' Jamie countered. 'I don't know what's got into me, Charlie. I'm sorry. You're not going to believe this,' Jamie dodged two drunks who were lying asleep across the pavement, 'but we haven't even . . . you know. Nothing. So why am I feeling so guilty?'

Charlie's eyebrows pulled together in a crease. 'Not a thing? What about the other night?'

'We slept together – as in asleep.'

'Non-consummated adultery? Now there's a novel concept.'

'It isn't through lack of inclination,' Jamie elaborated hurriedly.

'Mmm,' Charlie said. 'I see.'

'How can you see, if I don't see?' Jamie said crossly.

'You feel guilty, because you are guilty,' Charlie explained.

Jamie's face darkened. 'I don't want to have to hit you again, Charlie.'

'Well, I suppose I should be thankful for that.' Charlie looked sideways at him. 'It's because it's premeditated, dear boy. You can't plead diminished responsibility, because your responsibility isn't diminished. This isn't a flash in the pan, is it? This isn't carnal manslaughter – one moment of madness and you're left with a body that you don't know what to do with, and blood on your hands. This is inching step-by-step to its ultimate conclusion, every move precisely planned. This is first-degree adultery that you're planning to commit. Every jury in the land would find you guilty. If there was still capital punishment, you'd swing.'

Jamie looked stricken. 'If you're trying to cheer me up, Charlie, I have to say it isn't working.'

'I'm merely trying to point out the facts of the case.'

'Not only do you look like Columbo, you're starting to sound like him too,' Jamie said tersely. 'Anyway, I don't know why I'm telling you all this.'

'Because I'm your best friend.' They stopped at the office door. 'Because I'm your *only* friend. And because, even though I think you're a prize prat, you know I'll be there to help you pick up the pieces when it all goes horribly wrong.'

Jamie punched him playfully on the shoulder. 'And don't hit me again,' Charlie said tetchily. 'I mark easily.'

Chapter Thirteen

Teri was sitting on the toilet seat. Clare was in the bath surrounded by an over-indulgence of bubbles which bobbed rhythmically round her chin and showed a blatant disregard for the economies of a water meter. There was a bright yellow duck with an orange beak at the taps end which was struggling to keep its head above the froth.

The bathroom was the only room that Teri hadn't yet tackled. The suite was yellow – primrose yellow rather than duck yellow – and someone had gone overboard, covering every conceivable remaining surface with three-inch white tiles erratically veined with the same yellow. It was truly nauseating and would be hellishly expensive to put right. The bathroom needed a new suite and new tiles – albeit not on the scale of the current acreage. She'd tried sponging and stippling and Artexing, and she could put up a shelf that actually stayed up, but tiling was something that Teri felt was beyond her limited Do-It-Yourself ability. That was definitely a job for someone else.

Teri twisted the top on and off the foaming bath gel. It was an aromatherapy one, optimistically called 'The Source of Life' and the blurb on the back assured her it was enriched with oils of ylang ylang and sandalwood to relax troubled spirits and soothe the tired mind. She'd used gallons of it since Clare arrived. It had made not the slightest bit of difference. Her 'troubled spirit' was still about as relaxed as a poltergeist and her 'tired mind' rather than being soothed felt perilously close to exploding. Clare had also used a gallon of it and it hadn't done anything to make her easier to live with either.

Teri glanced at her friend. She was resting with her eyes closed, a dreamy look on her upturned face, curiously decapitated by the froth. Teri went back to twisting the cap. 'Look, this is going to be really hard for me to say.'

Clare opened her eyes. 'It's about the milk, isn't it? I know I used it all yesterday morning. I'm really sorry, but I think you ought to get some more delivered. There's just not enough, and dry Weetabix is no one's idea of a fun breakfast.'

Teri sighed and counted very quickly to ten. 'It isn't about the milk.'

Clare's brow crinkled. 'It's the ironing board, then.' A hand appeared from beneath the water and she cleared a path in the bubbles just in front of her mouth. 'I can tell you exactly how it happened.' Clare's gabbling was legendary. 'David rang just as I was pressing my jeans and I don't know how but it must have just fallen over. I didn't notice until I could smell the burning.'

'I didn't know you'd burnt your jeans.' A look of concern crossed Teri's face.

'I didn't. It missed my jeans and burnt a hole in the ironing-board cover. I swear I'll buy you a new one though. Just as soon as I get paid.'

Teri closed her eyes. She could feel a headache coming on. A severe one. 'It's not about the ironing-board cover either.'

'I can't think of anything else I've done.' Clare tried to sound innocent and failed.

'I can,' Teri replied tetchily, 'but it isn't anything you've done either.'

'Then what is it?'

Teri took a deep breath. 'I don't think this is working out.'

'What?'

'Us – sharing.'

'Oh really, Teri, it's fine,' she said soothingly. 'You're so considerate. I hardly notice you're here.'

Teri put the bath gel on top of the toilet. 'That's my point, Clare. You hardly notice me and it's my house.'

'But I'm in and out all the time. I'm not exactly under your feet. I'm the perfect lodger.'

'That, unfortunately, is a matter of opinion.' Teri rubbed her temples. 'I never know when you're in or when you're out or when you're likely to be back.'

'You sound like my mother,' Clare said testily. 'And what's more, it isn't attractive.'

'You come in at all hours of the day and night and drink my milk.'

Her friend's eyes narrowed. 'I *knew* this was about the milk!'

'The milk's just one of many irritating little things, none of which add up to the sum of the whole.' Teri sighed heavily. 'I need my privacy back.'

'Oh, I see.' Clare put on her Sister Mary Bernadette look. 'I get it now. You mean you need somewhere to bonk!' A superior expression spread over her face. 'This is about him, isn't it? This Jamie. This *married* man.'

'Partly,' Teri conceded reluctantly.

'How can you do this to me? I thought you were my best friend.'

Teri spoke very quietly and rationally, although it was a struggle to do so. 'We need somewhere to spend some time alone together.' She put her hand on her chest and patted it for emphasis. 'This is my house.'

Clare was indignant. 'I have been abandoned by my husband, but you don't give that a second thought. You want me to move out so that you can move someone else's husband in. Is that what we're talking about here?'

'Pretty much,' Teri admitted. 'Though it sounds much worse when you put it like that.'

'This isn't very nice, Therese Carter, is it? *Is it*?'

'No, it isn't,' she agreed. 'Happy now?'

'Happy! You're kicking me out into the streets with nowhere to go and you ask me if I'm happy.'

'I love him, Clare. I want to be with him. I thought you'd understand, but all you do is make snide comments about him.'

'Don't talk to me about love, Teri. I know all there is to know. It's like a nasty dose of bindweed that spoils the garden of romance – it creeps in innocuously, obliterates everything in sight and is an absolute bastard to get rid of.'

'For a brief moment I thought you were quoting Shakespeare,' Teri said derisively.

'No, this is pure Clare Owen! Educated at the university of life and much better use to you than some poncey old bloke in tights.'

'I can't stand your disapproval any longer.' Teri could feel tears prickling behind her eyes. 'I thought you'd be there for me.'

'I've always been there for you, Teri.' Clare also sounded

close to tears. 'I was there for you when Michael Lacey poured our playtime bottle of milk on your head in Mrs Whittle's class. I told on him for you!'

'It was *you* that dared Michael Lacey to pour it on my head in the first place,' she reminded her.

Clare paused to think about it and then continued, 'I was there for you when Janet Starkey tied you by your plaits to your front gates and left you there.'

'Clare, you came and cut all my hair off! It took months to grow. My mother wouldn't let me out of the house for three weeks.'

Teri waited while Clare sorted through the various files in her brain. She was getting red in the face and Teri was sure it wasn't just the temperature of the bathwater – although she wouldn't mind betting a pound on the fact that she'd probably be washing the dishes in cold water again tonight. Finally Clare said, 'I've been there for you lots of times.'

'I know.' Teri tried pleading, 'And I'm asking you to be there for me now.'

'No, you're not! You're asking me to *not* be there for you. You want me to leave. How much more not being there do you want?'

'I'm sorry.' It was all she could think of to say.

'We could work out time constraints – a rota.' Clare looked completely crestfallen. 'I'll make myself scarce when he's here.'

'It wouldn't work,' Teri said firmly. She had decided on this days ago; it was just a matter of breaking it to Clare. 'I want him to be free to phone me without hearing you tut-tutting in the background.'

'You're wasting yourself on him, Teri,' she warned. 'This will end in tears. The trouble with married men is that they promise you the earth and all you end up with is a handful of poxy little pebbles.'

'He hasn't promised me anything,' she said defensively.

'Then you're an even bigger fool than I thought.'

They looked away from each other. Clare stared at the yellow-veined tiles on the wall by the side of the bath and Teri stared fixedly at the ones in front of the toilet. Several of them were cracked. It was Clare who spoke first. 'I don't know where to go,' she said quietly.

'I've bought the local paper. I thought we could look through it together. You might be able to get somewhere closer to the airport.'

'Shit!' Clare snapped. 'You're all heart!' She kicked the duck out of the bath and it landed with a startled look on its face on the bath mat. 'I don't know if I'll ever forgive you for this, Therese Carter. You're a tart, a harlot and ruthless adulteress. Now get out and let *me* have some privacy.'

Teri stood up and slowly left the bathroom. She leaned with her back against the wall at the top of the stairs and let the tears roll down her cheeks to drip unhindered on the front of her blouse. At this moment, she didn't think that she would ever forgive herself.

'It's me.' His voice was familiar at once.

'Oh Jamie, thank goodness you've called. I've just had a blazing row with Clare. I asked her to leave and she's actually packed her stuff and gone tonight. She's taken it really badly.' Teri sniffed. 'She was in a terrible state when she left. I shouldn't have let her go.'

'Why did you ask her to leave?'

'Oh Jamie, she's been so awful about you. I couldn't stand it any longer. And I wanted my house back to myself so that we could, perhaps, spend some time together.' There was a long pause at the end of the phone. 'Jamie? You do want that, don't you?'

There was a heavy sigh before he said, 'Of course I do.'

'Where are you ringing from?'

'The phone box just down the road from the house. I'm out with MacTavish.'

'MacTavish?'

'The dog.'

'I wish you were here,' Teri blurted out.

'I wish I was there, too.'

Teri's throat was tight and she could feel herself starting to cry again. 'I'm going to do something really silly and take British Telecom's advice. If they think it's good to talk, we'll see how it works.' She took a deep and unsteady breath. 'I think I'm falling in love with you, Jamie,' she said hesitantly.

There was another long silence. Too long. Uncomfortably long. 'I think I love you, too,' Jamie eventually replied. He sounded sad rather than elated, she thought. 'Look, I've got to go,' he said rather too briskly. 'MacTavish has only so much patience and he's starting to do his starving hound impersonation. I'd better get back and feed him. I only phoned to say that I'll see you in the morning.'

They saw each other every morning, so when he managed to phone in the evening it was entirely superfluous and, therefore, all the more welcome.

'I love you,' Teri said. It was easier the second time round.

'I love you, too.' It didn't sound as if it had been any easier for Jamie. The phone went dead.

Teri sat with her head in her hands staring at the wall. Damn, she had blown it! What a stupid thing to say. The guy phones for a few minutes' illicit chat at great personal expense and she comes over all heavy and gives him the complete heebie-jeebies. Why did she never learn to keep her big trap shut when she was tired and emotional? What a berk! Why on earth did she ever think that BT knew what they were talking about? She was going to throw a brick at the television next time that bloody chirpy Bob Hoskins popped up on it.

Jamie pulled MacTavish away from the crisp packet that he had hopefully buried his nose in and started to walk back home. It was a bitterly cold night with a full moon and the crisp whiteness of a hard ground frost, and he pulled his scarf up towards his ears. It was the beige cashmere that had been returned to him on the regretful demise of Frosty the snowman and he was eternally grateful for it – as Frosty had probably been.

His hands were cold and his heart was as heavy as a bowling ball – the heaviest one you could get. In fact, this was much like his first, and last, experience at the Megabowl Alley. It was like slithering down the highly polished lanes in smooth-soled shoes and being totally out of control, unable to get a grip with your feet and being equally unable to let go of the ball, but knowing full well that before long you were going to smash headlong into the waiting row of skittles.

The only difference was that at the Megabowl, with a lot of luck and a following wind, he had eventually managed to chalk up – or log on the computer-aided display – an excruciatingly low score. With Teri he hadn't managed to score at all yet. The really frightening thing was that this unfamiliar out-of-controlness wasn't an entirely unpleasant feeling.

Charlie was right. He had to end it before it became a way of life, before he turned into another Gordy. How could he be doing this to Pamela and the children? What sort of pathetic lech sneaked out of the house on the pretext of walking the dog to phone a beautiful, young, free and single woman who should be out on the town chasing young, free and single men – not sitting at home waiting on the off chance for him to call?

This sort of pathetic lech, whose stomach turned to ice at the thought of Teri with another man, yet who lacked the conviction or the courage to commit to her himself, Jamie concluded bitterly. How could it be possible for him to feel like this about Teri and still profess that he loved his wife? And yet he did. There was nothing inherently wrong with their marriage, they'd just got into a rut, a routine – that happened to everyone. But not everyone went round panting after some young bit of fluff – mental apology to Teri for the political incorrectness – like a lovesick teenager.

It was highly probable that a man could love two women equally – but it just wasn't on in practical terms. Not to mention the slight conflict with the marriage vows: there was nothing in those about 'to love, honour, cherish and to chase skirt' . . . Perhaps he should become a Mormon. They were still allowed a dozen or so wives, weren't they – or was it the Jehovah's Witnesses? Jamie shuddered. Imagine a dozen wives! It was difficult enough trying to juggle two women.

And what kind of monsters were they both turning into? Teri had thrown her best friend out of her house while he had done a totally unreasonable Frank Bruno impersonation and had laid *his* best friend out for some petty little remark. Pamela deserved better than this, Teri deserved better than this, the kids deserved better than this, their friends deserved better than this and even MacTavish deserved better than this.

It would have to end. He would have to call on all his depleted reserves of willpower and walk away from this. It was going to hurt like hell, but it would be for the best in the end. He only hoped Teri would see that, too.

'Come on, doggers,' Jamie said, with a weariness that was embedded deep into his bones. 'Let's get you home, my true and faithful alibi, and give you a nice big bowl of Chum.' MacTavish wagged his tail appreciatively. 'Otherwise we'll both be in the dog-house.'

Chapter Fourteen

'I still don't know why you agreed to work late. You've never worked late before,' Jamie said, labouring the point. He was lying across the bed watching his wife as she got dressed.

Pamela fastened the buttons on her blouse. 'I told you, it's a new contract that's come up. A big oil company's moving into Milton Keynes and they want us to quote. Tom and I need to discuss it.'

' "Tom and I need to discuss it",' Jamie mimicked silently behind Pamela's back. Aloud he said, 'Why can't you discuss it during normal office hours?'

Pamela smiled sardonically. 'Jamie, you're a fine one to talk. If anyone should appreciate that there just aren't enough hours in the day, it's you.'

'Well, I hope he's paying you overtime,' he said petulantly.

'He isn't. That's why he's taking me for a nice meal to make up for it.' She wriggled her skirt over her stockings and smoothing it over her hips, zipped it up.

'Stockings?' Jamie queried. 'You never wear stockings.'

'Don't be silly. Of course I do! It's just that you never look any more.' She slipped her feet into her high heels and hid a smile as she saw Jamie's frown deepen. 'We're going to the new Thai restaurant – the one in the old James Hunt racing-school building.'

'The one with the hideous red and white roof that looks like a bloody circus tent?'

Pamela brushed her hair. 'I believe it's lovely inside.'

'Well, it'd better be. Nice meals don't pay the kids' school fees.'

She turned and looked at him. 'I do believe you're jealous, Jamie Duncan.'

'Bollocks,' he said emphatically. He put the Thomas the Tank Engine he was toying with on the bed. 'It's just that, well, don't you think you're a bit kitted up for a business meeting?'

'I thought you'd be pleased that I'm going out.' She bent to clip her earrings on in the mirror. 'I get precious little chance to dress up these days. The playgroup might be surprised if I turned up in sandwashed pure silk and pearls.'

'You don't think you might give him the wrong idea?'

'I work for him, Jamie; we respect each other.' She fastened her watch on to her wrist.

Jamie snorted. 'Give him an inch and he'd take a mile. I know all about the Tom Pearsons of this world.'

Pamela stifled the urge to say, 'I bet you do.' Instead she said sweetly: 'Tom's all right if you know how to handle him.'

'I'd rather you didn't handle him at all!' He picked up Thomas again. 'Don't you think I should come with you?'

'No, I don't.' Pamela turned to him. 'For goodness sake, Jamie, it's one night! Who'll look after the children?'

'I'll get Melanie in from next door.'

'It won't kill you to look after your own children for one night,' she said, exasperation making her voice sound harsh. 'Jack's already asleep and Frankie will be too, as soon as you read her a story. I don't know why you're making such a fuss. I thought you came home early for me especially.'

'I did.' A scowl settled into his features. 'I just don't like you going out. You never go out.'

'All the more reason for you to be pleased for me and give in gracefully.' She kissed him lightly on the cheek. The sound of crunching gravel heralded a car pulling into their drive. Pamela peeped out of the window. 'He's here.'

Jamie got off the bed and strode to the window. 'Typical. Why do all British businessmen drive German cars? Where's their sense of patriotism?'

'It's very comfortable. Lovely and smooth and quiet,' Pamela said, admiring herself in the mirror.

'How do you know?'

'He took me out to lunch in it last week.' Jamie stood open-mouthed. 'Eternity or Passion?' she said, holding up two bottles of perfume.

'Don't you think that's a bit over the top?' His eyebrows knitted together as he surveyed the perfume bottles.

She chose the Passion and sprayed it liberally over her throat.

'You won't need plates,' Jamie said sarcastically. 'He'll be eating out of your hand.'

'Then perhaps I'll ask for a pay rise,' Pamela quipped. She twirled in front of him. 'Tell me I look nice.'

He hadn't seen her so excited in years. There was a girlish bloom to her face and a pinkness to her cheeks that he didn't entirely approve of. 'You look beautiful,' he said truthfully.

She kissed him on the cheek. 'I won't be late. I should be back by eleven.'

'Have a nice time,' he said reluctantly.

He heard Pamela skip down the stairs – yes, skip – and then the front door slammed, despite the fact that the kids were in bed. Pulling the curtain back, he watched as she slid her elegant legs into Tom Pearson's Mercedes and there was a sick and sinking feeling in his stomach. As he saw his wife kiss her boss on the cheek he let the curtain drop. Slowly, he walked through to Francesca's room, where he could hear her having a loud and exaggerated conversation with Barbie about the untimely demise of Take That.

'How did it go?' Tom said as Pamela settled herself into the luxurious surroundings of his car.

'Like a dream.' Pamela looked totally perplexed. 'If I hadn't seen his face for myself, I would never have believed it. It was a picture.'

'And not a pretty one, I'll bet.' The car crunched out of the driveway. 'What did I tell you? There's nothing like a touch of the green-eyed monster to give a flagging marriage that extra bit of spice.'

'You're a wily old dog, Tom Pearson.' Pamela shook her head and her hair tumbled round her shoulders. 'I know now that I should listen to you more often.'

Francesca had been easily placated with a few pages of her storybook and he had left them both in peace – Francesca sucking her thumb and Barbie looking as wide-eyed and bimbo-ish as always. Jamie eyed Barbie dispassionately. Her proportions would be humanly impossible. Scaled up, she would probably have a forty-eight double-D chest, a ten-inch waist, size two feet and legs like a giraffe. Shopping at Sainsbury's would be hell for her.

He could understand why Pamela objected to Barbie as a plaything. She said the doll encouraged girls to become anorexic. He thought she would probably have the opposite effect. Having seen what Barbie was like, and the fact that she could only pull a gimpish-looking bloke like Ken, he hoped Francesca would eat sensibly and have aspirations to become a brain surgeon. In future, he would try to support Pamela in her quest for more educational and challenging toys. Barbie was totally unrealistic.

But then, who ever wanted to play with things that were realistic? Wasn't that what play was all about – escapism? Perhaps that was why people had affairs . . . the adult version of play, when you reached an age at which escapism could no longer be achieved with wide-eyed, large-breasted dolls and Meccano. When Lego gave way to a leg-over. Was it the only chance adults had to escape from reality? To lose yourself in another person who didn't notice that you were going grey, had more flab than a Sumo wrestler and needed to mainline Phyllosan before you could tackle anything more energetic than mowing the lawn? To have someone think you were Tom Cruise when you actually felt ready to settle for nothing more strenuous than a Caribbean cruise was something that could quicken even the most stagnant heart. Had the fact that Teri obviously saw him as someone interesting and attractive made him forget for a short while that he was a boring, staid insurance executive with unfulfilled dreams, family responsibilities and an insanely high mortgage? To his wife, Jamie was nothing more than a meal ticket, a provider, financial security. That was reality. And reality wasn't all it was cracked up to be these days.

He had gone into the lounge – a tribute to interior

design magazines – where MacTavish had greeted him with a welcoming wag. At least someone wanted to spend the evening with him. Jamie poured himself a whisky and sat on the sofa, staring into the embers of the fire burning in the inglenook fireplace that dominated the room, and wondered where it had all started to go wrong.

He had never seen Pamela looking like that before – well, not for years. She had behaved like a schoolgirl out on her first date and it worried him more than he cared to admit. When she took the time, she scrubbed up very nicely. And she certainly had taken the time tonight. She had looked absolutely beautiful for her date – correction 'business meeting' – with Tom Pearson.

Was that what was irking him, the fact that she never took the time for him, and yet had pulled out all the stops for another man? Was that what Pamela wanted now – a so-called 'open' marriage? Was she really having an affair with that smooth cockney slime-ball? Was Tom her 'plaything'?

The thought made Jamie shudder. He'd never trusted Pearson, not since she'd started working there. And anyway, the chap was a good twenty years older than Pamela. Okay, so he didn't look it – but the age-gap was there nevertheless. He had never been so blatant about Teri; he had been the very soul of discretion. Then again, if Pamela *was* having an affair, would she be quite so transparent? She could be very devious if she put her mind to it. Perhaps it was just a purely innocent business meeting . . .

Jamie tasted his whisky and contemplated the fact. Business meeting, my eye! he thought viciously. She had been so obvious she might as well have said that she was going mountaineering in Holland. And to think he had been going to call a halt to his relationship with Teri!

He had been on the verge of telling her today, but his courage had failed him at the last minute. How could he announce to her in a crowded commuter train or in the sweaty smoke-laden atmosphere of Steamers that their beautiful friendship was destined for the dung heap before it had really started?

By asking Clare to leave, she had cleared the way for them to become more intimate – and what had he done about it so far? Zilch! Was that what he was frightened of? One more step and he would be off the end of the cliff and tumbling through the air into the tempestuous sea of infidelity, without the benefit of a safety net. No more pretending that this wasn't really an affair.

How much longer could he hide behind the nice, safe, secure meetings which they currently indulged in? Travelling together on the train – how quaint – morning coffee at the End of the Line Buffet and a quick drink at Steamers on the way home – no risk of being overcome by an urge to have sex on the table there. Especially not with all those beer stains . . .

He'd been torn for months between his desire to remain loyal – and faithful – to his wife, and his desire to take Teri home, tear her clothes off and ravish her on the Axminster. So far, Pamela had been winning.

He had thought, naively, that she needed him, but he was labouring under a complete misapprehension there. Pamela needed no one. She sailed through life like a stately galleon, while all around were mere jet-bikes – tossed and flipped repeatedly into the sea by little waves and wholly inadequate to deal with the storms of life. Pamela remained unaffected, aloof, unsympathetic and totally upright. His wife could sail life's charted course unaided. All she needed was a generous maintenance allowance.

* * *

Jamie watched television until midnight – or, more accurately, alternated between the clock and the television from eleven o'clock onwards when Pamela had said she would be home.

He had watched *World in Action*, *Take Your Pick* with Des O'Connor – not a patch on Michael Miles (or was it Hughie Green?) – a wildlife programme about predatory animals – very appropriate – some awful chat show hosted by Barbie's big sister that wheeled out equally vacuous celebrities intent on promoting their new film, highlights of a football match between two countries he'd never heard of – still rubbish, but better rubbish – and he'd just finished listening to Jerry Paxman harangue two inept politicians who deserved everything they got.

He went to the phone table in the hall and took out the *Yellow Pages*. There was an appointment card from 'The Hair Cut' by the phone, that showed Pamela had also been to have her hair done today – she was really pushing the boat out. He hadn't noticed and that had probably gone as a black mark against him to be used in later skirmishes of Alphabite warfare.

Jamie looked up the telephone number for the Thai restaurant. Its advert featured a stylised line drawing of an ornate Thai building rather than the re-hash of the old James Hunt racing school that it really was. He spent the next ten minutes vacillating about whether to phone or not.

He didn't want his wife to think that he was checking up on her – which he was. Nor that he was worried – which he also was. Pamela never stayed out late. In fact, she never went out in the evenings at all without him – except to school things and that didn't count.

'That makes it sound even more painful than normal,' he winced. 'No, I'm not.'

'Funny, I thought you might be.'

'I never got round to it,' he said pathetically, as if he were talking about returning an overdue library book rather than emasculating his manhood.

'There are some Durex in the bedside drawer,' she said. 'They're probably near their expiry date. I bought a twelve-pack ages ago in the vain hope that I would get seriously lucky at least once a month. You'll probably notice that they're still in their cellophane wrapper,' she added ruefully.

Jamie rummaged through the drawer – even Indiana Jones would have had trouble finding anything in here, he thought. Fighting his way through tubes of cream, lipsticks, headache tablets – hopefully she wouldn't need those tonight – roll-on deodorant – too phallic by half in his opinion – and sundry other cosmetic appliances, he eventually found the box of condoms.

He unwrapped it reluctantly. 'I haven't used one of these since I was at university,' he said, examining one of the small, neat envelopes distastefully under the bedside lamp. 'It always reminded me of having a bath in a plastic mac.'

'Is that something you do often?' Teri smiled.

'What?'

'Have a bath in a plastic mac?'

'No. And this isn't something I do often either,' he added sheepishly.

'Then put those down and come here.' She drew him towards her. 'We won't be needing them just yet.'

Jamie lay back against the pillows and stared at the ceiling.

'It's at times like this that I wish I smoked,' he said wistfully.

Teri snuggled against him. 'If that was what having a bath in a plastic mac feels like, then I'm going to abandon 'The Source of Life' aromatherapy bath gel and go straight down to Millet's to buy a cagoule.'

He squeezed her to him. 'Why does forbidden fruit taste so sweet?'

'For precisely that reason. Because it's forbidden.' She twisted the hairs on his chest between her fingers. 'If you could have it every day, it would be like any other boring old banana.'

'What an interesting analogy.' He kissed her hair.

They relaxed in silence, luxuriating in the nearness of new naked skin until Teri said, 'Tell me about your family.'

'Now?' Jamie was surprised. 'It seems a funny time to talk about my home life. I thought you didn't want to know about it.'

'I didn't,' she admitted, 'before. I feel part of you now and I want to know everything about you.' She trailed her finger lazily over his chest.

Jamie sighed. 'What do you want to know?'

'We could start with something easy,' she said. 'What's your house like?'

He shrugged underneath her. 'Big, expensive and a mixture of architecture that would look totally out of place anywhere other than Milton Keynes – or possibly Savannah.'

Teri draped her leg over his. 'Tell me about the kids.'

'Jack's three and is a little devil.' Jamie stroked her shoulder absently. 'Francesca's six going on thirty-six and she's a little madam.'

'Do they look like you?'

'Francesca does. Jack looks like Pa— my wife.'

'You can tell me her name if you want to,' she said softly.

'If I do that she'll become real, and right now I can pretend for a short while that she doesn't exist.'

'I want to know what she's like.'

Jamie sighed wearily. 'Pamela is Pamela.' He looked at Teri accusingly. 'There – you've made me say it!'

'Go on,' Teri prompted him with a nudge in the ribs. 'In the true tradition of Magnus Magnusson, you've started so you might as well finish.'

'She's self-contained, aloof and distant. And she doesn't understand me one bit.' Jamie held up his hand. 'I know it's a cliché and you did voice that very vociferously on one occasion, I seem to remember,' he said wryly. 'But she doesn't. We've nothing in common any more. She doesn't understand why I find *Men Behaving Badly* the funniest programme on television or how I can even laugh at *Absolutely Fabulous*. She doesn't understand why I weep openly at something like *Toy Story*, and yet can't cry at funerals. She doesn't understand why I find working for an insurance company the most stifling experience in the world. She doesn't understand why I, along with the children, don't like her home-made granary bread and long for shop-bought bleached and chemically adulterated white sliced loaves. She doesn't understand why I find playing golf a relaxing way to unwind. Neither does she understand that although I enjoy watching football I have lost all desire to kick one.'

He turned and buried his face in Teri's neck, tasting the salty sweetness of her flesh. 'And most of all she wouldn't understand why I need you.'

She arched towards him and his body met with hers.

181

They made love again, without the urgency of the first time and without the judicious intervention of latex. It was a wild and reckless thing to do, he thought as he lay beside her later. Particularly for a man who works in insurance.

Teri was slumbering softly when he stroked her breast to wake her. 'I have to go,' he murmured.

She made an appealing groaning sound and went to get up. 'You stay here, I'll let myself out.' He kissed her shoulders. 'I'll see you tomorrow.'

He crept out of the bed and pulled his clothes on. 'Do you want me to close the curtains?'

'No,' she answered sleepily. 'When I was Francesca's age, I was afraid of my curtains. The patterns on them used to make monsters and give me nightmares. I still sleep with them open.'

He smiled. 'Okay.' He kissed his finger and touched her nose. 'Sleep tight.'

He had driven to Leighton Buzzard Station that morning to meet Teri so, thankfully, the Volvo was now parked conveniently outside her house.

You could tell the sort of man he was from the car he drove. A Volvo – a reliable, roomy family car. Ideal for child car seats, carry cots, pushchairs, picnic hampers, bikes, balls, Barbie and all the other bloody paraphernalia they took with them whenever they moved out of the house. It was engineered for safety and always fared well in traffic accidents. An insurance man's dream. And the most sensible car in the universe.

He wished momentarily that he drove a Ferrari. Red and sexy. Too small for anything else but a chick with a tight skirt and long legs. And certainly no room for his conscience.

It was a cold night, but there was no frost and it was good to think that spring might be just around the corner. He turned the car heater up, so that as soon as the engine warmed it would be blasting out hot air. It was frightening to think that he had reached the age where he also appreciated the fact that the car seats were heated. The night seemed all the more chilly for his having just got out of a warm and comfortable bed . . .

It was late, but not suspiciously so. There would be time for a night-cap and a chat with Pamela before they went to bed. He wondered if he would be different now he had taken this irrevocable step into a life of deception. The actual deceitfulness became easier in practical terms, but the mental side seemed to grow steadily worse. Where was this going to end?

He thought of Francesca asleep at home, blissfully unaware of her father's duplicity. Would it change her life? Was she afraid of her curtains as Teri had been? There seemed nothing scary about fabric with Beatrix Potter characters on it to him – only the price of it – but then he wasn't six. She had nothing else to worry about. There had been no crises in her life other than the inadvertent loss of an idolised hamster called Gazza up the vacuum cleaner. She had a mother who fretted over her every move and a father who catered for all the material needs her mother could ever dream up for her.

And what of Jack? *His* only worry was overcoming the so-far unfathomable joining of Duplo. Jamie hoped to God that nothing would happen to change that.

As he drove back from his lover in Leighton Buzzard to his wife in Milton Keynes, he prayed fervently that his children would always enjoy deep and dreamless sleep. At the moment he was having enough night-time terrors for them all.

Chapter Sixteen

The Tom Pearson Ten-Step Plan for Rehabilitation of Errant Husbands wasn't working. The daily crooning in the Calypso Power Shower was growing even more forceful than the steaming jets of water that coursed over Jamie as he lathered his body. He was stuck on slushy love songs of the seventies and had worked his way through 'How Deep Is Your Love' – the Bee Gees' version, not Take That's, 'Three Times A Lady' – Commodores – 'All Of Me Loves All Of You' – Bay City Rollers (worrying) – most of 'Saturday Night Fever' and several of the more sentimental songs of Gladys Knight and the Pips. An alarming deviation had been 'Great Balls of Fire'. It wasn't only Gladys Knight who had the pip.

Pamela combed her hair and stared at her pale reflection in the mirror. They used to have sex in the shower. Years ago, when they were first married. She couldn't understand why now. It was a tiny shower in their first house and they used to bang their elbows and knees on the tiles and the Perspex cubicle door. Finally, a bottle of Vidal Sassoon's 'Wash and Go' had hit her on the head and that had been an end to it. They had a much bigger shower room now, but the urge to make love in it never seemed to arise.

Tom had suggested another evening out, to solve the current crisis. She thought this excessive, and there was also a faint whiff of ulterior motive about it. But what else was she to do? It had worked so well last time. She could tell that Jamie had been jealous, but since then his zeal for working long hours and sneaking out to make late-night telephone calls with MacTavish had simply increased.

The discovery about the phone calls had come when she had been forced to take MacTavish on his nightly constitutional due to Jamie's lateness. The poor dog had been crossing his legs and howling balefully at his lead and, ever mindful that the future displays of daffodils that were sprouting in tender infancy through their soil wouldn't benefit from a watering with MacTavish's urine, she had reluctantly donned her Barbour and walked him down the road.

It was when he had stopped at the phone box and refused steadfastly to budge until she had gone through the pretence of making a phone call that the penny dropped. It was with a leaden heart and a lump in her throat that she marched him home and rewarded him with a large bowl of Chum for his treachery. And they say a dog is a man's best friend! MacTavish was obviously unfamiliar with that concept.

It was disconcerting that when she told Jamie she was going to the Thai restaurant again on another business meeting with Tom there was a distinct lack of batting of either of his eyelids. 'Fine,' he said – and he sounded as if he meant it.

So here she was, dressed up to the nines again and going out with her boss when she would rather be staying in with her husband on the one night he managed to get home early – although, if Tom's hare-brained plan actually worked Jamie would soon be coming home early every night.

Pamela went slowly downstairs and waited uneasily in the lounge. Jamie didn't flinch as the majestic Mercedes swept into their drive. She was the one that did.

The restaurant was busier than last time. There was a party from one of the large computer companies doing some particularly raucous bonding following a seminar on 'Lateral Thinking in the Nineties'. Bottles of wine were being passed across the table with an intent that was almost savage in its ferocity. The only thing this lot were likely to be doing laterally tonight was sliding under the tables.

As Jamie had pointed out, from the exterior the restaurant looked rather like a circus tent, with the addition of two gold lions – or were they dragons? – placed strategically at the front door to give it an Oriental authenticity. Inside, it had been transformed from a sea of functional chrome and plastic that said 'racing school' into a Far Eastern wonderland of hastily carved rosewood and precarious bamboo canopies.

Tom and Pamela were shown to a table as far away from the inebriated lateral thinkers as possible, on a raised platform towards the back of the restaurant. Two tiny waitresses in traditional costume fluttered round them like exotic butterflies. They ordered a set menu because Tom had forgotten his reading glasses and she was feeling too disinterested to choose.

'So it's not working too well?' he said when the waitresses had left.

'No,' she sighed. 'It seemed to have the desired effect briefly, but then matters sort of escalated. He's staying out late – very late – and coming home smelling of Chinese food and 'Obsession'.'

Their own food arrived. 'Perhaps you're not playing the part convincingly enough,' he suggested, as he dipped a fish cake into one of the sauces which had been placed alongside them.

'I never said I was Dame Judi Dench.'

Tom unwrapped a piece of chicken from some sort of sturdy foliage. 'We might have to take this one stage further.'

'Why do I think I'm not going to like the sound of this.'

Tom shrugged nonchalantly. One thing she had learned early in life was never to trust a salesman when he shrugged nonchalantly. 'Perhaps we need some realism injected into this.'

'Now I *know* I don't like the sound of this.'

The butterflies cleared their plate of starters which had been decimated mainly by Tom and brought the main course. He covered her hand with his. 'You're a very beautiful woman, Pamela.'

'And you're an attractive man.' She moved her hand away. 'A *married* one.'

One of the lateral thinkers crashed to the floor on his chair. Tom moved his closer to her and spooned some noodles languidly on to her plate while not taking his eyes from hers. It was obviously a practised move and, as such, was quite impressive to watch. 'I've always wanted to get to know you better.'

His eyes had taken on the hard-edged glint of a predator. 'Don't do this to me, Tom. Please.'

'What harm could it do?' He was beginning to sound oilier than Italian salad dressing.

'I'm in a deep state of confusion and emotional strain

as it is. If I even consider placing one more card on the top, the whole wobbly pile will collapse.'

'Can I be frank with you?'

'I'd rather you weren't. I'd rather you were just Tom. The Tom I know and *don't* love.'

'I don't think you've been properly fulfilled as a woman.'

Two of the lateral thinkers started singing 'Agadoo' and the restaurant's owner hovered nervously round their table.

'I'm perfectly fulfilled as a woman, Tom,' she said tightly. 'And if I wasn't, I would be looking to my husband to fulfil me. The answer to my current domestic predicament isn't a quick bonk in the back of a well-built German car.'

Tom looked slightly deflated. 'So you don't think a full-blown revenge affair is a good idea?'

'No.'

'Wouldn't it be fun finding out?'

'No.'

'I just—'

'*No.*'

His face took on a look of pained honesty. 'I want to make love to you really badly.' He was sounding desperate.

She didn't have the heart to tell him that she'd rather be made love to really well, and that if anyone could do that it was Jamie. Instead she said, 'Tom, exactly which part of the word *no* is it that you're having trouble with?'

His fixed expression, she guessed, was meant to convey deep and painful longing. It looked instead like he had deep and painfully trapped wind. 'My arms ache for you.'

'I thought it was somewhere lower down the anatomical scale that was supposed to ache.'

'My whole body aches.'

'At your age, Tom, that's just a touch of rheumatism not love – or even lust.'

He fell silent. His face deflated as though he had just had a gaseous release. Perhaps she'd been right about the trapped wind after all.

'I don't know what I'm doing here at all.' She dropped her fork on the plate of untouched food. 'The whole thing has been a catalogue of crassness and stupidity. I should never have listened to you. You didn't want to add a bit of extra spice to my marriage, you wanted to throw the whole damn chilli pot on it and make it totally bloody unpalatable.'

She pushed back from the table. 'I don't want to fall out with you, Tom, I like working with you, but I think if I don't go now we'll both say things that we'll regret.'

'Not so fast, lady.' It was a loud voice for a small restaurant – booming out with a broad and less than chirpy cockney accent. Pamela looked round stunned, but nowhere near as stunned as Tom was. It stopped the lateral thinkers in their tracks and even the Agadoo-ers stopped Agadoo-ing. She hadn't met Tom's wife Shirley before, but she had heard enough about her to know that it was Shirley who stood in front of her now.

'I know your game,' Shirley said menacingly.

'Shirley, sit down,' Tom hissed. 'You're showing yourself up.'

'*I'm* showing myself up?' Her neat, over-made-up face was red with anger. 'You can talk. Business meeting!' Shirley spat the word out and some spittle landed on Pamela's cheek, but she was too terrified to lift her hand and wipe it off. She could feel it glistening in the seductive lighting, obvious to all the lateral thinkers who were staring at them with mouths gaping wider than the Dartford Tunnel.

Tom lowered his voice to a whisper. 'Of course it's a business meeting! You know Pamela's my secretary.'

She put her hands on her hips. 'So this is Pamela?'

'Pleased to meet you,' Pamela said quietly, and offered her hand.

Shirley looked at it as if she had been offered rat poison. Pamela retracted her hand.

'Secretary, personal assistant, typist – they've all had different names and guises – blondes, brunettes and now a redhead,' Shirley continued unabated. 'I don't think you've had a redhead before.'

The restaurant was deathly silent. The reassuring chink of cutlery and glasses had ceased completely. She could hear the faint hum of the heating system and somewhere a chair scraped uncomfortably over the polished wooden floor.

'Mrs Pearson,' Pamela pleaded in hushed tones. 'Shirley. You've made a terrible mistake.'

'The only mistake I made was marrying this mangy old tom cat.' She checked that everyone had heard her. 'Tom by name, tom by nature!'

'Shirley!' Tom was affronted.

The two butterflies had stopped flitting and were frozen to the spot, supporting the restaurant owner who looked perilously close to fainting.

'This is not what it seems,' Pamela said calmly. But what was it? Would it really help to tell Shirley that she was pretending to have an affair with *her* husband to make her own husband jealous and stop him having an affair . . . but that all along Tom had secretly fancied his chances? No, she thought it wouldn't. It all sounded terribly complicated and she wasn't sure she understood it herself. It didn't strike her as very convincing either, once you looked at it closely.

'Well, you can have him.' Shirley was obviously not in the mood to be placated or reasoned with. 'You deserve each other.' She pointed aggressively at them both. Tom winced. Shirley lunged at the table. 'And you deserve this.'

The bowl of Thai green curry was tipped on Pamela's head before she knew it. The delicate fragrance of lemongrass became overpowering as it ran past her nose to drip on her skirt. It was warm and creamy. If she had been eating it she would have been tempted to complain that it wasn't piping hot. As it was, she was grateful that it was only tepid. The noodles were hotter, but they landed in her lap and would only ruin her skirt rather than give her third-degree burns.

Tom was wearing the sweet and sour chicken before the restaurant manager galvanised himself into action and grabbed both of Shirley's arms.

'I call the police!' he shouted.

'Naff off!' Shirley kneed him in the groin and he fell to the floor like a sack of King Edwards. 'You!' She pointed at Tom. 'You don't need to bother coming home. I'm going to the solicitor first thing in the morning and I'm going to have an injunction served on you!' She marched past the restaurant manager who was doubled up in agony and crashed out into the night.

The lateral thinkers hooted and hollered and broke into spontaneous applause. They started a raucous chorus of 'I can't stand losing you' alluding to The Police the pop group, rather than the police the law-enforcement group.

Tom looked perplexed. He stood hands on hips, orange sauce running from his once-pristine white shirt on to the floor. A piece of carrot hung from his gold neck chain like a limp goldfish.

'I think you'd better go after her,' Pamela said, smoothing Thai green curry from her face.

'Do you think . . .' He took three steps towards the door. 'What about you?'

'I'll get a taxi.'

'I could run you home. Another five minutes won't make any difference, will it? I'll square it with Shirley as soon as I get home.'

Pamela looked at him in pure astonishment. The man had skin thicker than a whole herd of rhinoceroses. Or was it rhinoceri? 'Fuck off, Tom,' she said with unconcealed malice. 'Just fuck off.'

Tom, as instructed, did fuck off. Without paying the bill. She settled the account herself stoically, dripping curry on to her chequebook and trying not to cry. The restaurant manager, once he had recovered his dignity, called a taxi for her. For the next twenty minutes, she was forced to endure him ineffectually, but thoughtfully, sponging her down with a damp J-cloth, and the guffaws of the lateral thinkers while she waited for it to arrive.

The lights were still on when she reached home – which wasn't surprising as it was only an hour and a half after she had left. Jamie would gloat. How she wished she could have sneaked past him and cleaned herself in the steaming waters of their shower before he saw her. Unfortunately, the crunch of the gravel heralded her arrival and he stood with the door open as she paid the taxi fare. The driver hadn't taken kindly to her stinking his cab out with Thai green curry and noodles and, shamefacedly, she tipped him heavily to compensate him for his trouble, which he hadn't hesitated to point out.

'You're ear . . . ly,' he said, as she emerged from the darkness into the harsh light of their hallway. His eyes travelled over her, slowly, from head to foot, taking in the white creamy sauce, the shredded basil leaves and sundry bits of chilli that still adorned her. 'I didn't know it was fancy dress,' he said jovially. 'What have you come as?'

Pamela started to cry. 'I don't want to talk about it.'

Jamie's face softened. 'Come here.' He went to put his arms around her, but she pushed him away.

'I don't want you to touch me either.' She stifled a sob. When MacTavish appeared from the lounge and started to lick her legs, she gave him a swift kick and he ran for the sanctuary of the kitchen. It was bad enough to lose one's dignity like this without being mistaken for a doggy treat.

'Is there anything I can do?'

'Stop smirking.'

'I'm not smirking.' Jamie face tightened. 'I'm concerned.'

'Then don't be.'

Jamie leaned against the wall. 'What happened?'

'It's none of your business.'

'I'm your husband!'

Pamela's face tightened. '*That* is a matter for debate,' she said tartly.

Jamie sighed heavily.

'I'm going to bed,' she said wearily, and climbed up the stairs with as much haughtiness as a walking menu can muster.

'Do you want a hot drink?' Jamie shouted after her.

Her heart melted. He could be so sweet when he wanted to be.

'Perhaps some Jasmine tea?' he suggested.

For the third time that night, and the third time in her life, she used the F-word.

Chapter Seventeen

Jamie allowed his body to be buffeted by the movement of the tube train, swaying his weight from foot to foot to keep his balance. He didn't strap-hang, so that people would be able to tell he belonged in London and wasn't just some country bumpkin who was up for a day in The Smoke. Not that you could call it strap-hanging any more – 'rubber-ball-and-spring-hanging' just didn't have the same ring. But what did it matter, anyway. He would soon be with Teri and she would pour oil on the troubled waters at the end of his day. For a short while he would be able to forget he was married, with a mortgage the size of the national debt of a small Third World country.

Pamela was still refusing to discuss what had happened at the Thai restaurant with Tom. There had been several phone calls when she had slammed the phone down with a force that was quite unnecessary, and several answer-phone messages in which a doleful-sounding Tom had begged her to return his calls. As far as Jamie knew she hadn't done so. Nor had she gone into work for the last three days, which was a worrying trend. She assured him that she was using up her holiday, but even he could see that was something of a coincidence following the curry-wearing episode.

To placate Pamela he had tried to be as helpful and cheerful around the house as possible. It had worked to a certain extent in that the Alphabite combat had tailed off to a half-hearted effort in which Pamela limited herself to 'git', 'sod' and 'pig' – words not normally in her vocabulary, but at least brief and to the point.

Tonight he had promised to be home in time to go to Francesca's school concert. She was playing the recorder with the music group from year one. It was destined to be a hideous cacophony of ill-timed shrills and peeps through which Mrs Rutherford wandered with the original melody of the tune on the piano with a level of skill that would provide no obvious threat to Barry Manilow.

Jamie knew this from bitter experience of 'The Christmas Extravaganza' – a two-hour endurance test of lisps and lapses as the school performed, Mrs Rutherford announcing stoutly, 'Favourite Carols, Old and New'. Mothers oooed and aaahed appreciatively at their off-spring's attempts at entertaining, while fathers generally made nuisances of themselves recording the moment for posterity with the latest in video camcorder technology. Tonight it was to be 'Spring into Springtime', and Jamie shuddered at the thought. Francesca was the only one with any talent among them. But then he would think that.

On reflection, Teri wasn't likely to be in oil-pouring mode when he explained that he couldn't spend any time with her tonight before going home. He had tried to call her all day but she was apparently 'in programme rehearsals' – which probably wouldn't help her temper either. It was with a heavy heart that Jamie let himself be swallowed by the crush from the underground, squashed up the escalators and then finally spewed out, battered and broken like a recycled tin can, on to the Euston main line concourse.

She was there, waiting at the End of the Line Buffet. When she saw him she drained her coffee and walked towards him – her small tight walk, confident and vulnerable at the same time. His heart lurched and his stomach turned, and it wasn't the fact that he'd eaten nothing since his pork pie and pint with Charlie in the Clog and Calculator. How long had this been going on for now? And it still didn't feel any more right or any more wrong.

Teri passed him a polystyrene cup of coffee with a lid on it as she greeted him with a light kiss. 'Hi,' she said.

'Shitty day?'

She nodded. 'The worst. And you?'

He shrugged. 'Same as ever.' He noticed the carrier bag bulging with shopping and gave her back the polystyrene cup so he could take the bag from her. 'It's going to get worse.'

'What?'

'Your shitty day.'

'Oh.' Her face darkened. They set off down the slope towards the platform.

'I can't come back with you tonight.'

'Jamie!'

'I know, I know. I've been trying to ring you all day. I promised Pamela that I'd be home in time to go to Francesca's school concert.' They got on the train and found seats opposite each other. He pushed the shopping under his legs hoping that she would forget about it.

She missed nothing. 'You can give that to me.' She pulled the bag from under his legs and pushed it under her own. Glowering, she thrust his coffee back at him.

'Thanks,' he said meekly, and took a swallow of the warm, foul-tasting liquid.

The nights were getting lighter. A true sign – other than Francesca's concert – that spring was on its way. It enabled you to see the full squalor and decay of London as you travelled in and out of Euston, a pleasure that could be forgotten – if only briefly – during the darkness of winter. It enabled you to enjoy the full impact of the mindless psychedelic graffiti that was sprayed over everything that didn't move.

Willesden INTERCITY maintenance depot was a prime target, where all the broken trains bore the indecipherable legends NOS, FIG, SUB and DUNE and something that looked remarkably like SYRINGE. Though why anyone, even of limited intelligence, would want to boast of the tag SYRINGE was totally beyond him.

Once you were past Watford Junction you started to leave behind the depressing scenes of urban decay – the car-breakers' yards, tumbledown workshops, boarded-up factories and the backs of crumbling terraced housing. In fact, once you had hit the Ovaltine factory – which blinked the time and temperature at you in tangerine digital dots – the journey became quite pleasant.

Past the faded station at Hemel Hempstead, things became positively rural. Fields, that did actually roll. Trees, lots of them, dotted about the actually rolling fields. Not the spindly, jam-packed newcomers of Milton Keynes, but old majestic ones with tree trunks like proper tree trunks and room to spread their magnificent branches. Trees that had been there for centuries before anyone thought of railways.

And cows . . . not the concrete ones of Milton Keynes, but real ones. Cows that you could tell the weather by, although he could never remember whether it meant rain if they were sitting down or standing up. He usually stuck to Michael Fish, who was probably no more accurate, but at least these cows had the potential for weather prediction. That was the point.

There was the man-made meandering of the Grand Union Canal, complete with ducks and swans and quaint lockside cottages, and the brightly coloured narrowboats moored along its sides. You could get a quick glimpse of the ruins of Berkhamsted Castle if the train wasn't going too fast and you didn't blink. It was a shame that very often the train windows were so grimy, that everything was viewed through a veil of smeared mud and dirt . . . although so few people ever looked up from their newspapers that it would probably be a waste of water to wash them.

Teri was staring out of the window, jaw set, watching the discarded milk cartons, Tango tins and shopping trolleys as the train clanked slowly out of Euston. Eventually, she announced through gritted teeth: 'I have spent all day listening to temper tantrums from the universally hated Richard Wellbeloved, and non-deleted expletives from Jez, and I am trying very hard at this moment not to start shrieking myself.'

'I can understand that,' Jamie said quickly.

'No, you can't!' she shouted under her breath. 'The few precious minutes I did manage to snatch for lunch I spent *shopping*,' she pointed at the bag between her feet, 'for a meal for us tonight.'

'I tried to call,' Jamie ventured again.

'I bought smoked salmon, tiger prawns,' she counted the items off on her fingers, 'rainbow-trout mousse, a small but nevertheless expensive tin of caviar, a box of cute-shaped biscuits, champagne and, to finish off with, some tiny but highly calorific caramel meringue things with fresh cream and chocolate in them.'

Jamie looked guilty. 'Won't it keep?'

'No, it won't!'

'Would it make you feel better to know that I'll probably be having abusive Alphabites and burnt sausages?'

She smiled reluctantly. 'It might.'

He took her hand and tutted softly. 'You know I can't help this. This is one of the hazards of being involved with a *married*' – he mouthed the word silently – 'man. I wish *you* could come tonight. It would be wonderful.'

Teri's eyes widened. 'Oh yeah, wonderful,' she echoed sarcastically.

She was right. Why on earth would his mistress find it wonderful to sit and watch his child and her valiant attempts to come to terms with the mysteries of the recorder? Sometimes he wondered if he was losing what slender grip he had on reality.

He squeezed her hand comfortingly. 'What will you do tonight?'

'I'll stay at home and eat all this myself and sulk. Then I'll watch numerous repeats on the television and go to bed early still miserable and discontented with life.'

He smiled sadly. 'I'll make it up to you,' he promised.

'How?'

'I don't know.'

Teri settled into her seat. 'Well, start thinking. You've got two stations and it had better be good.'

'You're merciless!'

'I'm hurt,' she said.

It was just outside Cheddington that he finally said, 'What about if I come to stay for a whole weekend?'

Teri leaned forward, excited. 'Friday to Monday?'

Jamie looked unsure. 'Saturday and Sunday.' And when Teri slumped back in her seat, 'I'll come early Saturday morning and stay until as late as possible Sunday night.'

She looked at him warily. 'Promise?'

He crossed his heart. 'Hope to die.'

'This weekend?' Teri asked.

'That only gives me a couple of days.' Jamie fidgeted in his seat. 'It might be difficult to arrange at short notice.'

'This weekend,' she demanded.

'That's unreasonable!'

'This weekend!'

'This weekend,' he agreed. 'You drive a hard bargain, Therese Carter.'

'I'm a hard woman.'

He rubbed his temples. 'What am I going to say?'

'You'll think of something.' They were pulling into Leighton Buzzard Station. 'You're a clever and inventive man.'

Jamie snorted dismally. 'You mean I'm deceitful and an inveterate liar.'

'If you insist.' She stood up and kissed the top of his head. 'Tomorrow?'

'Tomorrow.'

Teri jumped from the train and banged the carriage door. Jamie pulled his newspaper from his briefcase and settled back in the seat, flicking the paper open at the sports page in one deft move. The train moved off.

Out of the corner of his eye, he saw Teri running along the platform keeping pace with the departing train. She was waving and blowing kisses and he could tell that she was shouting, 'I love you'. He smiled and lowered his paper. 'I love you too,' he shouted.

The words froze on his lips and he spun to face the rest of the carriage, realising too late what he had done. Everyone else had lowered their newspapers; there were some smiles and some ill-disguised sneers and most of them looked at him expectantly. He attempted an embarrassed, but light-hearted laugh, but it stuck in his throat and came out like an embarrassed cough.

Reddened and suitably chastised, Jamie huddled behind his newspaper. The muffled announcement for Milton Keynes Central Station couldn't come quick enough.

Her arms were at least a foot longer, having dragged the unnecessary and expensive bag of shopping up the hill. Teri massaged her forearms, which twinged painfully, through her dressing gown. She dipped in the carrier bag and spread the goodies she had bought in for her and Jamie on the coffee table.

Originally, she had thought they might eat them in bed – it was the sort of romantic thing they did in films. As she took the lid off the caviar she realised it was probably as well to eat them downstairs in front of the telly – in films you didn't appreciate the fact that it would leave the bedroom stinking of fish for weeks.

She popped the cork of the champagne and let it fizz over into one of her tall best glasses without spilling too much on the lounge carpet. It was very melancholy, the sound of a cork being popped by one person. Traditionally, it was the signal for celebrations, parties, romantic couples – not commiserations and nights in by yourself.

Perhaps she should have tried to phone Clare. She'd managed to track down one of her friends at the airport who had reluctantly divulged Clare's new number. She could have pretended that all this was part of a peace offering . . .

Teri bit into a heart-shaped biscuit piled with smoked salmon and caviar, cracking the livid green face pack that she had smeared lovingly over her skin. She tutted, swallowed the rest of her biscuit, ate two tiger prawns and swilled them down with a gulp of champagne. Even Clare wasn't that dim. She would have seen through her immediately and would have gone all Sister Mary Bernadette-ish again. No, ultimately, it was better to over-indulge oneself alone.

She used the remote control to switch on the television. Repeats of *Dad's Army*. ITV? Repeats of *Heartbeat*. Channel Four? Repeats of *Cheers*. BBC2? Cricket – England versus Pakistan. Not a repeat, but not exactly a wild night's viewing either. *Dad's Army* it had to be. Rainbow-trout mousse on a fish-shaped biscuit this time. And one tiger prawn.

Teri wound tissues between her toes. She found the bottle of nail polish hiding behind the champagne bottle and filled her glass in passing. Caviar on its own piled on a boring round biscuit. She put her feet on the coffee table and painted each toe bright red, being careful not to paint the coffee table in the process. Caviar topped with smoked salmon on a diamond-shaped biscuit. Three prawns.

She wondered what Jamie was doing now. Was he enjoying playing the dutiful father? Would Mr and Mrs Duncan be arm in arm looking on tenderly and misty-eyed as Francesca did her party piece? Would it make him realise that Teri was superfluous to his life? She was outside his family unit and why did he need her? Or would he be numbed by the drudgery of it all, stupefied by the singing six-year-olds, and realise that he wanted her, only her and his freedom?

But what if he did leave Pamela for her? Wouldn't the whole jolly circus just start all over again? Teri wanted children. She wanted to go to school concerts. She wanted to go home to a house full to the brim of family commitments. What would happen then? Would he meet someone else – another willing, wistful woman on another packed commuter train?

Jamie never talked of the future. He had never promised her anything, except for this weekend. Smoked salmon topped by rainbow-trout mousse topped by a tiger prawn *and* caviar on a frilly-edged biscuit. After burping, Teri excused herself with a swig of champagne.

Dad's Army really was quite hilarious. Fat Captain Mainwaring swaggering about, and all that 'They don't like it up 'em' – it was enough to make even the most depressed and disappointed person in the world laugh. Teri had some more champagne and started on the caramel meringues. Perhaps they were a little too rich on top of half a pound of smoked salmon, a tub of rainbow-trout mousse and two dozen tiger prawns – but it was only one teeny-tiny tin of caviar, and besides . . . they were such a temptation and it was true what she'd said to Jeremy . . . er . . . Jamie. Cream didn't keep!

It was at the end when they started singing the theme tune that Teri began to feel ill. When they sang that they were on the run, Teri had to run, too. She was doing quite well until she reached the bottom of the stairs on her way up to the bathroom and the phone started to ring.

What should she do? Charge upstairs, answer her call of nature and forget about the phone? But it could be Jamie. He would worry if she didn't answer. Or should she answer and face the prospect of redecorating the hall?

Desperately searching her dressing-gown pockets for tissues that didn't resemble Ryvitas, she decided to answer the phone. It was a decision she would live to regret.

Chapter Eighteen

Jamie threw his briefcase into the hall and slammed the door. 'What time does it start tonight?' he shouted.

The house was amazingly quiet. Strains of classical music floated through the hall – Vivaldi's *Four Seasons* – 'Spring'. Perhaps Pamela was getting herself into the mood for tonight. There was no MacTavish trying to whip Jamie's legs from under him. No incessant babbling from Francesca about how horrid Jack had been to her. Instead there was a funny smell. No, not funny, just unusual. It was cheesy – in the nicest sense of the word. And garlicky. It smelt like proper food. Not Alphabites or Alphabetti Spaghetti or even fish fingers. Adult food.

A puzzled look crossed Jamie's face. They couldn't be expecting anyone for dinner – they were going out. He took off his jacket and hung it over the banister – he would risk Pamela's wrath later – and went into the kitchen.

'What time— What the blazes!' Jamie was struck speechless.

Pamela was standing serenely in front of the cooker concentrating on stirring something in a pan. It was a halogen cooker and there were red lights coming on and going off everywhere, indicating a hive of activity on the hob front – either that or an alien spacecraft was about to

209

land in the kitchen. She was wearing a tight black dress – or rather a tight black dress was wearing her – and five-inch black stiletto heels. Her legs, which looked surprisingly long in heels that high and a skirt that short, were encased in fine fishnet and her stocking tops were just visible at the hem of her skirt.

Jamie loosened his tie as it seemed to be making his eyes bulge. The dress had a low-cut neck and her breasts, balanced on top of the neckline, were pale and plump and misted damply from the steam in the kitchen. Jamie gulped. She wore a tiny white frilled apron which obviously wasn't designed to cope with major domestic spillages. Her deep auburn hair was wound in a knot at the back of her head, which made her neck look incredibly long and slender, particularly as there was such a long way from her chin to the start of her dress.

'What are you doing?' It was an inane question, but the best he could manage in the circumstances.

'Cooking dinner.' Pamela smiled sweetly. 'Have you had a good day?'

It certainly wasn't one of his best, but at this rate it would probably count as one of his most memorable. He shrugged. 'Okay.'

'There's a bottle of red wine breathing in the utility room.' He hoped it was doing better than him, Jamie thought. 'Why don't you take a glass up with you? Dinner will be ready as soon as you've showered.'

Jamie's eyebrows met in the middle. 'I thought we were to be entertained by our budding James Galway in "Spring into Springtime" tonight?'

'I lied.' Pamela smiled sweetly again. 'That's next week.'

Jamie was dumbfounded. He looked round perplexed. 'So where is everyone?'

'The children are at my mother's.'

'Your mother's?' Jamie decided he would try the wine. 'What did she think about that?'

'She thought it was time we were alone as man and wife.' Pamela held the spoon to her lips, tasted it delicately then ran her tongue over her lips. They were red and glossy.

Jamie licked his lips.

'Man and woman,' she added seductively.

Jamie swallowed hard. 'And the dog?'

'MacTavish is next door for the night.'

Jamie popped into the utility room and found the bottle of wine. A good bottle, too. The wineglasses were in the cupboard next to the cooker and it meant he would have to go within close proximity of the Lycra creation and the pinny. He didn't know if he was up to it without breaking into a sweat.

Pamela normally wore silk and chiffon – floaty things. They were stylish but shapeless, covered in a profusion of muted flowers that finished somewhere round her ankles just before they reached her flat, sensible shoes that she had worn since she had given birth to Jack – because her back had never been quite the same. He didn't think he would ever be quite the same either. If he had seen his wife's bottom in Lycra before, he didn't remember it – and he was sure that he would have. It was tight and small and very touchable.

He yanked the cupboard open, grabbed two glasses, slammed the door shut and retreated to a safer part of the kitchen to busy himself with the process of pouring out the wine with trembling hands. He noticed that the table in the conservatory had been set for two. There were candles on it, and red roses in a crystal vase they had been given as a wedding present. The festoon blinds had been lowered slightly. He took a hearty swig of his wine and offered Pamela hers, too, in the vain hope that she might break her vow of temperance. She nodded demurely.

'Go and shower,' she said. 'I'll be ready when you come down. Don't be long.'

There was a sardonic twist to his smile as the wine started to relax him. 'May I just ask you exactly what you're cooking up?'

'It's from *Cosmopolitan*.'

'I might have known.'

' "How to liven up your home-cooking by giving it a more continental flavour." '

'Was the outfit *Cosmo*'s idea too?'

'No.' Pamela flushed attractively. 'That was my own idea.'

He took her glass of wine and placed it next to her, then stood behind her taking in the sweet cloying smell of her perfume and the even sweeter and more appetising smell of her cooking. He kissed her neck and felt her tremble. Nipping her earlobe, he whispered, 'Then I'd better go and slip into something more comfortable, too.'

Jamie wasn't sure what the male equivalent of a French maid's outfit was, so he settled on smart casual instead. Fawn trousers. A light silk shirt. Okay, so it had golf-type things all over it, but it was subtle – it didn't scream golf and therefore was less likely to annoy Pamela. He put on black underpants in an attempt to look sexy. They hadn't made love in months, but it was obviously on the menu tonight. He went downstairs with mounting trepidation – no pun intended.

Pamela had lit the array of candles in the conservatory and he had to admit that it looked very romantic. She brought in the steaming *Cosmopolitan* dish of continental delights and he was sure that she bent over further than she absolutely needed to while she was dishing up, given her back complaint. Perhaps it was just those shoes throwing her centre of gravity out?

Cosmo's idea of home meets continental cooking, it turned out, was nothing more threatening than a combination of shepherd's pie and spaghetti bolognese. The mince contained tomatoes, mushrooms, garlic and the other necessary components of bolognese sauce, and the mashed-potato topping was heavily flavoured with Parmesan cheese. It smelt divine and Pamela had taken the trouble to pipe 'I love you' on top of the mashed potatoes.

They ate slowly, watching each other's mouths as they did so. Pamela seemed light-hearted, she laughed when he told a joke, even if it was a bad one, and he realised it must have been an effort for her. He wondered nervously what he had done to deserve this and what the bill, when it eventually came, would be.

Pamela had abandoned *Cosmopolitan* for the dessert and had instead taken the advice of Delia Smith – goddess of calories, cream and cholesterol – and produced tiramisu. As he licked his spoon, Jamie marvelled at how Pamela had managed to fit it all within the constraints of the Lycra.

She cleared the dishes, then returned and took his wine glass from him and placed it alongside hers on the sideboard. Elegantly, in one supple move, she hoisted herself on to the table and laid back seductively on the tablecloth, which was the one his mother had bought them for

Christmas, and pulled her husband towards her by the lapels of his favourite golfing shirt.

Obligingly, he undid her apron, throwing it manfully to the floor – there was going to be no dishwashing tonight – and joined her on the table. She unbuttoned his shirt.

'Supposing the neighbours see us?' he asked tentatively. It wasn't every day that people made love on the breakfast table in the conservatory in full view of Fraughton-next-the-Green.

'You are an old stick-in-the-mud, Jamie Duncan.' She turned and blew out the candles in the candelabra. In the moonlit darkness he watched carefully as his black underpants sailed across the conservatory. His secretary had told him all about *Animal Hospital* again, a few days ago. Rolf had watched enraptured while the vet – the nice smiley one that she liked – had extracted a pair of Thomas the Tank Engine underpants from the stomach of a labrador puppy. Apparently, it was touch and go whether the dog would make it. Jamie's Thomas-free underpants landed on the floor in the corner. His last thought before he surrendered was that he must remember to retrieve them in the morning before MacTavish came home and ate them for his breakfast.

They were in bed, Pamela curled against him. The lights were off, but they were both awake. Jamie cleared his throat. 'I have to go away this weekend on a course. For work. Just Saturday and Sunday.'

Pamela snapped her bedside light on. 'A course?' Her hair was loose on her shoulders. She still had her make-up on, but her red glossy lipstick was gone, kissed away by Delia's tiramisu and his own traitorous lips. 'This weekend? Why didn't you say something earlier?'

Jamie's throat was dry. 'It hardly seemed appropriate.'

'You know what I mean.'

'I know it's short notice, but it really has only just come up.'

She pulled her hair away from her face and stared at him. He could hardly withstand the intensity of her eyes. She was naked and suddenly he couldn't bear to look at her. 'I don't believe you.'

'What?' He could hear his heart pounding. Why was he doing this? They had just had a wonderful evening – flirting, teasing, making love as if they were teenagers again.

'I said I don't believe you,' she repeated.

'Look – what's brought this on? We've just had the best evening together in a long time.'

'Exactly! We should be sharing a moment of intimacy and caring.'

'Is that another one of *Cosmo*'s ideas?' He couldn't believe he was sounding so heartless. Was it his suspicion that this sudden reawakening of sexual interest could have more to do with Tom Pearson than with him? The thought of Pamela doing erotic things on dining-room tables with her boss was making him feel sick.

'No, it's one of my ideas – and I hoped it would be one of yours. I don't know how you can do this.'

How *could* he do this with a ravishing woman, his wife, next to him? He didn't know himself, so how on earth could he expect Pamela to understand? Did adultery lead directly to insanity? It certainly seemed to be doing so in his case.

'What course is it?' she asked tightly.

'Management Ethics.'

'Management Ethics!' Pamela snorted. 'It should be a short course then.'

Jamie remained silent. It was the first thing that had come into his head and he wished it hadn't been.

'Show me the joining instructions.'

'The what?'

'The joining instructions. For this course.'

'I can't.'

'Why not?' Pamela was kneeling in front of him, clutching the duvet.

'I haven't got any.'

'You're a liar, Jamie Duncan. There are no joining instructions because there is no course.' She had started to cry and her sobs wrenched his soul from his body, but he was powerless to move, to comfort her, his limbs frozen by his own culpability. 'I know where you're going and you know I know where you're going.'

'I'm going on a course!' he insisted. What sort of course? A collision course.

She jumped from the bed and pulled her dressing gown round her, hiding her nakedness. 'I'm going to sleep in Francesca's room.'

'You'll be cold,' Jamie warned, unable to think of anything more useful to say.

'No colder than I feel now.' Pamela's eyes narrowed. 'I don't know how I'm ever going to trust you again.'

It was Jamie's turn to shout. 'And how do you think *I* feel, knowing that you're with that cockney oil-slick!'

Pamela looked shocked. She reeled slightly and steadied herself on the doorframe.

'Don't come the goody two-shoes with me, Pamela,' he went on self-righteously. 'It won't wash. I thought you wanted it this way. You can't change the rules whenever it suits you!'

She walked out of the room quietly and sedately. He

flung himself back on the bed, dejected and despising himself. He had ruined Teri's evening, he had ruined Pamela's evening and he had ruined his own evening. How soon would it be before he stooped to the level that Charlie had said he would, and ruin *all* of their lives completely?

Chapter Nineteen

'She's left me,' he said flatly, staring at the view of neat parallel roads interspersed with derelict strips of land waiting expectantly for someone to come along and build another chrome and glass monstrosity on them. 'Shirley's left me.'

Pamela sighed and perched on the end of his desk. 'Would it help if I talked to her?'

'Only through a medium.' Tom's eyes twinkled mischievously.

'This is serious!'

Tom shook his head. 'I've tried everything. I've explained the situation over and over again, but she just won't listen.'

'I thought you said she was understanding.'

'She was. Until she met someone else.' Tom rubbed his eyes. They were reddened and swollen, either from lack of sleep or from crying, she couldn't tell which. 'She's got a lover. What a joke! Can you believe it? After all this time. When I'd finally gone straight.'

'Don't push the point too far, Tom.' They exchanged rueful glances.

'Well, you know what I mean. You were a challenge. I had to give it a go. Don't blame me for that.'

Pamela crossed her legs. 'Jamie thought you'd succeeded.' She turned to look out of the window with Tom. 'He thinks you and I are having an affair.'

Tom looked thoughtful. 'I take that as a compliment.'

'I shouldn't if I were you,' Pamela warned. She crossed her arms as well as her legs. 'I did what you suggested. I dressed up like something out of *Allo, Allo*, legs akimbo, breasts heaving. We had a wonderful evening. We weren't exactly conservative in the conservatory. It was a re-enactment of *The Postman Always Rings Twice* in Fraughton-next-the-Green. It worked a treat. I wish you could have seen it.'

'So do I,' Tom said earnestly.

'Then afterwards he announced that he's going on a course this weekend. Saturday and Sunday.' Pamela humphed. 'A course! I couldn't believe it – not after what we'd just done.'

'Bastard,' Tom agreed.

'Then you know what really surprised me? Really took my breath away? He said he thought it was what I wanted, and how could I accuse him when I was having an affair myself? I was stunned, Tom, honestly I was.'

Tom smiled sadly. 'Is it so hard to imagine having an affair with me?'

Pamela flushed. 'It's not that.' She waved her hand dismissively. 'You *are* an attractive man.' She felt herself flush deeper as she said it. 'I thought he'd know it was just a charade, a pantomime, done purely to get him back. Deep down, I thought he knew that. He *must* know that. I was astonished that he actually thought I was capable of having an affair. Doesn't he know me at all, Tom?'

Her boss slid back into his ostentatious leather chair. 'I could ask the same about Shirley. For the first time in my life she's actually accused me of having an affair when I haven't laid so much as a finger on you. And, to top it all, she's now playing away from home. *My* Shirley. What is the world coming to?'

'It feels terrible to be unjustly accused, doesn't it?' Pamela commiserated.

'Disgusting!' Tom crossed his feet on the desk and chewed on the end of his pen.

'Wait there,' she suddenly instructed him – although Tom didn't look as if he was about to go anywhere. 'There's only one way to put this right. I'll be right back.'

Pamela flicked open the address book on her desk and ran her finger down the pages. She put the receiver to her ear and tapped a number into the phone. After speaking she put the phone down again thoughtfully and went slowly back through to Tom's office. His lower lip was pouting and his face bore an expression of utter misery.

She leaned on the doorframe and took a deep breath. 'Do you still want to make love to me badly?'

'Yes,' he said uncertainly.

'Let's go and have a therapeutic tumble then.'

His feet crashed to the floor. 'I can't believe you just said that.'

'I've booked a double room at The Happy Lodge.'

He closed his eyes and opened them again. 'I had to check I wasn't dreaming.'

'If we're being accused of it, we might as well do it. Surely it's better to be hanged for a sheep as a lamb.'

'I still can't believe you're suggesting this.'

'Neither can I.' She picked up her handbag. 'Come on, let's get going quick before I change my mind.'

They drove across Milton Keynes to The Happy Lodge

in stunned silence. Tom kept both eyes fixed firmly on the road, both hands fixed firmly on the steering wheel. The cassette player was strangely silent too, its usual diet of graunching country and western music trapped mutely inside its security coded system.

The reception staff at The Happy Lodge weren't. They were as miserable as sin – or at least as miserable as Tom had been. A blonde-haired girl, chewing gum like a languorous cow chews grass, handed them the key card to their room and looked disdainfully at them for their lack of luggage. It made Pamela feel all the more determined.

'Room four oh five.' She was Irish.

Tom looked puzzled. 'Room Four?'

'No. Four *oh* five. 'Not four *or* five. It's on the second floor.'

They took the lift up to the second floor. The lift was carpeted halfway up the walls, the rest was mirrored and Pamela thought how pale they both looked. Barry Manilow warbled unevenly in the background from a tape that was either badly stretched or was heedlessly being chewed by the distant tape machine.

Pamela followed Tom along the corridor until he found their room, which was bland and innocuous – it would impress no one and offend no one. It was painted in pale blue and beige with a dark blue carpet that would show no stains. The walls displayed two similar paintings of blurred landscapes in blues and beiges that she suspected were also present in every other room. It was a no-smoking room and the air was thick with the artificial sickly-sweet smell of lavender air-freshener.

Not knowing what else to do, they undressed each other briskly and she hid a smile as Tom broke away from their passion to fold his trousers into the trouser press.

'Are you sure you want to do this?' was the only thing he said to her.

'No,' she answered, before they guided each other to the blue and beige bed.

He didn't make love to her badly as he had insisted he wanted to. He made love to her gently, confidently and professionally. Proving he was an expert lover, as somehow she expected he would be. Afterwards, wrapped in a thin white towel with *The Happy Lodge* embossed on it, she made coffee from the little packets provided in the room along with fiddly cartons of long-life milk. They sat up in bed and nursed their cups until it was cold enough to drink and ate the two packs of McVities' Digestives that were also provided, containing two biscuits each. Pamela admired the swirling pattern of the Artex which hung in tiny stalactites from the ceiling.

They slept for an hour curled together like spoons. Tom showered and dressed alone and then sat and watched cricket on the television while she had the bathroom to herself. She luxuriated in the bath, using all the miniature bottles of foaming bath gel that had been provided and twisting her hair into the thin plastic shower cap that was also part of The Happy Lodge complimentary toiletries.

After drying herself, Pamela sat and looked in the mirror. She was surprised that she looked no different. She didn't feel any different either. No older, no wiser, no more wanton. No less in love with Jamie.

Her mouth was full, slightly bruised from the insistence of Tom's kisses, and she ran the tip of her finger over her lips to make sure that it was her mouth that was reflected. There was a flush on her throat that usually rose there as she orgasmed, increased by the heat of the bath. But it could have been someone else's throat that she was looking at. It didn't feel as if it belonged to her.

Was this how Jamie felt after making love with his mistress? There was a vague detachment from reality. She felt no guilt, no pain, no love. There was pleasure, satisfaction, even release. It had been pleasant rather than earth-shattering. But although the earth hadn't exactly moved, it had wobbled a bit. And while they were making love, Jamie hadn't existed. She hadn't thought it was possible to make love to one person without falling out of love with the other. But it was. Responsibilities were forgotten, children, cooking, cleaning, committees – all receded to nothing. No one was hurt. No one was any the wiser.

Except perhaps she was, after all. Was it always so easy to slip effortlessly into adultery? That was the only thing that shocked her. One minute you weren't an adulterer and the next you were. It was quicker than going round Sainsbury's.

Barry Manilow hadn't changed either. He still warbled unevenly in the lift. Tom squeezed her hand as they descended to Reception.

'Do you feel any better?' she asked him.

He bit his lip before he answered. 'No,' he said truthfully. 'Do you?'

'No. But I don't feel any worse.'

The lift doors opened and they strode across the crisscross carpet in Reception to pay their bill to the disinterested girl who was still chewing gum. The cost of an afternoon's adultery was £66.50 plus VAT. Tom insisted on paying and folded the receipt into his wallet. Tax deductible too. Pamela smiled and said thank you.

They drove back to the office in silence too. She needed to pick up her car to go and collect Jack from nursery. Tom twisted towards her as he stopped the car.

'You know it can't happen again,' she said.

'I know,' he answered. 'But thanks anyway.'

'Friends?' she asked.

'Friends,' he agreed. He picked her hand up and lightly kissed her palm.

She sighed. 'You know what you should do now?'

'What?' He looked less tired and drawn than he had before.

'Go and buy the biggest bunch of roses you can find and take them home to Shirley.'

He smiled. 'I think I might just do that.'

'Tell her how much you love her.'

He placed Pamela's hand back in her lap. 'I do love her, you know,' he said quietly.

'I understand that now.' She understood Jamie's situation too. She understood it, but she still didn't like it.

She got out of the car and stood leaning into the open door. 'There's one other thing that you ought to do too, Tom.'

He raised an eyebrow in query.

'This time make an appointment with Relate.' She blew him a kiss and closed the door.

Chapter Twenty

Jamie felt like a complete heel as he drove away from the house to Leighton Buzzard on Saturday morning. Francesca and Barbie were waving wildly. Pamela stood holding Jack on her hip, looking suitably forlorn and abandoned.

He hadn't seen Teri since he had promised to spend the weekend with her. She hadn't been on the train for two days or waiting at the End of the Line Buffet with his usual polystyrene cup of warm battery-acid coffee. And she hadn't been into work.

At night he had sneaked out with MacTavish to the public phone at the end of the road, but the line had been constantly engaged. MacTavish, who wasn't known for his enduring patience, whined incessantly despite all manner of hideous threats, and Jamie had been forced to return home without being able to find out if the weekend was still on.

He had wanted to cancel. Heaven knows, this had gone far enough. Charlie had given him another pep-talk about the ethical and moral responsibilities of marriage and fatherhood, and this time he had listened. Truly listened. It was just so much more difficult to end than it had been to start.

He parked outside Teri's house feeling more like a prisoner on his way to execution than a lover on his way to a secret tryst. He pulled his holdall from the boot of the car. Pamela had remained tight-lipped in the kitchen as he had packed the few paltry things that he needed.

He rang the doorbell and leaned against the wall surveying the row of identical houses, individualised only by the differing colour of their front doors. Even then, white seemed to be the most popular choice.

An elderly woman opened the door, which took Jamie by surprise. She was small and tubby, and had wiry grey hair curled in the same style as the Queen, which made her look older than she probably was – just like the Queen. Someone should get them both a new hairdresser, Jamie thought absently.

'You must be the television repair man,' she said affably, glancing at his holdall. 'Therese said she was expecting you. Come in, dear.' She turned and went inside.

'No, I'm . . .' Jamie looked round to check that she wasn't talking to anyone else and then followed her, perplexed.

Teri was lying on the sofa, covered by a duvet and looking suitably pale. 'Hi,' she said feebly. 'You've come to fix the television.'

Jamie's eyes widened in disbelief.

'Would you like a nice cup of tea, dear?' the Queen's sister said.

He nodded and he wasn't sure why.

'I'll go and put the kettle on then.' She went out into the kitchen and left the door open behind her.

'Be careful what you say,' Teri advised in a whisper. 'She's got ESP.'

Jamie looked impressed. 'ESP?'

'Extra Sticky-beak Power.'

'Oh.' Jamie lowered his voice. 'TV repair man?'

Teri gave a resigned look. 'Sorry,' she mouthed. 'It was the first thing that came into my head.'

He eyed the duvet suspiciously. 'What *is* the matter?'

'My mother,' she mouthed silently.

'I can see that, but what the hell's she doing here?' he whispered. 'Now? *This* weekend?'

Teri sank into her pillow. 'It's a long story.'

He tapped his foot impatiently and watched the kitchen door, whence a badly hummed rendition of *The Archers* theme tune was wafting. 'Well?' he urged, when she seemed reluctant to say any more.

She rolled her eyes and propped herself up on her elbows. 'I came home and ate all the food I bought the other night.'

'All of it?'

'And drank the whole bottle of champagne,' she added regretfully.

'What, you mean *all* the smoked salmon?' he whispered incredulously. Teri nodded. 'And the tiger prawns?' She nodded again. 'The rainbow-trout mousse too?'

'And the caviar and all of the caramel meringue thingies.' Teri had gone green.

'I'm surprised you weren't sick!'

'I *was* sick,' Teri snapped, 'just as my mother happened to phone. I thought it was you and made the fatal mistake of answering it, and it was *her*!'

On cue, Mrs Carter popped her head round the door. She waved a J-cloth like a lace hanky. 'Don't let me keep you from your work, dear. The tea can be brewing while you fix the set. I don't want to miss the omnibus episode of *Brookside*, do I?'

Teri collapsed back on to her pillow.

'What am I supposed to do now?' Jamie hissed.

'Turn the telly on. Look like you're fixing it.'

'I wasn't talking about the television, I was talking about us,' he said, as he obediently turned the television on and it blazed into life. 'Hey – there's nothing wrong with this.'

'I thought you knew nothing about televisions?'

He shot her a withering glare. 'I know a bloody healthy one when I see it. How am I supposed to look as if I'm fixing it?'

'Turn it to the satellite channels and keep flicking through them – they're all ghosting like mad at the moment. There must be a storm brewing.' He treated her to another glare which she ignored. 'Tell her that it's due to atmospheric pressure and that normal viewing of *Brookside* will be totally unaffected. That should do the trick. It's mainly MTV that's squiffy anyway and I don't think she'll want to watch that. Unless Tom Jones is on it,' she added thoughtfully.

'I've been trying to phone you, but it's been permanently engaged,' Jamie said, trying to keep one eye on the door and the other eye on scanning the channels.

'As I was saying, she phoned just as I was being sick. She was on the first train down from Lime Street the next morning and has been phoning all my relatives the length and breadth of the country ever since to tell them how desperately ill I am. She thinks it's food poisoning. She's convinced that you can only get salmonella from smoked salmon. How can I tell her all I had was a ruddy great hangover brought on by my married lover abandoning me with nothing for comfort but a surfeit of fine food and cheap champagne?'

Jamie looked at her reprovingly.

'Don't look at me like that,' she said through her teeth. 'I normally watch my diet very carefully, except when I'm bingeing.'

'You could have phoned.'

'Oh yes – how? What could I say? "Sorry to disturb you, Pamela, but my interfering mother has turned up so could you possibly tell Jamie our weekend love-in is cancelled." ' Teri twitched her head towards the door. 'Old Miss Marple in there doesn't miss a trick.'

'Milk or sugar?' her mother called.

They stared at each other blankly. 'Just milk, please,' Jamie replied.

'She'll be here for days,' Teri said tersely. 'She's harder to get rid of than curry breath.'

Her mother appeared with a tray of tea. 'Haven't you fixed it yet, dear?' she asked Jamie. 'It is taking you a long time.'

'Nearly finished,' he said tightly.

'Can't we offer Jamie a biscuit, Mum?'

'Jamie, is it? My, we're little miss friendly.'

Teri closed her eyes momentarily. 'Jamie is a friend – an *old* friend. I told you. He fixes televisions for a lot of people I know.'

Jamie scowled at her blackly.

'Do you like Jaffa Cakes?' Mrs Carter asked, nose wrinkled. 'All she ever has is Jaffa Cakes.'

Jamie smiled sweetly. 'They're my favourites.'

'I can't stand them myself,' her mother said, and disappeared into the kitchen.

Jamie waited until she had gone. He turned to Teri and asked his original question again. 'And what am I supposed to do now?'

'I don't know.' Teri sounded exasperated. 'Go home.'

'I can't do that. I'm on a course.'

'What sort of course?'

'Management Ethics,' he said reluctantly.

'Management Ethics,' she repeated incredulously.

'That's what Pamela said,' he snapped. 'It was the first thing that came into my head. So that makes us equal for the television repair man.'

'If you can't go home, go to a hotel then.'

'Thanks a bunch!' Jamie punched at the channel buttons.

'Look, I'm really sorry. There's nothing I can do about it.' Teri turned to check the kitchen door. She lowered her voice. 'This is exactly how I feel when you let me down. It can't be helped. We'll have to do it another time.'

'You have no idea what it has cost me to get here for you this weekend, do you?'

'I take it we're talking emotional cost here rather than petrol money?'

'Have you done this to punish me?'

Teri sagged against the pillows. 'Oh Jamie, don't ever think like that – if you do, we're finished.' Her eyes were bright with tears. 'You know I'm as disappointed as you are.'

'Here are your Jaffa Cakes, dear.' Her mother waltzed back into the lounge and put the plate on the coffee table after dusting it with the J-cloth. 'It's nice to see you've put a bit of colour back in her cheeks. She looks all pink and flushed.' A worried look crossed her mother's face. 'You're not going to be sick again, are you, dear? I'll get the plastic bucket if you are.'

Teri's face went from pink to puce. 'No, I'm not going to be sick.'

'Look, I'm finished here.' Jamie picked up his holdall. 'I'll be on my way.'

'No Jaffa Cakes?' The older woman looked hurt.

'No, thank you.' Jamie started to back out of the room.

'I hope it's nothing I've said to put you off.' Her brow was wrinkled. 'I thought they were your favourites?'

'They usually are.' He glared at Teri. 'I'm suddenly not hungry.'

Teri's mother followed him with the plate of biscuits. 'Just one?'

'No, thanks.'

'Just a little one?'

'No, really.'

'There's hardly any calories in them.'

'Well, okay then.' He took a Jaffa Cake, realising that he wasn't going to be let out until he did. 'Thank you.'

Mrs Carter glanced at the television. 'This still doesn't look right to me. There's all wiggly lines and shadows.'

'Ghosting,' Jamie said, confidently pointing at the screen with his Jaffa Cake.

The woman's eyes followed a solitary crumb that fell to the floor. 'It's due to atmospheric tension,' he added meekly.

'Pressure,' Teri snapped.

He grabbed the remote control and switched to Channel Four. 'Look – perfect.' He smiled encouragingly at Teri's mother. 'No problem with *Brookside* now.'

'Good,' she beamed benevolently. 'I can't live without my weekly dose of emotional turmoil, can you, dear?'

'I could give it a try.' He glanced meaningfully at Teri. 'Goodness, is that the time?' He looked at his wrist and realised he wasn't wearing his watch. 'So many televisions to fix and so little time.'

'Well, it was very nice to meet you, young man,' Teri's mother said. 'It was almost worth having a broken television for, wasn't it, dear?'

Teri, blanched against the pillow, had closed her eyes.

'Say goodbye, Therese,' her mother instructed.

'Goodbye Therese,' Teri said without opening her eyes.

Her mother tutted. 'I'll show you to the door.' She ushered Jamie outside, where she whispered conspiratorially, 'You ought to pop round again. We'd like to see you and Therese makes a very nice casserole. Not just stew, casserole. She's a very good cook. She takes after me.'

'Thank you, I'll remember that.'

'Well, goodbye now,' she said loudly and winked.

'Yes,' Jamie said uncertainly. 'Goodbye.'

He was back in the Volvo clutching his holdall and his Jaffa Cake, not knowing what to do with either of them before Teri's mother closed the door. 'Shit,' he said loudly to himself and stuffed the whole Jaffa Cake into his mouth.

Teri's mother peeped out of the curtain as Jamie started the car and drove off down the road. 'He's a very nice young man.' She turned to Teri, who had not yet dared to open her eyes.

'He's not a young man – he's thirty-seven,' she said tartly.

Her mother bristled. 'That's young in my book.'

Teri remained silent.

'Anyway, at least he's not got three earrings in every ear like most of them have these days. And he watches his figure. I had to press him to take one tiny little Jaffa Cake.' Mrs Carter reluctantly let the curtain drop back into place. 'You ought to find yourself someone like that,

Therese. You're not getting any younger.'

'Thank you, Mother.' She would ring Clare as soon as she was better and beg her forgiveness.

Her mother wagged her finger. 'You mark my words, young lady, he'd make someone a very nice husband.'

Teri opened her eyes. 'You had better get that plastic bucket – I think I *am* going to be sick, after all.'

Chapter Twenty-One

Jamie took the scenic route back to Milton Keynes, twisting through Soulbury before crossing over the Grand Union Canal and heading up the hill, past the golf club and through Great Brickhill. It was a sharp, sunny day and groups of golfers pulled their trolleys round the course that bordered the canal – which was probably half-full of their golf balls. Jamie envied them, wishing he'd had the sense to keep a set of clubs in the boot of the Volvo. Bright shoots of green sprouted from the hedges along the tight lanes and spoke of the promises of youthfulness and hope. It depressed Jamie intensely.

He had hit the roundabout at the bottom of the A5 before he decided where he was going to go. Briefly, he considered phoning Charlie Perry and bumming a room for the weekend, but two things had persuaded him against that course of action.

For one, Charlie was unlikely to be up at this hour, given the normal aftermath of his Friday-night entertainment, and secondly, he was bound to give him a lecture – an even longer one than he had dished out last time and Jamie wasn't sure he could stomach that just now.

Teri was right, he had to go to a hotel. How could he

return home now, especially after Pamela had been so scathing about Management Ethics. No way could he simply turn up and announce that the course had been cancelled. She could dine out on that story for the rest of the year. Anyway, she might have organised a wild night in, out or shaking all about with the grease-ball. It was hardly fair of him to pour cold water on that, just because his own extramarital aerobics had failed to get off the ground.

How on earth could Gordy *enjoy* having affairs?

Jamie groaned aloud. It was beginning to feel like a nightmare from which he would never wake up.

Driving through Milton Keynes on a Saturday was like driving through a ghost town. All it lacked was a bit of tumbleweed blowing down the dual carriageway. Most of the activity seemed to be centred round the shopping centre and there were never any traffic jams anyway – except when there was a pop concert on at The Bowl, when the whole of the city became gridlocked.

The city was like a little bit of America plopped down in the middle of a flattened square of Buckinghamshire countryside – a maze of vertical and horizontal roads that looked completely identical. There were no distinguishing features or landmarks, which meant that visitors got hopelessly lost. You couldn't say to someone, 'Turn left at the Dog and Duck,' because all the Dogs and Ducks were secreted away in housing estates. Instead, the roundabouts had been given names to try to help matters, but this had failed miserably.

The sun glinted off the glass slab-sided buildings, which had all been restricted to low-rise elevations; they epitomised the total lack of character of the city. The exception was The Point, an entertainment centre shaped like a pyramid that could be seen for miles around when all of its red neon lights were working.

As a student, Jamie had travelled a bit – it had once been one of his aims in life 'to travel'. He hadn't ever seen himself in a cottage in North Wales playing ball on a wind-lashed beach with two hyperactive children and a depressed wife. He had spent one summer in India, one in Morocco. Lands of gaudy colours, the gaggingly pungent smell of stale spices and unwashed bodies, the deafening babble of incoherent sounds and stomach-churning sights to assault the senses.

There are no snake-charmers in Milton Keynes. Or water-sellers to harass you into buying water that tastes as if it has been produced by themselves. Or amateur dentists pulling teeth out on the streets with nothing more than a pair of pliers. Or hands that clutch at you as you walk, raking you with hard eyes more intimately than is comfortable, dirty un-innocent faces hissing aggressively '*Rupee, rupee*' or '*Dirham, dirham*' – the mantra to part you from your money. In fact, there aren't any people on the streets at all. But there are roundabouts – lots of them – and trees. Millions of them. At one time there were more trees than people. Although Jamie wasn't sure if that was the case any more. So many of the trees had been vandalised.

In Milton Keynes everything is monochromatic, straight and neat and the air smells of nothing. To make up for this absence of environmental stimulus there are the concrete cows. They stand in a field near the main London to Glasgow line and are black and white-splotched – more manic Dalmatian dog than a true representation of a British dairy herd. Stiff-legged and angular, they looked like the sort of painting Francesca would do of a cow.

Jamie drove past them, feeling melancholy for the days when all cows in fields had been real, but they could no longer be seen clearly from the road due to the millions of trees. He followed the V's and H's – vertical and horizontal roads – until he came to The Happy Lodge. It was a sad brick building that resembled an abandoned Tesco's. He took his pathetic-looking holdall and went inside.

The bored blonde on Reception popped her chewing gum in one side of her mouth as he approached.

'Do you have a room vacant? Just for tonight.'

'Four oh five.'

Jamie shrugged. 'Four?'

'No. Four *oh* five.'

'Sorry,' Jamie laughed. 'I thought you said . . .'

She glared at him ferociously.

'Never mind.'

'Second floor.' She handed him the key card and went back to chewing the cud.

Room 405 on the second floor. Shouldn't it be on the fourth floor? Looking at the top of the receptionist's head, he decided not to pass comment. Jamie found it, surprisingly, on the second floor. It was a pleasant room. The same as any hotel room in any hotel in any city, anywhere in the world – but pleasant nevertheless.

After unpacking his holdall to give him something to do, he then wondered how he would fill the next twenty-four hours. He examined the wicker basket in the bathroom filled with minuscule toiletries, checked his nearest fire exit from the diagram on the back of the door, read the hotel directory from front to back, glanced at his watch and still only ten minutes had passed.

He opened the mini-bar and pulled out a cold beer –

despite the fact that the sun was nowhere near over the yard-arm. Kicking off his shoes he lay on the bed and reached for the television remote control, struggling to find the right button to switch it on. So much for the TV repair man in him.

It wasn't the same watching *Grandstand* without Jack bouncing on his lap or Francesca trying to plait his hair. He could actually hear what the commentator was saying – and what a load of old twaddle it was! – and watch the motor racing without two grubby fingers trying to explore his nose. Damon Hill had just spun his car on a practise lap and he had been able to watch all six of the slow-motion action replays without having to read something out of *Thomas the Tank Engine* in a forced Ringo Starr accent. It was altogether too peaceful.

He drained his beer and padded across the room, bringing the entire contents of the mini-bar back with him, cradled in his arms. He dumped all the bottles on the bed. There were three more beers. Two whiskies, two brandies, two vodkas. Two tomato juices, two lemonades and two Dry Gingers. Two ordinary Cokes and two sugar-free, caffeine-free Cokes – which presumably meant two tins of fizzy coloured water and a load of E numbers. Two packets of honey-roasted peanuts, two packets of cashew nuts and two packets of pork scratchings – which looked suspiciously like old toenail cuttings. There was also a bar of expensive Swiss chocolate which was too cold to bite into; when he tried, he decided to leave it until it had warmed up a bit, rather than risk losing a tooth.

Perhaps he should follow the Therese Carter School of Therapy and drink all of the attractive little bottles in front of him as a means of attaining oblivion from his current predicament. He started on another beer.

Suddenly there was a high-pitched giggle from the room next door and the creak of bedsprings as something heavy – and still giggling – was dropped on the bed. These walls were paperthin. Jamie turned Murray Walker up.

A steady, rhythmic banging began in the next room, and the headboard beat a familiar tattoo against the wall behind Jamie's head. He groaned and increased the volume of Murray Walker, who was also winding himself up to a climax of feverish incoherence. The banging became quicker and so did Murray. On the screen Murray shouted ecstatically about Damon Hill. In the next room someone shouted ecstatically, 'Oh yes!'

There was a brief respite during which Jamie's jangled nerves started to recover. He left the television on loud in the hope that the lovers would realise there was someone within earshot and would curb their passion – or at least curb their noise. But there is something about unbridled lust that makes one oblivious to anyone else's discomfort . . .

When the headboard and the earth started to move again, Jamie resignedly drained his beer and reached for the last one. After this it would be on to the hard stuff. What sort of perverts came to The Happy Lodge on a Saturday afternoon and bonked themselves senseless anyway? *Lucky ones*, Jamie thought bitterly.

Chapter Twenty-Two

Pamela answered the telephone. It was a man's voice.

'Could I speak to James Duncan, please?' She didn't recognise the voice. It was refined, clipped.

'I'm afraid he's away for the weekend. On a course,' she added without thinking.

'Oh.' There was a long pause.

'This is his wife. Can I take a message?'

'It's very important that I get hold of him.'

'I haven't got a contact number for him.' It was a lie; she knew exactly where he was. The thought made Pamela feel irritable. 'Who am I speaking to?' she said shortly.

'You don't know me,' the man answered. 'My name's Richard Wellbeloved. I'm a . . . a friend of Charlie Perry's. I'm afraid I have some bad news.'

'There's a woman on the phone for you, Therese,' her mother said. 'Very posh, won't say who she is.'

Teri struggled from beneath the weight of the duvet and stretched like a contented cat before walking to the phone – despite the fact that she was still feeling less than contented.

'Teri Carter,' she said, much more brightly than she felt.

No one spoke for a few seconds, then the woman said: 'This is Pamela Duncan.' Her voice was tight. 'Can I speak to Jamie, please?'

There was another uncomfortable silence as Teri tried to find her voice which, coward that it was, seemed to have deserted her. 'He isn't here,' she said eventually.

'Don't play games with me,' Pamela snapped. 'I need to speak to him urgently.' There was another pause and Jamie's wife sounded as if she was struggling to control her emotions. 'I wouldn't have phoned otherwise. I'm not in the habit of humiliating myself unnecessarily.'

'I'm being serious,' Teri said. She smiled at her mother and kicked the door closed. Her smile died. 'He wasn't able to stay.'

'Where the hell is he then?'

'I don't know. I think he was going to find a hotel.'

'Do you know where?'

'No. No, I'm sorry I don't.'

'Well, if he contacts you, tell him to get his lying backside home as quickly as possible.'

'Is there something wrong?' Of course there was – why else would she phone?

'Nothing that need concern you.' The phone went dead.

Pamela put the phone down with shaking hands. Her stomach was twisted into a tight knot and her mouth was dry. The girl had sounded even younger than she had on the answerphone, but less confident than Pamela had expected.

Why wasn't Jamie there? What had gone wrong? If he hadn't been able to stay, why hadn't he come home?

Even through the unanswered questions there was a

faint hope pushing up like a weed through a pavement. He hadn't spent the weekend with Her.

But where the hell was he? Teri said she thought he had gone to a hotel. Pamela pulled the *Yellow Pages* out of the drawer. She would try the most obvious place first. The place where pain and pleasure met, sin and solace, love and lust. The Happy Lodge. She dialled the number.

They had been at it for more than three hours, virtually non-stop. Jamie was feeling exhausted just listening to them. Murray Walker had given way to another less exuberant commentator, presumably while he refreshed himself in the BBC's hospitality suite. Even Murray couldn't keep going for three hours unabated.

Soon the shred of plasterboard that separated the two rooms was bound to give and spill the copulating couple right on to his bed. Jamie had tried banging back on the wall – although it made him feel like a complete spoilsport – but this had done nothing to quell their ardour.

He was sipping the second of the miniature whiskies straight from the bottle, alternating it with sips from the Dry Ginger bottle in his other hand when the telephone rang. He put the whisky bottle between his teeth, turned down Muddly Talker's counterpart with the remote control and put the receiver to his ear.

'Hello,' he said into the whisky bottle.

'It's Pamela.'

He swung guiltily off the bed and put the whisky down. 'How did you know I was here?'

'I've just spoken to Teri. After that it was an educated guess.' She sounded philosophical rather than annoyed.

'Oh.' Jamie was confused. 'Is everything all right?'

'No.' Now he could hear the strain in her voice.

A lump blocked his throat. 'Is it the kids?' He would never forgive himself if anything happened to them.

'No, they're fine, but you need to come home right away.'

'I can't.'

'What do you mean, you can't?'

Jamie answered sheepishly. 'I've been working my way through the mini-bar. I'm not in a fit state to drive.'

'Oh, for goodness sake, Jamie!'

'I'm sorry.' It seemed an inadequate thing to say in the circumstances.

'Look, I'll come and get you. I'll see if Melanie's around to look after the children.'

'Can't you tell me what's wrong?' There was a feeling of dread rising in him, darkening his mood.

'It's Charlie,' was all she said.

'I'm in room four oh five,' Jamie offered. 'Pamela, are you still there?'

Her voice was barely audible. 'I'll be with you as soon as I can.'

Chapter Twenty-Three

Charlie lay deathly still on the bed. His face was as white as the hospital sheets and there were dark unnatural circles round his closed eyes. His normally effervescent curls were plastered flat to his head with sweat, making it look as if someone had shaved his skull. He looked older and more haggard than he normally did after a night on the tiles – and that was really saying something. Upturned on the bed, his wrists swathed in bandages still seeped tell-tale lines of blood.

'Good grief,' Jamie said. 'You look like Uncle Fester from the Addams Family.' He pulled the nearest plastic chair over to Charlie's bed and sat down heavily.

Charlie opened his eyes and smiled. It was a weak, feeble smile that didn't reach his eyes. 'What are you doing here?'

'I'm here on behalf of the Mutual and Providential management to make sure that you're not just skiving.' Jamie picked some grapes off the bunch from the bedside table next to Charlie's. The occupant was asleep and unaware that his fruit was being pilfered. 'Actually, you asked for me when you were coming round. Richard phoned to tell us.'

Charlie stared at the ceiling, where a whirling fan made

an ineffectual attempt to provide a breeze in the stuffy, disinfectant-scented heat.

'I don't know what to say, Charlie. I had no idea.'

He looked squarely at Jamie. 'What – that I was gay or that my lover had left me?'

'Both, you silly bugger. Oh, sorry.'

Charlie grinned. 'It's all right, dear boy, you can still be politically incorrect with me.'

Jamie sighed. 'So how long have you been . . .'

'Homosexual?'

'If you want to put it like that.'

'Years, dear boy.'

'But I thought we were best friends, Charlie! How come you never told me? I thought you were one of the lads – a man's man and all that sort of macho crap.'

'Some of us are.'

Jamie's brow was furrowed. 'And what about all those busty blondes you brought to the office parties?'

'All front, old chap – me, not them.'

He looked at Charlie's mutilated wrists and twitched his head. 'So what caused this?'

'Richard left me – two weeks ago.' He cleared his throat. 'We'd been together ten years. He came back last night to collect his things. That's when I decided to do a re-enactment of *Psycho* with me playing Norman Bates *and* Marion Crane.'

Jamie looked puzzled. 'Marion Crane?'

'She was the one in the shower,' Charlie explained. 'Janet Leigh. It was her finest moment. Don't tell me you're too young to remember. If I remember, so should you.' Jamie still looked blank.

Charlie shook his head impatiently, then sighed heavily and bit his lower lip. 'I made a terrible mess of the grouting.' His eyes filled with tears. 'Richard's set up home with a twenty-one-year-old television presenter called Jez with pierced nipples and a sperm whale tattooed on his penis. How can I compete with that?'

Jamie shook his head incredulously. 'I'm not sure that you should want to.'

'Perhaps you're right,' he said listlessly.

'Why didn't you say something, damn you! You should have said you were feeling so . . .'

'Suicidal?' Charlie smiled ruefully. 'You can't just drop something like that into the conversation. Besides, you've got problems of your own, love.'

Jamie stole some more grapes. 'Tell me about it.'

'I didn't think you'd take kindly to my moralising if you'd realised that my own life was more tangled and shredded than clothes in a clapped-out washer-dryer.'

'I didn't take kindly to your moralising anyway, but only because what you were saying was true.'

'This is the sort of thing that happens, Jamie, when love goes wrong.' Charlie held his wrists up. 'This is the reality of affairs. The pain of broken promises. It's not all hearts and flowers and forgiveness and friendly little tête-à-têtes over the custody arrangements. Speaking of which – where is the lovely Pamela?'

'The lovely Pamela is sitting in the rather seedy-looking café just down the hall, nursing a coffee and probably contemplating which particular vice of mine to cite on her divorce papers. Do you want me to get her?'

Charlie shook his head. 'I'd rather she didn't see me like this.' He plucked disdainfully at his NHS nightie. 'Just give her my love.'

'I think I need to give her *my* love before anyone else's,' Jamie said wearily.

'Are things any better?'

'I don't think they've ever been worse,' he admitted. 'She knows about Teri.'

Charlie winced.

A look of concern crossed Jamie's face. 'Are you in pain?'

'No. I'm wincing for you, not me.' Charlie waved his bandaged wrist dismissively and winced again.

Jamie settled back in his chair and popped another grape in his mouth. 'Do you think things can ever get back to normal?'

'What's normal, dear boy?'

'Now there's a question.' Jamie rubbed his chin. It was heavy with stubble. 'You know, just Pamela, me, the kids, the mortgage.'

'I think that's really down to you, Jamie.'

Jamie stretched and yawned till the tears came to his eyes. 'You don't fancy getting out of that bed and going for a walk, so that I can have a nice lie down?'

'No, I don't.'

'I thought you'd say that.'

'It's time you were running along – you don't want to keep Pamela waiting. I'll be all right.' Charlie glanced at the slumbering occupant in the next bed. 'It would be nice if the fractured femur had some grapes left when he woke up, too.'

'Are you sure you'll be okay?'

Charlie nodded.

'Has anyone else been to see you?'

'No. I've told Richard to stay away.' He gestured at the nurses. 'These poor creatures have enough to deal with, without my histrionics.'

'What about your parents?'

'Mater and Pater? They don't know my circumstances. Old school, you know. Not sure that women should have the vote, men should still do National Service, bring back hanging. I don't think they'd understand. They think I'm a reprehensible rogue, nothing but a debauched dilettante. And I *do* have my reputation to keep up.'

'I'll come again tomorrow.'

'That would be nice.' He looked exhausted. 'Bring some grapes.'

Jamie put his hand on top of Charlie's. 'I love you, Charlie.' His voice was choked with emotion.

Charlie's eyes widened. 'That's a poofy sort of thing to say.'

'Naff off, Charles.' Jamie was embarrassed. He brushed his eyes with the back of his hand. 'You know what I mean.'

'I've never fancied you anyway. You're not my type.'

'I'm glad to hear it.'

'Go on, go and be nice to your wife.'

Jamie stood up. 'I'd shake your hand,' he nodded at the bandages, 'but I'm afraid it would come off.'

'Still firmly attached, old boy. I'm not much good at that either,' he said sadly.

'Stick to insurance then.'

'I'll take your advice, if you take mine.'

'No more amateur butchery?'

'Wouldn't dream of it, dear boy.'

'Good. I'll see you tomorrow.'

Charlie closed his eyes. 'Tomorrow.'

Jamie patted Charlie's hand and walked slowly down the ward. Charlie opened his eyes and watched him – his broad straight back and his mop of dark unruly hair even more unkempt than usual. He saw the nurse's eyes follow him, her attention distracted from the mundane task of tucking the man with the bandaged head and two black eyes back into his bed.

Charlie put his hand to his mouth. 'I love you too, James,' he said quietly.

Chapter Twenty-Four

Neither Jamie nor Pamela noticed the car parked just further down the road in Fraughton-next-the-Green. Teri had been sitting there for half an hour already. She had lured her mother from the house with the promise of an hour's shopping in Marks & Spencer's, but Mrs Carter was less than pleased when rather than the girlie expedition of retail therapy she expected, Teri had dumped her at the store's doors and promptly disappeared.

It had taken her ages to find Fraughton-next-the-Green. She knew her way to the shopping centre and back with her eyes closed, but once you strayed off the beaten track in Milton Keynes you were in uncharted territory. You could end up going round and round in circles for days and never find the place you wanted. All the houses looked the same, all the roads looked the same. And not knowing whether you wanted to be Vertical or Horizontal was a bit like not knowing your elbow from another part of your anatomy. She had even taken the precaution of studying her map book before leaving, but it was out of date and Fraughton-next-the-Green was marked as a pink blob with the words *Undeveloped Land* stamped unhelpfully on it.

Eventually, she had stumbled across it by accident and

at first she had thought it was a mirage brought on by severe disorientation. Fraughton was indeed next-the-Green. It was also next-the-olde-worlde-pub and next-the-village-pond, across which two swans swanned majestically. White-clad men played cricket on the Green, while people sat around in deck chairs and straw hats and clapped genteelly. Wild flowers grew in the neat grass verges and there was no litter or graffiti on the bus shelter. It was as if Milton Keynes had been involved in a head-on crash with *Trumpton*.

Jamie's house was set further down the road than the Green – away from the main 'action'. He was right when he said the house was a mix of architecture. It looked as if someone had cut several pictures out of *Homes and Gardens*, thrown them up in the air and then built what landed. There were pillars and porticoes, balconies and balustrades, all topped with a thatched roof – a peculiar blend of Regency, Georgian, Suffolk and Southfork.

The house had a circular gravel drive with a circular lawn in the middle of it, and in the middle of that Jamie pushed a Flymo about with purpose. Behind him Francesca followed with a child-sized rake. Jack sat in a plastic car with blue wheels and a yellow roof and Pamela helped him as he struggled to steer it through the gravel. She looked how she sounded. Cool, confident, controlled.

Collectively they looked like something out of Disney. All the scene needed was a few talking flowers and some cartoon rabbits hopping about, and they would have had their next blockbuster on their hands.

Pamela disappeared indoors and reappeared moments later with a tray of drinks. The family huddled together as she benevolently dished them out. Jamie took his drink and squeezed her affectionately round the shoulders. He squeezed Teri's heart painfully at the same time. Mr and Mrs Bun the Baker and their chubby-cheeked children Master Bun and Miss Bun had been less of a happy family than this lot.

How could she ever have thought that she was destined to share any part of his life? This was her dream – big house, two big cars, two angelic children, a look of quiet contentment and a hunk of a husband. This was what she thought about when she lay awake at night in her seventies box, imagining Jamie's humped shape slumbering beside her in the bed. It was her dream – but someone else was living it in her place.

So much for his wife not understanding him. It was the oldest line in the book and she had fallen for it. He was never going to leave all this for her. She must have been a fool to think that he ever would. Clare would put on her Sister Mary Bernadette voice and say, 'I told you so.'

As far as she could tell, Jamie had made only three lapses from utter perfection in his life. One was marrying another woman before he'd given himself the chance to meet her. The second was buying this house – which wasn't so much a statement of sartorial taste as a demonstration of cash over common sense. It was a house that screamed 'First Division footballer' – not 'insurance executive'. She could picture the architect now – the type of man who would park a Ferrari in the drive and would consider circular houses *de rigueur*. The type of man who would design the rooms with the lounge in between the kitchen and the dining room without a thought to the mess the transient food would make on the shag pile. It must be more his wife's style – although she'd had the good taste to marry Jamie.

The third slip was the flea-bitten hound that had just bounded into the Disney film set. It should have been white and fluffy and wagged its tail in time with the catchy signature tune written by Tim Rice that also should have been tinkling away in the background. This mutt was a cross between a doormat and the sort of Afghan coat that was briefly fashionable among the less discerning hippies during the late seventies. It clearly had more varieties than Heinz could ever hope to offer. Its fur stood on end, giving the impression its nose had recently been pressed into a live electric socket, and its tail wagged erratically in short staccato bursts that enhanced the effect.

This dog was the only thing that bound them all to earth. Its tatty presence reassured her that she hadn't slipped quietly into a virtual reality game of 'Mr and Mrs Perfect and their perfect lives'. This dog was the only anchor to sanity.

She looked away from the tableau in front of her. How was she going to face Jamie on the train tomorrow? It would be best to avoid him, but she needed to find out what had happened yesterday. She could consider commuting by coach. There was a coach that left from the end of her road at some ungodly hour in the morning. It took hours to get into London, but it was a fraction of the cost and they all drank whisky and played poker and had wild affairs with each other to pass the time. The locals called it 'The Love Coach'. She had tried it once. Whether it was the lure of cheap travel, whisky or the possibility of a wild affair, she was unsure now. On the first morning she had been violently sick just outside Hemel Hempstead and the driver had been forced to stop for her. Everyone had been very cross and unsympathetic and late for work, and she hadn't dared try it again. Not one of the men had looked like potential affair material anyway.

She drove away from Fraughton-next-the-Green unsure why she had come, and now that she *had* come, unsure exactly what she would do about it. Her biological clock was ticking away as loudly as the clock in the crocodile's mouth in *Peter Pan*. Except that unlike Peter Pan, this clock was reminding her that she was aging. She could feel her collagen fibres binding as she spoke. Her hormones were hurtling her headlong into hirsuteness – her oestrogen was on the way out and her progesterone on the verge of pulling the plug. That was why she was so desperate for a promotion: if she had fulfilment at work and a grotesque amount of money, perhaps there wouldn't be this empty yearning inside her, this desire to wear Laura Ashley smocks and float round the garden cutting roses, this ache to know that Braxton Hicks wasn't a character in *Dallas* but a kind of contraction, and talk about breaking waters and *not* mean the seaside . . .

Her mother, spent up at Marks & Spencer's, for once had the sensitivity not to break the solemn silence in the car. The deluge would probably come, but she seemed to realise that now wasn't the time, and Teri's heart went out to the chubby, elderly lady next to her who had the unfortunate affliction of sharing the Queen's hairdo.

The telephone was ringing as they pushed through the pile of free newspapers and leaflets advertising double-glazing bargains behind the front door. Teri was sure that every time she went out – even for five minutes – people leapt out of hiding in her bushes and pushed free newspapers and junk mail through her door. When she answered the phone, it was Clare.

Her friend sounded bright and bubbly, which made Teri feel even flatter. 'I'm sorry I haven't phoned, Teri. I've been terribly busy.'

'I thought you were sulking.'

'Me? No! I know that you can be thoughtless, heartless and totally selfish when you want to be, Therese, but I'm not one to bear grudges. Besides, I've been far too busy to sulk.'

'Go on then. What have you been doing?' Teri settled herself on the bottom stair. Her mother made a capital T with her fingers and Teri nodded.

'David came back to me!' she shrieked.

'Oh Clare, I'm so pleased for you,' Teri said gaily. Her heart sank deeper into the pit of her stomach. 'What happened?'

'Well, I decided to play it cool, after a month of sweating by the telephone, forcing myself not to ring. You know, Teri, I'm sure that giving up someone you love is worse than trying to give up chocolate – the withdrawal symptoms are terrible!'

This was just what Teri wanted to hear. Her mother opened the door and passed her a cup of tea. She mouthed, 'Thank you.'

'Anyway, after a month of no contact whatsoever – I didn't reply to his solicitor's letters, estate agents' calls, no midnight tearful phone calls, nothing – he simply abandoned the nubile bitch Anthea and begged me on bended knee to take me back. Can you believe it?'

'I'm really pleased for you,' she said numbly. 'What made him change his mind?'

'Sex,' Clare stated baldly. 'They were having it for breakfast, lunch and dinner with only a break for a Pot Noodle in between. And as you well know, Teri, Sister

Mary Bernadette always used to say "man cannot live by Pot Noodle alone".'

Teri twisted a tendril of hair round her finger. 'Actually, I think it was bread.'

Clare was affronted. 'I thought that was Marie Antoinette?'

'Er – that was cake.'

'Whatever,' Clare said dismissively.

Teri changed the subject. 'So how's it going now?'

'Heaven! I clasped him back to my bosom, Teri. I've ironed his shirts, I've performed sexual athletics in the bedroom, and in the back garden – but that's another story. I've fed him sumptuous specials from Delia Smith every night for dinner. Take it from me, Teri, even in the nineties the way to a man's heart is still first and foremost through his stomach rather than his genitalia.' Clare sighed. 'Generally, I've pandered to his every whim.'

'It sounds more like hell than heaven.'

'He has been languishing in my boundless stream of love and has thrown himself at my feet declaring himself a fool for ever leaving me.' Clare was jubilant.

'So everything in the garden of romance is rosy again?' Teri said with a twinge of jealousy.

'Absolutely marvellous,' she agreed triumphantly. 'I threw him out two weeks ago.'

'*What!*'

'Well, he was a bloody idiot! I knew that, you knew that, I just wanted him to realise it too.'

'So where is he?' Teri was stunned.

'I don't know. He's been phoning every night since declaring undying love to my answerphone.'

'I can't believe you,' Teri breathed. 'You're on a different planet from the rest of us.'

'You know he always had the hots for you, Teri. I'm surprised he never made a pass at you.'

'What's that got to do with anything?' she said warily.

'Mind you, I used to think you encouraged it sometimes.'

'That is grossly unfair – and untrue!'

Clare swept on, oblivious to her protest. 'Anyway, he's free now if you're interested.'

'Why should I want your cast-offs?'

'I seem to remember you rushing off with Stephen Whitely not five minutes after I'd broken his heart.'

'That was different! He had a Chopper bike and I was fickle then,' Teri seethed. 'Some of us have moved on since the playground.'

'Some of us have, Teri. Some of us,' Clare said benevolently. 'Still, that's another chapter of my life closed. Onwards and upwards. I'm dating a pilot called Dermot who, thankfully, is neither gay nor married. How are you and Thingy getting on, by the way?'

Teri checked that her mother was out of earshot. 'Jamie!' she snapped at Clare before relenting. 'I think it's grinding to a slow and painful halt. You can put on your Sister Mary Bernadette voice and say "I told you so".'

'Well, I hate to remind you, Teri, but I *did* tell you so.' She was right back at The Sacred Heart of Jesus primary school. 'If you would only listen to your Aunty Clare you'd save yourself a lot of pain. Remember when Michael Lacey wanted to meet you behind the bikesheds and I warned you that he was only after your body?'

'Clare, I was ten at the time.'

'And what did you get? Nothing but a quick snog and a—'

'Yes, thank you, Clare. I remember it very well.'

'You've suffered from cold sores there ever since.'

'Yes, you're right! I should have listened to you then.'

'And you should listen to me now. I'm so much wiser in the ways of the world than you are, Teri. You're an innocent abroad.'

'You were calling me a tart and a harlot and a ruthless adulteress last time we spoke.'

'I was cross because you were making me homeless. After begging me to come and stay with you –' Teri didn't actually remember any begging '– you then had the cheek to fling me out. Sometimes you can be so perverse.'

'You've spent months luring your husband back from the arms of another woman for the sole purpose of proving what a good thing he was missing – only to throw him out after two weeks – and you have the nerve to call *me* perverse!'

'I didn't phone to argue, Therese.'

Teri laughed. 'Why did you phone?'

'I want us to be friends again.'

'We never stopped being friends.' Teri sighed. 'I'm going to have to go, my mother's here and it sounds as if she's trying to demolish the kitchen.'

'Oh, give my love to her. I used to get on well with your mother.'

Teri nodded at the telephone. 'You have such a lot in common,' she said sweetly.

'Phone me,' Clare said.

'I will.'

'Teri,' Clare shouted, just as she was about to put the phone down.

'Yes?'

'Good luck with Jamie.'

'Thanks.' She was going to need it. Why did human

beings insist on making life unnecessarily complicated for themselves? It would be so much easier if we just simply fell in love with people who loved us back, who didn't have wives and children and life-threatening mortgages and emotional baggage and hang-ups and roving eyes and wandering hands and uncontrollable urges.

Teri padded back into the kitchen. Her heart still heavy from seeing Jamie in 'Toytown' with his wife and children. It put on a few more pounds when it saw what her mother was doing. Mrs Carter had removed the entire contents of the fridge, had spread them over every available work surface and was busy wiping down the inside with a J-cloth. 'How's Clare?' she asked, without looking up.

'Oh, she's . . . she's Clare,' Teri said philosophically.

'Good,' her mother replied. 'That's nice. I always liked Clare. She's got so much more *about* her than you have.' Teri stuck out her tongue at her mother's back.

Mrs Carter shook the J-cloth out. 'I'm going home tomorrow, Therese. You'll take me to the station, won't you, dear? You're looking much better now.'

She started to put the contents back into the fridge, examining them carefully – or as carefully as she could without her glasses – and wrinkling her nose at anything that looked remotely spicy.

'I think it was that nice young man who came to repair the television, myself.'

'Really?' Teri said sardonically.

Her mother ignored her. 'He seemed to buck you up no end. You know, you should ask him for a date. I watch *Top of the Pops*.' Mrs Carter wiggled her bottom. 'Take him to a rave or something – that's the sort of thing young people do these days.'

'That's the sort of thing sixteen-year-olds do these days, Mother. I'm over thirty years old.'

'Then you should have more confidence. You never used to be backwards at coming forwards. This is the nineties.' She wiped each egg with the J-cloth before putting them back. 'You've got equality. A boy only had to buy you two ounces of Uncle Joe's mint balls in my day and you were as good as engaged. One kiss outside the gate and the lights in our front room would be flashing on and off like the Blackpool illuminations. Things have changed. There's no need for you to sit on the shelf and wait for someone to take you down and give you a good dusting.'

'Thank you, Mother, I'll bear that in mind.'

'By the way, I bought some nice bits and pieces in Marks & Spencer's food hall. It's wonderful food, but I don't know how you can afford to shop in there all the time.'

'I can't.'

'I certainly can't on my pension. Anyway, you owe me thirty-two pounds and fifteen pence.'

'Thirty-two pounds and fifteen pence? What on earth did you buy – gold-plated chicken drumsticks?'

'I told you. Some nice bits and pieces.' Her mother lifted the Marks carrier bag on to the work surface and started to pull out the items one by one. 'I got some smoked salmon. Not my sort of thing really, but I'll force it down. I'd rather have a nice steak and kidney pudding, but I know you like it. Some rainbow-trout mousse. Some big prawns and some fancy-shaped little biscuit things.'

Teri had gone very pale. 'You haven't got any caviar in there, have you?'

'Don't be silly! Do you think I'm made of money? I did

get some sickly little meringues. Oh, and a bottle of their cheapest champagne. Still, it looks all right.' Her mother pulled the bottle out of the bag with a flourish. She frowned. 'What are you looking for, Teri? Is it your purse you're after?'

'No,' Teri said faintly. 'I suddenly don't feel very well at all, and this time I'm definitely going to need the plastic bucket.'

Chapter Twenty-Five

Pamela was going through his suit pockets. It was something that she had managed to avoid doing so far. She had also avoided pressing the last number redial facility on the phone every time he was out of the house, prising open his locked desk drawer and rifling through the contents of his briefcase – now that she had managed to work out his combination. He'd used their anniversary date – not very original, really.

However, this suit did need cleaning and Jamie had the habit of leaving a pile of business cards secreted in one of his pockets. There was something unavoidably grubby about commuting. She crammed his wardrobe with 'fragrance sachets' – nothing too flowery, woody scents of sandalwood, rosewood and patchouli – to dispel the lingering aura of city grime and diesel fumes. Despite using Sketchley's Gold Service, Jamie's suits could usually stand up by themselves within days. Collars and cuffs turned black at an alarming rate. Anti-perspirants might work well on television adverts showing people running around in the fresh air, but the manufacturers should do a bit of product-testing on commuter trains in the summer, when hot air belts out from the heating ducts unabated, and sweaty bodies are squashed together like

Swedes in a sauna. Just recently there had been an unseasonal hot spell, and the trains had been delayed all week.

There was a handkerchief in the top pocket of the suit – folded neatly, but decidedly dirty. Pamela pulled it out gingerly, holding it between her immaculate fingernails. It had been washed – but not by her. Whoever had done this didn't use Persil Automatic. There were faded red stains all over it that were probably lipstick, and when she shook it out to examine it further, a tidy little note fell out.

It was neat handwriting. Neat and girlish. She closed her eyes and tried not to look at it. This was a personal note between Jamie and his lover – she knew she shouldn't look, but it taunted her and teased her and tempted her to read it. She had found her mother's diary once – coincidentally, when she was looking for a handkerchief. It was hidden in the back of her underwear drawer, beneath the silky petticoats and sensible-sized knickers, and the lure of it had proved too great.

Pamela had read of things she shouldn't – her mother's irritation with her father, how they struggled to make ends meet despite the affluent lifestyle they'd adopted and how, although she tried to love her children equally, her mother couldn't help favouring Pamela's sister, who reminded her so much of herself. Pamela blew her nose hard on the handkerchief that she eventually found. Returning the diary to its secret place, she closed the drawer quietly, firmly and she never looked at it again.

It was with the same sense of foreboding that she viewed the note she held in her hands. She should tear it into shreds, she knew that. But now that she had seen the tiny, perfect script she wanted to know what it said. Jamie was downstairs. She listened for his footsteps, but none came. All she could hear was the faint murmur of the television drifting up from below. It was a comedy programme and someone was laughing too loud. She spread the square of paper on her lap and smoothed it out.

Her eyes filled with tears until the writing was blurred and she could read no more. Pamela sat on the bed, the grubby hanky looking up accusingly from the crisp cotton whiteness of the duvet cover. The note spoke of dreams. Shared dreams. Unfulfilled dreams. No protestations of love, no lustful lamentations, no sordid or smutty thoughts. Just sadness and regret – for opportunities missed, chances wasted and plans turned to dust.

Pamela held the note cupped in her hands. She could tear it up, destroy it, obliterate it – but what would that achieve? What was written would still be in her mind, waiting there for the darkest moments to regurgitate itself.

Was this what Jamie had really wanted from life? Had *she* crushed his ambitions, his goals, his spirit as easily as she could crumple this note between her fingers? Or had he simply abandoned them to devote himself to family, responsibility, commitments, duty? That didn't mean his dreams had gone away. Perhaps he felt them more keenly now that he knew they would never be achieved. She felt devastated. Why could he tell his lover about his innermost thoughts and dreams when he had shared nothing of this with her, his own wife?

She needed to see Teri. She needed to know what made her so special. She needed to know why Jamie could share with her things that he had never mentioned to another living soul. Now that she had spoken to her, it only made matters worse. Her voice was etched into Pamela's brain as if it had been scored deeply in cut-class. Was she dark? Was she blonde? Would Pamela be consumed with jealousy when she saw her, or simply wonder why Jamie had chosen her?

Pamela folded the note, following the previous creased lines carefully, like one does with a road map or a knitting pattern. She went to Jamie's wardrobe and put it back in the pocket of another suit that hung silently expectant in the wood-scented air.

Jamie was sprawled on the sofa, reading the remains of the Sunday papers and sipping a therapeutic whisky. He had been to see Charlie in the hospital again and had returned home pale and drawn. Pamela sat by his feet. 'I'm going to come into town with you tomorrow.'

Jamie lowered his paper. 'Why? You hate going into London.'

'I've got things to do.'

'What things?'

'Just stuff.' She picked up the glossy magazine which he had discarded on the floor. 'I wouldn't mind coming into your office,' she said over-casually. 'Perhaps we could meet for lunch.' Her face had coloured and she leaned earnestly over the magazine so that her hair would drape forward and hide it.

'You've never wanted to come to the office before.'

'Well, perhaps now is a good time to start.'

Jamie put his paper down. They had lit a fire to dispel the chilliness of the evening – a legacy of a clear, cloudless day. The embers cast a golden glow across the room which pooled where Pamela sat and picked out the unseasonal autumnness of her hair. Her face was pinched, her cheeks flushed, her pain transparent. 'I don't work with her,' he said.

Pamela started to protest and changed her mind.

Jamie massaged his hairline. 'I met her on the train.'

'I need to see her,' Pamela stated flatly.

'What good would it do?'

'None.'

'Then why?'

'It's a woman's thing.' She looked into the fire and her eyes flickered with the reflected dying flame. 'Like calories and hormones and stretch-marks.'

'Like masochism.'

She turned to Jamie. 'If it were me, you'd want to know, wouldn't you?'

'I *do* know!' Jamie tossed his paper to the floor. 'And believe me, it doesn't help one bit.'

Pamela sighed. She should explain about Tom, that it had all been a silly, stupid plot – a pretend revenge affair – and get this whole damned sordid business out into the open. Except that now she didn't want it all out in the open. She only wanted certain bits out in the open and, when pressed, would she feel the urge to confess?

However hard she tried, her Catholic upbringing would never really go away; there was always the underlying urge to purge the soul of stains of sin and guilt. Would it help or would it hinder? Could she really stand there and play the innocent party when she had courted the danger of temptation all along? And had finally not only succumbed but had actually instigated it? How could she explain to her husband that they both had more than a passing interest in room 405 of The Happy Lodge?

'Do you want to talk about it?' she asked.

'No.' Jamie sighed. 'My brain's about to explode as it is. I can't stop thinking about Charlie.' He had swung through the ward doors and had been at Charlie's bed before his friend had noticed him. The true pain had been shining through there too, before he had put his carefree mask back on. He was bruised, bandaged and bereft.

At this moment, Charlie was a sadder character than Gordy. And that was so sad, it made you want to weep. Jamie had taken some grapes and a Get Well card, and they were the only things Charlie had received.

'So,' Pamela broke into his thoughts, 'do you mind if I come tomorrow?'

'Yes,' Jamie said. 'But you'll come anyway.'

Pamela hated railway stations – and airports. To her they were the epitome of purgatory. A place of disembodied coming and going – as many people happy and reunited with loved ones as there were devastated ones, cast out and abandoned, starting a life of enforced, eternal separation. These places were always so bleak. Bleak and windy, with the sort of wind that clings to your bones and chills you right down to the marrow. At least at airports there was the Duty Free to cheer you up.

Her thoughts turned miserably to Jack and Francesca, whom she had dragged screaming from their beds at an even earlier hour than normal to deposit – still protesting – with a bleary-eyed and infinitely obliging Kathy from next door. She and Jamie would be late home too and Pamela had asked Kathy to give the children whatever they wanted/demanded for their tea in the vain hope that copious amounts of junk food would buy their forgiveness for indulging in this selfish pilgrimage.

It was drizzling, and at her insistence they were waiting for the train – which was late – in the unpleasant waiting room, a cold glass box made up of windows two feet wide, banded by garish red aluminium. Three of the windows had no glass in them and the wind whistled peevishly through the gaps; the jagged edges of the broken glass looked like an evil smile. The floor was strewn with old newspapers and empty burger boxes, and it stank of urine. As soon as she had walked in, Pamela wished they had waited outside in the wind and the rain.

Jamie was subdued. No, morose. He hadn't tried to dissuade her from coming, but he hadn't spoken all the way to the station in the car, although he had held her hand as they queued to buy her a ticket. Now he stared out of the windows, peering past the numerous unmentionable substances that were smeared across them. When the commuters on the platform started to shuffle towards their favoured spot, Jamie and Pamela went out to greet the impending arrival of the train.

You could always get a seat this early. It was something Pamela had learned over countless dinners with friends who also commuted. They talked endlessly about the vagaries of British Rail and now Railtrack, the price of their season tickets and the comparative time they travelled. Their lives were measured by the length of their journeys. If yours was longer, more expensive and more hassled than your colleagues', you were lauded rather than ridiculed. It was worse than having dinner with a group of struggling golfers. (No. It was bad, but perhaps it wasn't *that* bad.)

The doors closed automatically, beeping like a demented microwave, and the train sped off towards London through the urban dereliction that was once Bletchley – a place not yet swallowed up by the greedy expansion of Milton Keynes, but no longer sufficiently attractive or economically viable to support its own town centre or to compete with the burgeoning megastores that crowded its limits.

It was at Leighton Buzzard that she got on. Leighton Buzzard – erstwhile scene of the Great Train Robbery and now the great husband robbery too. Teri – her husband's lover – swung on to the train jauntily, despite the fact that it was still only just after six-thirty in the morning. She looked as if she should be in a Tampax advert, with the strains of 'It's my life' following her and the confidence to wear white on days she really shouldn't. Her style was casual but expensive, and Pamela was surprised at the absence of the power suit she had imagined. She looked small and vulnerable and nice.

Her body was angled towards them as she moved between the seats and the train jerked out of the station. She shook the rain from her hair, flicking her eyes over the occupants of the carriage. When they rested on Jamie, who was looking suitably ashen-faced behind his paper, she smiled – but it froze on her face as she spotted Pamela.

Recognition was instant. Clever as well as beautiful. But it didn't give Pamela the pang of malice or jealousy she had expected. There was just a deep and abiding sadness to know that this woman, this girl, had been intimate with her husband. Intimate with his body and intimate with his thoughts. She would know the birthmark on his shoulder that looked like a map of Japan. Had Teri run her fingertips over its smooth, ragged outline and then lovingly nipped it as she once used to do?

Pamela tore her eyes away from the other woman and fixed them instead on the stylised mural at the end of the carriage, which seemed to depict the Swiss Alps and stippled clouds floating above what appeared to be two nuclear bunkers surrounded by navy-blue grass.

When she could bear it no longer, she glanced at Jamie and saw that he was mortified. It had been wrong of her to come. She shouldn't have done this to him. Throughout her childhood, Pamela's mother had insisted on accompanying her into the classroom and helping her to hang up her coat while all the other children had struggled valiantly with theirs alone. The final ignominy had been a warm, wet kiss on her cheek as her mother disappeared with a flourish of skirts. It had branded her a wimp in front of the class and she had longed for her maturity into junior school and out of such excruciating oppression. She could feel the same emotion emanating from Jamie and throbbing through her veins. It had been wrong.

At Euston the train stopped abruptly and the impatient commuters spilled out on to the platform. Teri left the train without looking at them. They followed at a polite distance, Jamie fussing with his newspaper to give her a head-start. Pamela watched Teri's hair bobbing in front of them, passing the hanging baskets over-flowing with garish red and yellow plastic geraniums, following the crowd of commuters through the ticket barriers like sheep being herded into a pen.

When she broke away from the mass of people and jogged up the slope into the main concourse, Pamela turned to Jamie, who was pretending not to watch her. 'You can go after her if you want to. I don't mind.'

'No,' Jamie said lifelessly. His face was a blank screen from which all trace of emotion had been erased. 'I'll stay with you.'

He tried phoning Teri all morning, but all he got was her jolly answerphone message, which said: 'Teri Carter isn't at her desk right now,' but infuriatingly offered no further enlightenment.

The office was very quiet without Charlie, and Jamie

listened to his secretary's dissection of *Animal Hospital* with even less fervour than usual. It was nearly midday when Joyless Lovejoy came out of his office and announced that he wanted to see Jamie in private straight away. He was staring out of his office window at the pigeons on the roof opposite when Jamie followed him in and closed the door.

'What do you know about Charlie?' he said, without turning round.

Jamie sat down. 'He's getting better. He should be out of hospital in a day or two. They've been keeping him in for observation.'

Joyless turned round and perched on the windowsill. He looked remarkably like one of the pigeons outside. Pointy-nosed, beady-eyed and grey – overwhelmingly grey. 'Is he mentally stable?'

'He's as stable as you or me,' Jamie answered laconically.

Joyless's head snapped up and he scrutinised Jamie's face for any sign of sarcasm. 'This is very inconvenient of him,' he said.

Jamie bristled. 'That's one way of looking at it.'

'Is he fit to do your job?'

'*My* job?'

'We need to be sure of a replacement before we can promote you.'

'*Promote* me?' He was aware that he was beginning to sound like Little Sir Echo.

Joyless glared at him. 'We're merging with another insurance group. All hush, hush. It'll mean reassessment, restructuring, reintegration, reorganisation and recentralisation. We want you to head up the IT Department.'

Jamie swivelled in his chair. 'I'm flattered.'

'We want you in Macclesfield next Monday.'

'Macclesfield!'

'Didn't I mention relocation?'

'No,' Jamie said. 'You mustn't have *re*-membered.'

'So you'll go?'

'Do I have a choice?'

'Yes.' Joyless nodded joylessly. 'Redundancy.'

'Chester?' Pamela's voice rose in disbelief. They were on the train on their way home. Jamie was feeling tired and emotional, and the last thing he wanted was a scene. His wife was nursing an ominously large Harrods carrier bag, which he was trying very hard to ignore.

'Well, near Chester,' he answered cagily.

'How near Chester?'

'Macclesfield.'

'Macclesfield!' Pamela's expression was pained. 'Chester sounds terribly salubrious. Macclesfield doesn't sound salubrious at all.'

'We live in Milton Keynes, for goodness sake. How much worse can Macclesfield be?' He was trying to keep his voice down. 'I think it would be a good move for us.'

'But the children will grow up speaking with Northern accents.' He wished Pamela would try to keep hers down too.

'*I* have a Northern accent.'

'Yes, but far enough north to have a certain rustic charm.'

'I'll take that as a compliment,' Jamie said tersely.

'It was intended to be.'

'Having a regional accent is hardly life's biggest handicap, Pamela. Even the BBC allow their presenters to veer from Queen's English these days.' Jamie gesticulated expansively. 'Take Michael Fish – there are days when I can barely understand the man. And these so-called "youff" programmes have presenters that are complete gibbering morons – they're totally unintelligible! If we keep letting the kids watch these they'll grow up being unable to string two sentences together – despite your best attempts with the Alphabites.'

'You've made your point,' Pamela said.

Jamie stared silently out of the window as they rushed through Watford Junction. It was a rare thing – rushing through Watford Junction. He normally liked to stop and read the platform sign which said PASSING TRAINS CAUSE AIR TURBULENCE. It made him smile and wonder how you could even swallow a train, let alone *pass* one. And heaven knows, he was in need of something to smile about today. 'I could stop commuting and live nearer to the office.'

'Is that some sort of veiled promise?'

'Yes, it is.' Jamie lowered his voice further. 'I would have thought with our current domestic predicament that you would relish the chance of moving away. Unless of course, there's something – or someone – that would keep you here.'

Pamela ignored the barbed reference to Tom. 'I didn't say I didn't want to move. I was just expressing distaste at Macclesfield.'

'What does it matter whether it's Mars or Macclesfield? This gives us a chance to make a fresh start.'

'Does that mean you're going to end it?'

Jamie looked around. The sea of raised newspapers and best-selling paperbacks jogged along with the steady motion. There was a pale-skinned Pre-Raphaelite redhead further down the carriage, with one button too many of her blouse undone. She had her face to the fluorescent tubes, rosebud mouth parted expectantly, eyes dreamily closed, and picked her fingers constantly until they were red raw at the quick. Or what about the man diagonally across, who had chain-eaten painkillers since Carpenders Park washed down with Diet Coke. Were they struggling to hold their lives and their sanity together? He looked at the blank, expressionless faces and wondered how many of them were disguising difficult domestic situations that were straight out of *Brookside*. Probably all of them.

'We shouldn't be having this conversation on the train,' he said.

'Does it?'

'Yes.'

Pamela's eyes brimmed with tears and she started to cry. Slow, silent tears poured out of her eyes, rolling languorously down her cheeks and splashing on to her skirt.

'Oh, hell!' Jamie muttered. 'Don't cry.'

'You shouldn't tell someone not to cry,' Pamela sobbed. 'It negates their emotions.'

'You've been reading *Cosmo* again, haven't you?' He searched frantically in his suit for a handkerchief and finally pulled one out of his top pocket. The shock of recognition showed on his face. *It was the hanky panky*.

He hesitated in handing it over. What had once been white and pristine was a terrible mess now, anyway – stained and spoilt. Ruined. It was unlikely that Pamela would want to have it anywhere near her.

His wife had stopped in mid-sob and was staring at him. Reluctantly, he shook it out. A tiny, folded piece of paper dropped out of it and fluttered delicately to the grubby floor of the carriage. They both watched it, mesmerised by its meandering descent. He passed her the hanky, unable to take his eyes off the note on the floor. She took it but didn't use it, crushing it into a ball and twisting it between her fingers.

All the way to Milton Keynes the note lay on the floor between them, like a lone scrap of confetti, forgotten after the wedding had long since ended. Jamie listened to the wind-rush buffeting against the train, braced himself against the vicious jolt of a passing express and tried not to think of Teri.

The train slowed for Milton Keynes Central Station. Commuters gathered their belongings – newspapers, briefcases, coats from the overhead racks – and crushed towards the doors for their final burst to freedom. Jamie put his arm round Pamela to steady her as the train stopped. 'I need one last night,' he said. 'Just one night and then that's it. No more working late.'

Pamela chewed determinedly at her lip and nodded. A barely perceptible movement of the head, but a nod nevertheless. She was still wringing the hanky between her hands and there were dark smears of mascara under her lower lashes. The harsh fluorescent lights that flattered no one picked out the fine lines on Pamela's face. Jamie's heart twisted into a tight line like a wrung-out J-cloth. He swallowed the lump that threatened to fill his throat and helped her – and the still unmentioned Harrods bag – off the train.

The tiny note went unheeded, blackened and crushed beneath the weight of alighting feet. As the automatic doors closed, an eddy of wind caught it, whipping it and blowing it out of the train after Jamie and Pamela. It circled in the air, wheeling and soaring briefly before it plummeted to the platform. The train moved off and the wind blew along the dusty, grimy concrete, making the note skip animatedly. For a moment it teetered on the brink of the platform beyond the safety of the yellow line, before a final gentle gust tipped it over the edge.

The train was disappearing from view – whisking its passengers off towards the more exotic destinations of Crewe, Runcorn and ultimately Liverpool Lime Street. The scrap of paper lay on the track, forgotten, invisible, unnoticed by the people who pushed down the stairs on to the platform, cursed their bad timing and waited impatiently for the next train to come along.

Chapter Twenty-Six

'Jamie!' It was the tenth time he had called, but the first time he hadn't been answered by a recorded message. 'I didn't expect you to call.'

His heart still went into somersault mode at the sound of her voice, and it did a triple backflip now so that he wasn't disappointed. 'I need to see you.'

'I wasn't sure what to think after yesterday.'

He cut across her, impatient to get this over with. 'Can we meet tonight?'

'Of course we can.' She lowered her voice, so there must be people around her in the office. 'I'm sorry about what happened at the weekend.'

So much had happened he wasn't sure exactly what she was referring to, until he realised that Teri was still in the dark as far as most things were concerned. She still didn't know where he had gone when he left, or why Pamela had needed to contact him so urgently. He wasn't keen to shed any further light either.

'Is everything okay?' she asked, when he didn't answer straight away.

'Not really.' He sounded miserable.

'Do you want to tell me now?'

'Not really.'

'Shall I get some food for tonight?'

'No.' How was he ever going to break this to her gently? 'I thought we'd go to Steamers for a drink.'

'Neutral territory?' She wasn't just beautiful, she was razor-blade sharp.

'Something like that.' The silence hung heavy between them. 'I'll meet you outside the office.'

Teri's voice was quiet and he could tell it had nothing to do with the hindrance of eavesdroppers. 'I'll see you later then.'

He hung up and twirled round in his chair, propping his feet up on the desk. Why the hell wasn't Charlie here when he needed him? He would know what to do, what to say. He was aware that he was sounding like Joyless Lovejoy. Charlie was doing all right. The bandages had come off, revealing dark crusted slashes that would ultimately heal to nothing more than faint white reminders of a love gone tragically wrong.

One of the young nurses had been fussing around him, surreptitiously administering lavender oil to his wounds. They would heal quicker that way, she had told them earnestly. It was something she had learned on the part-time aromatherapy course she had done so that she could supplement her meagre National Health Service pay. Jamie wondered if lavender oil could help the mental scars too.

He sat alone in the corner of the Clog and Calculator at lunchtime, not noticing the tasteless pint of bitter that sat in front of him and avoiding Gordy and three more of his cronies from the office. They were talking loudly and laddishly about the barmaid's breasts, while she leaned lazily on the pumps, absently picking peanuts from the dish on the bar and popping them into the red gash of her mouth. He had taken a detour on his way back to the office and had stopped at the flower shop – Blooming Marvellous – which announced: *Say IT with Flowers!* in the window. Which flowers were suitable for saying his particular IT, was anybody's guess.

He chose roses, the blooms of lovers. How romantic. They were deep dark red, the colour of let blood. The colour of hearts torn and mangled. The colour of the congealing wounds on Charlie's wrists. The soft, velvet plush petals deceived the unwary and made them prey to the spiking thorns on the stems.

The florist offered to trim the thorns, but Jamie refused. They summed up perfectly the way he was feeling, particularly when she cheerfully pointed out that there were always more thorns on roses than there were petals. It was a thought that sent him further into his depression.

The florist wrapped the roses in copious layers of paper tissue and bound them tightly with a scarlet bow. He paid and clutched the bouquet to his chest. As he stepped on to the street, a thorn pushed through the protective layers and drew blood from the finger on which he used to wear his wedding ring. Blooming marvellous.

The roses spent the afternoon unfurling on the office floor, while Jamie went over in his head the best way to tell Teri that it had to end. By the time he left, they had gone from tight curled buds to full-blown but tired-looking blooms. He knew how they felt. The heating in the office was rather like that on the trains. It made sure they froze to death all winter, and with the onset of the balmy days of spring it miraculously burst into life and fried them all through the summer. Armpits sweated, shirt collars chafed and shoes squelched. It was a blessed relief to be standing in the fume-choked, car-filled excesses of Euston Road waiting for Teri.

She burst out of the revolving doors chatting animatedly to a colleague and, despite the fact that he had made up his mind to do it, he wondered how he was going to manage without her. He kissed her cheek and gave her what was left of the dying roses. They walked up Euston Road arm in arm, making no attempt at conversation. At the station the concourse was, as usual, thronged with people. They made their way across towards Steamers. Jamie opened the door and a wall of sound met them – the high-pitched hubbub and hearty laughter of aimless conversation.

'Not in here.' Teri pulled his arm. 'If you're going to end it, the least you can do is afford me some dignity.'

Jamie's face crumpled. 'How did you know I was going to end it?'

'I may be green, Jamie, but I'm not entirely cabbage-coloured.' She smiled at him wryly. 'Come on, I've a bottle of fizz in the fridge at home and I have got something to celebrate too.'

Jamie hesitated. 'I promised Pamela.'

She looked straight at him. 'It's far too late to start worrying about telling porky pies now, Jamie. One more isn't going to make the slightest bit of difference. We'll both be prodding the coals in hell as it is, and you'll be lined up by that tiny little guillotine. Come on, or we'll miss the train.'

Chapter Twenty-Seven

There was a policeman on the screen wearing a fluorescent yellow vest which said POLICE INCIDENT OFFICER in bold capital letters.

Pamela looked up from her sewing. It was nine o'clock and the first time she had sat down that night. Jack and Francesca had squabbled incessantly since teatime and had forced her brow to crease into a permanent furrow and subsequent headache. Now she was stitching name tags into Francesca's school sweatshirts in the vain hope that she might at the end of term have the same ones she started with.

It was the tangled mass of trains and the mention of Euston Station that made her prick up her ears and prick her thumb. In the background, ambulance sirens wailed, the surging discordant noise still sounding strangely American rather than British. There were shots of bloodied, bandaged people being stretchered away from the trains by men in tight-fitting orange jumpsuits who whisked them into waiting helicopters. In the background, firemen held clear plastic drip bags attached to patients lying bleeding on the ground – they looked like something they had won at the fairground and should have had the orange flash of a goldfish swimming round in them.

Horrified, Pamela learned that this was the 18.07 out of Euston – a packed commuter train that had crashed into an empty goods train heading south from the depot of Bletchley. The collision was just south of Watford Junction. The train had been carrying over four hundred people. There was one fatality and over one hundred other injuries. The POLICE INCIDENT OFFICER said that it was a miracle more passengers weren't killed. Pamela's throat went dry.

The news cameras switched to a harassed BBC reporter, standing outside Watford General Hospital. Every ambulance that arrived at the ugly grey concrete building was greeted by a swarm of nurses in pale blue uniforms and matching plastic aprons who fussed around the casualties and hurried them inside. A large red sign bearing a large red arrow said: WALKING WOUNDED THIS WAY, PLEASE.

Pamela couldn't hear what the reporter was saying. There was blood rushing in her ears and she scoured the faces of the injured, imagining them without their bandages. One fatality. *Oh God, please let it not be my Jamie.*

The news flash continued interminably – eyewitness reports of crashing sounds and flying glass and flowing blood. The trains hung precariously from an embankment, looking like toys sadistically smashed by a child who hadn't yet learned how to play nicely. In the houses below the carnage, people had been evacuated while they were having their tea. One man complained to the reporter about his chips going cold.

A haggard-looking spokesman from the Railways Inspectorate made a vacuous statement to the camera, citing unblemished safety records and assuring the general public that an internal enquiry was being launched. He, too, echoed the sentiments of the Incident Officer that it was a miracle there weren't more dead, then delivered his well-rehearsed uncomfortable condolences to the families of the dead and injured. Already the press were looking for someone to blame. All Pamela was looking for was Jamie.

Chapter Twenty-Eight

Teri found the only vase she owned, which was lurking at the back of her under-sink cupboard gathering dust. She unwrapped the fading blooms, which were now shedding their petals due to the warmth of the train and the battering they had taken because they had both been forced to stand until Watford Junction. It was a shame that the only flowers she'd had in years seemed destined to be a farewell present.

She clinked two lone ice-cubes from the tray into the vase and tossed the tray into the sink. Somewhere she had read that ice could revive wilting flowers. This lot would need a small iceberg to do the trick by the look of them. Either that or a small miracle.

What would revive a wilting love affair, she wondered. Certainly not an iceberg: this relationship was beginning to feel as though it had been struck a cruel and fatal blow by one. It seemed unlikely to survive. Look at the *Titanic* – how indestructible that had seemed at the time. Had she and Jamie ever seemed indestructible? No, she had to admit, they hadn't. They had always been a leaky tub – the water of commitment and loyalty seeping in too steadily for them ever to venture too far from the shore.

She had seen this coming. After the debacle of the

weekend and then Pamela on the train yesterday, what else could she expect? They were up to their ears in water – the moment of sink or swim. There was no question about what Jamie would do – there never really had been. It was why she loved him – the kindness, the loyalty, the inherent goodness. She had vowed that she would be brave and smiling as their ship slowly sank. Jamie would strike back for the safety of the shore and she would silently and with dignity let the water engulf her.

Teri tucked the champagne under her arm and carried the vase into the lounge, where Jamie was perched uncomfortably on the edge of the sofa, scattering petals across the carpet as she went.

'Here, you can open this.' She passed him the bottle and slid two slender glasses across the coffee table at him. 'Open it carefully. I don't want another dent in my ceiling.'

He squeezed the cork expertly out of the bottle and poured the champagne into the glasses. 'What are we celebrating?'

Teri took a glass and knelt on the floor in front of him. '*We're* not celebrating. *We're* in mourning. *I'm* celebrating.' She lifted her glass. 'May I propose a toast to the new presenter of City Television's most popular youth culture show – *Out and About!*'

A smile creased Jamie's face and his eyes sparkled with the reflected bubbles from the champagne. 'You got your promotion!'

Teri sipped the champagne and put it to one side. 'And about time too!'

'That's incredible.'

'I know. It was such a fluke too. My producer – I told you about him – Richard Wellbeloved . . .'

Jamie's blood ran cold. 'I don't believe it,' he said.

'Thanks!' Teri pouted. 'You need an ego the size of a very large house to be on television, and at the moment mine's already smaller than my downstairs loo!'

'That wasn't what I meant.' He waved his hand dismissively. 'Carry on!'

'Well, he's gone! Under a cloud, by all accounts. The rumour is, he's been given the big heave-ho from on high. Gross misconduct. And that irritating little twerp Jez – I told you about him too. Gone! Apparently, they've run off together . . .' Teri prattled on, but Jamie was only half listening.

How could he tell her about Charlie now? Why did it always work out that one person's pain was another person's pleasure? Why was one man's grief invariably another man's glory? One's loss another's gain. Was that why funerals were so much like weddings? Flowers, cars, hymns, crying and slap-up food afterwards. No one wore black at funerals any more and everyone seemed to wear black at weddings – with the possible exception of the bride. And even that wasn't a certainty. As far as he was concerned, there was only one obvious difference – one was most definitely an end and the other was a beginning. And, of course, no one tended to video funerals.

'. . . There was some scandal involving the programme controller's desk, some cocaine and a banana. But you know what office gossip is like. You can't believe everything you hear.'

'It's true,' Jamie said.

Teri's eyes widened. 'What – even about the banana?'

Jamie shook his head. 'I don't know about the banana – or the rest of it – but Richard Wellbeloved has definitely run off with Jez.'

'Well,' Teri said, 'who would believe it?' She shot bolt upright. 'How do you know?'

'That's why Pamela was looking for me on Saturday. Charlie's in hospital. Richard was his lover, partner – I don't know – whatever you call it these days. Charlie's taken it very badly. He tried to top himself.'

'We *are* talking about Charlie "I'm one of the boys, tits and bums, ten pints of bitter and big-breasted ladies" here?'

'The very same one.'

'And he's gay?'

'As Elton John. He just doesn't play the piano as well.'

'I'm stunned.' Teri looked it. 'I was going to try and fix him up with Clare.'

'It's just as well you didn't.'

'I can't see why Richard Wellbeloved is attracted to Jez. Charlie is a much better catch,' Teri said philosophically.

'Apparently, he's got a sperm whale tattooed on his penis.' Jamie filled his glass again.

'Richard Wellbeloved?' Teri's voice was a squeak.

'No, Jez. And pierced nipples.'

'That figures.' Teri pulled her fringe away from her face. 'But I still can't see the attraction.'

Jamie shrugged and smiled. 'Perhaps it's a life-sized sperm whale.'

Teri stopped to think about it, then: 'Look, I'm not going to sit here all night discussing other people's love lives when our own is on the brink of catastrophe.' She took his glass from him. 'Come upstairs and make love to me.'

'I can't.' He put his face in his hands. 'It would only make things worse. I think it would be best to end it quickly.'

'No, it wouldn't.' She pulled him towards her by his tie. 'It's best to end it slowly and seductively. Then at least we can look back when we're sitting in our rocking chairs reminiscing in our Alzheimer-riddled heads and remember what irrational and irresponsible ravers we once were.'

There seemed no appropriate moment to tell her, so Jamie blurted it out. 'I'm moving to Macclesfield.'

'Macclesfield!' She let go of his tie and he recoiled on to the sofa.

'It isn't the end of the world. Or even the end of civilisation as we know it.' He adjusted his tie, tidying it back into the right place. 'Though Pamela thinks it is.'

'Why Macclesfield?' Teri shook her head in disbelief.

'My company's relocating.'

'That still doesn't answer the question.'

'I don't think there is an answer – other than why not?'

Teri's face had fallen and she looked as if she was about to cry. 'We'll never see each other again.'

He could tell he wasn't making a very good job of breaking this gently. He suspected bulls in china shops broke things more gently than he did. 'That was the general idea.'

'I didn't think it would be so final.'

He pulled a petal off one of the roses and rolled it absently between his fingers. 'You can't end an affair and then still go on seeing each other – it doesn't work like that.'

'I thought we might at least accidentally bump into each other sometimes on good old Platform Eight. You know, you could ladder my tights and sprain my ankle again. And I could ruin another one of your hankies. It would be just like old times. And we could shoot the

293

breeze over a coffee at the End of the Line like good buddies do.'

Jamie shook his head. 'You know it wouldn't work.'

'I must say you're taking this very calmly.'

'I'm not calm – my insides are churning more than they do when I've had a chicken vindaloo.' He discarded the petal which was bruised and broken. 'I'm just resigned. There's a difference.'

Teri twisted and leaned against his legs. 'Did you ever love me?'

It was a stupid thing to ask. She should know he did. He had risked everything for her. But he could feel the uncertainty prickling from her like the edgy palpable static electricity that comes from VDU screens. He smoothed her hair with his hand, expecting it to crackle under his fingers. It didn't.

'You know I did. I still do,' he whispered.

'More than Pamela?'

How did he ever think this was going to be easy? He didn't answer and when she looked up at him, his eyes were closed and he was resting his head back against the sofa.

'More than Pamela?' she repeated.

'I love my wife,' he said, without opening his eyes.

'Look at me and say that.'

Jamie turned his head and his eyes met hers and he said levelly, 'I love my wife. I always have.'

'You bastard.' Teri sounded sulky. 'You do, don't you?'

Jamie nodded wordlessly. 'It's a different love. There's not the need – the greed. It's steadfast and stoic. It's corny and dated – and it's, well, it's *there*.'

'So a bit like Rolf Harris, really.'

Jamie sighed. 'A lot like Rolf Harris – but without the

didgeridoo.' He bent down and kissed the top of her head. 'I wish I could turn back the clock. I wish that we'd never met and then I wouldn't have to hurt you now.'

'I wish you wouldn't keep making wishes. I've already told you once that you're too old. The last ones you made didn't come true or we wouldn't be in this situation now.'

He wrapped his arms around Teri and pressed her to his chest. Her body was tight and angled, every muscle taut with tension under his hands. She felt considerably less in control than she sounded. 'How am I going to live without you?'

She looked up at him. 'I used to think that about Häagen Dazs ice cream, but somehow I managed.'

'You just eat Ben and Jerry's instead now, don't you?'

Teri looked puzzled. 'So I do.' It was an analogy that Jamie didn't care to dwell on.

She lay watching his sprawled dozing body on her bed, remembering every line of his face, the way his hair curled, the birthmark that looked like a map of Japan on his shoulder. This would form the Polaroid photograph that she would store in her memory. She had taken no proper photographs of him and it seemed too late and too sad to start now. How could she ask him to smile and say cheese when that same mouth would say goodbye to her in just a few short hours?

His heart was beating loudly and solidly in the silence and she strained her ears to listen in case it was one of her neighbours with their bass boost turned up too loudly. Teri kissed his ear lobe and he swished his hand as if to swat an irritating fly before he opened his eyes and realised it was her.

He smiled, a lazy, lopsided smile – *store in the memory* –

and his eyes crinkled. Three more lines to memorise. She kissed him full on the mouth. There was a need inside her that was more raw than a plateful of sushi. 'Make love to me again.'

'I don't know if I can.'

She trailed her hand over the flat of his stomach. 'Just one last time.'

He held her away from him. 'This is the third time you've said that.'

'We all have to find previously untapped reserves of strength during times of adversity.' She padded to the stereo, seemingly unaware of her nakedness, and put on a CD – *Touch Me in the Morning*. 'Indulge me before you break my heart.'

'Teri!' He looked at her accusingly. 'This is a real tear-jerker!' She came back to the bed and Jamie took her hand. 'Don't torture yourself like this.'

'I'm not torturing myself. It's you that's torturing me. Besides, if it was good enough for Diana Ross it's good enough for me.' She lay beside him on the bed, head nestling on his chest. 'Anyway, I'm a big girl now. I'm not going to cry.'

'Come here,' he said gruffly.

This time they made love silently and seriously – afraid to touch each other unless one of them should shatter into a thousand brittle fragments. The tears slid silently down her face and Jamie's face was wet, too – although she couldn't tell if it was from her tears or his own.

He traced the line of her tears over her cheeks. 'I thought you said you weren't going to cry.'

'I lied,' she said.

When she had laid curled in his arms for some time he said gently, 'I have to go.'

He prised her away from him and twisted out of bed and sat with his back towards her. She pulled the sheet over her head and stayed there. Jamie went into the bathroom. She could hear the tap running into the sink and solitary splashes of water, but there was no singing like there usually was. Eventually, he returned.

'I'm ready to go.' His voice was tight with emotion. There seemed a necessity for this sharp cruelty, this detachment from the pain, if he was ever going to be able to go at all.

'Goodbye,' Teri said from beneath the covers.

'Don't let me go like this.' Jamie pulled at the sheet tucked tightly over her head. 'Come out and say goodbye like an adult.'

'I don't feel like an adult. I was going to be brave and sophisticated and light-hearted but I can't.' Diana still crooned on the CD player.

He pulled the sheet down. Her eyes were red-rimmed, her face tearstained. He brushed her hair from her face and kissed her forehead. 'I love you,' he said and walked out of the door.

Teri closed her eyes and hot tears squeezed through her lashes again, burning a track across her already feverish cheeks. 'I wish you weren't married, that we weren't hurting anyone by loving each other, and I wish more than anything that when I opened my eyes you'd still be here.'

She opened her eyes at the same time as the front door slammed brutally and irrevocably shut behind him.

So that was it. Their brief encounter was over. Trevor presumably chuffed unhappily away alone on his train, while whatsername stood pathetically waving a damp hanky. It was bound to be something like that. It always was.

Life was nothing but a bitter journey on the rails to nowhere. A series of horrible tacky stations, unexpected delays and, sometimes along the way, the odd devastation of a major derailment. That's what Jamie had been – a major derailment on life's tortured track.

Anyway, she'd never know how the stupid film ended – and what's more, she no longer cared. How could she ever bear to watch it now? Whatever happened THE END would come up in big white capital letters. And she'd reach for the man-sized Kleenex once again.

Chapter Twenty-Nine

The emergency number that they gave out for friends and relatives was constantly engaged. She sat with the phone in her hand, pressing and re-pressing the redial button and imagining that by sheer will she could force the incessant, negative bleeping to change to a comforting, informative ring.

There was a news update every half-hour, and still she hadn't recognised Jamie among the battered and tattered travellers. Surely, he wouldn't be on that train. This was to be his last night with *her* – with Teri.

What were the chances of them being trapped and tangled together on the train? A million to one? There was more chance of them winning the National Lottery.

Somewhere, she had read that it was more likely for a thirty-seven-year-old man to die of a heart attack immediately after buying his lottery ticket than it was for him to win 'The Big One'. For one mad moment, Pamela clung to the safety of that thought.

Jamie must surely have been well on his way to Teri's place by the time the train crashed. You're hardly likely to hang around at the office if there's a passionate night of sex on the cards, are you? To Pamela it seemed a cruel and ironic twist to be praying fervently that her husband was safely tucked up in bed with his lover. Somehow, she thought hysterically, it wouldn't be what Relate advised.

For the last time she tried to get through to the emergency number, but it was still frustratingly unavailable. There was only one other option. She stared at the phone, wrestling with her indecision. Perhaps he would come home soon? Safe and well and hopefully sexually unencumbered, too.

The minutes squeezed by on the hall clock in exquisite slowness until another twenty had passed into the vacuum of oblivion and there was still no sign of Jamie. She had lasted out this long, sweating and trembling beside the phone like a heroin addict who tries to prolong her fix as much as possible – but knowing full well that she will eventually succumb. Her hands trembled as she dialled Teri's number for the second time that week.

'Hi.' A quiet, subdued voice answered the phone.

Pamela swallowed. 'Is that Teri?'

'Yes.' Her voice was instantly cautious.

It was horrifying how nice she sounded. Pamela wanted to hate her and be set against her but she couldn't find it in her heart. 'I promise I won't make a habit of this,' she said politely. 'Is Jamie there?'

'No.'

Oh my God. Pamela tried to breathe deeply. She closed her eyes to keep the blackness at bay. 'There's been a train crash, at Watford Junction. I just need to know that he's safe.' She steadied her voice again. 'Has he been with you?'

There was a moment's hesitation before Teri answered. 'Yes,' she said. 'He's safe. He's already left.' She paused and Pamela heard her clear her throat. 'He's on his way home to you.'

Pamela stood against the wall, her emotions scattered like a tub of hundreds and thousands dropped on a kitchen floor. Relief flooded through her, making her giddy with happiness. 'Thank you,' was all she managed to say. 'Thank you.'

'You love him very much, don't you?'

'Yes,' Pamela said. She was crying and smiling at the same time. Tears of joy, of relief, of sadness and regret.

'I do too,' Teri said sadly. 'I'm sorry about all this. We never meant it to happen.'

'These things can take us all by surprise sometimes,' Pamela said. She thought of Tom and Shirley, of Jamie and herself, and her heart went out to the sad and lonely young woman at the other end of the phone.

'You're a very lucky woman, Mrs Duncan.' It sounded as though she was crying.

'I know,' Pamela said softly, and put down the phone.

Chapter Thirty

Jamie drove home along the main roads. His mind was too full of images of Teri to risk the twists and turns of the village roads in the darkness. The yellow-orange glow of the street-lamps soothed him, and the concentration of his driving helped to stop him thinking too much.

He wondered how they would settle down in Macclesfield. It would be good for them to make a fresh start. He would make it up to Pamela – and the children. The thought of how close he had come to blighting their lives made him shudder. He had never wanted them to become just another blip on the broken-home statistics.

How could he have coped with seeing Teri on the train and not holding her and smelling the fresh, clean scent of her hair – pretending that they were just friends and that they had never really been lovers? Would there come a time when he would be able to remember something she had said, but not be able to hear her voice, its tinkling intonation and the effervescence of her laugh? Would he remember the colour of her eyes, but not be able to picture her as sharply as he could now? Would he ever feel the softness of silk against his skin and not think of her? Would there be a time when he would look back and know that what he had just done was the right thing? Or would she remain gouged in his heart for ever like the initials carved on a tree by a young and hopeful courting couple? Although he was married to someone else, the scar would remain with him always – lessening, fading with age but never entirely disappearing.

As he turned into the drive and pulled up at the garage doors, the security light flashed on, flooding the sweep of gravel with a harsh glare, picking out the colours of individual pebbles. It had been fitted for them by Secure Home Limited. There had been precious few perks in Pamela's job, except for this state-of-the-art burglar alarm and a house that had more security lights than a NATO base. It was funny how they had taken so much trouble to defend their house, yet had left themselves so open and vulnerable to attack. He hoped Pamela would be able to forget Tom. She hadn't been into work since the curry-flinging episode, and there hadn't been any 'hang-up' phone calls, so he was quietly optimistic.

He parked the car and set the alarm, closing the garage door behind him. This was one thing he wouldn't miss about Milton Keynes – the car crime was rife here. Although he doubted that Macclesfield was very much better. You probably would have to move to Mars these days if you didn't want your car to be nicked. If the truth was known, they probably already had little green joyriders there.

Jamie pondered briefly how many vehicularly challenged juvenile delinquents would want to half-inch a Volvo with infantile vomit all over the upholstery and a baby seat in the back. No street cred or what. Still, there was something intrinsically embarrassing about having to make a claim of your own when you worked in insurance. It was better to be safe than sorry. And he had always been a cautious man.

* * *

Pamela was waiting in the kitchen. She heard the car and the crunch of his feet walking heavily across the gravel. Her face was freshly washed and her make-up re-applied. There was an envelope in front of her and she fingered it tentatively, brushing unseen specks of dust from its surface with shaking hands.

The envelope contained tickets for the Monaco Grand Prix. In Monte Carlo. A million miles from Milton Keynes or Macclesfield. She had stretched her flexible friend to the limits of its pliability and had booked a five-star hotel too. It would be her last wanton extravagance, and it would be worth it. The room had a jacuzzi – perhaps they would make love in it.

There were only two tickets and they would abandon the children to the tender mercies of her mother and go alone. Husband and wife. Man and woman. The tickets had been difficult to get hold of and extortionately priced, and she would probably hate it – the noise, the crowds, the cloying smell of oil, the environmental pollution, the French. But she would go for Jamie's sake and she would make sure that she enjoyed it and that he enjoyed it too.

Pamela realised it was a small and hideously inadequate gesture, but it was an attempt to compensate for the things Jamie had sacrificed for them. The things that his heart most desired. The things that he had confided to Teri and hadn't been able to tell her. It was an attempt to say that she would try to make more time for him, to understand him and to show that she really did love him.

They would have a smaller house in Macclesfield, she decided – one without an *Alien* mortgage. One that didn't strangle the life out of their relationship and make a prisoner of their dreams.

She heard his key in the lock and as she turned to greet him, her eyes glanced along the work surface. The stained and ruined handkerchief was lying on top of the pile of bills that waited patiently for someone to pay them.

'Hi, I'm home,' he shouted breezily. She heard the catch in his voice and the way it didn't quite match the heartiness of his words.

She picked up the hanky and clutching it tightly in her hand, she walked to the swing bin. Pushing the lid deftly to one side, she dropped the hanky inside.

Chapter Thirty-One

Teri went back upstairs to the bathroom. There was a wet towel on the floor – it was clear no man was perfect – and a sprinkling of Johnson's Baby Powder on the carpet that looked like a case of seriously bad dandruff. How could he think of using baby powder at the moment their relationship was turning to dust? There was a damp footprint in it – a Jamie-sized one – and she put her own foot down inside it and a flurry of soft white talc clung desperately to it.

She had bought them both new toothbrushes. A pink toothbrush and a blue toothbrush – a jokey reference to the old Max Bygraves song. She picked Jamie's blue toothbrush up and threw it in the bin. Her own looked so forlorn now. There was nothing in this world sadder than a toothbrush-holder with only one toothbrush in it. It summed up the essence of loneliness. If only life was as easy as Max Bygraves had made it sound . . .

Teri ran her hands over the flatness of her stomach. Was she the only person in the world who was becoming fraught about a continued lack of cellulite and stretch-marks? She sighed and opened the bathroom cabinet. The box she had bought a few days ago sat staring at her insolently from the shelf. There were only so many early-morning vomiting sessions that could be blamed on an excess of champagne and smoked salmon and tiger prawns and cream-filled meringues.

Teri lifted the pregnancy test out of the cupboard. It was quite predictably called THE PREDICTOR and she thought it sounded like the latest Arnold Schwarzenegger film. Perhaps the baby would burst forth from the birth canal brandishing an Uzi eight millimetre and blast the obstetrician into oblivion. Perhaps not. She placed it on top of the toilet. Perhaps she would use it tomorrow. Then again, perhaps not.

She felt no guilt or shame or regret. Which for a Catholic, convent-educated girl was quite a departure from how she had conducted most of her life. The Catholic ethos seemed to her to be one wrought in guilt and shame. It had been enforced wholeheartedly by a mother who had in a former life been a Spanish Inquisitor, and a best friend who prided herself on being an incarnation of Sister Mary Bernadette – commandant of The Sacred Heart of Jesus primary school. If there was a child, it would be born with pride and joy.

She would call Clare and grovel and ask her to come back. Stoically, she would listen to all that crap about bindweed in the garden of romance again and she would agree that Clare had been right all along, and that she could have avoided all this pain and suffering if she had only listened to her in the first place. And, for once, she would probably be right.

If the test was positive she would tell Clare first, knowing that her friend would scold her and bully her and support her. And she would be there for her as she always was. Clare would get drunk and Teri would sip a glass of orange juice so as not to inflict any damage on the brain cells of the tiny tadpole inside her that would miraculously turn itself into a child.

They would work their way steadily through a box of man-sized Kleenex and pontificate about what heartless bastards men really were. But she would say quietly to herself so that Clare couldn't hear – *not Jamie*. If Jamie had been heartless, he would be here right now and not with his wife and children where he belonged.

With unfaltering fingers she unwrapped the cellophane on THE PREDICTOR. She would definitely do it tomorrow. The sooner she knew the better.

It was a good job that she had signed her contract for *Out and About* as soon as she had received it. She wondered what her new producer would think of a children's television presenter who was not only unmarried but pregnant, too.

It would certainly be more trendy than John Craven had ever been.